THE LAST OF US
AND PHILOSOPHY

The Blackwell Philosophy and Pop Culture Series
Series editor: William Irwin

A spoonful of sugar helps the medicine go down, and a healthy helping of popular culture clears the cobwebs from Kant. Philosophy has had a public relations problem for a few centuries now. This series aims to change that, showing that philosophy is relevant to your life—and not just for answering the big questions like "To be or not to be?" but for answering the little questions: "To watch or not to watch *South Park*?" Thinking deeply about TV, movies, and music doesn't make you a "complete idiot." In fact, it might make you a philosopher, someone who believes the unexamined life is not worth living and the unexamined cartoon is not worth watching.

Already published in the series:

THE LAST OF US
AND PHILOSOPHY
LOOK FOR THE LIGHT

Edited by

Charles Joshua Horn

University of Wisconsin Stevens Point
Stevens Point, USA

WILEY Blackwell

Published by John Wiley & Sons, Inc., Hoboken, New Jersey.
Published simultaneously in Canada.

For general information on our other products and services or for technical support, please contact our Customer Care Department within the United States at (800) 762-2974, outside the United States at (317) 572-3993 or fax (317) 572-4002.

Wiley also publishes its books in a variety of electronic formats. Some content that appears in print may not be available in electronic formats. For more information about Wiley products, visit our web site at www.wiley.com.

Library of Congress Cataloging-in-Publication Data Applied for
Paperback ISBN: 9781394221929

Cover Design: Wiley
Cover Image: © EOL STUDIOS/Adobe Stock

Set in 10/12pt SabonLTStd by Straive, Pondicherry, India

SKY10081157_080524

Contents

Contributors

Survivors

Peter Admirand, like Ellie, enjoys comic books and wanted to be an astronaut as a child, but unlike her, he fears tight spaces, heights, the dark, and pun books. Enduring and surviving, he is a theologian, Deputy Head of School, and the Director of the Centre for Interreligious Dialogue at Dublin City University. Most recently, he authored a book examining the comics *Y: The Last Man* and *Saga* and is the editor of the forthcoming *Theology and The Last of Us: Violence, Ethics, Redemption*? If a fungal pandemic arises, his wife and five children know it's safer to stick with her no matter how many Clickers he supposedly ambushed.

Federico Dal Barco is a PhD candidate in philosophy and the history of ideas at the University of Milan "San Raffaele" and the LMU München. Fearful of Cordyceps, he spends most of his time in a quarantine zone where he writes articles about modern philosophy and reviews for an Italian videogames journal. Surviving in the academic world is sometimes more challenging than dealing with raiders, but Immanuel Kant helps him to cope with the infections of editors and reviewers!

Steve Bein got infected by philosophy in his senior year of high school. From his brain it spread swiftly into his spinal column and extremities. These propelled him all over the planet, to contract various philosophical contagions in Illinois, Germany, Japan, Hawai'i, Minnesota, New York, Texas, and now Ohio. There, he is Patient Zero at the University of Dayton, transmitting his now hideously complex syndrome to hundreds of unsuspecting students every year. He infects countless others through skin contact or aerial contact with his written work, which includes chapters in twenty-two books and a handful of the top journals in the field. Though he obtained a doctorate in philosophy, he has been unable to develop a vaccine. There is no known cure.

Lance Belluomini is mostly known for having published the only academic essay on *Tenet* in *The Palgrave Handbook of Popular Culture as Philosophy*.

He's also contributed chapters to a variety of Wiley Blackwell volumes, most recently on *Ted Lasso* and *Mad Max*. Immediately after watching *The Last of Us* pilot, Lance went on Atkins (like Joel) to improve his odds of surviving any large-scale fungal outbreak.

Mary Bernard is a Registered Mental Health Counselor Intern in private practice in Florida, where she counsels from an existential and feminist orientation. Mary was first infected by the philosophy bug as an undergraduate at Stetson University, where she majored in philosophy and French literature. An avid gamer, Mary binged the first season of *The Last of Us* after recognizing the title from various video game awards. A completionist at heart, when she was offered the epic quest of contributing to this volume with Dr. Susan Peppers-Bates, she accepted without hesitation.

Enea Bianchi obtained his PhD at the University of Galway (Ireland), where he teaches in the Italian Department. He has published a book on the thought of Italian philosopher, Mario Perniola, and contributes to journals including the *British Journal of Aesthetics* and *Journal for Cultural Research*. He's currently researching the aesthetics of catastrophe and traditional archery (being an archer himself). Perhaps that's the reason why he finds solace in exploring post-apocalyptic realms with bow and arrow, and that's also why he felt a twinge of sadness when he realized that, alas, neither Joel nor Ellie uses this weaponry in the TV show. Dear Mr. Mazin and Mr. Druckmann, can you please consider incorporating this element in season 2?

Armond Boudreaux is Associate Professor of English at East Georgia State College. His publications include *The Last Revolution* technothriller series, and contributions to several volumes in the Blackwell Philosophy and Pop Culture series. He has been on the verge of becoming a full-blown prepper for a long time, and writing this chapter might have been the thing that tipped him over the edge.

Per F. Broman is Professor of Music Theory at Bowling Green State University, Ohio. He never wanted to become a singer, but grew up playing his four-string violin on the firefly-infested porch. He likes to lose his mind in film music, modernist art music, and aesthetics, intertwining music theory, musicology, and philosophy with the harsh lessons of academic endurance and survival. As he walked through the scholarly valleys in Sweden, Canada, and the United States, he published on filmmaker Ingmar Bergman's use of music and biographies of composers Karin Rehnqvist and Sven-David Sandström. If somehow the Lord gave him a second chance in those moments, he would do it all over again.

Matthew Crippen grew up along the Nottawasaga River in a stretch of woods, not unlike where Bill lives in *The Last of Us*. Because his parents are biologists (among other things), he got to look at interesting organisms through microscopes from a young age. Though he's never dealt with a zombie apocalypse, he was in Egypt for a revolution and later a coup, and saw both the good and bad ways that people deal with crises. Since then, he's moved to Busan—famous for the zombie movie, *Train to Busan*—and taken an interest in how East Asian ideas contributed to the trajectory of classic American philosophies.

Michael K. Cundall Jr. became a philosophical zombie at age fourteen. His parents thought it was a phase, but the questions grew from sporadic to full fungal by the time he reached college, where he found the right growth conditions under which to pursue philosophy to its evolutionary zenith. He spends his time working on philosophical issues related to humor, laughter, and mirth. His recent book is *The Humor Hack: Using Humor to Feel Better, Increase Resilience, and (Yes) Enjoy Your Work*, and he's currently working on a monograph exploring humor and the common good. When not watching *The Last of Us*, he can be found carving spoons and bowls. His favorite woods to carve have beautiful spalting—and that's no joke.

Yassine Dguidegue was born and raised in Morocco, where his passion for understanding why certain religious beliefs promise heaven for some and hell for others took root. His deep interest in diverse cultural, religious, and national groups led him to explore and engage with their stories. Inspired by Ellie and Joel's narrative in *The Last of Us*, Yassine felt a connection to their struggles with not completely fitting into Quarantine Zones (QZs). This connection fueled his desire to write a chapter depicting the paternalistic actions of quarantine zones and their respective social institutions.

Darci Doll is Professor of Philosophy at Delta College in Michigan. She has written extensively on pop culture and philosophy, including on Anthony Bourdain, *The Handmaid's Tale*, Queen, and *Better Call Saul*. When she's not writing or teaching, she's really poetic and losing her mind with the people she loves.

Mariya Dvoskina is a psychologist in Denver, Colorado. Her work involves providing training, consultation, and therapy. When she is not head-shrinking, she enjoys annoying her husband with mid-movie plot analysis. She is a fan of dystopian fiction and consumes it in all its forms. Or does *it* consume her? Mariya is also a trained mushroom hunter (owing to her Russian heritage), so beware, Cordyceps!

Mackenzie Graham is Senior Research Fellow at the Ethox Centre, University of Oxford. He works primarily in practical ethics, and the philosophy of trust. He is a huge fan of video games in the post-apocalyptic genre, though he probably wouldn't last very long in a real zombie apocalypse.

Lucas Hinojosa-López is a philosopher of biology at the University of Valparaíso, Chile. His research focuses on the impact of the mutualistic relationship between plants and fungi on their ecosystems. He seeks to evaluate whether the emergent abilities of plants in this relationship can be defined as cognitive. As an avid mushroom forager, he has inhaled countless spores while doing fieldwork in the forests of Chile, showing no signs of infection ... yet. Some people claim that he talks to plants, but he claims that this is not a symptom of infection.

Charles Joshua Horn is Professor of Philosophy at the University of Wisconsin Stevens Point. He specializes in seventeenth- and eighteenth-century philosophy (mostly focusing on the thought of Spinoza and Leibniz), metaphysics, and philosophy of religion. He also regularly plays and researches all sorts of video games. He has previously published several articles connecting philosophy to video games like *The Legend of Zelda*, *Bioshock*, and *God of War*. Aside from Joel and Ellie's journey, the only other escort mission he's ever liked is the one with his children, Sophia and Jonah, even though sometimes they're more trouble than Cordyceps or raiders.

Daniel Irwin is an aspiring screenwriter and filmmaker. In his free time, he loves building Lego sets, hunting for collectibles around the neighborhood with his dog Duncan, and (of course) playing video games. When he played *The Last of Us Part I,* he was younger than Ellie in that game, and now he's older than Ellie from *Part II.*

William Irwin is Professor of Philosophy at King's College in Pennsylvania and is the General Editor of the Blackwell Philosophy and Pop Culture series. In addition to his work on popular culture, Irwin has published the novel *Little Siddhartha* and two books of poetry, *Always Dao* and *Both/ And.* Like Joel, Bill loves music, has a goofy sense of humor, and maybe shows a bit of bias toward his family.

Clint Wesley Jones teaches philosophy at Capital University in Columbus, Ohio. His scholarly work focuses on environmental problems, utopianism, pop culture, Marxist philosophy, and issues in critical social theory. He has contributed to several Blackwell Philosophy and Pop Culture volumes, including those on *Inception* and *Mad Max*. His most recent book,

Contemporary Cowboys, is an edited volume that examines the changing role of the cowboy in contemporary cultural mythologies. Though he one day hopes to be a survivor in a zombie apocalypse, he is equally sure that he doesn't want it to be one started by Cordyceps.

Tim Jones is Course Leader for the BA in Psychology with Sociology at City College Norwich in the UK, where he also lectures on their Access to Higher Education Diploma in the Humanities and Social Sciences. His absolutely ideal module would take a speculative look at the new social forces and structures impacting individuals in a world devastated by Cordyceps, but he's instead stuck lecturing on digitalization and climate change. He lives with his wife and two cats, who'd totally have ripped Ellie to shreds if she'd dare go near them with a shiv.

Quân Nguyen is a teaching fellow at the University of Edinburgh in Scotland. He researches feminist philosophy and climate ethics, and has worked as a climate campaigner—but he also hates mushrooms, so he was extra excited about a video game and TV series that both cover climate and environmental change and at the same time serve as a warning about the dangers of fungal life forms.

Alberto Oya is Investigador Doutorado Contratado at the Instituto de Filosofia da Nova (Universidade Nova de Lisboa, Portugal). He is the author of *The Metaphysical Anthropology of Julián Marías, First-Person Shooter Videogames*, and *Unamuno's Religious Fictionalism*. He has published over thirty papers in professional philosophical peer-reviewed journals. It saddens him that Ellie from the video game didn't get the chance to play in a working arcade.

Susan Peppers-Bates is Associate Professor of Philosophy and Chair of the Philosophy Department at Stetson University, where she teaches and splits her research between Nicolas Malebranche, feminist philosophy, the philosophy of race, and the philosophy of religion. Though she loves most science fiction, she loathes most horror and only agreed to watch *The Last of Us* so her partner could prepare for its house at Halloween Horror Nights. To both of their surprise, she was immediately infected and so craved yet more fungal contact that she sought out the video games and tracked down the editor of this anthology. Her children, Robin and Anne-Marie, alas share her horror of horror and won't be reading her contribution.

Traci Phillipson is Assistant Professor of Philosophy at Loras College in Dubuque, Iowa. She specializes in the history of philosophy, especially medieval philosophy in the Latin and Arabic traditions, while also working in ethics and the philosophy of religion. She isn't sure that she'd survive a Cordyceps outbreak, or that she'd want to.

Remis Ramos Carreño teaches philosophy at the Universidad Alberto Hurtado in Santiago, Chile. He has expended most of his experience points upgrading his philosophy of mind and cognitive science skill trees, researching how and why humans and other animals are able to acquire abstract mental representations and concepts. He has been playing video games since he was a nerdy little kid in the early 1980s, when arcade machines were a staple in every neighborhood instead of being a distant relic of the past.

Juliele Maria Sievers is Professor of Philosophy at the Federal University of Alagoas, Brazil. She has unlocked several achievements during her character arc. After graduating and getting her Master's Degree from the Federal University of Santa Maria in Brazil, she moved on to the hard mode of doctoral studies at the University of Lille 3 in France, followed by a legendary mode working as *Wissenschaftlicher Mitarbeiterin* at the University of Konstanz in Germany. After that, her character's journey brought her back to her homeland, where she was a postdoctoral researcher, before beginning to work in her current position. She is interested in the connections between philosophy and literature and normativity, has published works on philosophy and video games, sci-fi films and series, and is constantly researching about other ways of doing and playing with philosophy.

Dylan Skurka is a philosophy PhD student at York University in Canada. His research focuses on the intersection between transcendental phenomenology and the philosophy of psychiatry, perilously straddling the line between the Continental Philosophy Fireflies and the Analytic Philosophy Disaster Response Agency (or APEDRA, for short) in their post-apocalyptic battle in the unforgiving wilderness of academic philosophy. He heads his school's graduate student philosophy blog, *Brainwandering*, and his work has been published in *Philosophy Now*. In his spare time, he enjoys infecting his wife Sasha and their baby on the way with bad jokes and incoherent rants about Edmund Husserl.

Acknowledgments
Thank Who You Can Thank

Unlike the survivalist, Bill, I couldn't have accomplished this project alone. I'm very thankful to each of the authors who contributed thoughtful and original chapters that were even better than what I had in mind when I envisioned the book. The chapters were a pleasure to read, teaching me a lot and heightening my appreciation of the video games and the show.

A special thanks to my former professor, Scott Davison, too. In 2003 (over 20 years ago!), I started my undergraduate work at Morehead State University, and he had just published an essay in *The Lord of the Rings and Philosophy*. Davison's essay was on how Tolkien could help us think about the nature of evil, and it helped make sense of some of the earliest philosophical questions I had from growing up in the Bible Belt in Eastern Kentucky. Davison's work, and the Blackwell Pop Culture and Philosophy series more generally, had a profound impact on my education and interests, and inspired me to continue studying philosophy. It's my sincere hope that this volume has the same impact on young philosophers, too.

I also want to thank William Irwin, the editor for the Blackwell Philosophy and Pop Culture series, who has been a tremendous source of support and encouragement from the first moment that I proposed this volume in 2014, not long after *The Last of Us* was released. With his guidance, patience, and keen insight, there wasn't an instance where I felt lost in the darkness.

And, of course, a special thanks to my children, Sophia and Jonah, who give me hope for Future Days. Daddy loves you, baby girl and boy.

Introduction
No Questions Left Behind

The Last of Us is a story wrapped in contradictions. It's dark, but hopeful. It's simple, yet has layers upon layers of complexity. And it depicts humanity both at its worst and its best. Using a fictional post-apocalyptic setting during a fungal pandemic, the story of *The Last of Us* follows Ellie, a young girl immune to the Cordyceps infection.

Ellie's story couldn't be told without her protector, Joel, who lost his daughter, Sarah, on the first day of the outbreak. Over the course of the first video game and the first season of the show, Joel grows to love and care for Ellie as if she was his own daughter, culminating in a pivotal moment when he kills the Firefly doctors who were going to sacrifice Ellie's life in hopes of finding a cure for the infection. After rescuing her, Joel doubles down on his morally questionable actions and lies to Ellie, telling her that the Fireflies found others immune from the infection like Ellie, that they couldn't find a cure, and that they have stopped looking. Lying to Ellie was the only way to protect her from going back to the Fireflies to sacrifice herself for the greater good.

Joel's choice to kill the doctors has been controversial ever since the first video game was released in 2013, leading some to wonder whether we were unwittingly playing the villain of the story all along. It's quite reasonable to think that Joel's actions were morally blameworthy. After all, he killed doctors trying to save humanity and then lied about it. And it's quite reasonable to think that the doctors were morally praiseworthy for thinking of the greater good. Ellie's death, while tragic, might have led to saving countless people. On the other hand, some might quite reasonably argue that Joel was protecting Ellie because his moral obligation was not to the world, but to the young girl he loved and promised to protect. Maybe Joel's actions weren't praiseworthy, exactly, but they weren't blameworthy either. In other words, Joel might not be a hero, but he isn't a villain either.

In *The Last of Us Part II*, the second video game in the series, we find Abby, the daughter of the main Firefly doctor, seeking revenge against Joel. In the earliest moments of the video game, Abby finds, tortures, and kills

Joel in front of Ellie. The second video game is primarily a story about revenge and its costs, as it follows Ellie and Abby, whose stories mirror each other in complicated and compelling ways. Ellie, like Abby, has lost a father in moments of cruel violence in the name of justice. We might wonder whether their revenge is morally justified, and more broadly, whether morality and justice even exist in the world of *The Last of Us*.

The Last of Us is filled to the brim with great characters, but they don't exist in a vacuum. They grow and develop together. People need each other—community is necessary for being human, and it's even more necessary in a world filled with Clickers, Bloaters, cannibals, raiders, slavers, and more. But how is it possible to have trust and genuine relationships with others when there are threats around every corner? How can we genuinely care for others, when such care may get us killed, infected, or worse? And perhaps most importantly, is there more to living than just *surviving*? Looking to Bill's relationship with Frank, we have to ask what good security is if you don't have someone to share it with. Sometimes a packet of strawberry seeds might just be more important than a gun.

Because the characters are connected with each other, we can think of their actions not just in moral terms, but political terms, as well. So, in addition to considering whether our favorite characters are moral or immoral, we can also ask questions about the broader systems that govern their world. Is FEDRA a legitimate political power? Does Marlene have legal authority over the Fireflies? Are the rules imposed in the quarantine zones legal or just? Addressing these questions about the *Last of Us* can help us make sense of the moral and political questions in our world, too.

As much as *The Last of Us* is about the morally complex and controversial actions of characters like Ellie, Joel, Abby, and others, it is also about understanding and appreciating the softer moments that speak to our humanity. Can beauty still be found in a world ravaged by disease and the collapse of society? How does Ellie's joke book help to develop her relationships with Riley and Joel? How does Joel's guitar and playing music to Ellie help him recover and heal from the loss of his daughter? More succinctly, how important are art, music, and humor to humanity?

On the surface, *The Last of Us* is a story about surviving in a post-apocalyptic setting, but looking deeper we see it is much more than that. *The Last of Us* helps us to confront and understand what makes us distinctly *human*. What is the proper way to understand concepts like love, justice, hope, responsibility, community, and forgiveness? These and other questions await. So, throw on your backpack and come along for the journey. With this book as a guide through the darkness, we'll look for the light together.

PART I
JOEL'S CHOICE

1

Joel's Choice
Apocalyptic Fantasies, Dystopian Hope, and the Post-Human Question

Clint Wesley Jones

Apocalyptic stories are generally fun escapist forms of entertainment, and this is especially true of the apocalyptic stories that have dominated popular culture for more than two decades now. Zombies in varying forms, emerging from divergent sources, and aimlessly shambling about a broken world, infest the contemporary imagination.[1] But *The Last of Us* stands apart from the typical zombie stories of the last few decades, and serves as a unique contribution to the genre of apocalyptic literature and media. In *The Last of Us*, the Infected aren't generated from industrial catastrophes such as nuclear fallout, chemical spills, or lab-created diseases, but rather from the accelerated global climate shift that alters the environment enough that Cordyceps can migrate beyond its "natural" boundaries to a new environment—the human.

To properly understand apocalyptic fantasies like *The Last of Us*, it's important to read them within the framework of capitalist-driven social forces, because it's easier to imagine the world ending than it is to imagine capitalism ending. As Jeffrey Jerome Cohen argues, "Apocalypse is a failure of the imagination, a giving up on the future instead of a commitment to the difficult work of composing a better present."[2] Cohen is pointing to "dystopian hope" which resides at the heart of contemporary apocalyptic stories.[3] Dystopian hope resonates with consumers as escapist *and* renders catastrophic futures *as desirable*, as the only way to "reset" civilization so that we (the survivors) can right the wrongs of society.

Joel's ultimate refusal to save humanity, stripping the survivors of the reset they desire, and, instead, opting for a post-human existence in the aftermath of Cordyceps, puts *The Last of Us* in a unique position to answer what the right thing to do is in the aftermath of an apocalypse. Joel's decision to save Ellie is justified by rejecting the dystopian hope that resonates with consumers of apocalyptic stories. Joel is a different kind of survivor.

The Last of Us and Philosophy: Look for the Light, First Edition.
Edited by Charles Joshua Horn.
© 2025 John Wiley & Sons, Inc. Published 2025 by John Wiley & Sons, Inc.

It's Different in the Daylight

Devastation and revelation are the two sides of apocalyptic storytelling. "Apocalypse" is generally understood to be a revelation of some sort, usually divine in nature, but this needn't be the case. In fact, on the devastation side, some catastrophes are described in apocalyptic terms even though they don't meet apocalyptic standards. For instance, in the wake of a Category-5 hurricane, news reporters might describe an apocalyptic landscape. Such descriptions compel the imagination. So when someone is confronted with an apocalyptic story, they conjure up similar ideas, while omitting more relevant or pertinent details necessary to understand an apocalyptic world. For instance, an apocalypse can't be localized, but must be global and total in its reach; everyone may be affected to different degrees, but everyone must be affected.

A dystopia can come into existence without any apocalyptic underpinnings just as surely as an apocalypse could occur without causing undue destruction in its wake. Dystopias and apocalypses are usually conceptually linked because the world is often depicted as falling apart. It's critically important that, when addressing apocalyptic stories, we remember that utopian and dystopian communities both exist. Utopias and dystopias are sociopolitical arrangements, while apocalyptic forces are imposed on communities and are totalizing in their destruction.[4]

A destructive apocalypse would certainly destroy the world as we currently know it, but the way people chose to live in the aftermath would be describable in utopian and dystopian terms. The aftermath of many destructive apocalypses would most likely be a dystopian setting. *The Last of Us* doesn't depict the aftermath of the apocalypse in dystopian terms except for the abandoned cities we're shown. The larger world seems to have escaped the destruction of the Cordyceps infection and serves as the basis for dystopian hope.

The Last of Us is an apocalyptic story, albeit a unique one, and our first task is understanding what makes this apocalyptic tale substantially different from, say, *The Walking Dead*.[5] *The Walking Dead* is one of the most popular apocalyptic stories ever told, but the focus of the story is squarely on the time immediately *after* the fall of humanity. This is generally true of most apocalyptic stories that use some variety of infected as the apocalyptic catalyst for society's downfall. In Robert Kirkman's narrative the reader goes from normal to zombie apocalypse in the first page turn, which accounts for roughly six weeks. *The Last of Us*, by contrast, jumps forward twenty years and forces us to contend with a significantly different set of questions about the post-apocalyptic world. Not only that, but it generates its apocalyptic catalyst from an environmental force derived from climate shift, or, what we might think of as a genuinely green apocalypse.

When You're Lost in the Darkness

While it might seem like all apocalypses are the same, the reality is that not all end-of-the-world stories are similar.[6] *The Last of Us* eschews the usual approaches by simply allowing Cordyceps to evolve beyond its natural boundaries. As Dr. Neuman points out in 1968 in episode 1, there is no cure for something like a fungal outbreak. Fast-forward to September 24, 2003, and Dr. Ratna Pertiwi in Jakarta, at what is ostensibly Ground Zero, says the only reasonable response to the infection is to "bomb" the city. Dr. Ratna's response indicates that there still isn't a cure available for a Cordyceps fungal infection. In fact, that her first thought is to bomb a city suggests that she may not believe a cure is even *possible*. Here we get the seeds of a typical apocalypse.

Simultaneously across America and, presumably, the world, people transform into monsters and begin spreading the fungal infection, causing widespread chaos.[7] The chaos is depicted in the military response, houses ablaze, planes falling from the sky, and a massive conversion of uninfected to infected in a short time span.[8] Life as we know it is over. If *The Last of Us* were a typical "zombie story," then most of its narrative would follow survivors of the initial outbreak as they attempted to navigate the immediate post-apocalyptic world. Instead, *The Last of Us* jumps forward twenty years and presents a world well beyond the immediate aftermath of social collapse.

For instance, we know that the military bombed most major cities to contain the spread of Cordyceps, yet all the Quarantine Zones (QZs) are in major cities. These facts suggest that the bombs dropped weren't nuclear, but also that there weren't many dropped; otherwise, the major population hubs, like Boston, Atlanta, Kansas City, or Pittsburgh, would've been leveled, something which clearly isn't the case. Moveover, if the Cordyceps infection happened at roughly the same time, as Joel suggests to Ellie, then given the nature of the infection and how widespread it is, it's unlikely that chemical plants, oil refineries, nuclear facilities, mining operations, and so on would have been safely shut down or taken offline in the chaos that would have ensued from the start of the infestation and the days immediately afterward.

These facilities and their adjacent problems—like slurry ponds or soil or air toxification—would devastate the world in the aftermath of an apocalyptic event, especially since most of these types of industry are in or near major population centers which were being bombed. Even if all of these industries were properly shut down, the bombs would've destabilized them and the major population centers would've been uninhabitable in the immediate aftermath. But *The Last of Us* avoids these problems which might cease, in many instances, to be life-threatening problems after two decades, and this goes for a whole host of problems that would typically emerge in the immediate aftermath of a post-apocalyptic world. The essence of dystopian hope that *The Last of Us* emphasizes so well is that the world will survive a catastrophic apocalyptic event and we can go on living in it with concerns only for the monsters and marauders that populate the planet.

When looking at the world that emerges in *The Last of Us*, it's clear that the frailty of human civilization has impeded the ability of communities to navigate the world. In such a world, highly specialized knowledge, in many communities, would vanish. Medical expertise, various types of engineering, high-level mathematics, agriculture, history, technology, and philosophy would be hindered in growth, development, and their ability to adequately handle Cordyceps as a common and pervasive enemy. The frustration of not being able to handle the state of world is made explicit by Joel when he tells Tess, "Vaccines, miracle cures. None of it works. Ever."

Over two decades, once vanquished diseases would reemerge in human society without vaccines and qualified people to administer them. Building and building maintenance would be incredibly difficult, especially as heavy machinery became unusable. Communication would be increasingly difficult as batteries failed, and travel would not only be dangerous due to raiders, hunters, slavers, and Cordyceps, but also, after two decades, roadways, dams, bridges, and other infrastructure would fall apart. These changes would mark a return to a more natural, that is, less human environment. In short, the world would be incredibly hostile to humans *regardless* of the threat posed by Cordyceps. Dystopian hope, perhaps evidenced best by the community in Jackson, Wyoming, would lead us to believe that we can turn things around, control for the worst, and do better than merely subsist. We would believe we can conquer the world anew.

We Always Win

Though the Infected are the main feature of the collapsed world in *The Last of Us*, the significant difference between this story and other similar narratives is how they approach dystopian hope. The problem with contemporary apocalyptic storytelling is that stories often trade on the same trope—with the end of civilization as we currently understand it, there's the possibility for something better. Once the apocalypse happens, if we can just weather the post-apocalyptic landscape for a couple of years, then we can rebuild society and build it back better than it was. All we need is a little time and the right plucky group of survivors to remake the world.[9]

These types of stories invite us to consider what we would do differently and, importantly, *why* we would do things differently. Everything can be called into question. Every social stigma can be erased, every injustice wiped clean, and everybody gets a fresh start if you can just survive a year or two. *The Last of Us* depicts no such opportunity. Twenty years of battling the elements, each other, Cordyceps, and so much else, and human society is still teetering on the edge of total collapse. We can see this examination of dystopian hope in the communities that Joel and Ellie interact with throughout their story. These communities encapsulate the essence of why apocalyptic and dystopian fictions are problematic, but they also help explain why Joel's choice to save Ellie is incredibly significant.

Dream of Sheep Ranches on the Moon

In *The Last of Us Part I* and season 1 of the show, the vaccine is central, as it is in most stories of the genre. The critical difference between *The Last of Us* and its counterparts is that the solution to the apocalypse of infected is left in the hands of Joel. Having begun to see Ellie as a surrogate for Sarah by the time they reach Salt Lake City, Joel can't sacrifice her for the greater good.[10] Joel's reluctance to deliver Ellie to the Fireflies overrides her desire to follow through because, "it can't all be for nothing." Once Joel learns the truth from Marlene, that the fungus must be removed from Ellie's brain, resulting in her death, he must decide whether to allow her to be sacrificed for a possible vaccine or attempt to save her from the Fireflies by any means necessary. Joel's decision is the most significant break with other apocalyptic stories because Joel doesn't give in to dystopian hope, but rather, effectively ends humanity's chance to return to pre-apocalyptic fantasies.[11]

It's abundantly clear, regardless of which community you view it in relation to, that there is no going back to the way things were and there is no bringing civilization back better than before. Not only have several QZs been overrun by infected or revolutionaries, but several have also been abandoned. After twenty years, this instability certainly indicates an ongoing backsliding into primitivity for those still living in the shrinking QZs. Access to material goods, the loss of manufacturing, increased population density or, worse, the loss of people, all tally up to increased hardship and the inability of FEDRA to provide security for people.

Tommy's group, to the extent it would be possible, has no designs on expansion, evidenced by their unwillingness to allow outsiders to join their collective. Perhaps with a vaccine, they would change their mind, but Joel's decision to save Ellie effectively eliminates that possibility. However, the vaccine *would* help the Fireflies. The Fireflies openly recruit people, have a large network of cells that could draw people away from the QZs, or use those people to overthrow FEDRA, allowing the Fireflies to take immediate possession of FEDRA's resources. Marlene's willingness to sacrifice Ellie hinges on this vision and the promise of a return to pre-apocalyptic civilization. That Marlene doesn't see the world as irrevocably broken in the way that Joel does is apparent in their exchange in the parking garage of the hospital. Marlene tells Joel that Ellie "lives in a broken world that you could have saved."

Joel refuses to sacrifice Ellie because he no longer thinks of her as cargo and doesn't suffer from dystopian hope.[12] But Tess clearly does when she reveals her bite to Joel and demands that he make and keep a promise to deliver Ellie to the Fireflies. She may have been without hope before, but Ellie's immunity has restored it. At the end of their journey, Joel still doesn't believe a vaccine is possible, and even if it is, he doesn't believe the world could ever go back to the way it was. Joel's choice to save Ellie is motivated by the wrong reasons, his care and concern for Ellie, but he ultimately chooses to do the right thing; with or without a vaccine, we can't return the world to its pre-apocalyptic condition.

Not Today You New-World-Order Jack-Boot Fucks

Joel helps us see that dystopian hope is flawed. His choice isn't just to save Ellie, but to force humanity to rethink how it's going to live in a post-apocalyptic world.[13] There are many similarities between *The Last of Us* and other apocalyptic tales, but the significance of *The Last of Us* is that it doesn't ask us to think of how we would rebuild the world into something better. Rather, it asks us to consider how we're going to inhabit a post-apocalyptic world in which we're not the most dominant force for change. Joel's choice to save Ellie places all the survivors into a post-human condition where being human must begin to mean something radically new.

Notes

1. Ashley Dawson, *Extinction: A Radical History* (New York: O/R Books, 2016), 16.
2. Jeffrey Jerome Cohen, "Grey," *Prismatic Ecology: Ecotheory beyond Green* (Minneapolis: University of Minnesota Press, 2013), 285.
3. For a more thorough examination of this concept see my *Apocalyptic Ecology in the Graphic Novel: Life and the Environment after Societal Collapse* (Jefferson, NC: McFarland & Co., 2020).
4. Though I won't pursue the dystopian aspect of *The Last of Us* further, for more on dystopian social arrangements, see Gregory Claeys, *Dystopia: A Natural History* (Oxford: Oxford University Press, 2017). For more on the intersection of dystopia and apocalypse see my *Apocalyptic Ecology in the Graphic Novel: Life and the Environment after Societal* Collapse.
5. Robert Kirkman, *The Walking Dead: Compendium One* (Portland, OR: Image Comics, 2009).
6. Nuclear origins betoken a different post-apocalypse than does a viral one; say, the world of *Snowpiercer* versus *The Walking Dead*. Human-made viruses can become apocalyptic in different ways which might hinge on how fast the virus is able to spread or who is at risk, as in stories like *Y: The Last Man* or *Sweet Tooth*. Even stories that rely on climate shift usually focus on rising oceans or unbreathable air to draw attention to the perils of our current situation.

7. This claim is grounded in the narrative of the HBO show rather than the video game, given the Jakarta story arc which sets the foundation for the outbreak in the show.

8. The timespan of the Cordyceps apocalypse is a somewhat difficult thing to nail down. In the video game, there is a boy's journal that is discoverable in Bill's town which insinuates that the apocalypse still hasn't reached the town several weeks after the outbreak. However, the HBO show seems to insinuate that things go from bad (Jakarta) to worse (apocalypse) in about thirty-six hours, and is widespread and simultaneous, although this is complicated by the flashback scene at the beginning of episode 3 which shows the military "evacuating" Bill's town with no Infected in sight.

9. Most zombie stories opt for incredibly high numbers of the population to be infected with whatever makes people zombies, the point being that the world is overrun with zombies. However, in stark contrast, there is a discoverable military missive in the video game which puts the infection rate at approximately 60 percent. This is far lower than similar tales and means that there are somewhere between 3 and 4 billion survivors. In the United States that would leave about 130 million people uninfected. Unfortunately, I do not have the space to pursue this further, but this does complicate both my analysis of *The Last of Us* and also its fit in zombie end-of-the-world narratives.

10. Though there isn't space for it here, there is an interesting way to think through Joel's reluctance to sacrifice Ellie using Jacques Derrida's meditation on sacrifice in *The Gift of Death* (Chicago: University of Chicago Press, 1996).

11. Joel repeatedly says that trying to save the world is "a pipe dream" (see episode 4) and his realist outlook on the state of the world after twenty years is a foreshadowing of his inability to sacrifice Ellie.

12. Though there isn't room for an analysis of it here, Joel's development of feelings for Ellie raises important questions for how people interact *in a world* and especially a world where nature is defined by the Anthropocene. The end of the Anthropocene, which I am arguing takes place in *The Last of Us*, would likely fundamentally change *how we love one another*. For an excellent introduction to this idea, see Dale Jamieson and Bonnie Nadzam's *Love in the Anthropocene* (New York: O/R Books, 2015).

13. For more on the Anthropocene and how it relates to apocalypse see Dawson, *Extinction*, 20–21.

2

Justifying Joel
In Defense of Love and Favoritism

Daniel Irwin and William Irwin

"To me, he did the right thing for him," video game and show co-creator Neil Druckmann said in an interview with Todd Martens of the *Los Angeles Times*. When explaining Joel's decision, Druckmann said, "As a parent, if I found myself in that same situation, I would hope I could do what Joel did."[1] Joel's defining choice to save his surrogate daughter, Ellie, at the cost of humanity's future has sparked debate among fans of *The Last of Us* for over a decade. Yet the single most prominent voice behind the story firmly believes Joel's decision was correct. The video game, after all, only has one ending—the player must murder a hospital full of Fireflies to save Ellie.

Series co-creator and co-writer, Craig Mazin, echoed Druckmann's sentiment, saying that "If I were in that situation as a parent, I would try really hard not to, but I probably would."[2] Of course, the appeal of *The Last of Us* is that a player/viewer can take away a different conclusion—one that doesn't align with the creators' own opinions. Ashley Johnson, the actress who played Ellie in the video game, has a more conflicted reaction to Joel's decision. She says, "it's harder to sort of take in the decision that Joel makes ... I don't know if I could give somebody away that I love so much for this cause, but I don't know if I would be able to go on a rampage like that."[3] Druckmann and Mazin are both parents, whereas Johnson is not. So maybe Joel's instinctual reaction to Ellie's peril is paternal—a decision only another parent could understand. After all, the video game actor who played Joel, Troy Baker, claimed that he was at a "disadvantage" when making the first video game in not being a father. Yet after having a son of his own, Baker now believes, "If I had the opportunity to save [my son] ... I would do anything to save him."[4]

The strength of Joel's paternal bond is surprising when we consider that he's only Ellie's father figure for about a year. He met her when she was fourteen, and he had no relationship with her mother. Unlike Marlene, Joel hasn't known Ellie since birth and didn't see her grow up. Ellie's mother, Anna, was her lifelong friend, and her dying wish to Marlene upon having

Ellie was to "make sure that she's safe." In the series premiere, Ellie even asks Marlene, "You my fucking mom or something?" Marlene's job is to be a mother to Ellie just as much as to be a leader of the Fireflies. Yet when she's faced with the same choice as Joel, Marlene values her obligation to the world over her promise to Anna.

So who's the villain? Marlene for cutting off her human feelings or Joel for dooming humanity? By framing Joel as the story's protagonist, the video game and show creators make Marlene the obstacle, the antagonist, which reflects Druckmann and Mazin's own beliefs. But Joel's decision isn't just appealing because of the framing of the narrative or his role as a father. Joel's choice is appealing because his unparalleled care, favoritism, and empathy toward Ellie are a product of his love. And such love is profoundly human.

Utilitarian Leaders

Let's first look at Joel's decision from a utilitarian perspective. Utilitarianism is a moral philosophy that says we should always act to produce the greatest good for the greatest number of people. Marlene is clearly a utilitarian. As Druckmann says, she's "a leader that can make the hard sacrifices for the betterment of humanity."[5] When discussing Marlene's goal to eradicate the fungus and re-democratize America, Mazin said that "she has to be a utilitarian" to achieve it. When it comes to sacrificing Ellie for the world's greater good, that's what Marlene precisely is—not a mother or even a human, but rather, a utilitarian leader.[6] When faced with the same decision as Joel, Marlene sacrificed Ellie like a good utilitarian.

The decision Joel faces can be seen in terms of the trolley problem, a classic thought experiment in philosophy, devised by Philippa Foot (1920–2010) and developed by Judith Jarvis Thomson (1929–2020).[7] The problem considers a scenario like this: You watch as a trolley hurtles down a track that will collide with and kill five people. In front of you is a lever that can switch the trolley to a different track with only one person on it. You can't get anyone off the track in time to save them or stop the trolley from moving. Your only choice is whether to pull the lever. What is the morally right action? If all you know is the number of people involved, then the utilitarian answer is clear: pull the lever to save more lives, because it allows you to maximize goodness and minimize suffering. Joel's dilemma is similar, but more complicated. He must choose between saving one person and saving many, but that one person is Ellie. Instead of five people at a distance with a lever, he must kill a hospital full of people to save the one, and he is effectively killing countless more by removing the world's chance for a vaccine. Of course, as we will discuss later, Joel's not a utilitarian. But Marlene is. She promised Anna to protect Ellie, but, as Mazin says, "she's willing to sacrifice her own morality and what she believes is right"[8] to ensure a brighter future for humanity.

Marlene overrides her emotions in the name of the greater good, but she isn't cold and calculating. In fact, Marlene expresses guilt, telling Joel, "I promised her mother that I would save her child. I promised. So, I do understand. I'm the only one who understands." If she can empathize with Joel, why doesn't she come to the same conclusion? Most obviously, because she hasn't just traveled across the country with Ellie and formed a lifelong bond. As a result, Marlene isn't conflicted because of her attachment to Ellie. She's conflicted because of her attachment to Anna and the promise made to her.

In the first season's finale, Marlene promises her dying best friend, Anna, to find someone to look after her infant daughter. But, as Mazin puts it, "Marlene didn't pick a person to raise Ellie. She picked FEDRA," her enemies. Distancing herself from Ellie in this way is a prime example of Marlene's instincts as a utilitarian leader. As Johnson puts it, Marlene "doesn't fully have the maternal thing," because being a mother would directly conflict with her role as a leader.[9] In the video game, a hardened Bill, bitter over the death of Frank, says something that could provide insight into Marlene's psyche, as well as his own. Bill explains that "Once upon a time, I had somebody that I cared about. It was a partner. Somebody I had to look after. And in this world, that sort of shit's good for one thing: gettin' you killed." While this is a warning to Joel, it also applies to Marlene. She distances herself from Ellie while still doing everything possible to ensure her safety. Marlene keeps her promise but avoids the attachment.

At the end of the video game, the player can find two voice recordings from Marlene in Saint Mary's Hospital. The recordings are personal logs that shed light on what was going through Marlene's mind when the Fireflies found Ellie. In one recording, Marlene speaks directly to Anna, Ellie's deceased mother. Marlene says, "I need you to know that I've kept my promise all these years ... despite everything that I was in charge of, I looked after her. I would've done anything for her, and at times ..." In this recording, Marlene never once refers to Ellie by her name, further supporting the idea that Marlene's attachment to her is limited. The recording depicts Marlene coming to terms with her decision. She claims it was the doctor's choice, and that their "asking [her] was more of a formality." Like most of her recording's contents, this claim is a case of self-deception. (For more on the role of self-deception in *The Last of Us*, check out Chapter 15.) In *The Last of Us Part II*, we see a flashback conversation between Marlene and Dr. Anderson that occurs soon after the Fireflies find Ellie. Dr. Anderson is "begging" Marlene to allow him to perform the surgery, but she has the final decision. While she struggles to forsake her promise to Anna, Marlene sees Abby, Anderson's daughter, enter and drop off dinner for her dad. At this moment, Marlene lets go of her obligation to one dead person, in favor of her obligation to the greatest number of the living. She gives Anderson a decisive "do it."

Loving Protectors

Marlene's utilitarianism leads her to sacrifice Ellie, but why does Joel choose to *save* Ellie? When discussing Joel's identity and his desire to protect Tommy, Sarah, and later Ellie, Mazin says, "this is Joel's purpose: he has to have somebody to save."[10] *The Last of Us* depicts many protectors. Bill protects Frank, Henry protects Sam, and Abby protects Lev. All these pairings serve as reflections of Joel and Ellie. The protectors are willing to sacrifice everything to save one person they care about. Henry steals valuable medicine to treat one person with a near-untreatable case of leukemia, and for her part, Abby turns on and murders her own faction to protect a member of that faction's sworn enemy. Should such actions be condemned as immoral? No, not necessarily, because Joel and these other protectors are deeply human in favoring the ones they love.

In "The Myth of Universal Love," the contemporary philosopher Stephen T. Asma argues that "Empathy is not a concept, but a natural biological event."[11] Citing current research in neuroscience, Asma explains that empathy is not a "limitless reserve" for humans to pull from, but is instead a very "limited resource."[12] In *The Last of Us*, Joel exhibits a lack of empathy right from the prologue. Before and during the outbreak, Sarah is the one person he cares for above all others. We see Joel's favoritism when he, Tommy, and Sarah try to make it to the highway exit. They pass a group of strangers, and Tommy slows down to help them. He says, "They've got a kid, Joel." Joel responds, "So do we," and urges Tommy to keep driving. Joel's so concerned with his daughter's safety that he can't empathize with a family much like his own in need of help.

As another example of the human capacity to empathize, consider the part of the video game when Joel and Ellie escape Pittsburgh with Henry and Sam. Chased by hunters, the group must climb a ladder onto some shipping containers to get out of the city. Henry gets up first, followed by Sam. As Ellie climbs the ladder, it detaches from the shipping container, leaving Joel stranded. Instead of finding another way for Joel to get up, Henry grabs Sam and runs to safety, unconcerned about whether Ellie comes along. This action may be selfish, but it also expresses simple human favoritism. Henry's a protector, and just like Joel and every other survivor in the world, he values the life of his favorite over anything else. Ellie returns to save Joel, and they later reunite with Henry and Sam. Fending off a furious Joel, Henry explains, "You had a good chance of making it, and you did. But coming back for you meant putting him at risk.... If it was the other way around, would you have come back for us?" In his book *Against Fairness*, Asma writes, "It is human to prefer. Love is discriminatory."[13] Henry acted out of love for his kin, and Joel would do the same. Love overrides utilitarian calculations of the greatest good for the greatest number.

Like any human, Joel only has so much empathetic reserve. But what determines who he loves and protects? Sarah is Joel's daughter, and he's bonded tightly with her. Much of the science behind human attachment involves oxytocin, "the love hormone."[14] As Asma says, oxytocin is a hormone "absolutely vital in human bonding" that "helps the brain form attachments."[15] While oxytocin levels are higher in women, both men and women experience its effects, especially when bonding with children. "Our brains are actually biased toward our families," Asma says, regardless of our other relationships.[16] At its core, Joel's profound connection to Sarah is a product of the human pursuit of social bonds and the pleasure we receive from forming relationships with our kin—"the main ingredient in human happiness is not wealth, property, pleasure, or fame, but strong social bonds," Asma says.[17]

But what about Ellie? Joel's attachment to his surrogate daughter has two concurrent explanations. The first cause behind Joel's attachment is compelling for anyone who's watched the show or played the video game. When discussing how we create bonds outside immediate family members, Asma says that "favorites (friends) can only be created by spending time together, sharing experiences, and immersing in each other's lives—and *time*, sadly, is a finite resource."[18] Finite time goes along with finite empathy. Asma explains, "Biology can bond people together, but so can history—so can shared habits, emotions, and values, as we respond to life events."[19] As Joel spends time with Ellie, so does the audience, and we grow to care for her in a way that Marlene, by her own volition, never does.

The additional catalyst for Joel and Ellie's mutual love involves "the flexibility of biological bias," as Asma discusses.[20] When we find the characters twenty years into the apocalypse, despite having lost their biological parent and daughter, respectively, Ellie and Joel need that kind of connection. The canon prequel comic, *American Dreams,* which follows a younger Ellie as she arrives in Boston, depicts her restless desire for a parent. The comic starts with Ellie asking a soldier, with whom she's built a relationship, to take her with him. The soldier maintains, "I got my own family to look after," and leaves Ellie alone in the QZ. In response, Ellie tells herself, "I can manage just fine on my own." However, upon meeting Riley, Ellie can't help but look up to her. The comic illustrates Ellie's desire for someone to lean on and trust. Riley is the closest thing to a parent Ellie has, though later their relationship will evolve into a romantic one.[21] We can assume that Ellie has been searching for a protector her entire life before this, as she famously says to Joel, "Everyone I have cared for has either died or left me." Ellie's desire for a parent is explained by Asma when he says that even when a child doesn't have a relationship with their parents, "*someone else* in close proximity ... may have unknowingly built the ability (to bond) in the otherwise deprived infant."[22] Whether she recognizes it or not, Ellie has been searching for a protector her whole life, and Joel's the one to satisfy that need.

Joel, it turns out, needs Ellie just as much as she needs him. Joel tragically lost his daughter, but "our bias defaults do not set like cement," they "remain open to new experiences," as Asma says.[23] The protector still needs someone to protect, someone to extend his empathy toward, but that doesn't mean that Joel just moved on after Sarah. It wasn't until he met Ellie that Joel became a father again. Joel's scar on the side of his face represents his ability to heal and bond again. In the season 1 finale, Joel reveals to Ellie that he "was the guy who shot and missed," leaving the scar. Joel "couldn't see the point anymore" after Sarah's death and decided to end his life. But as he pulled the trigger, he flinched. Sarah's death left a scar on Joel, but part of him wasn't ready to die. Twenty years later, Joel begins to heal and find purpose, but as he tells Ellie, "It wasn't time that did it." Joel and Ellie were drawn to each other because "Strong friendships and family bonds are unparalleled in providing people with happiness."[24] In a desperate world, Joel attests that "you keep going for family," and when faced with the choice between saving Ellie or everyone else, Joel saves his surrogate daughter.

In Favor of Favoritism

Favoritism is out of fashion in contemporary America, where we try to be as fair and impartial as possible. But that is not the way it has been in all times and places. For example, Asma explains that "Favoritism is the groundwork of Confucian culture. The model of the good person is not the saintly world-saver, but the devoted family member."[25] So is it possible to argue that saving Ellie makes Joel a good person?[26]

Druckmann and Mazin are candid about their favoritism toward their children, so it makes sense that *The Last of Us* expresses approval of human bias. Nonetheless, the video game and show depict the ugly consequences of favoritism. Joel's rampage through the hospital to rescue Ellie isn't portrayed as a heroic act. It's tragic, violent, and relentless.

The show also explores this theme in "When We Are in Need," the episode with cannibalistic narcissist, David. Toward the end of the episode, David explains to Ellie that he was shown the world's truth not by God, but "by Cordyceps." He asks her, "What does Cordyceps do? Is it evil? No. It's fruitful. It multiplies. It feeds and protects its children, and it secures its future with violence, if it must. It loves." David isn't just describing Cordyceps; he's describing a protector. Cordyceps represents the often-ugly reality of our nature. From the opening scene of the series, *The Last of Us* depicts the conflict between Cordyceps and humanity over dominance of the planet. It was likely global warming that caused Cordyceps to mutate and be able to infect humans. The fungus, like Joel, isn't killing people because it's evil; it's ensuring its survival by its natural impulse to love.

The shot of Tess being kissed by an Infected illustrates this theme. At the end of episode 2, an Infected Runner turns Tess not by biting her, but by gently kissing her. It's horrifying, but Druckmann, who directed the episode, wanted to "shoot it in the most beautiful way."[27] In response to this shot, Mazin says "the fungus loves too. It makes more of itself. That's what we do when we love each other."[28] Like Joel, the Infected discriminates against others for the survival of its own kind. For Cordyceps and humanity, discriminatory love is natural and good.

Of course, David is among the least redeemable antagonists in an otherwise morally grey universe. We shouldn't accept his words as gospel. That said, the idea of the beauty and horror of Cordyceps pervades *The Last of Us*. The opening credits sequence played at the beginning of every episode is a stunning animation of Cordyceps sprouting and blossoming as it spreads across America. The opening is paired with Gustavo Santaolalla's haunting and beautiful main theme. The idea that this fungus is taking over the country is disturbing for any human, yet the sequence doesn't portray the fungi's flourishing that way. The sequence ends with two sprouts of fungus, one a bit taller than the other, standing alone against the rest of the country—a representation of Joel and Ellie. *The Last of Us* illustrates the persistence of the Cordyceps fungus as reflective of our human compulsion to endure and survive.

The Last of Us tells us that we survive to love, and we love to survive. No matter how hard we fight it, nature wins. Cordyceps wins over humanity, and Joel's love triumphs over Marlene's utilitarian righteousness. Joel's love for Ellie preserves the world's humanity. The consequences are costly, but that's what the world of *The Last of Us* and love is—beautiful, painful, and horrifying. Sometimes all at once.

Paradoxical

When playtesting the original *Last of Us* video game, Druckmann would end the session by asking players, "What did you think of Joel's choice?" According to Druckmann, "If the player was not a parent, it was 50/50 as to whether they agreed with what Joel did."[29] However, "If the player was a parent, a hundred percent, with zero exceptions, they agreed with Joel."[30] While we've tried to highlight the complexity of Joel's choice, chances are that if you're a caring parent, you understand Joel. Does that make the 50 percent of non-parent players wrong in their assessment of Joel's choice? Of course not. The fact that there was such an even split between those players speaks to how impossible the ethical quandary is to reconcile for human beings. "The point of a dilemma," Mazin says, "is it ain't easy, and there isn't one right answer."[31] That's why we continue to debate *The Last of Us*. Sometimes, nature is paradoxical. Just as Cordyceps need a human host to survive, we need love. And for both Cordyceps and humanity, that one thing we need in life is the one thing that might get us killed.[32]

Notes

1. Tracy Brown, "'The Last of Us' Game Ending Divided Fans: Here's Why It Feels Different on TV," *Los Angeles Times*, March 13, 2023, at https://www.latimes.com/entertainment-arts/tv/story/2023-03-13/last-of-us-finale-video-game-reaction.

2. Roxana Hadadi, "'We Have to Interrogate How We Feel About Our Heroes': *The Last of Us* Co-Creator Craig Mazin Questions the Inherent Positivity of Love," *Vulture*, March 12, 2023, at https://www.vulture.com/article/last-of-us-craig-mazin-season-finale-ending-interview.html.

3. Louise Griffin, "The Last of Us Star Ashley Johnson 'Devastated' by Final Episode," *Radio Times*, March 13, 2023, at https://www.radiotimes.com/tv/sci-fi/the-last-of-us-ending-newsupdate.

4. Anthony Wood, "Troy Baker's Perspective on The Last of Us Ending Changed after Having a Child," IGN, November 28, 2022, at https://www.ign.com/articles/troy-baker-joel-miller-the-last-of-us-ending-daredevil-game.

5. Troy Baker, host, "Episode 9—'Look For The Light,'" *HBO's The Last of Us Podcast*, March 13, 2023, at https://listen.hbo.com/the-last-of-us-podcast?c=3Z9AtEp-R4F_xkzpvfSlKg&h=111e969fbd0c35d10.

6. Baker, "Episode 9—'Look For The Light.'"

7. Philippa Foot, "The Problem of Abortion and the Doctrine of Double Effect," *Oxford Review* 5 (1967), 5–15, and Judith Jarvis Thomson, "Killing, Letting Die, and the Trolley Problem," *The Monist* 59 (1976), 204–217.

8. Baker, "Episode 9—'Look For The Light.'"

9. Baker, "Episode 9—'Look For The Light.'"

10. Troy Baker, host, "Episode 4—'Please Hold To My Hand,'" *HBO's The Last of Us Podcast*, February 6, 2023, at https://listen.hbo.com/the-last-of-us-podcast.

11. Stephen T. Asma, "The Myth of Universal Love," *New York Times*, January 5, 2013, at https://archive.nytimes.com/opinionator.blogs.nytimes.com/2013/01/05/the-myth-of-universal-love.

12. Asma, "The Myth of Universal Love."

13. Stephen T. Asma, *Against Fairness* (Chicago: University of Chicago Press, 2013), 7.

14. Asma, *Against Fairness*, 27.

15. Asma, *Against Fairness*, 29.

16. Asma, *Against Fairness*, 32.

17. Asma, *Against Fairness*, 154.

18. Asma, *Against Fairness*, 96.

19. Asma, *Against Fairness*, 63.

20. Asma, *Against Fairness*, 35.

21. Neil Druckmann and Faith Erin Hicks, *The Last of Us: American Dreams*, #1 (April 2013).

22. Asma, *Against Fairness*, 35.

23. Asma, *Against Fairness*, 35.

24. Asma, *Against Fairness*, 154.

25. Asma, *Against Fairness*, 102.

26. For another defense of Joel's decision in terms of his role as father, see Charles Joshua Horn, "*The Last of Us* as Moral Philosophy: Teleological Particularism

and Why Joel Is Not a Villain," in David Kyle Johnson ed., *The Palgrave Handbook of Popular Culture as Philosophy* (Cham: Palgrave Macmillan, 2021), 1–16.

27. Troy Baker, host, "Episode 2—'Infected,'" *HBO's The Last of Us Podcast*, January 23, 2023, at https://listen.hbo.com/the-last-of-us-podcast.
28. Baker, "Episode 2—'Infected.'"
29. Baker, "Episode 9—'Look For The Light.'"
30. Baker, "Episode 9—'Look For The Light.'"
31. Baker, "Episode 9—'Look For The Light.'"
32. We thank Stephen Asma and Joshua Horn for their feedback that helped us to improve this chapter.

3

"He Who Fights with Monsters"
Inner-Circle vs. the World in *The Last of Us*

Dylan Skurka

ELLIE: If you don't think there's hope for the world, why bother going on? I mean, you gotta try, right?

JOEL: You haven't seen the world, so you don't know. Keep going for family, that's about it.

Imagine you're a brilliant physicist, making a name for yourself as the leader of a group of world-class researchers working with nuclear fusion to help tame the devastating effects of climate change. You understand that the fate of countless people may rest on your shoulders, and the only way for you to succeed is to essentially dedicate the entirety of your life to your job. One day you fall in love, and a few months later you find out that you are going to be having a child, leaving you in quite the predicament: To be the best parent and partner you can be, you realize you will need to neglect your demanding job so you can spend quality time with your family. To be the best scientist you can be, though, you will need to be a poor parent and partner, neglecting their needs so you can immerse yourself in your meaningful work. If you could only choose one path, then, which one would it be? Would you prioritize the well-being of your inner circle at the expense of the wider world, or would you help the wider world at the expense of your inner circle?

The Last of Us is about a deadly fungal pandemic rather than climate change, but the underlying dilemma between the inner circle and wider world is the same. As a result, nearly all the characters in *The Last of Us* can be divided into two camps: the "tribalists" are those who choose to put their inner circles first, while the "joiners" are those who prioritize the wider world. One of the most pressing questions that unfolds in the show and video game is how one can justifiably choose between tribalism or joinerism when both sides are defensible positions.

The Last of Us and Philosophy: Look for the Light, First Edition.
Edited by Charles Joshua Horn.
© 2025 John Wiley & Sons, Inc. Published 2025 by John Wiley & Sons, Inc.

The Joiners and the Tribalists in *The Last of Us*

Tribalists in *The Last of Us*, such as the anti-hero, Joel, tend to be the most cynical and untrusting characters we encounter, often due to a combination of personal disposition and past experiences. Long before the fungal infections, for example, Joel had already been jaded by his time spent fighting in the Gulf War, enduring grueling combat that he would come to learn was unnecessary and thankless. Thousands of people would die, and thousands more, including Joel, would be scarred for life.

Joiners, in comparison, are optimists and ideologues who are drawn to fight for bigger causes that imbue their lives with meaning. "Tommy's what we used to call a joiner. Dreams of becoming a hero," Joel says mockingly when talking about his younger brother, who volunteered to fight in the same war that he did, albeit for very different reasons.

Rather than explicitly championing tribalism or joinerism, *The Last of Us* refuses to show its hand, taking a cryptic stance toward both sides by criticizing one perspective one moment, only to support it the next.

In the first episode of *The Last of Us,* when the fungal infection begins to spread in their neighborhood, Joel, Sarah, and Tommy are speeding in a pickup truck to find safety. As the three passengers make their way through a dark, desolate landscape, a disheveled young family suddenly appears in front of them on the road. A woman, they see, is hugging her young child, and a man is waving his arms in primal desperation, pleading with Joel's group to pull over to help them. Joel, Sarah, and Tommy only have a few seconds to make a collective decision, and as Tommy begins tapping the breaks, disagreement ensues:

> JOEL: What are you doing?
> TOMMY: They've got a kid, Joel.
> JOEL: So do we! Keep driving.
> SARAH: We can put them in the back …

Before Sarah can even finish her thought, the stranded family is already well behind them, the father's increasingly pained howls now fading into white noise. Avoiding his younger brother's disappointed eyes, Joel fumbles for an excuse, knowing that what he's about to say is going to be a lie: "Somebody else will come along."

As bad as we may feel for the stranded family, the context undergirding Joel's decision—the risk of getting infected and the limited time to find safety—makes it easy to sympathize with his tribalist sensibilities. All he's trying to do is protect his family. What's so bad about that?

Shortly after they drive past the stranded family, Joel and Sarah, now separated from Tommy, are forced to abandon their vehicle in an infection hotspot. With an infected man chasing them, they wind up in a deserted field where a fully armed military officer shoots their deranged pursuer and proceeds to point his gun at them:

OFFICER: Don't move!
JOEL: My daughter's hurt. Her ankle ...
OFFICER: Stop right there!
JOEL: Easy now—we are *not* sick.
OFFICER (SPEAKING INTO HIS WALKIE TALKIE): I've got two civilians by the river.... Yes, sir.... Yes, sir.
JOEL: We are not sick.... Sir.... WE ARE NOT SICK!

In one of the saddest scenes of the entire show and video game, we see the officer ignore the screaming man in front of him and unleash his weapon. The bullets only graze Joel, but the result is much worse; he is suddenly left with no choice but to cradle his daughter in his arms as she slowly bleeds to death—a parent's literal worst nightmare.

In this scene, it's difficult to think of the military officer as anything but evil for what he does to a father and child pleading to be spared. But if the officer is evil, why isn't Joel equally evil for what he did to the family pleading for help beside the road? It certainly can't be ruled out that the military officer—a man with a family of his own—was concerned Joel and Sarah were infected and believed he did what he had to do out of self-protection, or that defying his superior's orders meant he would be punished for insubordination. Wasn't the military officer doing the same thing that any good soldier does when he shot at Joel and Sarah: following his superior's orders?[1] Why is it then that no matter how hard we try to understand where the military officer is coming from in this scene, Joel still unambiguously comes across as the more sympathetic character?

One way to make sense of the conflicting feelings that result from both scenes is to note that we feel compassion for Joel when he abandons the stranded family because we're viewing his decision through the lens of his inner circle—if the lives of a few strangers must be sacrificed so that Joel and his family can protect themselves, then so be it. In a masterful twist, though, this inner circle that we are so invested in suddenly trades places with the stranded family and they become the few strangers who must be sacrificed for the interests of the inner circle of the military officer! In other words, we are led to believe that Joel's tribalism is clearly the morally superior position to joinerism, but once Joel is harmed by the tribalism of someone else, we suddenly view joinerism as the morally superior position.

FEDRA, the Fireflies, and Utilitarianism

In the years following the spread of the Cordyceps fungal outbreak, when resources are scarce, throngs of people are left dead and infected, and civil society collapses on itself, the Federal Disaster Response Agency (FEDRA) emerges as a powerhouse authoritarian regime that institutes Quarantine Zones (QZs) around the country. In response, the Fireflies gain momentum as an anti-authoritarian militia group that violently resists FEDRA's political control and devises a plan to develop a vaccine for the infection.

Diametrically opposed as they may be at first glance, both FEDRA and the Fireflies are proponents of joinerism to the extent that their underlying motive is to save humanity; it's just that, for the former, the most expedient way to achieve this end is through meticulously managing the world's remaining resources, and for the latter, the best way to serve humanity is to focus on eradicating the infection altogether.

Philosophically, FEDRA and the Fireflies lean heavily toward utilitarianism, an ethical theory that holds that the morally right thing to do is to maximize happiness for the most people. Although most utilitarians are willing to admit that we should give *some* special consideration to friends and family when making moral decisions, a key component of this theory is its emphasis on impartiality. We shouldn't, from this point of view, merely benefit those we love and occasionally help strangers, but rather *always* think about how we can best support those in need beyond our inner circle. In fact, the contemporary utilitarian philosopher, Peter Singer, contends that we have a moral duty to help the most vulnerable people in the wider world right up to the point that we would completely sabotage our own quality of life if we kept on going, or, as Singer puts it, "sacrificing anything of comparable moral significance."[2] Utilitarians like Singer have often been criticized for how demanding their theory is.[3] If we take Singer's words to heart, for example, we might be compelled to donate huge sums of our money to impoverished people across the world who we don't even know, only stopping if we would become impoverished if we continued to donate.

It's inspiring, then, to see the demanding moral aspirations of FEDRA and the Fireflies, who dedicate their lives to helping as many people as possible, whether they know these people or not. "No matter what anyone out there says or thinks, we're the only thing holding this all together," reasons the head of a FEDRA school, Captain Kwong. "If we go down, the people in this zone will starve or murder each other. That much I know." In risking their lives by defying FEDRA's orders so they can end the pandemic, the Fireflies courageously demonstrate their willingness to fight for a greater cause as well.

Tribalism, Communitarianism, and Aristotle

It's also easy to admire the tribalists in *The Last of Us* when we look at the world through their eyes and see how far they're willing to go for those within their inner circle. Henry, for example, brims with humanity when he consoles his eight-year-old brother, Sam, exuding a calm confidence, even though he is painfully aware of how unsafe they are. Joel, too, proves to be heroically loyal to his family when he resolves to go on a dangerous mission across the country to save Tommy.

Some communitarian philosophers would support key aspects of Henry and Joel's tribalist ethos by emphasizing the importance of partiality in moral decision-making. Echoing Aristotle's (384–322 BCE) thought that humans are social animals, communitarians stress the integral role that our family, friends, and broader community play in shaping our identity, and the special obligations we have toward them as a result.[4] In his *Nicomachean Ethics*,[5] Aristotle expands on his "social animal" portrayal of humans by noting the indispensable role that close relationships play in attaining a flourishing life.[6]

With these considerations in mind, it's easy to root for the tribalist characters even when they act in arguably morally objectionable ways. For example, Henry represents the tribalist mindset when, to get medicine for his younger brother, he informs on the beloved leader of a rebel group who promises to save Kansas City from a particularly corrupt QZ leader that has "raped and tortured and murdered people for twenty years." Surely Henry's actions inadvertently led to the deaths of many who could have been saved by this leader and contributed to keeping many others stuck in a cycle of oppression and injustice. And yet, it's fair to wonder what the purpose of saving the world is if your own tribe isn't any longer part of it. When the world only promises disappointment, the only way to get by is to "Keep going for family," as Joel says in defense of tribalism. "That's about it."

When You Gaze Too Long into the Abyss

Although *The Last of Us* doesn't explicitly conclude whether it's more praiseworthy to be a joiner or a tribalist, it says a lot about how doing bad things, even for justifiable reasons, can turn ordinary people into monsters, adopting the Nietzschean warning that, "He who fights with monsters should be careful lest he thereby become a monster. And if thou gaze long into an abyss, the abyss will also gaze into thee."[7] Entrenched in the utilitarian calculus of saving as many people as possible from getting infected, FEDRA's joiners become monsters when they decide to round up uninfected men, women, and children under the false pretense of bringing them to safety, only to kill them with the senseless rationale that "dead people can't be infected." Marlene, the leader of the Fireflies, reveals the dark side of joinerism as well when she lures a young Ellie to a hospital so she can kill her to extract a potential cure for the infection from her body. Even worse, Ellie's mother was Marlene's life-long friend whose dying wish was for Marlene to protect her daughter at all costs—a promise Marlene vowed not to break.

When tribalism goes too far in *The Last of Us*, the result is the twin-headed monster of narcissism and nihilism, best exemplified by one of the show's most evil characters, Kathleen. Named the commander of the rebellion group in Kansas City after her brother is killed, Kathleen essentially funnels all of her tribe's resources toward capturing Henry, her brother's informant, characterizing every problem they face in the show as somehow leading back to him. She tells her compatriots, "This is Henry's work, understand? And he won't stop until *we* stop him." Like FEDRA and the Fireflies, Kathleen murderously abuses "the ends justify the means" reasoning to betray other people's trust in her bloodthirsty quest for Henry. In one memorably horrific instance of this, she promises to spare a group of prisoners if they inform her of his whereabouts, only to order for them to be shot and their bodies burned once she squeezes a confession out of one of them.

Besides the ruthlessness she displays toward those who she deems enemies, Kathleen's fanatical tribalism makes her a poor leader for her in-group as well. Not only does she misrepresent Henry as a constant threat to her community's safety, but she also ignores obvious signs of the actual threat of a deadly onslaught of infected people, recklessly putting her people in grave danger. Appropriately, when the onslaught eventually happens, Kathleen ignores her opportunity to escape so that she can finally kill Henry, only to get pulverized by an infected ghoul the moment she is about to pull the trigger. Blinded by revenge, Kathleen gazed too long into the abyss; and in return, the abyss gazed right back at her.

Appreciating the Beauty of the Other Side

Perhaps the lesson of *The Last of Us* is that, when taken to extremes, both tribalism and joinerism turn us into monsters even scarier than those infected by the Cordyceps. In what might be the most enduring and ful-filling relationship of *The Last of Us* though, Bill and Frank discover a purpose that eclipses anything joinerism or tribalism can ever hope to offer. Bill and Frank wisely come to understand that finding peace isn't about overpowering your enemies or righting every wrong—it's about accepting that, despite our differences, we should attempt to find common ground and humanize others. If we can learn from Bill and Frank, there might just be hope for our world too.

Notes

1. Some might think the distinction between killing and letting die is important and that the military officer makes the more evil decision than Joel because he tangibly kills Sarah while Joel merely lets the family on the side of the road die.

I'm inclined to agree with James Rachels (1941–2003), though, who argues that whether one kills someone or lets them die is not as important of a consideration, ethically, as the *justifications* underlying one's action. Since the military officer has at least equally good reasons for killing than Joel does when he lets the family die, Joel's passivity on its own isn't more justifiable than the military officer's act of pulling the trigger. For more on this argument, see James Rachels, "Killing and Letting Die," in Lawrence Becker and Charlotte Becker eds., *Encyclopedia of Ethics,* 2nd ed. (New York: Routledge, 2001), 947–950.

2. Peter Singer, *Practical Ethics,* 2nd ed. (Cambridge: Cambridge University Press, 1993), 229.

3. See, for example, William Shaw, "Consequentialism," in Hugh LaFollette ed., *Ethics in Practice: An Anthology,* 5th ed. (Hoboken, NJ: Wiley Blackwell, 2020), 31–39.

4. Daniel Bell, "Communitarianism," in *The Stanford Encyclopedia of Philosophy,* at https://plato.stanford.edu/archives/fall2023/entries/communitarianism.

5. Aristotle, *Nicomachean Ethics,* trans. Terence Irwin (Indianapolis: Hackett Publishing, 2019), Book VIII.

6. This isn't to say that communitarians and Aristotle think that special relationships should be the only consideration when making moral decisions. For Aristotle, for example, being virtuous entails considering several different morally relevant factors on a case-by-case basis. So, even if close relationships play an integral role in our lives, as Aristotle suggests, that doesn't mean that he thinks that there aren't instances when the virtuous person should justifiably put the wider world's interests before the interests of their tribe.

7. Friedrich Nietzsche, *Beyond Good and Evil,* trans. Helen Zimmern and Paul Cohn (Ware: Wordsworth, 2008), §146.

4

Is Humanity Worth Saving?
Philosophical Pessimism and Joel's Choice

Quân Nguyen

TESS: Joel, save who you can save.

At the end of *The Last of Us Part I*, Joel chooses to protect Ellie's life rather than sacrifice her for a potential cure for the Cordyceps infection. In both the video game and show, the moment forces players and viewers to reflect on responsibility, love, violence, and what ultimately makes us human. Joel, a self-admitted bad person who lost his daughter Sarah to the authoritarian response to a worldwide fungal pandemic, survived through murder and theft. Accordingly, a thoroughly dark, pessimistic view guides his actions in a world where humanity has lost itself. But after encountering, escorting, and protecting Cordyceps-immune Ellie across the former United States, he seems to change and become more caring—and it's precisely this change that makes him choose Ellie's life over a cure for humanity.

As we'll see, philosophical pessimism can help us understand Joel's thoughts and actions in terms of the question he faces: Is humanity worth saving?

Pessimism and *The Last of Us*

HENRY: The plan is good!
JOEL: The plan is good? We've been down here two seconds, we don't know anything.
HENRY TO ELLIE: Your dad's kind of a pessimist ...

Let's unpack this exchange in the sewers to see whether Joel is really a pessimist. Normally, we understand a pessimist as someone who thinks

The Last of Us and Philosophy: Look for the Light, First Edition.
Edited by Charles Joshua Horn.
© 2025 John Wiley & Sons, Inc. Published 2025 by John Wiley & Sons, Inc.

that things are going to get worse. While this characterization certainly fits Joel's outlook in some way, the exchange with Henry reveals something deeper about how Joel approaches the world and the future.

Pessimism is an old and complex philosophical school of thought. To understand the appeal of philosophical pessimism, consider its historical opposite, philosophical optimism. The German philosopher and mathematician, Gottfried Leibniz (1646–1716), addressed the problem of evil, the question of how an all-knowing, all-powerful, benevolent God could allow pain, evil, and suffering in the world. In short, his answer was that we live in the best of all possible worlds.

Leibniz thought that God allowed so much pain, evil, and suffering partly because, in the grand scheme of things, the goodness of the world outweighs the badness of creation, even if we cannot see it. Moreover, any flaws we might see in the world must exist for a greater purpose that we may not understand from our limited perspectives. Or in the words of David, the cannibalistic cult leader in *The Last of Us*, "everything happens for a reason," even the emergence of a brutal fungal pandemic that almost wipes out humanity.

In response to Leibniz's optimism, Voltaire (1694–1778) penned his novel *Candide*, in which he ridiculed and satirized the idea that we live in the best of all possible worlds. Building on this rejection of philosophical optimism, pessimists ask us to take seriously that for many, *life is often not worth living* due to pain and suffering, and that we should *reject false hope and narratives of progress*.[1] The former element of pessimism can be called value-oriented pessimism, and the latter element can be called future-oriented pessimism.

Why should we be pessimists? First, following Voltaire, we might find it insulting and patronizing to tell those who suffer that their pain is part of a grander purpose, that things could not possibly be better. Second, following the classic pessimist, Arthur Schopenhauer (1788–1860), if we only focus on the good, the bright, and the hopeful aspects of our existence, then we'll ignore much of the suffering in the world that we need to alleviate. We may also start resenting our fellow humans in their imperfections, as they do not resemble our brightly shining ideals. A pessimist ethic takes people's suffering seriously, acknowledges the pain in the world, and doesn't try to see purpose in evil; this ethic may be better suited to console us, and build a moral community between fellow sufferers.[2]

Both value-oriented pessimism and future-oriented pessimism allow us to situate Joel's choice as a rejection of philosophical optimism. By philosophical optimism we mean the view that life is worth living despite all the pain and suffering, and that, while not guaranteed, progress in life is possible. Hoping for deliverance isn't a silly thing to do.

Recall that value-oriented pessimism is the view that life often isn't worth living due to the hardships we experience. Value-oriented pessimism goes to the heart of the question of whether humanity is worth saving, and

The Last of Us offers a clear answer—no, humanity is already lost. Clearly, humanity has lost its battle against Cordyceps. Additionally, in fighting the fungal disease, humanity has also lost itself and embraced brutal authoritarianism, violence as the primary means to solve conflicts, and a general inhumanity in those who didn't turn into Infected.

Value-oriented pessimism is especially visible when *The Last of Us* shows us something that looks like a community on its surface, but instead turns out to be a cannibalistic cult led by the sadistic pedophile, David. In short, even those who were not infected turned into monsters of a kind, including Joel and Tess, who are "bad people" by their own admission. An awareness of the loss of humanity in every person shapes Joel as a person and informs his agency throughout the video game and series. The ultimate statement of value-oriented pessimism is his choice to save Ellie because humanity has already lost itself. A pessimist's evaluation of the world in *The Last of Us* tells us that humanity has lost in the fight against Cordyceps, and also in the struggle for a meaningful human existence beyond mere survival. If we interpret Joel as a pessimist, then saving Ellie isn't selfish. Rather, it's a rational decision to save someone he loves rather than a human race that isn't worth saving and doesn't deserve to be saved.

Recall that future-oriented pessimism is a stance of skepticism against narratives of progress and promises of salvation. Clearly, Joel adopts this view, cautioning all his companions against having expectations. His future-oriented pessimism is perhaps most clear when it comes to the promises of a cure delivered by the Fireflies. Upon learning of a possible cure for the Cordyceps fungus, Joel tells Tess, "We've heard this a million times—vaccines, miracles cures, none of this works, ever."

After living through the breakdown of civilization, and experiencing too many broken promises and false hopes, Joel simply expects nothing good. Hence, he warns Tess and Ellie not to expect salvation from the promise of a cure. Additionally, he cautions Ellie against expectations about their other fellow survivors, making clear that they may be just as dangerous as the Infected. When seen through the lens of future-oriented pessimism, Joel's choice to save Ellie is an act with moral depth. For a pessimist in a world where humanity already lost, expecting salvation is a form of false hope that needs to be resisted. For a pessimist like Joel, losing Ellie for a promise of salvation isn't worth it.

Seen through the lens of philosophical pessimism, Joel's choice isn't personal and selfish, but rather a decision that weighs the state of the world in *The Last of Us* with the promises of saving humanity against the real bonds of love he has with Ellie. As a pessimist, Joel decides that humanity has already lost, and expects no cure to work against infection. He therefore saves Ellie. We can grasp the moral depth of Joel's choice. However, a question remains open: Is Joel correct? Is humanity indeed not worth saving?

The Drive to Be Optimistic

ELLIE: This place actually fucking works.

In the video game, the verdict seems clear—humanity is beyond saving and has fallen to barbarism in the face of the fungal apocalypse. However, the TV adaptation of the video game makes some significant changes to the world of *The Last of Us* that makes a pessimist evaluation more nuanced. The show depicts instances where humans can build a life of meaning that goes beyond mere survival. Yes, the TV series shows authoritarianism and cannibalism, but it carefully contrasts those with hints of communities that make life worth living. The different depictions of certain communities are showcased in episode 6 when Joel and Ellie arrive in Jackson and spend time with Tommy and Maria. In the video games, there is a sense of constant danger and vulnerability in their community, but in the TV series we get a greater sense of a community that is able to build a shared life of care and solidarity.

The same emphasis on a meaningful life is most visible in episode 3, where the story of Bill and Frank marks one of the show's major departures from the video game. In both the video game and TV series, Bill is a lone wolf who survived the pandemic by being an isolated prepper. In the video game, he's on his own, having lost his partner, Frank. In fact, he tells Joel that caring for others is a weakness to overcome: "Once upon a time I had somebody I cared about. It was a partner. Somebody I had to look after. And in this world that sort of shit is good for one thing. Gettin' ya killed. So, you know what I did? I wisened the fuck up. And I realized it's gotta be just me."

His partner Frank left him and committed suicide before turning into an Infected. In his note for Bill, Frank wrote, "Well, Bill, I doubt you'd ever find this note cause you were too scared to ever make it to this part of town. But if for some reason you did, I want you to know I hated your guts. I grew tired of this shitty town and of your set-in-your-ways attitude. I wanted more from life than this and you could never get that. And that stupid battery you kept moaning about—I got it. But I guess you were right. Trying to leave this town will kill me. Still better than spending another day with you. Good Luck, Frank."

In the video game, the experiences of Bill and Frank confirm Joel's pessimistic worldview: a life of pain and suffering that punishes you for loving may not be worth living. Even if there had been good times in their relationship, in the end, only bitterness remains.

In the TV series, Bill and Frank are also partners, but they built and shared a loving life together, filled with gourmet cooking, fresh strawberries, and delightful music. They struggled and argued, but their differences never turned into bitterness, and they died together, ending their lives content on their own terms. In episode 3, Frank tells Bill, "I'm not going to give you the 'everyday was a wonderful gift from God speech.' I have had a lot of bad days. I had bad days with you, too. But I've had … more good days with you than with anyone else. Just give me one more good day." At the end of their final day together, Bill also drinks the wine prepared to end Frank's life and tells him, "This isn't the tragic suicide at the end of the play. I'm old. I'm satisfied. And you were my purpose." Frank responds, "I should be furious. But from an objective point of view … it's incredibly romantic."

Bill and Frank show that a meaningful, purposeful life beyond mere survival is possible during the apocalypse. Even in a world as dark as *The Last of Us*, someone as isolated and grumpy as Bill can find meaning and purpose if he opens up and lets himself care for others. Bill's rejection of pessimism is also shown in his letter to Joel. He writes, "I used to hate the world, and I was happy when everyone died. But I was wrong because there was one person worth saving. That's what I did. I saved him. Then I protected him. That's why men like you and me are here. We have a job to do, and God help any motherfuckers who stand in our way."

So, what does this mean for our pessimistic analysis? In the TV series, Bill's letter suggests that, despite the suffering, pain, and evil, life can still be meaningful; humans can find purpose with each other; and therefore humanity might still be worth saving. So, with this major divergence from the video game, the TV series seems to suggest that humanity can still be redeemed. Given this backdrop, our value-oriented pessimist conclusions about Joel's choice are less warranted than they would be in the video game.[3] But this doesn't mean that they are completely unjustified. Even in the TV series, it is hinted that Joel takes these messages, both at Bill's and in Jackson, with a grain of salt, cautioning Ellie and emphasizing the loss that everyone in the world of *The Last of Us* has experienced. And even if value-oriented pessimism isn't warranted, because life is more worth living than we thought it to be, and even if humanity is more redeemable than we thought, Joel might still be right in pushing back against false hopes and expecting salvation.

What Can We Hope during the Apocalypse?

TESS: How about you just take the good news? Can you do that?
     To think that for once, we can actually win?

Hope is the central concern for future-oriented pessimists, who demand that we should expect nothing. Pessimists caution against seeing purpose in suffering and evil, but that doesn't mean that they must renounce all forms of hope. The three most hopeful characters in *The Last of Us* are Tess, Ellie, and Marlene, and all three are driven toward optimism through their need for hope.

After she's infected, to give purpose to her own suffering and death, Tess needs the promise that Ellie can deliver a cure. She needs the hope for a cure to make sense of her life journey, and to give her the strength to sacrifice herself to allow Joel and Ellie to escape. She is driven toward optimism, in the form of a greater purpose in her sacrifice, to help her cope with her impending end, and to "set everything right—all the shit we did."

Similarly, Ellie is driven toward optimism because she needs to believe in the possibility of a cure to give purpose to the pain and suffering she has endured. After losing her friend and first love, Riley, to Cordyceps, losing her friend, Sam, right after she befriended him, and being forced to kill to protect Joel and herself, Ellie needs a sense of purpose, a deeper reason to her suffering. The promise of delivering a cure for humanity provides meaning for her suffering. Ellie's optimism is captured by her statement to Joel toward the end of their journey, "After all we've been through. After all that I've done. It can't be for nothing."

But as a pessimist, Joel knows that these hopes come out of desperation to make sense of suffering in a world that does not make sense anymore. As Voltaire and Schopenhauer taught us—there isn't any deeper sense or purpose to pain and suffering, neither from God nor from anything else. Suffering is just suffering, and optimistically asserting that there's a reason for the pain just serves to insult and patronize those who feel it.

Pessimism cautions us to be wary of false hopes that tell us about a greater purpose of suffering. But this doesn't mean that pessimists must give up all forms of hope. Pessimist philosopher, Albert Camus (1913–1960), warned against vertical forms of hope—hope for salvation from above by God, and horizontal forms of hope—hope for salvation from human progress.[4] According to Camus, both kinds of hope are false hopes, with the former being empty promises by the church and organized religions, and the latter embodied by Stalinists who accepted inhuman atrocities in the name of progress toward communism.

Vertical hope is hinted at with cannibal cult leader, David, who also asserts that everything happens for a reason. However, horizontal hope is central in The Last of Us, and is best represented by the Firefly leader, Marlene. When trying to convince Joel that Ellie's death would be tragic but still meaningful, Marlene says, "How long until she's torn apart by infected, or murdered by raiders, because she lives in a broken world that you could have saved. It's not too late, even now, even after what you've done, we can still find a way."

If we view Joel's choice at the end of his journey from a pessimist perspective, then we ought to be skeptical of horizontal hope in the promise of salvation for humanity through a cure. Real hope needs to be based on something other than expectations of progress and the promise of purpose. For Camus, hope lies in recognizing that suffering and pain won't end. Hope calls for us to embrace the possibilities and ways of life that are already present in our lives, our environments, and our surroundings, and to find the courage to use them to resist the systems that govern us.

Ellie is the person who brought Joel hope in his realization that he could protect and care for someone again. In Ellie, Joel finds someone who makes him human again, someone who enables him to love and care. Ultimately, the world of *The Last of Us* lacks both love and care. Both in the video game and the show, the world needs more people to care for each other, helping each other to be humans again so that they can make a meaningful existence beyond mere survival. What pessimism then asks us to do is to find the courage to protect those who make us human, even in a world as dark as *The Last of Us*.

Optimism or Pessimism?

An optimist could reply that all this stuff about hope and courage sounds suspiciously like a form of nuanced, complex optimism. The optimist might insist that Joel was a pessimist who rejected the naive optimism of the Fireflies. But after witnessing community and care in Jackson, he learned to embrace a more nuanced form of value-optimism that doesn't deny the darkness of the world, yet still asks us to persevere. Joel sticks to his future-oriented pessimism, and expects nothing from the future, but he overcomes his value-oriented pessimism by coming to see life as worth living. As a result of such nuanced optimism, Joel saves Ellie.

Optimists could go even further, arguing that Joel in the beginning was indeed a pessimist in both senses, but in the end, Ellie shakes him out of it, as he recognizes through her that life, despite everything, is worth living, and that there is purpose in his journey. His purpose is to love, care for, and protect Ellie. Tragically, this optimism then leads him to reject the cure for humanity.

So, after learning to care for Ellie, is Joel a hopeful pessimist, or a complex optimist? Both interpretations are possible, and you might find one or the other more plausible depending on whether you focus on Joel from the video games or Joel from the TV series. Was Joel's choice to save Ellie at the expense of humanity, correct? Philosophical pessimism doesn't give us a definitive answer to this question. Instead, it helps us recognize the moral depth of Joel's decision. Even if humanity isn't worth saving, it's still worth saving those we care for, and it takes courage to do so.

Notes

1. I recommend Mara van der Lugt, *Dark Matters: Pessimism and the Problem of Suffering* (Princeton, NJ: Princeton University Press, 2021) and Joshua Dienstag, *Pessimism: Philosophy, Ethic, Spirit* (Princeton, NJ: Princeton University Press, 2009) for a great historical overview on both value- and future-oriented pessimism.

2. Arthur Schopenhauer, *Parerga and Paralipomena,* trans. Sabine Roehr (Cambridge: Cambridge University Press, 2014), at https://assets.cambridge.org/9780521871389/frontmatter/9780521871389_frontmatter.pdf.

3. A recommended viewing on this is the video essay, "Why Apocalypse Stories Feel Different Now" by Like Stories of Old, analyzing the shift of apocalypse stories toward more hopeful tones, at https://youtu.be/1rvYYD9mlac?feature=shared.

4. See Albert Camus, *The Myth of Sisyphus and Other Essays* (New York: Vintage Books, 1955).

PART II
JUSTICE

5

Is Ellie's Revenge Ethically Justified?

Alberto Oya

The Last of Us Part II (Naughty Dog, 2020) maintains the gaming mechanics common to the action video game genre, including the customization of weapons, the acquisition of new abilities, puzzle-solving tasks, and some degree of platforming. The gameplay ultimately revolves around shooting at (and thereby killing) enemies. So, it's not its gaming mechanics that makes *The Last of Us Part II* an innovative video game, but rather its ability to challenge the narrative common to the action video game genre.

One common feature of action video games is that the narrative is set in what we might call a heroic light. In these video games, the player takes the role of a video game character who must face the honorable (and challenging) endeavor of fighting an evil force that threatens to destroy human life. This evil may take different forms, but it is always something that threatens human life and acts against commonly accepted moral standards. Importantly, the video game character is often presented as being the only one who can succeed in overcoming the evil force, not as a matter of free choice, but of fulfilling one's duty. Such a heroic narrative facilitates immersion in the gaming experience because it provides an ethical justification for the violence of the playable video game character. Thanks to the in-game heroic narrative, engaging in violent gaming mechanics does not require players *to suspend* their own ethical judgment. An in-game heroic narrative facilitates players' immersion in the video game since it allows them *to accommodate* their own ethical standards. Notably, the embedded nature of video games indicates that moral considerations are still relevant even when players are well aware of being immersed in a purely fictional scenario.[1]

The Last of Us and Philosophy: Look for the Light, First Edition.
Edited by Charles Joshua Horn.
© 2025 John Wiley & Sons, Inc. Published 2025 by John Wiley & Sons, Inc.

Endorsing Ellie's Quest for Revenge Is an Overtly Contradictory Ethical Position

At the beginning, *The Last of Us Part II* follows the heroic formula. During the first half of the video game, when players occupy the role of Ellie, the video game takes care to show Abby as the common cliché of the despotic and sadistic villain who doesn't even care about her comrades, and who enjoys torturing Joel to death. Abby is presented in a way that makes players feel justified in seeking to kill her. All in all, Ellie's revenge seems to be a just act.

However, in the second half of the video game, players occupy the role of Abby. It's then that players come to realize that Abby is not as cruel as she first seemed. In fact, Abby cares about others, even those who are not part of her own group, such as Lev and Yara. Most importantly, players become aware that Abby's motive for killing Joel was revenge for him having killed her father, an act committed by the gamer in the culminating moments of *The Last of Us* (Naughty Dog, 2013). So, it was the players who, while gaming as Joel, killed Abby's father.

By forcing players to alternate between Ellie and Abby as their playable character, *The Last of Us Part II* requires that players occupy overtly contradictory ethical positions. Given the evident parallels between Ellie and Abby, if players agree that Ellie is ethically justified in getting revenge on Abby for her having killed Joel (who is a father figure for Ellie), then players should also agree that Abby is ethically justified in getting revenge on Joel for him having killed her father. The argument can easily be extended: in the *hypothetical case* in which Ellie kills Abby (which she does not), if we agree that Abby is a sort of paternal figure for Lev, then players would also have to agree that Lev would be ethically justified in killing Ellie for the sake of revenge.

The problem is not that the cycle of revenge would end up generating, as the video game shows, an endless and increasing spiral of violence. The ultimate problem is conceptual, not just practical. That Ellie is ethically justified in killing Abby is itself a contradictory claim. Here's why. If Ellie is ethically justified in killing Abby, then Abby is ethically justified in killing Joel. But if Abby is ethically justified in killing Joel, then she cannot be blamed for it—and so Ellie cannot be ethically justified in killing Abby. The only way to avoid this contradiction is by accepting that it is ethically justified to punish a morally sound action; but this is also a contradictory claim.

Once players become aware of, or at least intuit, this contradiction, they come to realize that Ellie's aim of killing Abby is not an act of doing justice, as they probably thought during the earlier stages of the video game. Rather, it is nothing more than a matter of passionate revenge. It's in this way that players are progressively moved to the conclusion that all the violence they're engaged in during their own gaming experience is simply gratuitous and not justified by any honorable moral principle.

Retributive Justice and the *Lex Talionis*

The contradiction between the permissibility of Ellie's and Abby's actions cannot be resolved by assuming a retributive notion of justice. The core claim of retributive notions of justice is that wrongdoers should be punished according to the way in which they have offended. The intuition behind these positions is that there is a sort of pre-existing balance of justice, and that each time an offense is committed, the balance is broken and only restored when the offender receives a punishment that accords with the gravity of the offense.

The most straightforward example of a juridical principle based on a retributive understanding of justice is the so-called *lex talionis*. The earliest known juridical use of this principle was in ancient Babylon. It is also referred to in the Old Testament (Exodus 21:24–25; Leviticus 24:17–23; Deuteronomy 19:21).[2] The *lex talionis* states that offenders should face a punishment that is *equal* to the offense they have committed—"an eye for an eye and a tooth for a tooth." For example, according to the *lex talionis*, if someone murders another person, the murderer must be punished by their own death, thereby compensating one death with another and in doing so somehow restoring the balance of justice.

Just for the sake of the argument, let's grant that "an eye for an eye" is a sound moral principle, such that justice requires that wrongdoers be punished in exactly the same way in which they offended. To this effect, we may concede that the imbalance brought about by a murder is redressed by the death of the murderer, and therefore that killing a murderer is an act of justice and therefore a morally sound action. It is important to emphasize, however, that killing a murderer is a morally sound action because it restores the imbalance initially caused by the murderer. Killing the murderer's executioner is not ethically justified. The new murder would only serve to break the equilibrium once again, which is why the application of the "an eye for an eye" principle does not make "the world go blind."

Even assuming a retributive understanding of justice in the form of the "eye for an eye" principle, if Ellie was to succeed in killing Abby, then it would not be an act of justice. The restoration of the equilibrium that retributive justice seeks has already been achieved by Joel's death. Endorsing the claim that Ellie is ethically justified in killing Abby is tantamount to accepting that executioners should be sentenced to death.

It may be argued that Abby killing Joel was the act that broke the equilibrium of justice in the first place. If Joel was ethically justified in killing Abby's father, then Abby killing Joel would be an act of injustice— and, according to *lex talionis*, Ellie killing Abby would thereby become an act of doing justice, of restoring the equilibrium. This line of reasoning requires an argument to conclude that Joel was ethically justified in killing Abby's father, which itself would depend on whether Abby's father was ethically justified in sacrificing Ellie for the sake of finding a vaccine for the fungal outbreak. Otherwise, if Abby's father was justified in sacrificing Ellie, then it was Joel who first broke the equilibrium of justice, meaning that under the "eye for an eye" principle, Abby killing Joel would be ethically justified—and, in such a case, Ellie killing Abby would therefore not be ethically justified.

The most compelling argument for claiming that Joel's actions are ethically justified was formulated by Charles Joshua Horn in his article "*The Last of Us* as Moral Philosophy: Teleological Particularism and Why Joel Is Not a Villain."[3] In it, Horn convincingly argues that Joel's actions in the original *The Last of Us*, including the decision to rescue Ellie from the hospital no matter the cost, are morally defensible inasmuch as Joel has taken on the role of Ellie's father, and fathers have the moral duty to protect their children no matter what.

The argument is compelling and is probably the reason why most players do not see Joel as a villain, despite the brutality of some of his actions. However, the same reasoning can be used to justify Abby's father's decision to sacrifice Ellie for the sake of finding a vaccine. It may be argued that the ultimate reason why Abby's father intends to sacrifice Ellie is the fatherly desire to guarantee his daughter a safer and more peaceful world to live in—one in which there are no zombie-like violent mutant creatures.

We then face a contradiction similar to the one we faced when claiming that Ellie was ethically justified in killing Abby. For the same reason we might conclude that Joel is ethically justified in killing Abby's father, we should conclude that Abby's father is ethically justified in killing Ellie. But if Abby's father is ethically justified in killing Ellie, he cannot be blamed for it. So Joel cannot be justified in killing Abby's father.

The Requirement to Empathize with Abby

In order for players to realize that Ellie's aim of killing Abby isn't an act of doing justice, but simply a matter of passionate revenge, players are required to endorse Abby's perspective as much as they had endorsed Ellie's perspective during the first half of the video game. It's then that players come to realize that both characters are ultimately driven by the same kind of motivation—the obsessive desire to kill their father's killer. Otherwise, if players carry on seeing Abby as a one-dimensional, evil character, then they will fail to realize the evident similarities between Ellie and Abby. They will therefore feel no conflict about killing Abby. In fact, they will feel overtly contradicted when, while playing as Abby, the video game asks them to chase and fight against Ellie.

Even though the video game is clearly designed with the purpose of moving players to first condemn and later empathize with Abby, not all players are able to do the latter. Some players persist in seeing Abby as a one-dimensional evil character, despite the video game's efforts to show Abby as a much more complex character than just a sadistic and soulless clichéd villain. This can be explained by their strong attachment to Joel and Ellie during the original video game. Fans of the original *The Last of Us* were eager for a sequel that would allow them to see how the character of Joel, and his relationship with Ellie, had developed. What they were not expecting was a sequel in which they are forced to play as Joel's murderer.

This inability of some players to empathize with the character of Abby due to their strong attachment to Joel and Ellie explains why, in contrast with the highly positive reception the video game had from professional critics, who praised it for its complex but nonetheless enticing narrative, *The Last of Us Part II* faced a significant backlash from a segment of the fanbase of the original video game. The video game was subjected to "review bombing," an online phenomenon in which a large number of users post negative reviews online to lower the average score of the product—either as a collectively organized attempt to diminish its reputation or simply as a spontaneous way to express their discontent with the product. Despite having an average score of 95 out of 100 by professional reviewers and critics, *The Last of Us Part II* was given a score of 3.5 out of 10 by players on the review aggregator Metacritic, based on the almost 30,000 reviews posted within the first two days after its release.[4]

The inability to endorse Abby's perspective may not only impede the player's understanding of the overtly contradictory position they're assuming while endorsing Ellie's quest for revenge, it may also stop them from getting any enjoyment out of the video game. The reason for this is that players tend to distance themselves from what they consider to be immoral characters.

Players are willing to take on the role of an action character even if this character is not morally perfect, provided they are still ultimately driven by an honorable purpose. In *The Last of Us*, Joel is an excellent example of this. Although as a character he may be ethically questionable, all his actions during the video game are ultimately driven by the honorable fatherly purpose of protecting Ellie.

In contrast, very few players (if any) will find it entertaining to take on the role of an arrogant and soulless character who enjoys torturing people to death and mocks the suffering of their victims. Abby is first shown along these lines. She takes her time in slowly and brutally torturing Joel to death, and she seems to enjoy it. To Joel's request of "why don't you say whatever speech you've got rehearsed and get this over with," Abby replies, "You stupid old man.... You don't get to rush this."

The soulless and sadistic way in which Abby is first presented is the reason why all players are initially reluctant to play as Abby. However, most players overcome this initial reluctance as the story progressively reveals Abby's reasons and motives. Abby is shown to be a very similar character to Ellie, and just as complex. Moreover, as the story advances, players also discover Ellie has the same kind of need for gratuitous brutality as Abby has. For example, just before killing Nora, one of Abby's friends, Ellie claims that "I can make it quick, or I can make it so much worse" (which she does). By switching perspectives, players come to understand that if they are to empathize with Ellie, then, for the very same reasons, they should also empathize with Abby. And if they are to feel repulsion for Abby, for the very same reasons, they should also feel repulsion for Ellie.

The players who are unable to identify the obvious similarities between Ellie and Abby will be stuck in Ellie's subjective perspective, and continue seeing Abby as a one-sided and completely soulless character. For these players, taking the role of Abby is an undesirable and unrewarding gaming experience.

The entire gaming experience offered by *The Last of Us Part II* consists in forcing players to alternate between the roles of Ellie and Abby, so if players don't relate to both these characters, but instead feel repulsion for one of them, it's clear that this will diminish their interest in playing the video game.

A recent psychological study conducted by Valérie Erb, Seyeon Lee, and Young Yim Doh provides empirical evidence for the role of empathy in shaping players' responses to *The Last of Us Part II*.[5] The authors interviewed twelve players who completed the video game in order to explore the connections between the player–character relationship and the overall satisfaction with the video game. They found that players who were able to overcome their initial aversion to playing as Abby developed a deeper understanding and appreciation of her character as they progressed through the video game. They learned more about Abby's personal story, motivations, and relationships, which enabled them to empathize with her perspective and actions. The empathy for Abby enhanced their enjoyment of the video game and made them perceive *The Last of Us Part II* as a "meaningful emotional experience." In contrast, the players who were unable to empathize with Abby because of their strong attachment to Ellie and Joel expressed a general dissatisfaction with the gaming experience.

Challenging the Heroic Formula *While* Playing

Admittedly, *The Last of Us Part II* is not the first video game aiming to entice players to reflect on the ethical justification of their own gaming behavior. The most explicit and straightforward way in which video game designers have invited the player to reflect on the ethics of their own behavior is by compelling players to face an ethical dilemma during their play. The use of ethical dilemmas is interesting because it shows the attempt by video game designers to make the player's own moral intuitions an explicit part of the gaming mechanics.

One of the most well-known examples of the use of ethical dilemmas in video games is the first-person shooter video game *BioShock* (Irrational Games, 2007). One type of non-playable character that players encounter in *BioShock* are the so-called "Little Sisters"—young girls, aged somewhere between five and eight years old, who have been altered and brainwashed to collect from corpses, and later preserve in their own bodies, a substance called "ADAM." ADAM is used in the video game to enhance the abilities of the playable character. Whenever players get close to a Little Sister, they must decide whether to "harvest" her or to rescue her. Harvesting her means killing her to literally extract the valuable substance preserved in her body. Rescuing her means saving her life and restoring her humanity. Rescuing a Little Sister gives the players only half the resources that harvesting does. The difference in reward is highly relevant in the first stages of the video game. Each time players get close to a Little Sister, they are forced to choose between satisfying their own self-interest or sacrificing their self-interest for the sake of helping others. Although the video game becomes easier by harvesting the Little Sisters, the video game does not overtly advocate for a "correct" answer. The decision of whether to harvest or rescue a Little Sister ultimately depends on the player's own moral intuition.

In contrast to *BioShock*, the gaming mechanics of *The Last of Us Part II* do not require players to actively take a position regarding any ethical dilemma. The video game's entire storyline is linear and follows a predetermined path, meaning that there is no way that players can alter the events presented in the video game. However, even when giving players no room to decide, *The Last of Us Part II* still manages to entice players to reflect on the ethical justification of their own gaming behavior, and it does so by challenging the heroic formula so characteristic of action video games. As *The Last of Us Part II* unfolds, players become progressively aware that all the violence they have been engaged in throughout their own gaming experience is not an act of doing justice, but only passionate, unjustified revenge.

The Last of Us Part II is not the first action video game to take advantage of the common heroic formula to entice players to ethical reflection. In fact, the original *The Last of Us* already moved players to reflect on the ethical justification of Joel's last decision to save Ellie from the hospital. Other recent and well-known examples of this can be found in some of the titles in the first-person shooter video game saga *Far Cry*.[6] However, these video games do not move players to question the ethical justification of their gaming behavior until the game's very end, meaning that their aim is not to alter the player's gaming experience, but rather to complement it by allowing them to reflect on their own gaming experience after finishing the video game. In this regard, the innovative aspect of *The Last of Us Part II* is that the ethical conflict is embedded in the gaming experience itself, aiming to progressively move players to question their own gaming behavior *while* playing the video game.

Notes

1. For a detailed discussion on this topic, see my *First-Person Shooter Video Games* (Leiden: Brill, 2023), especially chap. 5 entitled "The Heroic Narrative in First-Person Shooter Video Games." My analysis there is specifically focused on the first-person shooter video game genre, although I think that in general it can be easily extended to action video games more generally. Among other claims, I argue that the inclusion of a heroic in-game narrative or background story in first-person shooter video games is explained because players would not enjoy the shooting gaming experience these video games offer if their own ethical standards were overtly contradicted—which indicates that moral considerations are still relevant even when players are well aware of being immersed in a purely fictional scenario.

2. There is some debate among theologians and biblical scholars as to whether the *lex talionis* should be understood literally, as stating that the punishment should be equal to the offense committed, or figuratively, as stating the more general requirement that the punishment should be proportional to the offense. For a first approach to this discussion see Alan Tzvika Nissel, "Equality or Equivalence: A Very Brief Survey of *Lex Talionis* as a Concept of Justice in the Bible," in Barry S. Wimpfheimer ed., *Wisdom of Bat Sheva* (Jersey City: KTAV Publishing House, 2009), 111–145.

3. Charles Joshua Horn, "*The Last of Us* as Moral Philosophy: Teleological Particularism and Why Joel Is Not a Villain," in David Kyle Johnson ed., *The Palgrave Handbook of Popular Culture as Philosophy* (Cham: Palgrave Macmillan, 2021), 1–16.

4. Riley MacLeod, "*The Last of Us Part 2*'s Metacritic Page Shows How Broken Numerical Scores Are," Kotaku, June 20, 2020, at https://kotaku.com/the-last-of-us-part-2-s-metacritic-page-shows-how-broke-1844106265. Notably, the average user score on Metacritic has since slightly increased. As of September 2023, *The Last of Us Part II* has a user score of 5.8 out of 10, based on over 160,000 reviews from players ("*The Last of Us Part II* for PlayStation 4 Reviews," Metacritic, September 5, 2023, at https://www.metacritic.com/game/playstation-4/the-last-of-us-part-ii).

5. Valérie Erb, Seyeon Lee, and Young Yim Doh, "Player–Character Relationship and Game Satisfaction in Narrative Game: Focus on Player Experience of Character Switch in *The Last of Us Part II*," *Frontiers in Psychology* 12 (2021), article 709926.

6. Alberto Oya, "*Far Cry 2*: Are You Sure about Being a Hero?," andphilosophy.com—The Blackwell Philosophy and Pop Culture Series, December 22, 2022, at https://andphilosophy.com/2022/12/22/far-cry-2-are-you-sure-about-being-a-hero.

6

Necessary Violence in *The Last of Us Part II*

Tim Jones

The opening lines of Pearl Jam's "Future Days" are heard throughout *The Last of Us Part II*, "If I ever were to lose you / I'd surely lose myself." These lyrics, about how the loss of a loved one precedes the loss of one's self, function as a particularly cruel piece of ironic foreshadowing—Ellie *will* soon lose Joel, and she indeed finds her mental state unraveling due to the actions she takes in response. The lines recur during the course of her revenge against Joel's killers, as she loses her humanity through her escalating orgy of violence. Ellie loses Joel, and her own identity falters further with each violent step she takes toward avenging him. Why can losing someone close to us send us down the sort of path Ellie takes? Why did loss turn a balanced and friendly young woman into a brutal mass murderer? Because we need to get revenge, right? But *why*?

No Woman Is an Island

Ellie's loss of her "self" is the spark that leads to her journey of brutality. To grasp why the loss of self is critical to violence, and to understand the deeper meaning in the lyrics, we can look to contemporary philosopher Judith Butler's exploration of the many facets of the relationship between loss and violence.[1] Butler argues that loss is *often* followed by violence, so we shouldn't regard Ellie's actions as particularly unusual or unlikely.

Butler discusses large-scale acts of violence that provoke nationwide mourning, like in the aftermath of the 9/11 attacks on the World Trade Center in 2001, but she also examines the more singular loss of a loved one that accompanies an individual death (though I guess any distinction we might draw here becomes a little slippery in the recognition that the former is ultimately just a huge collection of instances of the latter). Loss makes us uniquely vulnerable, and, according to Butler, leads us toward the possibility

The Last of Us and Philosophy: Look for the Light, First Edition.
Edited by Charles Joshua Horn.

of compensating for this vulnerability with acts of aggression toward other people—whether this be in the shape of military action against countries presumed to be responsible, or picking a fight with a group of strangers in a bar. Or, in Ellie's case, traveling hundreds of miles to butcher an army of German Shepherds (who we soon learn just want to play fetch all day) and stab a pregnant woman to death in an aquarium.

Take a moment to consider everything that defines you. And then consider how many of those things involve others. Ellie is the girl who *Joel* escorted all the way from Boston to Salt Lake City; the girl to whom he gave an unforgettable trip into space (sort of) to celebrate her birthday; the girl for whose safety *Joel* committed acts of violence; the girl who became no less than his surrogate daughter; the girl *Joel* taught to play guitar.

Ellie isn't an island. Much of her (and our) identity is bound up with other people. Because our identity isn't self-contained, the loss of someone dear to us causes a reduction of our own self. As Butler puts it, "It is not as if an 'I' exists independently over here and then simply loses a 'you' over there, especially if the attachment to 'you' is part of what composes who 'I' am."[2] Ellie doesn't lose herself by committing violent act after violent act— she loses herself the moment Joel dies and takes a part of her with him.

This interrelated concept of the self stands in stark contrast to much of what the modern Western philosophical and political tradition says about the autonomy and self-sufficiency of identity. For example, the atomistic conception of the mostly self-sufficient individual figured prominently in the political philosophy of Thomas Hobbes (1588–1697). And Henry David Thoreau's (1817–1862) idyllic image of withdrawing from society altogether to live in the woods emphasizes the possibility and promise of a peaceful, solitary (not lonely) existence.

Butler's view is quite different: the self is marked with imprints made by our connections with other people. For that reason, the solitary individual of Thoreau's *Walden* would inevitably lack key elements of what makes us fully human. In contrast to Hobbes and Thoreau, Aristotle (384–322 BCE) contends that nobody can be truly delighted with solitude unless they're a beast or a god—neither of which describes any of the main characters of *The Last of Us*. If they'd existed in solitude, they simply wouldn't be the complete, rounded characters who we've come to love, hate, or mourn.

Butler also sheds light on a special challenge for LGBT characters like Ellie. Members of groups who have long campaigned for the rights to do what they want with, and to, their bodies nonetheless have to contend with the inevitability that no one's body can ever be truly her own.[3] For all of us, the vulnerability that follows the death of someone close to us is the result of how hugely rupturing the loss is to our identity. Striking out violently as a response to such loss is one potential way of processing the rupture of our sense of self.

Other Pathways

But is such a violent reaction to loss truly that hard to avoid? Butler hopes that it might become easier to respond differently to loss. The moment of our ruptured identity does not necessarily have to push us toward compensatory violence. Instead, it can push us toward a process of reflection, if we can become comfortable enough with our own vulnerability to remain fragile long enough to hear where else it might take us. We must resist the desire to resolve the problem as quickly as possible through what Butler calls "a fantasy of mastery," like Ellie's revenge quest against Abby or the United States's retaliatory actions against countries that may or may not have had anything to do with 9/11.[4]

One form this reflective process might take is thinking anew about how we tell stories about what happened, especially when our loss has resulted from violence.[5] When we tell the story of 9/11, where do we start? Most narrative accounts begin on the day itself—"a group of terrorists flew hijacked planes into the Twin Towers and the Pentagon" and everything that comes next is a consequence of this statement. But what if we go back further and begin our account with statements that cast *this* statement, too, as only the consequence of a statement chronologically referring to the world before, like "The rise of the Taliban in Afghanistan was encouraged by the US as a result of its Cold War era foreign policy"?

Framing and interpreting the events of 9/11 more broadly doesn't excuse the terrorists. 9/11 still happened as a result of evil decisions that no one forced them to make. But recasting the events sets up an explanatory framework that might engender a perspective that leads to something better than more violence. The United States might realize that however diminished it felt after 9/11, it has made other countries feel similarly through its recent history. Such recognition might compel the United States to guard against making other countries feel that way in the future.

What if Ellie had learned to be comfortable with her vulnerability after Joel's murder, rather than immediately setting out on a revenge quest motivated by a desire to eliminate the feeling of vulnerability? Abby clearly hated Joel, just as Ellie now hates Abby. Focusing on this hatred, Ellie might have become curious. She might have sought to understand why someone's hatred would motivate them to trek across the United States to commit murder. That would certainly have been better than blindly becoming the same kind of person herself.

Forgive me if this sounds ridiculous (and I'll admit it would've made for a less entertaining video game), but what if Ellie then tried to sit down with Abby and have a conversation about her motivations? Ellie might have learned the one fact about Joel's murder that she never explicitly discovers at any point in the game—that Abby's father was the doctor who Joel killed to save Ellie.

"Abby killed the person I love most in the world" wouldn't be the opening sentence of the narrative Ellie tells about Joel's death. It's not as if
knowing Abby's motivations would make Ellie forgive Abby, or stop hurt-
ing from Abby's actions. But it could still matter to Ellie, by revealing their
shared connections. This chimes with Hannah Arendt's (1906–1975)
argument that "The practice of violence, like all action, changes the world,
but the most probable change is to a more violent world."[6] Joel's violence
against Abby's father creates the world in which Abby violently murders
Joel, which in turn creates the world in which Ellie murders Abby's friends,
as she moves in on her ultimate target. Killing Abby wouldn't change
anything, but would only create, in turn, a world in which someone who
loved Abby in the same way (like maybe Lev?) would be driven to murder
Ellie to deal with his own vulnerability in the face of his own loss.

Ellie's final decision not to kill Abby, made right on the brink of her
death, is a decision that will create, by however small a degree, a less
violent world. But because she's already killed several members of Abby's
crew and caused all their surviving friends or relatives to feel the vulnerability of their own diminishment, the world has still become more violent
than it would've been had Ellie reflected on her own loss earlier, instead of
pursuing revenge. How much more violence ensues (and whether Ellie will
become its victim) will depend on whether these friends and relatives
pursue the same course of action as first Abby and then Ellie, or whether
they are able to respond to their loss differently.

What If Violence *Is* the Only Way?

In the context of the Algerian struggle for independence from France,
Frantz Fanon (1925–1961) wrote controversially, but persuasively, about
the necessity of physical violence if former European colonies were going
to achieve freedom from their colonizers.[7] The international backdrop to
his argument doesn't mesh exactly with the personal conflict between Ellie
and Abby, but there are enough similarities for Fanon's points to explain
why the peaceful outcome that Butler would love to see the two characters
achieve isn't likely to endure much beyond the end of the second video
game. If Fanon was correct about growing beyond the long-term consequences of colonization, then Ellie would find her mind turning back to
violent intentions—violent intentions that would necessarily, for Fanon, be
shared by the friends and relatives of the victims of Ellie's own violence.

Fanon argues that colonization is itself violent, not only because the sub-
jugation of a native population involves a continual marshaling of actual
and potential physical violence, but also because the removal of native
customs, ways of life, and beliefs, and their replacement by those of the
colonizer, are a form of symbolic violence, through the literal erasure of a
people's ability to determine their own identity under the imprint of the

colonizer's own. The symbolic violence of colonization captures the impact of Abby's actions upon Ellie. Similar to a colonized country, Ellie can't understand her own story without casting it as the unwilling product of Abby's actions—of Abby's physical violence toward Joel, and the symbolically violent consequences of this violence upon everyone whose identity Joel was a significant part of. And we can think, too, of the colonizing impact of Ellie's actions upon the friends of her victims, who cannot think any longer of their own paths without Ellie looming large as the agent of their grief.

We are not only diminished, then, by the loss of those close to us; the agent of that diminishment rewrites our identity by making themselves a part of our story that we do not want. Ellie was the girl who *Joel* took across America, and she's now the girl stricken by grief because of *Abby*. Loss doesn't just diminish us, as Butler suggests. When achieved through the violent acts of another, loss fills the gap with the perpetrator's own insidious presence.

Those that colonize, whether the subjects of their colonization be whole nations, or individuals like Ellie, fill their victims with physical and symbolic violence. Fanon is clear that whatever follows, for colonizer or colonized, it's the colonizer that started the process, or who first filled the space with the violence that decolonization sees turned back on its creators. It might seem that just because the colonizers started the violence, that doesn't necessarily justify the colonized following suit. However, Fanon would suggest that such a "two wrongs don't make a right" level response is naive to the sheer necessity of violence for throwing off the colonial chains and becoming an independent, thinking agent who takes back control of his or her own identity.

It's not just that violence might practically be the only means of physically compelling a foreign power to abandon its claim on your land and go home—an argument more suited to France with respect to Algeria than to Abby, who presumably has no active wish to continue being a part of Ellie's existential territory, and who acquires no material or political gains from remaining so. It's also, Fanon writes, that, for the colonized, violence is a "cleansing force" that "frees the native from his inferiority complex and from his despair and inaction; it makes him fearless and restores his self-respect."[8] Violence restores agency and empowers those whom colonization had diminished. Violence doesn't just make us large again by filling empty space; it makes us large again by demonstrating to those who reduced us that we're no longer merely a page of *their* story, but again the writers of our own.

There's something about the desperate momentum of Ellie's hunt for Abby, to the point of abandoning what looks from the outside like the promising start of a new, peaceful life with Dina on a farm in Wyoming, that could confirm Fanon's arguments about the necessity of violence. There is a gulf between Butler and Fanon, who both explore potentially violent responses to different, though similar, forms of loss and diminishment. Butler sees violence as a precipice that we understandably find ourselves approaching, but should pull back from, by finding more peaceful, healthier forms of engaging with trauma. By contrast, Fanon sees alternatives to violence as a form of unhealthy compensation that will keep us small. Fanon admits that violence must cease once it has served its purpose, but there *is* a vital purpose that it needs to serve first.

Even though Ellie ultimately forgoes her violent mission at the end of *The Last of Us Part II*, the damage has already been done. Ellie can try to turn her back on violence, but this will be to little effect if the grief she's already caused creates a violent response in turn, against which she can only defend herself through, that's right, *violence*.

Loss and Violence

Butler might suggest that the closing scenes of *The Last of Us Part II* show that Ellie has found a more contemplative response to the loss of her identity than needing to kill Joel's murderer, and that, even at the very last moment, we can resist the call to violence. Fanon, by contrast, would almost certainly contend that we haven't yet seen far enough into Ellie's future to know if she will maintain her contemplative, non-violent attitude. If we accept the explanation of the intensity of Ellie's actions across the game through Fanon's arguments about the necessity of violence to exorcise the impact of colonization, then we might think it close to inevitable that violent intentions will creep back to the fore.

The narrative structure of *The Last of Us Part II* leads the player through experiencing the loss of the hugely popular Joel after spending so much time with him in the first video game, through wanting to see Abby dead for her brutal execution of Joel, and then to approaching some level of understanding that these same motivations are what guided Abby in the first place. If Ellie had reached that understanding it might have saved the lives of all the people she killed in her pursuit and saved their loved ones from having their identities impacted by violent loss. The video game ultimately has a lot to say about what we might learn if we reflect on the losses we experience in our own lives and the importance of remaining with the resultant vulnerability long enough for a period of reflection, instead of following Ellie into the immediate rush of (potentially violent) compensation.

And if the player can reach a lasting appreciation of Abby's motivations that endures in the days, weeks, and months beyond finishing the video game, rather than ultimately wishing that Ellie had stuck her knife in when she had the chance on Santa Barbara beach, then perhaps Butler's perspective will win out over Fanon's—and Ellie's turn away from violent revenge against Abby can likewise demonstrate a permanent change that could even point the way toward a more peaceful response from the people that she hurt.

Notes

1. Judith Butler, *Precarious Life: The Power of Mourning and Violence* (London and New York: Verso, 2004).
2. Butler, *Precarious Life*, 22.
3. Butler, *Precarious Life*, 26.
4. Butler, *Precarious Life*, 29.
5. Butler, *Precarious Life*, 5.
6. Hannah Arendt, *On Violence* (Orlando: Harcourt, 1970), 77.
7. Frantz Fanon, *The Wretched of the Earth*, trans. Constance Farrington (New York: Grove Weidenfeld, 1963), 35–95.
8. Fanon, *The Wretched of the Earth*, 94.

Natural Law and Positive Law
Marlene's Understanding of Law and Justice

Juliele Maria Sievers

One has a moral responsibility to disobey unjust laws.
—Martin Luther King Jr.

The Last of Us presents a world where law and social norms have disappeared or been reconfigured. The martial law imposed by FEDRA and the revolutionary militia of the Fireflies denies rights to people infected by Cordyceps. Marlene, the leader of the Fireflies, decides to sacrifice the life of Ellie, the daughter of her longtime friend, Anna, to create a vaccine from her antibodies, which could potentially save humanity from extinction. But is Marlene lawfully entitled to make such a decision? If there is no law, where does Marlene's authority come from?

Marlene's decision to sacrifice Ellie for the greater good fits with the utilitarian ethical principle of justice that demands the needs of the many outweigh the needs of the few. But Joel's opposition shows that a general abstract idea of justice can be difficult to accept in a particular situation. After all, are we willing to accept the consequences of a just decision when it causes death or harm to those we love most? If we aren't willing to accept those consequences, does that mean we're against the law?

Authority and the Force of the Law

In the video game, the player faces difficult situations and moral dilemmas where the course of events will depend on the choices made. *The Last of Us* doesn't provide narrative choice—the video game can unfold only one way—and yet, the player may still have to justify their own actions, through Joel. This dynamic puts us in a philosophically vulnerable position: What if we had to justify every decision made during the game? Are our

The Last of Us and Philosophy: Look for the Light, First Edition.
Edited by Charles Joshua Horn.
© 2025 John Wiley & Sons, Inc. Published 2025 by John Wiley & Sons, Inc.

choices and actions driven by the morality of the society in which we live, following what people tell us is right or wrong, or do we tend to be more legalistic and simply follow what norms and laws expect us to do, in terms of permissions and prohibitions?

There is often disagreement about whether our decisions can be morally accepted on the one hand, or legally prohibited on the other. Concerning moral evaluation, we call those actions just or unjust, and when it comes to a legal evaluation, we must simply say that they are in accordance with or against the law. In most of the world of *The Last of Us*, there seems to be no such thing as the law anymore. There's no governing body, police, trials, taxes, or any traces of a legal order as we know it, except in decentralized groups or organizations such as the village where Joel's brother Tommy lived or in David's cult-like society.

And yet, Marlene appears to possess *legal* authority. What is the nature of Marlene's orders and decisions in a world largely lacking legal institutions? If you find yourself within the Fireflies collective, are her commands mandatory to you just because she is the leader? Is she issuing binding norms that are grounded in her authority? Do the members of the Fireflies have the right to oppose her commands if they find them unjust?

In our time and place, Martin Luther King Jr. drew our attention to the need to cultivate our critical thinking when it comes to obeying norms. After all, history is full of examples of legitimized legal norms that shouldn't have ever existed from a moral point of view. There have been laws permitting slavery, genocide, segregation, and all kinds of prejudices. These laws were valid in the sense that they were derived from the governing bodies, and consequently, they were mandatory, binding on everyone in a sovereign territory. They were mandatory not simply because of their content, but because of their origin—they were issued by an authority, by those who were in positions of power.

Natural Law and Positive Law

In legal philosophy, two main theories diverge on the place that morality (that is, the notion of justice) occupies in legal matters: legal positivism and the natural law tradition. According to legal positivism, the notion of justice isn't and mustn't be linked to moral systems. Instead, it is defined in terms of legality itself—what is fair is stipulated by what is legally determined by the legal authority. In fact, actions taken under positive law will not always seem fair, such as enforcement of segregation. But positivists insist that the force of the law comes not because the law is *good*, but because the law was issued by a legitimate legal authority.

By contrast, in the natural law tradition, the notion of justice is "prior" to any legal system or law, as a rational principle with a moral basis. In other words, natural law looks to the moral principles underlying the legal system. However, morality frequently depends on subjective beliefs related to religion, which can also result in cases of injustice, such as the mistreatment of women in some societies.

In *The Last of Us*, Marlene's decision to sacrifice Ellie fits with the natural law conception of justification. As Marlene understands it, justice demands the sacrifice of the individual in favor of the collective. Marlene's duty as the head of the Fireflies was to lead the way out of the darkness, and the light was represented by the hope of developing a vaccine. Thus, killing an innocent person was legitimate and justified for the promotion of a greater good. The preference for saving the greatest number of people seems to be based on a kind of rational choice: it seems to be the "obvious" way out of this situation, and, in the bigger picture, it assures that justice is served.

Marlene was faced with a conflict between norms that we also face in our real world in our everyday actions. Because we are influenced by many different overlapping normative spheres, we are constantly following or breaking rules of etiquette, rules of courtesy, rules of work ethics, religious rules, and so on. These many types of rules may be different from the rules that the law prescribes, and may even conflict with them.

For example, according to their religion, members of Jehovah's Witnesses are not allowed to receive blood transfusions. However, there have been many cases in which children or young people hospitalized at risk of death ask their doctors to claim an injunction to perform the transfusion even without parental authorization. Their parents may believe that religious law should prevail even if it results in the death of their child. Which position is right and just? Lawyers and judges often disagree about what to do when there are normative conflicts. Sometimes legal decisions are interpreted and based purely on the text, and other times these decisions draw on more basic moral principles.

It's more difficult for us to understand the legal rather than the moral aspects involved in Marlene's choice because we don't know how the law functions in *The Last of Us*. Even the Firefly saying "When you're lost in the darkness, look for the light" is ambiguous. Is it a piece of advice, moral guidance, motivation, a moral imperative, or law?

There are some clear legal norms imposed and enforced in the world of *The Last of Us*. For example, the laws in FEDRA's occupied territory about killing anyone infected were probably justified on utilitarian grounds, just like other laws in Quarantine Zones. Of course, we might argue that not only are those laws unjust, but so are those who follow them. For example, in episode 1, the lost child looking for help is killed by FEDRA soldiers who are following orders and executing the law of their territory—a very disturbing justification perfectly aligned with a positivist conception of law, and often used in our real world too.[1]

Who Decides What's the Right Thing to Do?

Honoring Anna's request to kill her and then take care of Ellie, Marlene is a leader and authority figure who puts her emotions aside in favor of a "greater good." Eventually her decision to sacrifice Ellie is justified by the same moral principle, and the math justifies her. Marlene clearly explains her reasoning to Joel.

> MARLENE: No matter how hard you try, no matter how many people you kill, she's going to grow up, Joel. And then you'll die. She'll live. Then what? How long until she's torn apart by Infected or murdered by raiders? Because she lives in a broken world that you could have saved.
>
> JOEL: Maybe. But it isn't for you to decide.
>
> MARLENE: Or you. So, what would she decide, huh? 'Cause I think she'd want to do what's right.

In legal philosophy, the notion of justice, or "the right thing to do," is a central element in the theory of natural law. According to this tradition, justice is achieved when we reach a fact that is "self-evident" to us as rational beings. Historically, natural law theory tends to be linked to religious conceptions involving law, for example during medieval times when the West was under tremendous influence from the church. As a result of the influence of Christianity, the justification for legal decisions was often based on general religious principles that were seen as "universal" values. At that point in history, legality, morality, and religion had very blurred boundaries.[2]

Legal positivism began to displace natural law in the early nineteenth century as it developed largely out of the empiricist theory of knowledge. In fact, legal positivism was first developed in the thought of Jeremy Bentham, the famous utilitarian and political reformer. The main difference between legal positivism and natural law theory is that a positivist definition of justice is merely formal and neutral, not going beyond the limits of law itself to include elements from religion or morality. Positivists generally agree with empiricists and insist that the law, like everything else, should be limited to what can be observed. Justice simply means that similar legal cases must be treated similarly, and we can't appeal to higher-order moral principles.

But even if positive law is the theory that prevails today in most Western societies (a controversial claim, to be sure),[3] there is still a strong connection that we tend to establish between what is legally valid (according to legal positivism) and what is morally good or just (according to natural law tradition). The autonomy of legal systems in relation to other systems of rules such as morality or religions, as defended by legal positivists, comes with a cost. For example, the atrocities committed by the Nazi regimes were all legally legitimate, even though they were morally abominable. And yet, the moral principles mobilized by natural law advocates tend to be linked to a very conservative agenda that promotes, for example, the condemnation of the right to abortion, LGBTQ rights, and environmental policies, among others.[4]

With a basic understanding of the difference between legal positivism and natural law theory, we have a new perspective on Marlene's judgment of the necessity for Ellie's death. Her decision is grounded in a very attractive idea of justice based on utilitarianism.[5] But Joel has a very different idea of justice, not grounded in utilitarian ethical principles.

Should Justice Be as Blind as a Clicker?

In the final episode of season 1, we see how Marlene's plans are frustrated by Joel, who seems to have a very different conception of justice according to which justice demands that we do whatever is necessary to survive. Joel considered the loss of Sarah and Tess to be injustices which he wouldn't allow for Ellie. It's fair to say that, while Marlene was ready to kill Ellie to save the whole world, Joel was ready to kill anyone to save Ellie in the name of justice.

In criminal law, this scenario is close to what is called a "state of necessity," where there is a justification or an excuse for breaking the law. One famous case of a state of necessity occurred when a Uruguayan rugby team's plane crashed in the Andes mountains in 1972.[6] The survivors had to eat the flesh of their dead teammates to live until the rescue. None of the survivors were legally charged for cannibalism (which per se is not a crime but could be related to the crime of corpse desecration). Here we might think of David's religious community which also practiced cannibalism, though many members weren't aware. David covertly imposed cannibalism on his community under what appears to be a moral, religious, or even rational justification that whatever is necessary is also permitted. But is there room for disagreement in such a normative context?

It's hard to determine where exactly the state of necessity begins and ends. Even if we grant that Silver Lake was in a state of necessity, was the area 500 yards outside of Silver Lake in a state of necessity too? Perhaps it's not the *area* that determines the state of necessity, but instead the *people* who are starving. But that would mean that anyone starving to death, like those in Silver Lake, would have free rein to do anything for survival.

David is probably the clearest villain of the whole series, and Joel is clearly our hero. Yet, out of necessity, Joel kills dozens of people—some infected, some not—to protect himself and Ellie. Some of his victims were themselves killers, criminals, and terrorists, but all of them were also trying to survive. So, if they were all trying to endure in this scenario of despair and destruction, why did some lives seem to matter more than others? When Joel lies to Ellie after killing Marlene, he does so because he knows

Ellie wouldn't approve. He knows his conception of justice or "the right thing to do" is only legitimate for himself.

Many of us would probably behave like Joel under the threat of losing a loved one. But it's precisely for this reason that we need a legal system to ensure that it won't be up to us to judge ourselves. Under positive law, Marlene's actions, as well as Joel's, would be legally problematic. Both broke the law, even though their private motivations may be regarded as mitigating circumstances concerning the penalties to be applied. (Joel, for example, was first and foremost trying to save Ellie from being murdered.)

Morality is complicated in Marlene's world, and legal philosophy might be even more complicated. We don't know the status of the law, who constitutes a legitimate legal authority, or the relationship between law and morality. But in thinking about these questions in the context of *our* world, we might be able to make sense of them in the world of *The Last of Us*.

Notes

1. The most famous case concerning the conflict between the following of legal norms and the underlying morality is explained by German philosopher Hannah Arendt (1906–1975) in her book *Eichmann in Jerusalem* (New York: Viking Press, 1963). Arendt coined the term "banality of evil" to try to explain how one is ready to perform hideous actions under someone else's order and authority, like the Nazi soldiers and officials.
2. The main philosopher representing a naturalistic understanding of law during these times was Thomas Aquinas (1225–1274).
3. The most important author of legal positivism was Austrian jurist and philosopher Hans Kelsen (1881–1973). He was also the author of the Austrian Constitution, written in 1920 and still operating today.
4. One of the few defenders of natural law conceptions today is contemporary Australian philosopher John Finnis, whose problematic comments on same-sex marriage were the target of much criticism.
5. In ethics, utilitarianism is a branch of consequentialism, and was founded by English philosopher and jurist, Jeremy Bentham (1748–1832), which defined it by the preference for actions that maximize utility, happiness, well-being, benefit, the "good," and so on. It has received many reformulations since, being defended by many philosophers, including John Stuart Mill (1806–1873) and, more contemporarily, Peter Singer.
6. Emma Jones, "Society of the Snow: The Horrifying Story of the 1972 Andes Plane Crash Is Also One of Survival and Generosity," BBC (website), December 14, 2023, at https://www.bbc.com/culture/article/20231213-society-of-the-snow-the-horrifying-story-of-the-1972-andes-plane-crash-is-also-one-of-survival-and-generosity.

8

The Last of Us, Hobbes, and the State of Nature

Armond Boudreaux

Many philosophers have asked what life was like for humans during the time before they organized themselves into societies and created states for their governance. They call this ungoverned, prehistorical condition "the state of nature." How we think about the state of nature depends in large part on what we think about human nature. Are we basically good, so that we can imagine an Edenic time when people lived harmoniously as hunter-gatherers in a pre-social state? Or are we basically "evil," so that we imagine violence and barbarism in some dark prehistoric past? Do we need societies with strong governments to keep us in line? If *The Last of Us* is any indication, the philosopher Thomas Hobbes (1588–1679) may have been correct in his pessimistic view of life in the state of nature and the need for a strong government.

Maybe human nature means that whenever we find ourselves without a strong state governing us, we must create authorities like FEDRA to keep the worst aspects of our nature under control. After all, the post-apocalyptic world left in the wake of the Cordyceps pandemic seems to turn a lot of people into barbarians who will do anything—including killing and eating one another—to survive. In a world like we see in *The Last of Us*, should people be grateful for a powerful and sometimes oppressive authority like FEDRA to keep life from being intolerable for all?

You're an Animal

Hobbes's way of seeing humanity is illustrated in episode 8, when Ellie has been separated from Joel and taken prisoner by the people of Silver Lake, an isolated resort town in the Colorado Rockies.

The leader of Silver Lake, David, is a charismatic preacher with a gift for inspiring people to religious fervor. Having seen that Ellie is cunning,

The Last of Us and Philosophy: Look for the Light, First Edition.
Edited by Charles Joshua Horn.

determined, loyal, and violent, David says that he recognizes himself in her. He wants her to become his romantic and sexual partner, to lead the people of Silver Lake with him. "They follow me," he tells her, "and they would follow *us*. Lord knows I could use the help." It's a creepy offer—not least because of Ellie's age and the earnestness with which the middle-aged David makes it clear that he wants her as more than just a new member of his leadership team.

Ellie, of course, has no interest in his advances—especially since she's spotted a severed human ear on the floor of the room and surmised that the Silver Lake people are cannibals. David confirms Ellie's suspicion is true and says that he's ashamed of it, but defends his actions by laying out a bleak view of human nature. When Ellie calls him an "animal," he responds, "Well, yes, we all are. That's sort of the point."

To Ellie, humans acting like animals is a horror, but David thinks that he's seen the truth about humanity—and rather than hiding from it by indulging pleasant fantasies about morality or through sincere religious belief, he embraces it and uses it to survive. He says he's able to see violence in Ellie because it's the same thing he finds in himself. For a long time, he tells her, he resisted the violence in his own heart, but when the Cordyceps outbreak ended human civilization, the fungus showed him "the truth": "What does Cordyceps do? Is it … evil? No. It multiplies. It feeds and protects its children. And it secures its future with violence if it must."

But while we should probably join Ellie in condemning David as an "animal," his ideas about humanity aren't as easily dismissed as we might wish for them to be. In fact, his views have been anticipated by some of the most important thinkers in the philosophical tradition, including Hobbes.

Enter the Leviathan

Hobbes is most famous for his book *Leviathan*, which he wrote during a time of enormous social, political, and intellectual turmoil. England was in the throes of a civil war that would, over the course of four decades, transform it from a monarchy to a republic. European culture had seen important shifts in thinking as a result of the Protestant Reformation, revolutions in philosophy, and the development of modern science. In *Leviathan* (and in his earlier, lesser-known work *De Cive*), Hobbes set out to provide a justification for a strong government that would grapple with the political, religious, and intellectual challenges of his day (and especially to comport with the new science and jettison reliance on medieval philosophy).

For Hobbes, humans are barbarous by nature and can only avoid that barbarism by surrendering most of their natural freedoms to a strong state. This state might be a military dictatorship like FEDRA, or it might be a communitarian polity like the one in Jackson, Wyoming, where Joel finally finds Tommy. It might be an absolute monarchy or a liberal republic.

It might be socialist, or it might have a free market. But in Hobbes's estimation, we need a state strong enough to rein in our worst appetites and manage our aversions.

He calls this strong state the "Leviathan," and believes that we would willingly surrender most of the freedom we have from nature to that state in exchange for relative peace, order, and safety. As a FEDRA officer tells Ellie in episode 7, "No matter what anyone out there says or thinks, we're the only thing holding this all together. If we go down, the people in this zone will starve or murder each other. That much I know." In a sense, the officer is right. It's not that FEDRA is the only kind of government that can control the chaos that follows the Cordyceps pandemic. Theoretically, that role could be played by other forms of government. But it's clear that most people outside the Quarantine Zones are dangerous and willing to hurt, steal, rape, kill, or enslave their fellow human beings to survive.

Back to the State of Nature

So what was life like in the state of nature long ago? Did we live in peace with one another and in harmony with nature? Were we vicious savages who beat each other with clubs and lived in caves? Or was the truth somewhere in between those two extremes?

Hobbes answers these questions with a bleak picture of humanity. He says that the state of nature put us into bitter competition with one another for scarce resources—a "war of all against all,"[1] as he puts it in his book *De Cive*. Under these conditions, Hobbes reasons, there can't be any industry, agriculture, cultivation of knowledge, inventions, literature, or society. Humans in the state of nature only experienced "continual fear, and danger of violent death; and the life of man solitary, poor, nasty, brutish, and short."[2]

If this seems too pessimistic, Hobbes asks his readers to examine their own behavior even in a high-trust society like England. He points out that we all lock our doors and, even with our doors locked, we often secure our valuable belongings in locked chests (and we do this even though we have police to punish all wrongdoing against us). If we trust others so little in a civilized society, how much less would we trust others if there were no institutions to protect us from one another?

In Hobbes's view, "every man is enemy to every man"[3] in the state of nature because without a sovereign state to govern us, the only law is the rule of survival. He rejects all ideas of a *summum bonum* ("highest good") toward which human nature strives, substituting desires and aversions in place of the moral law of the philosophers and theologians. The most basic fact about our psychology is our appetite for scarce resources. We know that we need things. We know that others need those same things. We know that there often isn't enough to go around. These basic facts about human nature and the world create a relationship of distrust and fear between people because we know that just as we might be willing to do harm to survive, others are just as willing as we are (and maybe *more* willing).

Hobbes's view of humanity is represented in the suspicion and fear with which most people treat each other in *The Last of Us*. The survivors of the Cordyceps pandemic intuitively understand what Hobbes argues in *Leviathan* and in *De Cive*: scarcity of resources means that we're all in competition with one another, and without the rule of law and a system of exchange, our most obvious means of acquiring things we need isn't very nice.

They Got a Kid, Joel

Further incidents from the show seem to support Hobbes's pessimistic take on humans in the state of nature. In episode 1, for example, it takes less than a day for fear to reduce the entire population of Austin, Texas, to utter chaos. By the middle of the night, fires burn in the streets and crowds of people trample one another in their attempts to escape. As it becomes clear to everyone that the structures and institutions that keep us all safe from one another are rapidly collapsing, people revert immediately to the kind of behavior that we might expect from them in Hobbes's state of nature.

We see Hobbes's representation of human nature clearly after Joel, Tommy, and Sarah flee their home and look for a route out of the chaos of the city. At one point, they come upon a mother, father, and child standing on the side of the road, their vehicle broken down. Tommy slows down the truck, planning to help them, but Joel tells him to keep driving. "They got a kid, Joel," says Tommy. "So do we," says Joel. Sarah suggests that they could let the family ride in the back of the truck, but Tommy drives on, leaving the terrified father calling after them.

In this incident, we see two human urges—compassion for strangers and the instinct to survive—come into conflict with one another. Compassion moves Tommy to stop and help the family even though he knows that time isn't on their side. The longer they wait to leave town, the less likely it is that they'll be able to escape. Worse, he has no idea whether any of the stranded family members are already infected. Yet Tommy's first response to seeing the struggling family is to stop and help. When Joel tells him to drive on, he's motivated by the law of survival. If they stop, they risk not making it out and exposing themselves to infection.

It's easy to suppose that we can answer Hobbes's negative view of humans in the state of nature by pointing out that compassion seems to be just as much a part of us as the propensity for violence. After all, even though the world rapidly returns to the state of nature on September 26, 2003, Tommy, Sarah, and even Joel, feel compassion for the family in need.

Two observations will show why this doesn't really provide us with a refutation of Hobbes, however.

The first response to the objection regarding compassion is that it's easy to see how good people raised in a safe, orderly, free society would preserve their highest values and ideals once society collapses. Tommy, Joel, and Sarah are good people. Their sense of decency and sympathy won't simply disappear in a matter of hours. In fact, given how terrified people must feel in the face of society's utter collapse, it seems likely that many people would hang on even more tightly to their most precious values and ideals.

The second observation is that even though our heroes *feel* compassion as they come upon a family in need, the instinct to survive wins out. Tommy's desire to help withers and dies quickly in the face of the harsh reality that Joel forces him to see. Tommy and Sarah's resignation seems to show that the will to survive is more *basic*, more *fundamental* to our nature than compassion.

If You Don't Think There's Hope for the World ...

Just as someone might feel themselves on the verge of despair when they finish the first season of *The Last of Us*, fully accepting Hobbes's picture of humanity might lead us to a dark place. It can be awfully depressing to think that we need a strong government to keep us from eating one another. However, there *are* reasons to question Hobbes's understanding of the state of nature—some purely logical and others experiential.

One way we can cast doubt on Hobbes is to ask if we can *really* know what the state of nature looked like. Whatever and whenever the state of nature was, humans would have been in it long before writing or any other form of historical record. Nobody who lived in that condition has left us a record of what it was like. All we can do is speculate. And though we can make the argument that the world we see in *The Last of Us* is a good indication of what the state of nature is like, we might wonder whether the people who wrote the game and the show can give us an accurate picture of something they've never seen.

Another reason for doubting Hobbes's view of human nature comes from our experiences. Consider Bill's story from episode 3, for example. When troops remove everyone from his town right after the outbreak and execute them, Bill sets up his own personal fortress because he knows what comes next. In addition to the occasional Infected that shows up on his property, he expects raiders to show up sooner or later—people who will have no qualms about attacking him and taking everything from him if they can. So, Bill sets up an array of traps and weapons to protect himself and fully expects to have to kill to ensure his own survival. But then something happens to challenge Bill's well-armed, solitary existence. His surveillance system alerts him that someone has fallen into one of the pitfalls that he's hidden around his property. When he goes to investigate, he finds Frank, who is making his way to Boston. At first, he's suspicious of the newcomer, treating him as a legitimate threat. He doesn't know Frank, after all, and Frank could be a danger to him. He could have a hidden weapon. He could be a scout for a larger group of marauders. He could be carrying a disease. But when Frank tells him that he hasn't eaten in two days, Bill shows compassion. He gives Frank food and lets him stay in his house.

We might say that Bill's aid to Frank has more to do with sexual attraction or the desire for companionship than with any compassion that might live in the deepest recesses of the human heart. After all, Bill and Frank soon become lovers and life partners. But this ignores the basic facts of their initial meeting and the power of the survival instinct (especially Bill's hyper-developed survival instinct!). It's clear that Bill enters into a romantic relationship with Frank reluctantly at first, and his behavior when they first meet suggests nothing like attraction. By all appearances, he allows Frank into his home against his better judgment, and purely out of a sense of compassion for another human being.

Let's consider another example that might call Hobbes into question. Soon after Joel, Tess, and Ellie leave Boston in search of Tommy, Tess gets bitten by an Infected. She reveals her secret to Joel and Ellie only once they're about to be overrun by a swarm of Infected. Instead of shooting herself or asking Joel to kill her before she loses her mind, she insists on staying behind to slow and maybe stop the swarm while Joel and Ellie run.

At first, it might not be obvious why Tess's final act poses a challenge to Hobbes's view of human nature, but what she does runs counter to the picture of humanity's most basic instincts as described by Hobbes. We are driven by appetites and aversions, he says. We desire the resources to survive, but are also averse to suffering. The easiest thing for Tess to do would be to have Joel kill her so that she wouldn't have to suffer the horror of becoming a mindless monster. Instead, she willingly embraces her horrific fate. The thing to notice is that she sacrifices herself out of love—not only for Joel, but also for humankind, since in saving Ellie's life, she knows that she might be saving the lives of countless others. Unless we want to say that Tess's actions are driven by a self-interested desire to give meaning to her death, Hobbes's philosophy might have a hard time accounting for this kind of sacrifice.

Are We More Than Animals?

Do these examples provide enough reason to doubt Hobbes's account of human nature? Are we as brutish without the Leviathan state as he says we are? Are we as reprehensible as David and the Silver Lake people? Or do the examples of people like Bill and Tess show that humans are more than simply fleshy machines driven by appetites and aversions? Or are their actions simply driven fundamentally by self-interest? Are we just machines (or animals, as David puts it)? Does all of our behavior in the state of nature finally come down to our appetites and aversions, our self-interest and need to survive?

The answers to these questions are unclear, so perhaps it's best to conclude with some advice from Hobbes. In *Leviathan*, he writes,

> He that is to govern a whole Nation, must read in himself, not this, or that particular man; but Mankind; which though it be hard to do, harder than to learn any Language, or Science; yet, when I shall have set down my own reading orderly, and perspicuously, the pains left another, will be only to consider, if he also find not the same in himself. For this kind of Doctrine, admitteth no other Demonstration.[4]

Hobbes advises princes that if they want to govern a nation of people, they should understand human nature. But, he says, the only way to understand human nature is to "read" ourselves. He admits that this is easier said than done—after all, people are often poor judges of their own motivations and very good at deceiving themselves—but the only way to know whether someone's account of human nature is true is to compare that account with what we find in ourselves. So, when David offers Ellie his philosophy of human nature, she rejects it as false. Is that because she doesn't *want* to believe it? Or is it because she looks honestly at herself and finds something more than the ugly brutality that David thinks is in human nature?

Notes

1. Thomas Hobbes, *Man and Citizen: De Homine and De Cive*, trans. Charles T. Wood and Thomas S.K. Scott-Craig (Indianapolis: Hackett Publishing, 1991), 101.
2. Thomas Hobbes, *Leviathan* (United Kingdom: Broadview Press, 2010), 128.
3. Hobbes, *Leviathan*, 125.
4. Hobbes, *Leviathan*, 39.

9

Decision Making and Exclusion in *The Last of Us*

Yassine Dguidegue

In 2018 none of us would have predicted that we would soon find ourselves living through a viral pandemic, but those of us who had played *The Last of Us* had already thought about some of the issues that would confront us during the COVID-19 era. Now that we have survived, we have the opportunity to reflect on both the video game and reality. Specifically, this chapter will consider the human causes of suffering that result from dealing with a fungal or viral pandemic.

Perspective Matters

JOEL: They got infected trying to sneak into the zone.
TESS: Tsh. As much as everyone complains about it. You got all
        these poor bastards wishing they were living on the inside.

Joel and Tess navigate the restrictions and deadly enforcement policies of the Boston Quarantine Zone (QZ) by resorting to smuggling activities. On their way to finalize a smuggling transaction with Robert, a black-market dealer, Joel finds a note from a dead, infected person named Mark, explaining the circumstances around his struggles to sneak into the QZ and how he became infected while trying to run away from the FEDRA soldiers. Mark concludes, "I should've listened to you and come to the zone with you when I had the chance. Now it's too late." This poignant note paints a picture of the brutal realities endured by people outside the QZ, highlighting their yearning to gain access to its perceived safety.

Tess's commentary subtly captures the conflicting perceptions of the QZs, seen as confining social prisons by some and protective sanctuaries by others. Her words also show that she is aware of the diverging views. Those inside the QZs have their grievances, but the "poor bastards" outside

The Last of Us and Philosophy: Look for the Light, First Edition.
Edited by Charles Joshua Horn.
© 2025 John Wiley & Sons, Inc. Published 2025 by John Wiley & Sons, Inc.

face far more difficult conditions. Tess's comment reveals a touch of bitterness, stemming from her frustration with the daily struggles she has lived and witnessed. In essence, Tess's words provide a glimpse into the intricate feelings and perspectives of characters navigating the unforgiving post-apocalyptic world.

In the first game, the Fireflies' willingness to sacrifice Ellie can seem cold, but an exchange between Abby and her father in the second game puts a more human face on the decision.

> ABBY: You're doing the right thing.
> DR. ANDERSON: Yeah.
> ABBY: If it was me ... I'd would want you to do the surgery.

The dialogue above highlights Abby's moral approval of her father's decision. Dr. Jerry Anderson chose to perform the surgery on Ellie, despite being aware that it would ultimately cost Ellie her life. The Fireflies' acceptance and justification of sacrificing Ellie's life highlights that institutions formulate distinct missions, moral beliefs, and codes of ethics and instill them in their members. In contrast to the oppressive military measures enforced by the Federal Response Disaster Agency (FEDRA), the Fireflies' core mission centers around scientific research aimed at finding a cure for the Cordyceps fungal infection.

In contrast to Dr. Anderson, Joel hasn't been connected to the institutional and scientific mission of the Fireflies. More importantly, Joel was scarred by the loss of his daughter, Sarah. Even though they weren't actually infected, both Joel and Sarah were shot on mere suspicion of infection by a military officer following orders. This traumatic event had a profound and enduring impact on Joel's worldview and mistrust of institutional decisions. Joel's inability to reach closure regarding the death of his daughter partly explains his judgments and actions, most notably his decision to kill Anderson and the Fireflies' personnel to rescue Ellie.

In contrast to Joel, Dr. Anderson, as the leading scientist for vaccine development at St. Mary's Hospital QZ, considered Ellie's life to be morally expendable for the sake of developing a vaccine that could save millions. When Marlene confronted Dr. Anderson with the question of whether he would accept the same fate for his daughter, Abby, he was hesitant to answer. The response to Marlene's question came from Abby herself who assured her father that he was making the right decision and that she would want him to take her life if doing so led to a vaccine.

The conflicting worldviews of Abby and Joel lead to the drama of the second video game. Abby is resolute in her belief that she would have willingly undergone the surgery, even at the risk of her own life, if she'd been in Ellie's shoes. In her mind, this makes Joel's life not just expendable but deserving of elimination, as she pursues vengeance for her father's murder.

As we know, Ellie survives, but all is not well. Consider the pursuit of closure that is evident in Ellie's actions, particularly when she returns to St. Mary's Hospital. Her return to this pivotal location is a powerful symbol of her determination to uncover the details of how Joel intervened to stop the surgery and effectively "kidnapped" or "rescued" her from the Fireflies. Ellie's journey back to the hospital is an emotional narrative point in the video game, as it reflects her desire to come to terms with the moral complexities of her own existence and Joel's actions. Her perception of her own life as one worth sacrificing highlights the complexity of the question—when, if ever, does one's life matter? It's worth emphasizing that Ellie's life mattered for all the central characters, including Marlene, Dr. Anderson, Abby, and Joel. However, her life mattered to each of the characters for conflicting and divergent reasons.

Ellie's life mattered to Marlene on both emotional and scientific grounds. The emotional connection stemmed from Ellie's mother, Anna, who entrusted Marlene with Ellie's care after her tragic passing on the day Ellie was born. Anna's note, found by the player in St. Mary's Hospital, highlighted Marlene's character as someone capable and trustworthy to look after Ellie. However, Marlene faced a profound moral dilemma due to her commitment to honor Anna's wishes and her institutional allegiance to the Fireflies' scientific mission to develop a vaccine against the Cordyceps infection.

When Dr. Anderson presented the plan for a potentially fatal surgery on Ellie, Marlene grappled with mixed emotions regarding Ellie's value. On the one hand, Marlene saw Ellie's life as intrinsically valuable, and on the other she saw Ellie's life as less valuable than the greater good of saving humanity. Marlene eventually, hesitantly, accepted that Ellie's life matters more for vaccine development than for its own intrinsic right to be lived.

The significant impact of institutional affiliation on shaping one's moral decisions becomes evident through Marlene's allegiance to the Fireflies, greatly influencing her moral choice to accept Dr. Anderson's decision. Her commitment to the organization and its goals played a significant role in her support of Dr. Anderson's decision to sacrifice Ellie for what she believed was the greater good, in line with the Fireflies' objectives.

Dr. Anderson was driven by a utilitarian perspective, where the potential benefit to the majority outweighs the welfare of the individual. This utilitarian perspective was reinforced by the institutional scientific commitment to fulfill the mission of vaccine development. He believed that the sacrifice of Ellie's life could save countless others from suffering and death. And yet, he couldn't respond to Marlene's repeated question of whether he would perform the surgery on his own daughter, Abby, without her consent. Abby greatly admired her father's noble mission to save the world, and she was very supportive of his decision to conduct the surgery on utilitarian grounds as well.

Marlene, Dr. Anderson, and Abby all agree about Ellie's surgery, given their shared institutional mission of the Fireflies. However, Joel was excluded from these crucial conversations, and his opinion on Ellie's fate wasn't fully appreciated. This exclusion lies at the heart of the profound sense of injustice that Joel experienced, reminiscent of the injustice he felt when the military agent received orders to shoot him and his daughter, Sarah.

The Fireflies' disregard for Joel's deep affection and concern for Ellie amplified his determination to save her. Ellie had become his surrogate daughter, and he was not going to lose another daughter to a callous institutional decision. Joel's experience of betrayal by the Fireflies' institutional decisions unfolds in two pivotal moments in the narrative. First, in the video game version of the events, upon his arrival at St. Mary's Hospital, he was physically hindered while desperately attempting to rescue Ellie from drowning, intensifying the emotional turmoil of the situation. Second, after completing his mission and being released by Marlene, he was confronted with the harsh reality of being denied the opportunity to check on Ellie. The Fireflies' institutional directives and their decision to exclude Joel from discussions about Ellie's fate left him feeling alienated.

Marlene, Dr. Anderson, and Abby all regarded Joel's opinion as irrelevant to the decision-making process regarding Ellie's surgery. Dr. Anderson, for example, clearly remarks that he wasn't in favor of letting Joel know about the surgery. Joel was probably excluded from the decision-making process because he isn't a member of the Fireflies, highlighting how institutional affiliation plays a pivotal role in determining one's inclusion or exclusion in decision-making discussions. Joel, therefore, experiences the politics of exclusion as dictated by the Fireflies' mission.

It's worth emphasizing that all the characters were sincerely adamant about serving their causes. In the context of Ellie's surgery, Dr. Anderson exhibited a determination akin to Joel's in fulfilling his mission, even when faced with resistance. Dr. Anderson, with nothing more than a medical knife, passionately defended the surgery, stating, "I won't let you take her. This is our future. Think of all the lives we will save." He demonstrated his institutional commitment to the scientific cause of saving humanity before he was killed by Joel. Similarly, Marlene opposed Joel's efforts to take Ellie away, persisting until her last breath, underscoring her unwavering dedication to the mission of supporting the Fireflies' vaccine development. And Abby's relentless pursuit of vengeance against Joel for her father's murder showed her resolute commitment to her personal cause (seeking revenge for her father's death).

Who Decides?

The preceding analysis doesn't seek to justify the actions of characters like Joel, Dr. Anderson, Marlene, or Abby regarding Ellie's surgery. Instead, it aims to provide a framework for evaluating the moral acceptability of decisions by considering the process through which those decisions are made, rather than by merely focusing on the intrinsic merits of the decisions made. In other words, a decision may yield moral outcomes yet remain morally unacceptable if it's arrived at through methods that are unethical, exclusionary, dictatorial, or if it devalues the contributions of those affected by the decision-making process. This perspective highlights the significance of both the ends and the means in ethical evaluation. Participatory means of evaluation and decision-making are generally absent within QZs, as experienced by Joel and Ellie. The absence of participatory decision making can be explained by the prioritization of safety at the expense of human rights, namely the right to participate in decision making.

The exclusion of Joel from the conversations around Ellie's surgery is representative of the paternalistic exclusionary rules in QZs, which are justified by the QZs' presumed mission to care for and protect their citizens. But when political leaders focus too much on paternalistic safety measures, they end up alienating people and pushing them away instead of protecting them.

Minor characters in *The Last of Us*, such as Riley, Henry, and Sam, also deal with paternalistic actions. For example, Riley's story highlights the struggles individuals face to be part of a meaningful cause as a member of a community, and yet maintain their individual freedom. Her decision to join the Fireflies reflects Riley's desire for purpose and her willingness to take a stand against the harsh world by joining a meaningful community. However, as the story unfolds, Riley's perspective on the Fireflies begins to change. She witnesses firsthand the consequences of their actions and becomes disillusioned with their methods. This leads her to make a daring decision to leave the Fireflies. The symbolic act of breaking and dropping the Firefly necklace, which serves as a powerful emblem of the group, represents Riley's rejection of their ideology and her embrace of individual freedom. Riley's decision to leave both the Boston QZ and the Fireflies reflects her rejection of collectivist paternalistic institutions.

Sam and Henry have a different experience, as their hardships result from being left out by the decision of the military to abandon the Hartford QZ. It's not surprising that they seek community and stability, "safety in numbers and all that" (as Ellie puts it). After a period of bonding and shared struggles to escape the hunters, Ellie has a profound conversation with Sam, revealing her fear of abandonment. As she tells him, "I'm scared of ending up alone." Ellie illustrates a strong desire for community protection, while also preserving individual freedom, a struggle shared by many other characters, including Riley.

One major source of tension between Joel and Ellie is her rejection of Joel's paternalistic behavior. In a bar scene, a man named Seth confronts Ellie about her romantic relationship with Dina, and Joel intervenes to protect Ellie. However, Ellie interprets Joel's intervention as paternalistic, and is clearly angered by it. Ellie strives for independence and autonomy. In rejecting Joel's paternalistic tendencies, Ellie implicitly criticizes the pervasive authoritarianism that permeates the QZs.

Unite and Empathize

The Last of Us and the real-world COVID-19 pandemic point beyond the dangers of fungal or viral infections. To solve such medical problems, we need to overcome our tribalistic tendencies, prejudices, proclivity toward paternalistic authoritarianism, and exploitative behaviors. Sadly, in both the video game world and the real world, we see the dehumanization of, and discrimination against, certain groups of people who are deemed disposable or less worthy of protection. In the context of COVID-19 pandemic, the elderly, the poor, minorities, and frontline workers didn't receive adequate protection and care. Despite being called "essential workers," frontline workers were paid poorly and put at risk. Meanwhile people of Chinese or Asian background were stigmatized and physically attacked because the virus originated from Wuhan, China.

In both *The Last of Us* and the COVID-19 pandemic, we witnessed and experienced a profound search for personal and social freedom and acceptance within a world marked by division, fear, hatred, prejudice, and violence. The characters in *The Last of Us* navigated a post-apocalyptic landscape where fear and hostility were ever-present, forcing them to seek safety and acceptance amidst the chaos. Similarly, in the real-world COVID-19 pandemic, individuals grappled with the divisive impacts of the virus, encountering fear, discrimination, and prejudice. They sought to maintain personal freedom while adapting to new norms like mask-wearing and social distancing, and yet they also yearned for a sense of social solidarity and unity.

Individuals who contracted COVID-19 encountered stigma stemming from at least two distinct sources of bias: one related to misconceptions about their perceived carelessness and another linked to judgments regarding their health conditions, such as obesity and compromised immune systems. Stigmas also affected those who refused to get the vaccine or the subsequent boosters.

The Last of Us offers a profound lesson by emphasizing that our deeply rooted cultural divisions often constitute the true source of our suffering, rather than the pandemic itself. Throughout the video game series, the central focus remains on the conflicts between human factions, highlighting how people are pitted against each other in a world ravaged by infection. Even in the face of a deadly fungus, humanity's struggles with tribalism, prejudice, and power dynamics are the primary drivers of unethical decisions, chaos, and devastation. In the video games, the battles are not primarily against the Cordyceps, but instead against humans, serving as a reminder that our ability to unite and empathize can be just as crucial to survival as our resistance and resilience against external threats.

PART III
THE INDIVIDUAL
AND SOCIETY

10

Trust, Trustworthiness, and Betrayal in a Post-Apocalyptic World

Mackenzie Graham

At its core, *The Last of Us* is about trust and betrayal. While the Infected are the most physically grotesque enemies, and often the toughest, the greatest threat to Joel and Ellie is their fellow humans. They have no one they can really trust but each other. The relationship between Joel and Ellie, which grows and changes over the course of the video games and show, is palpable to the player and is a big part of what made *The Last of Us* critically acclaimed. It's also what makes Joel's decision at the conclusion of the first video game so complicated. How should we think about Joel's decision? Did Joel betray Ellie's trust?

To answer this question, we need to think carefully about what the concept of trust really means. Though we use the concept of trust all the time in our ordinary talk, and clearly have some sense of what trust is, philosophers continue to debate its nature. What does it mean to trust, and when is our trust well placed? Exploring these questions will help us to better understand and appreciate the complexity of the relationships within *The Last of Us*, and answer whether Joel betrayed Ellie's trust.

Trust in the World of *The Last of Us*

The events of the first video game, *The Last of Us Part I*, take place in 2033, twenty years after civilization has been devastated by the outbreak of the mutant Cordyceps fungus. Society, as we know it, has ceased to exist. Those who have avoided infection live either in authoritarian Quarantine Zones (QZs), in small, isolated settlements, or in itinerant groups of scavengers roaming the country. Government in the QZs is scant and its control tenuous. Where is there room for trust in a place like this?

Fundamentally, trust is a way of responding to a situation of uncertainty. Trust gives us a reason to depend on others, especially when we know there

The Last of Us and Philosophy: Look for the Light, First Edition.
Edited by Charles Joshua Horn.

isn't an outside force compelling them to act as we hope they will (otherwise, there wouldn't be a need to trust them). In large, complex societies, where many of our interactions are with strangers, it can be difficult to determine who can be trusted. Fortunately, laws and institutions can remove some of this uncertainty by providing assurances that people will behave as they should. The protections of laws and institutions can remove the need for trust in others and replace it with trust in institutions. For example, when I order my copy of *The Last of Us* online, I expect that it will be delivered to my house in working order, rather than in pieces (or that the box will be empty). This isn't a matter of trust in the video game seller. The background conditions (such as consumer protections and a well-established market-place for buying video games online) mean that trust doesn't even enter the picture. In a post-apocalyptic society like *The Last of Us*, however, where there are no (or few) laws or institutions to regulate behavior, trust in others may be the only reason we have to depend on them. Accordingly, trust within *The Last of Us* is primarily interpersonal trust.

Trust and Reliance

Most philosophical accounts of trust involve two assumptions. First, trust is fundamentally a three-place relation involving two agents and a task: for example, Ellie trusts Joel to take her to the Fireflies.[1] Second, trust involves expectations about competence and willingness. When I trust someone to do something, I take them to be both competent to do it, and willing to exercise this capacity as required.

Following Annette Baier (1929–2012), philosophers often distinguish genuine trust from mere reliance.[2] Reliance is a kind of prediction and roughly involves acting as though something will happen. For example, I rely on my video game controller to transmit the appropriate signal when I press the relevant button. We might rely on objects or people to behave in certain kinds of ways, and insofar as they behave predictably, they're reliable.

When we rely on other people, our reasons tend to involve things like the person's track record of reliability, or external guarantees of performance. Often, it's simply because we have no evidence that they're not reliable. For example, the reason Marlene relies on Joel and Tess to deliver Ellie to the Fireflies is because they have been effective smugglers before, and so likely will be again. And the reason Joel and Tess rely on Marlene is because she provides them assurances that they will receive the weapons they want in exchange for delivering Ellie (she shows them that she has them already, and so is at least *able* to give them those resources).

In contrast to reliance, trust is more than simply a prediction of behavior. When we trust someone, we take ourselves to have a special kind of reason for depending on them, one that goes beyond the evidence of their mere reliability. We might then understand trust as reliance plus some other factor, where it's this extra factor that explains why we're willing to depend on the would-be trusted person. Figuring out what this other factor is will explain why the relationship between Joel and Ellie is one of trust, and not mere reliance.

Distinguishing trust from reliance seems to clash with our ordinary usage. We often talk of trusting inanimate objects (such as trusting a rope to support our weight). Why do philosophers insist on the distinction between reliance and trust, given that we often talk about them in interchangeable ways? Most importantly, trust, but not reliance, is usually taken to matter morally. Trustworthiness is admirable, something to be aspired to; for some (but not all) philosophers, it's a virtue, something that's morally good without qualification. Reliability, on the other hand, doesn't carry the same moral weight. Because a reliable person or thing is simply predictable, one could be reliable in various unwelcome ways. After all, an Infected will reliably attack if it spots a person.

We can see the difference between reliance and trust by considering our reactions to when our trust, rather than our reliance, fails. For example, I might feel irritated, frustrated, or disappointed if my video game controller stops working (especially if an Infected is bearing down on me), but feelings of betrayal wouldn't be appropriate. Conversely, if I discover a trusted friend has been lying to me, I would rightly feel let down or betrayed. Philosophers refer to these kinds of responses to others' moral behavior as reactive attitudes. One explanation for why failures of trust and trustworthiness seem to merit reactive attitudes is because trust and trustworthiness, but not reliance or reliability, are moral.

What Is Trust?

What is the extra factor that distinguishes reliance from trust (and reliability from trustworthiness)? Several philosophical accounts of trust argue that a trustworthy person must have the right kinds of motives for acting as trusted, but disagree about what kinds of motives are the right kinds. One view, the "encapsulated-interest" account of trust, states that a trustworthy person is motivated by self-interest.[3] I take you to be trustworthy (and so, I trust you) because I believe you are motivated by self-interest to fulfil my trust. You have an interest in attending to my interests because you want our relationship to continue.

On the encapsulated-interest account of trust, the relationship between Henry and Joel seems to be one of trust. They can depend on the other's self-interest because both see that their best chance of survival in the short term is to depend on the other. In other words, Henry's survival depends on Joel trusting him, so he has a self-interested reason to do what is required for Joel to trust him. But do we really want to say that Henry and

Joel trust each other when they first meet, despite having a common goal? Probably not.

When the groups initially get separated, Henry and Sam don't show loyalty to Joel and Ellie. Instead, they abandon them to make their own escape. Once their interests diverge, and it's no longer advantageous to maintain the relationship, Henry isn't trustworthy anymore. Intuitively, trustworthiness is more robust than depending on someone out of self-interest; if someone is really trustworthy, they can be trusted even when it isn't to their advantage.

The weakness of the encapsulated-interest account is that it allows for the wrong kinds of motives (such as entirely selfish ones). Intuitively, trust requires that the trustee not be motivated entirely by self-interest. This intuition is behind the so-called "goodwill accounts" of trust.[4] On these accounts, I trust you to do something because I have an optimistic attitude about your goodwill toward me.

The presence of goodwill characterizes most of the core relationships in *The Last of Us* (Joel and Ellie, Joel and Tommy, Joel and Tess), and makes it easy to recognize these relationships as involving trust. Unsurprisingly, the people we tend to trust most strongly are those we care about, and that we believe care about us.

Yet, while trust is often motivated by belief in another's goodwill, goodwill seems neither necessary nor sufficient for trustworthiness. It's not necessary because we can trust people (and they can be trustworthy) without having goodwill toward us. For example, early in the video game when Joel is in need of a car, he seeks out the reclusive survivalist, Bill. Joel trusts Bill, though not because he thinks Bill has any sort of goodwill toward him. In fact, Bill makes it clear that since the outbreak he has only ever cared about one person (besides himself)—his erstwhile partner, Frank. However, Bill takes himself to have an obligation to Joel to repay a debt, and it's this obligation that grounds Joel's trust in him, rather than belief in Bill's goodwill. As Bill tells Joel in the video game, "But after this, I owe you nothin'."

Reliance on another's goodwill is not sufficient for trust either. First, someone trying to manipulate us can rely on our goodwill without trusting us. For example, when Ellie encounters David in the wilderness, he relies on Ellie's goodwill toward Joel to manipulate her and capture her. But we wouldn't want to say that he trusts Ellie (or that when attempting to escape, Ellie betrays his trust). Second, someone might have goodwill toward us, but be a poor judge of their own abilities to act as trusted, in which case we might not trust them, despite their goodwill. Third, we don't always want to be trusted by others (because trust can sometimes be burdensome, for example), even though we still have goodwill toward them.

Having the right motives seems important for trust, but doesn't tell the whole story. Non-motives-based views hold that trustworthiness is based on our normative expectations of the trusted person rather than their motives. The most prominent view of this sort comes from the contemporary philosopher Karen Jones, who argues that someone is trustworthy insofar as they are appropriately responsive to others' dependence on them, and are willing to signal to others that they are trustworthy. Jones calls this willingness to signal being "richly trustworthy."[5]

By the end of the first video game, both Joel and Ellie are responsive to the other's dependence, and are clearly trustworthy with respect to each other. For example, after Joel is wounded in the firefight in the Science Building at the University of Eastern Colorado, he and Ellie hide in a lakeside resort where Ellie manages to keep him alive. Joel is completely dependent on Ellie for his life, and Ellie is appropriately responsive to this dependence. She knows that Joel needs medicine, and is willing to trade with David. She also knows that Joel is vulnerable, and places herself at risk by remaining with David, so as to not lead David and James back to her camp. Ellie knows that Joel is counting on her for his life and acts accordingly—this is what makes her trustworthy.

Similarly, when Joel attempts to rescue Ellie from David's group, we can assume that Joel was responding to the fact that Ellie was counting on him. The fact that we don't *know* if Ellie was counting on Joel (perhaps she thought he didn't know where she was) highlights an important condition of responsiveness accounts of trustworthiness. Trustworthiness requires that the trustworthy person (in this case, Joel) be capable of recognizing that the other person is counting on them, and not merely *think* that this is so. A person's disposition to act in a trustworthy way needs to be properly mapped to others counting on them. For some philosophers, this is a limitation of the theory since it implies that we can't trust someone unless they know that we're trusting them.

An alternative to trust-responsiveness theories comes from Katherine Hawley (1971–2021), who argues that trust is about relying on others to keep their commitments, and that a person is trustworthy if they reliably fulfill the commitments they make.[6] For Hawley, motives don't matter for trustworthiness. A trustworthy person might be motivated by goodwill, selfishness, duty, or otherwise. Thus, Joel is trustworthy with respect to Ellie because he reliably fulfills his commitment to keep her safe. He isn't trustworthy with respect to Marlene because he doesn't keep his commitment to deliver Ellie to the Fireflies.

Trustworthiness seems to involve more than keeping one's commitments though. We often trust people to do things that they haven't committed to. For example, we might think that when Ellie and Sam get separated from Joel and Henry, Ellie shows her trustworthiness to Henry by protecting Sam, even though she has no commitment to do so. Moreover, we might reasonably think that trustworthiness requires knowing when to keep a commitment and knowing when to break it. For example, the close relationship hinted at between Joel and Tess suggests that they have various commitments to each other (including to protect each other), and explains why Joel is reluctant to leave her behind after she becomes infected. Joel might have kept his commitments to Tess, despite the futility of doing so, but this would seem to defeat the underlying purpose of the commitments. Trustworthiness seems to involve faithfulness to the values underlying the commitment, rather than rigidly keeping the commitment itself.

Did Joel Betray Ellie?

Having examined the foundational theories of trust and trustworthiness, and the relationship between trust and betrayal, we have all the tools we need to answer whether Joel betrayed Ellie at the conclusion of *The Last of* Us. The answer is simple: sort of.

It seems clear that by lying to Ellie about what happened with the Fireflies (that there were other people immune to the Cordyceps infection, and she wasn't needed for a cure), Joel has disappointed Ellie's trust. She trusted him to tell her the truth, and he failed to act as trusted.

Truth-telling isn't the only aspect of Joel and Ellie's relationship in which trust is at stake. Ellie also trusted Joel to safely deliver her to the Fireflies. On the face of it, it also looks like disappointed trust when Joel rescues/kidnaps her from the research facility.

But to say that Joel has betrayed Ellie is too simplistic. I suggested earlier that trust (and trustworthiness) are based on a shared understanding of the values and needs that underpin the task to be carried out. This conception of trust as shared understanding allows us to distinguish between trust that is disappointed and trust that is betrayed. Disappointed trust is when we fail to do the specific action or task trusted of us, whereas betrayal is when we fail to be faithful to this mutual understanding. This means we can betray someone's trust without disappointing it, but also disappoint someone's trust without betraying it.

For example, when Ellie and Joel reach Wyoming, and Joel reunites with Tommy, Joel attempts to persuade Tommy to take Ellie the rest of the way to the Fireflies. Joel has been trusted to get Ellie to the Fireflies, so as long as she reaches them, this trust hasn't been disappointed. Yet we can clearly see that leaving Ellie would be a betrayal of her trust, even though Joel thinks he's doing this out of good will. It's a betrayal because Joel fails to show proper concern for the values and needs underpinning Ellie's trust. Simply put, he is bringing about the result he has been trusted to bring about, but not in the right way.

Conversely, Joel's actions at the end of the story exemplify disappointed trust, but it's much less clear that they are a betrayal. At the beginning of the video game, the relationship between Joel and Ellie is purely instrumental. Joel and Ellie have experienced significant loss, and accomplishing the task of reaching the Fireflies provides each of them with a purpose—a reason to struggle on—at least temporarily. As the story develops, however, their relationship deepens, and they become each other's reason to struggle on. Being responsive to the shared understanding at the core of their trust relationship means that allowing Ellie to be sacrificed to the Fireflies is not what trust requires. In other words, for Joel, doing *what* was trusted is no longer consistent with acting *as trusted*.

Of course, the key to this conception of trust is that it's based on a *shared* understanding. It's possible that Joel's judgment of what he's been trusted to do in the situation is different than Ellie's judgment of what she's trusted Joel to do, and so even though Joel thinks he's acting as trustworthiness requires, he's mistaken. In this case, Joel's actions would be a betrayal. Whether Joel is blameworthy for this betrayal depends on whether we think Joel should be blamed for this mistaken judgment.

It seems much clearer that Joel betrayed Marlene, and so is perhaps *un*trustworthy with respect to her (unless we think that trust was never at stake between them). This potential for conflict in the requirements of trustworthiness (insofar as being trustworthy toward Ellie requires betraying Marlene's trust) points to a related question about whether trustworthiness is a virtue, that is, a morally excellent trait of character that leads its possessor to right action. If trustworthiness is a virtue, and untrustworthiness a vice, it shouldn't be the case that we're required to act in a way that is untrustworthy, since this would mean that we are morally required to act wrongly. The possibility of conflicting demands on our trustworthiness has led some philosophers to argue for a "non-moral" account of trustworthiness. Sometimes we morally ought to be trustworthy, but sometimes not.[7]

Epilogue

Trust is complicated. Paradigm cases of trust, like that between Ellie and Joel, can help us think more clearly about the concept, but there's still disagreement amongst philosophers about what exactly trust is and why it's important. Even when trusting doesn't require putting our lives at stake—as it often does in *The Last of Us*—warranted trust and distrust are an important part of the foundation of a good society. Of course, it can also come in handy on a cross-country journey through a post-apocalyptic wilderness.

Notes

1. Some philosophers also talk about "two-place trust" (for example "Ellie trusts Joel"), although there is debate about whether two-place trust is equivalent to three-place trust with the third element left unspecified.
2. Annette Baier, "Trust and Antitrust," *Ethics* 96 (1986), 231–260.
3. Russell Hardin, *Trust and Trustworthiness* (New York: Russell Sage Foundation, 2002).

4. Hardin, *Trust and Trustworthiness*.

5. Karen Jones, "Trustworthiness," *Ethics* 123 (2012), 61–85.

6. Katherine Hawley, "Trust, Distrust, and Commitment," *Nous* 48 (2012), 1–20.

7. Jones, "Trustworthiness." For an argument that trustworthiness is a virtue, see Alison Hills, "Trustworthiness, Responsibility, and Virtue," *The Philosophical Quarterly* 73 (2023), 743–761.

11

Caring for Ellie
From Cadet, to Cargo, to (Almost) Cure

Traci Phillipson

Even in a world as extreme as the one experienced by the characters in *The Last of Us,* people can't escape the need to give and receive care. Babies are born, orphaned children need taking care of, and adults need love and support. In episode 7 of the series Ellie has a discussion with Captain Kwong in which he seems to take a real interest in her future. He tells her that she can be something if she applies herself. He seems to care for her and to want the best for her future. But does he? Is his concern born out of genuine and ethical care, or out of a desire to serve FEDRA? What does it mean to genuinely and ethically care *for* or take care *of* (and not just care about) another person in a reality as harsh as that of *The Last of Us?*

The Ethics of Care is an ethical framework which can help us to examine the ethics underlying Ellie's relationships. Rising out of feminist philosophy and largely influenced by the seminal work of contemporary psychologist Carol Gilligan, care ethics holds that we can—indeed we must—place at the center of our ethical system our natures as relational, emotional, interdependent beings. It insists that we must understand ethics as related to particular situations, rather than absolute rules.[1]

One proponent of Care Ethics is the contemporary philosopher, Joan Tronto, who explains that "the ethic of care is a practice, rather than a set of rules or principles"[2] and that "care as a [moral] practice involves more than simply good intentions. It requires a deep and thoughtful knowledge of the situation, and of all of the actors' situations, needs, and competencies."[3] Tronto frames Care Ethics as a continual interaction between the four ethical elements of care: attentiveness, responsibility, competence, and responsiveness. These elements of care allow us to evaluate ethics situationally, rather than having to rely on blanket statements of right and wrong. As we'll see, Tronto's Ethics of Care framework sheds light on Ellie's relationships with Captain Kwong and Joel and can help us determine whether they care for Ellie in ethically relevant ways.

Captain Kwong: "I See a Leader in You"

Society in the United States after the outbreak is highly regimented, controlled by the Federal Disaster Response Agency (FEDRA), a military government that controls virtually all aspects of life. FEDRA maintains Quarantine Zones (QZs), kills anyone found to be infected, requires everyone else to work in exchange for ration cards, and institutes harsh penalties, including public hangings, for rule breakers. FEDRA claims these measures are necessary to slow the spread of the Cordyceps, maintain order, and ensure that everyone's basic needs are met. Everyone in this society must pull their weight, even children. Those children who don't have family to take up their share of the social burden are placed in FEDRA's military academy to be raised as future FEDRA soldiers.

The military academy is where Ellie, orphaned as an infant, grows up. Despite being raised within the strict FEDRA system and steeped in its propaganda, she's rebellious and strong willed. It's Ellie's spirit of rebellion that brings us to see her encounter with Captain Kwong, a FEDRA soldier responsible for the cadets, in episode 7. Does Kwong really care for Ellie though?

First, we can see that Kwong is, to some degree, attentive to Ellie's needs. Tronto defines attentiveness as "simply recognizing the needs of those around us."[4] Tronto notes that we can't begin to take care of someone if we don't know they need care. It's our responsibility as relational beings, beings who do or will have needs of our own, to recognize the needs of others; inattentiveness, even when it's the result of ignorance, can be a moral evil.[5] Kwong not only notices Ellie's basic needs—for food, shelter, and the like—but, more importantly, he also recognizes her rebelliousness as indicative of her psychological needs and/or need for a mentor or role model.

Second, Kwong takes responsibility for meeting Ellie's needs, at least insofar as he's part of the military structure which has taken on the practical aspects of raising orphans and ensuring their basic physical needs are met. More interestingly, he takes a personal interest in Ellie, meeting with her about her latest misbehavior, rather than simply sending her to the hole again. Kwong indicates that he has decided to take responsibility for her in a more direct way, beyond what is required in his job description.

Kwong's personal interest in Ellie is particularly important given Tronto's claim that responsibilities are different from obligations. Obligations generally have their basis in formalized laws, promises, or agreements, while responsibility rests on more informal social and anthropological expectations. We might take responsibility for some need because we are part of a social system which caused it, even if we didn't contribute directly to the creation of the need; or, "we might assume responsibility because we recognize a need for caring, and there is no other way that the need will be met except by our meeting it."[6] In other words, we may have no formal obligation to take care of an individual person or their needs, while still being ethically called to take responsibility for them.

As an orphan, Ellie doesn't have a parent who is obligated to take care of her, but she has people in her life who take responsibility for that task. Kwong is part of the system which has taken responsibility for meeting Ellie's basic physical needs. But, he seems to take responsibility for her mental and emotional care, too. We know he doesn't do this for all his cadets; he seems fairly dismissive of the girl who Ellie fought with, and Riley mentions that Kwong gave her sewage detail, not seeing her as capable of anything more. He tells Ellie that he sees a leader in her and encourages her to think about her future. This indicates that Kwong is doing more than fulfilling an obligation.

However, when Ellie asks him why he cares, Kwong's response isn't centered on Ellie's well-being or needs. He says, "I care because no matter what anyone out there says or thinks, we're the only thing holding this all together." Kwong reveals that he isn't really motivated by Ellie's expressed or actual needs, which are clearly needs for relationship and emotional connection. Indeed, he doesn't seem to care for Ellie as a person, but rather as a means to advancing FEDRA's ends. Thus, he fails to meet the ethical elements of competence and responsiveness.

Tronto argues that we shouldn't take responsibility for a need we can't effectively meet, even if it's the case that we don't see a way for those needs to be met some other way. She says, "Intending to provide care, even accepting responsibility for it, but then failing to provide good care, means that in the end the need for care is not met. Sometimes care will be inadequate because the resources available to provide for care are inadequate. But short of such resource problems, how could it not be necessary that the caring work be competently performed in order to demonstrate that one cares?"[7]

It's not enough to intend to do good or to try to take care of someone. For the caring to count as ethically performed it must be successful, at least within the bounds of the available resources. If this wasn't the case, Tronto notes, it would be easy for us to handle many issues by simply assigning someone—anyone—to "take care of it" regardless of their skills or ability.

Responsiveness, the final ethical element of care, involves the ability of the care giver and care receiver to enter earnest dialogue so that proper care can be assured, and burnout can be avoided. Because care relationships always involve inequality and vulnerability, with the care giver having a certain amount of power over the care receiver, it's essential that the care giver and the care receiver maintain a relationship built on dialogue and genuine responsiveness.

The Ethics of Care highlights the fact that human beings are not fully autonomous; we all rely on others for some things at some times. Often this reliance is hidden under political, economic, and social structures. However, when those structures collapse, we see the ways in which care occurs in our lives. In order to ensure that caring relationships don't fall into a pernicious sort of inequality—where the cared-for person's desires, wishes, or expressed needs are subsumed under what the care giver *thinks* the person's needs are—proper caring must be characterized by honest dialogue in which the care giver and care receiver "consider the other's position *as that other expresses it*,"[8] not as they assume it to be.

We can see clearly the failure of care in Ellie and Kwong's relationship. He has been attentive to the extent that he knows Ellie *has* emotional needs that are not being met, but his inability to enter earnest dialogue with her and discover *what* those needs are leads him to impose his own ideas and values onto their relationship. He clearly values FEDRA's mission and so his attempts to care for Ellie are centered on bringing her in line with his values, rather than allowing her to express her values and working to help her achieve them. Since he hasn't fully understood her care needs, he isn't able to competently meet them. Even if he were to correctly identify and understand what Ellie's needs are, we see no indications that he would be competent to meet them. Given his position in FEDRA and the fact that he clearly has many obligations already, Kwong may simply be emotionally ill-equipped, or lack the time needed, to take on a teenager's mental health struggles.

We may feel compelled to give Kwong a pass here. After all, he seems to genuinely try to connect with Ellie, doing the best he can under difficult circumstances. However, his incompetence may be blameworthy. Tronto argues that we must measure the adequacy of care on its success, not on the intent of the care giver.[9] Her example is that of teacher in a poorly funded school district who is ordered to teach a subject he knows nothing about. If we accept that the teacher means well, we end up in a position where competent care becomes impossible—everyone assumes that the issue is "taken care of" because there is a teacher in the classroom "teaching" the subject, even though the students are not actually learning it. Tronto would say the teacher is morally obligated to refuse to take responsibility for a need that he isn't competent to meet. Similarly, Kwong should advocate for additional mental and emotional health services for his cadets, rather than inadequately "taking care of" the issue himself.

Joel: From Cargo to Caring?

The relationship we see develop most deeply and over the longest period is between Ellie and Joel. In episode 1, we see Joel lose his teenage daughter on the first day of the Cordyceps outbreak. The loss of Sarah causes Joel to become cold and detached from most people. We know that he is trying to find his brother, Tommy, although their relationship seems to have become strained. He has a partner, Tess, with whom he works and lives, but there is clearly some distance. His initial meeting with Ellie occurs when he and

Tess are tasked by Marlene with smuggling her to a group of Fireflies outside the Boston QZ. Joel views Ellie as cargo and as valuable only because he will exchange her for the supplies he needs to find Tommy. He tells Marlene that he won't hesitate to kill her if he doesn't get what he wants. Once he finds out that she has been infected, Joel's even more distant, telling Tess that she must stop thinking about Ellie as if "she's got some kinda life in front of her."

Clearly Joel and Ellie's relationship doesn't have any of the ethical elements of care at this stage. While he protects her, he doesn't care about her in any meaningful way. He's willfully ignorant of her needs and refuses to engage when Ellie tries to connect with him on a human level; such willful ignorance is a moral evil within the framework of Care Ethics.[10] He refuses to take responsibility for her as a human being, let alone as a particular individual, seeing her as cargo—an object with no future, fit to be used for his own personal gain. Given the strong emphasis that Care Ethics places on the personal, relational, and contextual nature of ethics, the failure of personal connection between Joel and Ellie leaves no room for moral engagement or moral action.

Throughout the next several episodes, Joel begins to care *about* Ellie, although he keeps emotional distance and can't be said to care *for* her in an ethically relevant way. He has become attentive to her needs, but still refuses to take responsibility for them. It isn't until episode 6 that we see major ethical development in their relationship. In this episode, Joel is reunited with his brother Tommy, who has been living in a commune and has been able to emotionally heal from some of the trauma he and Joel suffered during their quest for survival in the early years of the outbreak. Tommy has become integrated into his new society and has even married; he's been able to accept the loss of his niece, Joel's daughter, without being consumed by it; his wife has done the same with the loss of her young son. Seeing Tommy in this environment allows Joel to work through some of his own feelings.

Significantly, Joel talks to Tommy about his fear that he's going to fail Ellie. He asks Tommy to take Ellie the rest of the way to the Firefly research facility. Although Joel's request may seem like he is abdicating responsibility and passing off care work to someone else, this isn't the case. Joel has listened to Ellie during their travels and understands at least some of her needs. He is responsive enough to understand her desire to accomplish the goal of reaching the Firefly facility and to help find a cure. However, he recognizes that he may not be competent to meet Ellie's needs. Although he isn't right about what her needs are—focusing on her physical survival over her need for relationship—he's still modeling the ethical element of competence; it is better to refuse to take responsibility than it is to simply do one's best, as Kwong was doing.

When Joel tells Ellie that Tommy will take her the rest of the way, and that he made the decision for her own good, they get into an argument.

Ellie feels that Joel is abandoning her. She indirectly expresses to him that he hasn't been properly attentive to her and misunderstands her needs. She asks him, "Do you give a shit about me or not?" and then goes on to clearly express her needs: "Everybody I have cared for has either died or left me. Everybody, fucking except for you! So don't tell me that I'd be safer with someone else because the truth is I would just be more scared." Joel responds by telling Ellie, "You're not my daughter and I sure as hell ain't your dad." He's afraid to allow himself to be truly attentive to her expressed needs and to take responsibility for them. And yet, he can't abandon her. He wakes up the next morning intending to steal a horse and leave without seeing her, but he can't bring himself to do it. He tells Ellie that she deserves a choice, and he accepts it when she quickly chooses Joel. He's deeply responsive to Ellie at that moment, allowing her to dictate the care she needs, rather than imposing his own view of what is best. Even though he doesn't fully understand what she needs, he's able to accept what she tells him. It's this responsiveness that leads to Joel's ability to be attentive to, and then take responsibility for, caring for Ellie.

As they leave the commune, Joel begins to open up to Ellie. He talks to her about life before the outbreak and about *his* life before the outbreak, even joking around a bit, telling her that everyone loved contractors. He may not understand what she needs or why, but he's responsive enough to take her lead in their relationship. He's attentive enough to notice her particular personality and fun-loving nature, and competent enough to meet her need for relationship through earnest and jovial conversation. However, their relationship development is quickly halted when Joel is injured, and Ellie is captured.

Eventually, they are reunited after Ellie has been deeply traumatized by her encounter with David's cannibalistic group in Silver Lake. Once they are reunited, Joel tries to connect with Ellie in the ways she needed before her capture. He tries to joke around with her, suggests he teach her guitar, and even opens up about his own grief and the trauma of losing his daughter. He addresses the fact that they don't have to continue; they can have the life that Ellie has been wanting. But her outlook and priorities have changed. She responds by saying, "After all we've been through. Everything I've done. It can't be for nothing. I know you mean well. I know you want to protect me. You have. And when we're done, we'll go wherever you want ... I'll follow you anywhere you go. But there's no halfway with this. We finish what we started." Clearly her needs have changed, and Joel isn't quite able to be attentive or responsive to them—it took him so long to be attentive to her need for relationship that we shouldn't be surprised that he isn't able to quickly be attentive or responsive to the type of care she now requires.

Soon after Ellie's traumatic experience in Silver Lake, they are ambushed and separated outside the Firefly hospital. When Joel wakes up, he's told by Marlene that the research needed to find the cure will result in Ellie's death. Despite Ellie's clear conviction and desire to complete their mission, Joel prioritizes his own feelings. He goes on a rampage, killing numerous Fireflies and rescuing Ellie. Marlene tries to stop him by asking him to think about what Ellie would want. In that moment, you can see it on Joel's face: he knows she would want to stay, but he shoots Marlene and leaves with Ellie. When Ellie asks what happened, he lies to her, telling her that the Fireflies found many immune people and discovered a cure was impossible. She doesn't quite believe him and reminds him of all the people she's lost and her desire to stop the outbreak. In the end, he swears it's true, she accepts it, and they make their way back to Tommy.

Joel's deception represents a setback in his ability to ethically care for Ellie. He has become less responsive to Ellie as he has become more attached to her. He has recognized the needs she had for family, but fails to recognize her newly developed need for a meaning to her suffering. He finally loves and cares *about* Ellie, but he can't care *for* her in the ethically right way.

Does Anyone Care for Ellie?

It seems that neither Kwong nor Joel fully or properly cares for Ellie. The four ethical elements aren't simply steps to be checked off in order— attentiveness, responsibility, competence, and finally responsiveness—they are a constantly shifting and integrating system of ethical factors to be used when making moral decisions in the context of relationships. Care is a practice, not a rule-based system. It involves conflict as the care giver and care receiver work together to integrate the four ethical elements, revisit and reevaluate their needs and expectations, and make judgments about what it means to care and be cared for.[11] While Kwong seems to take an interest in Ellie, he displays little effort when it comes to being attentive or responsive to Ellie's actual needs, let alone taking responsibility to meet them competently.

On the other hand, Joel comes very close to ethically caring for Ellie. We see moments of genuine attentiveness and responsiveness, he comes to genuinely want to take responsibility for Ellie, and we may even think he is competent to take care of some of her needs. Yet, he isn't able to make the necessary adjustments and reevaluations that arise from the fact that human needs differ and change as their context and experiences change. Once Joel thinks he's figured out what Ellie needs, he isn't able to maintain the level of responsiveness and attentiveness necessary to accept that her priorities and care needs have changed after her experiences with David.

Still, we might want to give Joel the benefit of the doubt. We might claim, for example, that Joel's own experiences of trauma and healing allow him to know that Ellie's depression—a potential cause of her willingness to sacrifice herself for a cure—isn't permanent. Or, we might say that Ellie is still a child and can't really know what she needs; she will thank him for saving her in the end. Yet, she's been treated like an adult up until this point and is able to clearly express her needs and desires. We know from the video game series that she doesn't come to thank him, but rather feels disrespected and betrayed by his inability to be a responsive partner in the care dialogue. Thus, in the end, Joel loves her, but he doesn't listen to her.

We might be tempted to claim that Kwong and Joel are doing the best they can in a difficult world. Perhaps it's simply impossible to achieve the level of relationship, dialogue, and deeply integrated ethical discourse necessary to Care Ethics in a world like the one presented in *The Last of Us*. It's impossible to be as attentive, responsive, and competent as Care Ethics requires when the world is falling apart. But we know this isn't the case. Frank and Bill's relationship provides an example of robust, genuine, and ethical caring, which demonstrates that it's possible to be truly ethical in this world. They are deeply attentive and responsive to one another, constantly reevaluating and discussing their needs. They take responsibility for meeting the needs they are competent to meet, even if they don't fully agree with what is being asked, trusting the other person to know what their own needs are. Thus, it's not the case that ethical care is impossible. Ellie has simply not found a person who can care for her in the way she needs, even if she has found, in Joel, a person who cares about her.

Notes

1. Carol Gilligan, *In a Different Voice: Psychological Theory and Women's Development* (Cambridge, MA: Harvard University Press, 1982).
2. Joan Tronto, "An Ethic of Care," in Ann E. Cudd and Robin O. Andreasen eds., *Feminist Theory: A Philosophical Anthology* (Oxford: Blackwell, 2005), 252.
3. Tronto, "An Ethic of Care," 255.
4. Tronto, "An Ethic of Care," 252.
5. Tronto, "An Ethic of Care," 252–253.
6. Tronto, "An Ethic of Care," 254.
7. Tronto, "An Ethic of Care," 254.
8. Tronto, "An Ethic of Care," 255, emphasis added.
9. Tronto, "An Ethic of Care," 254.
10. Tronto, "An Ethic of Care," 252.
11. Tronto, "An Ethic of Care," 255.

12

The Last of Love

Eudaimonia, Friendship, and Love in *The Last of Us*

Darci Doll

Unlike typical zombie stories, *The Last of Us* makes people the biggest threat. In episode 1, "When You're Lost in the Darkness," Joel, Tommy, and Sarah have several opportunities to help others trying to escape, but they don't. It could be that they're not sure of the scope of what they're dealing with, or that they don't know who's infected. It could also be the survivalist instinct that helping others would take away needed resources. However, it's most likely that they're right: people really *are* the danger.

This distrust of people evolves into trepidation as the series progresses. In "Long, Long Time" (episode 3), Ellie asks Joel what he's looking for, expecting it to be the Infected. But he simply replies, "People," telling her that people have a lot more in mind than robbery. Again in "Please Hold to My Hand" (episode 4), Joel and Ellie are attacked in Kansas City, and Ellie asks, "If they're not FEDRA, who are they?" Again, Joel simply replies, "People." The real threat in this episode isn't the Infected, but Kathleen's vengeance-fueled organization, which has overthrown FEDRA. As they're being hunted by Kathleen's resistance group, Joel makes an uncharacteristic move and joins forces with Henry and Sam. At first, their union is a cautiously pragmatic arrangement. Though Joel doesn't trust them, he sees them as a lesser threat than Kathleen, and knows they share the goal of needing to escape Kansas City. In "Kin" (episode 6) and "Left Behind" (episode 7), Joel and Ellie (having tragically lost Henry and Sam) are again hunted by *people*, and the Infected are merely a backdrop. The Infected are a catalyst for bringing out the worst in human nature, and we see what happens to humans when they can't depend on each other.

In the *Nicomachean Ethics*, Aristotle (384–322 BCE) wrote that good social systems and good relationships aid in the development of moral and

The Last of Us and Philosophy: Look for the Light, First Edition.
Edited by Charles Joshua Horn.
© 2025 John Wiley & Sons, Inc. Published 2025 by John Wiley & Sons, Inc.

intellectual virtues.[1] These virtues are fundamental for attaining *eudaimonia*, or flourishing.[2] According to Aristotle, a person can't flourish without external goods like wealth, power, family, education, and friendship.[3] These structures and relationships guide and mold a person toward goodness; without these external goods, a person can't become intellectually or morally good.

The Last of Us confirms that in the absence of reliable social infrastructure, the external goods that are needed for people to flourish are missing. FEDRA and the QZs try to provide some structure, but the overly militaristic, spartan approach falls short. The societies organized by Kathleen and David are survivalist and violent and don't contribute to people becoming good. The Jackson commune in Wyoming, however, seems to focus on providing the external goods that people need to become intellectually and morally good. In Jackson, people seem to be thriving, at least in comparison to other societies.

Seeing the quality of life in the different societies confirms Aristotle's assertion that we need external goods like morally good friends and romantic relationships to enable us to flourish and be the best versions of ourselves. Except for the community in Wyoming, the systems in place don't provide the conditions under which good relationships can be made. Without these relationships, we lose our humanity and become merely "people."

When We Are in Need

One challenge to a flourishing life for those in *The Last of Us* is that their existence is guided by pure survival and not intellectual pursuits, and there is a lack of good social systems. There is still education in the QZs, for example, but it doesn't aspire to provide for intellectual contemplation. The education provided in the QZs is mainly history and survival tactics. It's unclear what the educational system is like in the Jackson community, but with the other social structures in place, it's likely to produce better educational outcomes than FEDRA.

For Aristotle, a virtuous life is also dependent on external factors. A person can't expect to become virtuous unless they have opportunities to exercise and cultivate virtues into character traits.[4] For example, for a person to become courageous, they need opportunities to confront fears in a way that allows them to exhibit courage.

For Aristotle, the most important social structures and external goods that are needed for the development of moral virtues are friendships and romantic relationships. Since the ideal versions of both kinds of relationships are in short supply in *The Last of Us*, many people lack the conditions necessary to develop ethical virtues and therefore can't flourish.

Friendship and Flourishing

Aristotle says that we need strong social relationships to help us flourish, and he argues that *philia,* or friendship, is among the most important external goods that contribute to the development of both moral and intellectual virtues. Just as person's environment can shape a person's virtues, friendships influence a person's character and the degree to which they can attain virtues.[5] We develop our character partially in response to the character of our friends. Surrounding ourselves with good people will increase the likelihood that we can become virtuous; bad people increase the likelihood that we will become vicious.

In *The Last of Us*, moral development is stunted, in part, because the problematic social structures make it difficult to form good or true friendships. In "Long, Long Time," Frank says, "We're gonna make friends and we will invite them to visit." But Bill replies "We don't have friends, Frank. We will never have friends, because there are no friends to be had." Frank retorts, "Well, I've actually been talking to a very nice woman on the radio." Bill has given up on the idea of friendship, but Frank is still optimistic that such relationships are possible. Even after an apocalypse, Frank, like Aristotle, sees the value of friendship.

Aristotle distinguishes between three types of friendships, all of which involve a feeling of goodwill.[6] Friends want something good for each other. The first type of friendship is based on usefulness or utility. In this type of relationship, friends form relationships because they recognize they are mutually beneficial in some way. These relationships end once the relationship is no longer beneficial. We see this in *The Last of Us* when Joel agrees to work with Henry. Joel doesn't trust Henry, and vice versa. They're not concerned about each other's needs; however, they both see mutual benefit in working together. They join forces out of a sense of utility and of having a common enemy. Similarly, in "Long, Long Time," Joel becomes friends with Bill because there is a utility to their relationship. Joel and Bill don't trust each other, but there's still a recognition of mutual benefit and some semblance of respect.

The second type of friendship provides pleasure rather than utility. As with friendships of utility, friendships based on pleasure end when the pleasure ends. Ellie's relationship with Riley is a friendship based on pleasure. They enjoy each other's company and find pleasure together in their otherwise spartan lives. Ellie also has a friendship of pleasure with Sam, as they bond over comic books. There's also friendship of pleasure between Frank and Tess. While Joel and Bill are sizing each other up, Frank and Tess are enjoying wine, talking, and sharing in each other's lives. Tess says that even if they don't end up working together, it's nice to have a civilized meal and she "needed this." Because friendships of utility and pleasure are inherently subjective and vary based on the perceived benefit, they are limited. They can't really contribute to ethical character because they're purely transactional.

The third, and ideal, type of friendship for Aristotle is complete friendship. Complete friendships happen when two people of virtuous character have a reciprocal feeling of goodwill for the other's sake. Unlike with utility and pleasure, complete friendship is concerned with benefiting each other *because of the good character*, not external benefits.[7] These friendships are based on the recognition of virtuous traits and are most likely to influence the development and maintenance of virtues. Because complete friendships have the best chance to cultivate virtue, they're ideal and most likely to contribute to flourishing.

The lack of complete friendships in *The Last of Us* is part of the reason why the characters struggle with flourishing. After losing Sarah, Joel is, for lack of a better word, feral. Joel's relationship with Tess is stronger than all his other relationships, except Tommy. The trauma Joel suffered after losing Sarah indicates it was no small feat for Tess to earn Joel's trust and goodwill. They share intimacies, work together, and have common goals. Joel and Tess's relationship contains elements of all three kinds of friendships. They work together for common goals; they enjoy some pleasures together; and they seem to want what's best for each other. It's unlikely that Aristotle would call this a true, complete friendship, though, because, as Tess tells Ellie in "Infected" (episode 2), "Joel and I aren't good people. We're doin' this for us because, apparently, you're worth something. But we don't know what you're worth if we don't know what we have." Tess and Joel don't try to be good people and they don't pretend they are. They're bonded together and care about each other, but they're living in a way that isn't virtuous.

Despite having a strong relationship, Joel and Tess aren't morally virtuous people. When they first meet Ellie, they treat her merely as cargo. Joel tells Ellie this in "Please Hold to My Hand."

ELLIE: If you don't think there's hope for the world, why bother going on. I mean, you gotta try, right?
JOEL: You haven't seen the world, so you don't know. You keep going for family. That's about it.
ELLIE: I'm not family.
JOEL: No. You're cargo. And I made a promise to Tess. And she was like family.

However, by the time of episode 5, "Endure and Survive," Joel softens his attitude toward Ellie and even Henry and Sam. More importantly, though, Joel and Ellie seem to be enjoying each other's company. They're laughing and bonding.[8] When they get away from Kathleen and into safety, Joel invites Henry and Sam to continue the journey with them to Wyoming. Henry agrees and says, "Yeah, I think it'd be nice for Sam to have a friend." In the course of transporting Ellie to Wyoming, being with her through the loss of Tess, Joel has begun to remember the importance of friendship.

Three months later in "Kin," Joel has his first panic attack after learning that Tommy is likely dead. Ellie expresses worry and then reminds him, "If you're dead, then I'm fucked." One of the ways that we see the growth of the relationship between Joel and Ellie is later in the episode when they approach a dam and Ellie says, "Dam!" and looks for Joel's reaction. He replies, "You're no Will Livingston." And Ellie retorts, "Yeah, yeah, but who is?" They've developed a humorous interplay that shows growth since the early days of Ellie just being cargo.[9] Yet, Joel still won't talk to Ellie about Sarah. When they get to the Jackson commune, Joel asks Tommy to take Ellie to Colorado because he's afraid he'll get her killed. Tommy agrees, but Ellie hears about it and confronts Joel.

JOEL: I made this decision for your own good. You'll be way better off with Tommy. He knows the area better than I do—

ELLIE: Do you give a shit about me or not?

JOEL: Of course, I do.

ELLIE: Then what are you so afraid of? I'm not her, you know? Maria told me about Sarah and—

JOEL: Don't. Don't say another word.

ELLIE: I—I'm sorry about your daughter, Joel, but I've lost people, too.

JOEL: You have no idea what loss is.

ELLIE: Everybody I have cared for has either died, or left me. Everybody fucking except for you! So don't tell me I'll be safer with someone else, because the truth is, I would just be more scared.

JOEL: You're right, you're not my daughter. And I'm sure as hell not your dad. Now, come dawn, we're goin' our separate ways.

Part of Joel's concern is that he's starting to see Ellie as more than cargo, and feels guilty about not saving Sarah or Tess. If he starts to care for Ellie, he can lose her, and he likely can't handle another loss. The closer he feels toward her, the more he feels he must push her away. Joel decides to give Ellie the option to go with him or Tommy, and she chooses Joel. On the ride to Colorado, they begin to talk even more, and Joel opens up to her about his life before the infection, what he'd do once there was a cure. He's found a sense of ease with Ellie that wasn't there before.

Their friendship started as purely utilitarian but has developed into one of caring for each other, for each other's sake. Granted, Joel probably isn't virtuous, and maybe Ellie isn't either, but they're getting closer to Aristotle's ideal friendship. They are getting closer to the paradigmatic relationship because they're bringing out the best in each other and reinforcing more virtuous character traits.

In "Look for the Light" (episode 9), Joel begins to talk about having a future with Ellie. He talks about playing Boggle and teaching her to play guitar. He's beginning to see a hope for the future, and that future is with Ellie. Ellie provides something to Joel that Tess couldn't—there's an emotional side of Joel that has been blocked since the loss of Sarah that is beginning to manifest again.

Despite previously insisting that Ellie is just cargo, Joel tells Ellie that she doesn't have to go forward with finding the Fireflies to help develop a cure. She replies, "After all we've been through, everything I've done ... it can't be for nothing. I know you mean well. I know you wanna protect me. You have. And when we're done, we'll go wherever you want. Tommy's. Sheep ranch. The moon. I'll follow you anywhere you go. But there's no halfway with this. We finish what we started."

Joel agrees to continue with her and tells her about how hard things were when Sarah was gone. He confesses that the man who shot him in the head and missed was himself. He starts to tell her why he's telling her this. She says he doesn't have to; she already knows. Joel reckons she does. Ellie says, "so time heals all wounds, I guess." Joel replies, "It wasn't time that did it." After they exchange a look, Ellie responds, "Well, I'm glad that ... that didn't work out." And Joel simply responds, "Me too."

Joel acknowledges that his friendship with Ellie has enabled him to over- come trauma and become a better person. After Joel finds out what the Fireflies intend to do with Ellie, he slaughters them and rescues her, despite it being his "job" to deliver her. He's decided to build a future for the two of them instead of delivering Ellie. In the final scenes of "Look for the Light," Joel tells Ellie about Sarah, how he thought Sarah would like her because she's funny. Ellie tells him about having to kill Riley, and Joel says, "Look, sometimes things don't work out the way we hope. You can feel like ... like you've come to an end, and you don't know what to do next. But if you just keep goin', you find something new to fight for. And maybe that's not what—." Ellie interrupts, "Swear to me. Swear to me that everything you said about the Fireflies is true." But Joel lies and says, "I swear." Joel has moved on from seeing Ellie as cargo and has grown into a (somewhat) complete friendship where he wants good things for her because he sees the good in her.

Long, Long Time

Aristotle emphasizes non-romantic friendships as aiding in the development and maintenance of virtuous character. But romantic relationships are also important for the development of virtue.[10] Just as there are three forms of friendship (utility, pleasure, complete), there are three correlating types of romantic relationships. Just as in the complete or ideal form of friendship, in the ideal romantic relationship we recognize the good in each other and contribute to each other's flourishing and well-being.

The earliest romantic relationship we see in *The Last of Us* is between Ellie and her best friend, Riley. Early in "Left Behind," it seems that they're just best friends, friends of pleasure; after all, Riley says Ellie was the one thing she missed "from that fucking place, if it makes a difference." When Ellie confronts her after finding out she's working for the Fireflies, Riley breaks down and says Ellie doesn't know what it's like to have a family, to belong. Riley wants that sense of belonging again, and even if the Fireflies aren't what she thinks they are, they chose her, and she belongs.

Riley demonstrates that the society they're living in doesn't have the external goods needed to flourish. Both are looking for a place to belong, not just live. Riley matters to the Fireflies in a way that she didn't matter to FEDRA. Ellie replies, "You mattered to me first." Ellie later says, "You're my best friend. And I'll miss you." Then she tells Riley, "Don't go." Riley replies, "Okay." And they kiss. Their relationship has moved beyond just a friendship to a romantic, loving relationship. The two may not yet have the moral or intellectual virtues that Aristotle describes, but their desire to do what's best for each other for each other's sake puts them close to complete romantic relationship.

In "Infected," Tess asks Joel to take Ellie to Bill and Frank's. As a "survivalist" Bill has prepared for the apocalypse and set up his perimeter efficiently and as soon as possible. Even early after the outbreak and the collapse of society, Bill maintains an ordered life with a taste for the finer things—yet, it still lacks something. A stray human, Frank, falls into one of his traps and Bill decides to take a chance on him and give him food and a shower. Frank makes a move for the piano and plays some Linda Ronstadt. Bill takes over playing, wistfully. Frank asks, "So who's the girl? The girl you're singing about?" Bill looks even more wistful, "There's no girl." Frank replies, "I know," and then leans in for a kiss, with a tear running down his cheek while Bill quivers. When they move to the bedroom, Frank tells him, "I want you to know I'm not a whore. I don't have sex for lunches. Not even great ones. So, if I do this, I am gonna stay for a few more days. Is that ok?" Bill says "Yeah. Yes." We then see them three years later as a full-fledged romantic couple, bickering about Frank's desire to clean up the area and how he wants to have friends over.

Bill and Frank's relationship is the most important in the series in showing that love can help us develop a virtuous character and flourish. Bill was self-sufficient and was more or less content with the life he had built. Yet, through Frank, he found a side of himself that he hadn't experienced before. He learned to care for someone, to protect someone, and even opened up his home to strangers because having friends would make Frank happy. They both loved the good they saw in each other, and that love enabled them both to flourish even with the world falling apart around them. Bill expresses true joy when Frank surprises him with strawberries. He tells Frank, "I was never afraid before you showed up." The life he had built for himself paled in comparison to the life he built with Frank. It was riskier and less secure, but it allowed him to finally flourish. Their relationship may have started out as one of pleasure, but it evolved into a true love that brought out the best in both. In the end, Bill decided to give up the world he built because they weren't both going to be in it.

When You're Lost in the Darkness

The Last of Us shows us an example of what life could be like with a massive fungal infection causing the end of civilization. Social structures have fallen, trust is thin, and most relationships, whether friendly or romantic, are utilitarian or for pleasure, at best. In this environment, it's nearly impossible for people to form the relationships necessary for flourishing. But as Bill grew from loving Frank, and as Joel gave Ellie the family and sense of belonging she never had, we realize that friendship and love are still possible even if the world has fallen apart.

Notes

1. Aristotle, *Nicomachean Ethics*, trans. Sarah Broadie and Christopher Rowe (New York: Oxford University Press, 2002). It is worth noting that there is a competing interpretation that external goods aren't *required* but they contribute to the ability to cultivate the proper virtues. On this interpretation it's quite difficult to act virtuously if you are friendless, poor, etc. These external goods give the opportunities to act virtuously and without those opportunities it's nearly impossible to develop virtues.
2. Aristotle, *Nicomachean Ethics*, Book I.2.
3. Aristotle, *Nicomachean Ethics*, Book I.8., 1099b.
4. Note that the moral virtues are a key to attaining the more solitary-suited intellectual virtues. Additionally, as Aristotle notes, humans (unlike the gods) are not wholly self-sufficient and depend upon one another, which is why this is my main area of focus for this chapter.
5. Aristotle, *Nicomachean Ethics*, Book VIII.1, 1–13. See also I.7 in contrast with X.6–8 and VI.12, 1143b.
6. Aristotle, *Nicomachean Ethics*, Book VIII.2, 1155b.
7. While Aristotle doesn't really discuss it, a person of virtue could start a version of this type of friendship when they see the virtuous potential in another person. It's not what would be a complete friendship, but it is the potential for a complete friendship.
8. For more on the role of laughter in Joel and Ellie's relationship, see Chapter 22 in this volume by Michael K. Cundall Jr.
9. It should be noted that Aristotle also thought a good sense of humor is a component of a virtuous disposition. See *Nicomachean Ethics*, Book II.7, 1109a, IV.9, 1128a, and 1128b.
10. See Darci Lynn Doll, "A *Eudaimonistic* Critique of Heteronormativity" (Michigan State ProQuest Dissertations Publishing, 2020).

13

Ellie and Abby Are the Queer Feminist Icons We've Been Waiting For

Susan Peppers-Bates and Mary Bernard

The Last of Us depicts a protagonist who rejects the norms of pre- and post-apocalyptic society to strive toward a world built on feminist, queer, "otherwise" thinking. In actively fighting for her own self-determination, while pressured by forces on all sides that disregard her consent and autonomy, Ellie subverts the systemic hierarchies rarely questioned by those around her. By fighting for her autonomy, with force when necessary, but rejecting the violent use of power wielded by the leadership figures throughout the world of *The Last of Us,* Ellie imagines an "elsewhere," a future based in deconstructing and discarding the limits of power hierarchies previously seen as natural or inevitable. When Ellie comes close to losing herself in a haze of vengeance in *The Last of Us Part II,* her enemy, Abby, helps her transcend the path of destruction. Through their similar journeys of discovery, both women model a distinctively queer feminist ethics for the audience.

Ellie and Feminism

Ellie grows into the autonomy, self-respect, and insistence on equality that mark her as a feminist. But to understand Ellie's new brand of humanity and heroism, we need to unpack the philosophical terms "feminist" and "queer" in relation to *The Last of Us.* The feminist theorist bell hooks (1952–2021) argued that "feminism is a movement to end sexism, sexist exploitation, and oppression."[1] Sexism views men as superior to women and as the ones who should control women, children, and the world. Sexist exploitation and oppression speak to facts such as women making less money than men, the free labor women provide in child and elder care, and the high rates of rape and violence that women suffer at the hands of men.

The Last of Us and Philosophy: Look for the Light, First Edition.
Edited by Charles Joshua Horn.
© 2025 John Wiley & Sons, Inc. Published 2025 by John Wiley & Sons, Inc.

The pattern is always the same; when privileged group members dominate the positions of power within societies, that power is presented as natural and normal.

Before the fungal apocalypse, formal structures within society were dominated by men; and as society collapsed, a male-gendered ethos of power and control continued to dominate within the dystopian pseudo-government, the Federal Disaster Response Agency (FEDRA). The fight for survival appears to have pushed remnants of the US military and the rebels into fully including women. Even so, the women in power deploy that power in a way that mirrors the pre-fungal society's patriarchal norms of violence and domination. Ellie, who was left in a FEDRA orphanage and training center, has been brainwashed to a certain extent by their propaganda. However, from our first meeting with her, we see Ellie rebel against injustice, rules, and abusive power. She fights off Bethany, a bully who is much larger and stronger, and she is willing to listen to Riley despite her joining the traitorous Fireflies. Indeed, Ellie sneaks out with Riley on a regular basis—including when Riley returns to say goodbye. Yes, Ellie spouts a few pro-FEDRA platitudes, but her heart clearly isn't in it. She trusts her relationship with Riley above generalized rules and stereotypes. When we see Ellie yelling at Marlene that Fireflies are terrorists, she quiets immediately when asked "Was Riley a terrorist?"

Feminists reject the idea that one's sex (loosely one's biology or secondary sexual characteristics, genes, and hormones) determines one's gender role (the social expectations heaped upon one depending on one's assigned birth sex). Even in the post-fungal world, patriarchal cults like David's, and even the goddess-worshipping Seraphite cult, still embrace traditional gender roles. The few decades of time after the fungal apocalypse haven't been enough to wipe out millennia of traditional patriarchal gender norms. Ellie, however, defies conventional gender expectations. She's self-reliant and resourceful, rejecting all the trappings of stereotypical feminine wiles or emotionality. She's a young woman comfortable in her own skin, without—as Joel notes—being "girly." She forged a loving bond with Riley outside of gendered heterosexual norms, and she formed a family bond with Joel, flipping gendered expectations on their head by saving his life and her own. Eventually she will reject the benign paternalism of Joel and his violent protective style, especially his lying to her and taking away her choice of whether to sacrifice herself for the possible salvation of humanity. When she finally confronts Joel in the second video game about the truth of his "rescue" and his subsequent lies, she heatedly spits out, "My life would've fucking mattered. But you took that from me."

Ellie more dramatically rejects the malign paternalism of David, who physically abuses the teenage Hannah for challenging his authority as "father" of his "flock," and makes a pedophilic offer for Ellie to join him by his side (as his helpmeet, not as co-ruler). When he tries to punish her refusal with dismemberment and then attempted rape—telling her "I thought you already knew, the fighting's the part I like the most"—Ellie chops him to death with a machete. Violence for the sake of power and control isn't a feminist value, but the right to self-defense and to resist rape and dominance surely are. Ellie's trauma from David's violence, and her own violence in response, haunt her and temporarily silence her formerly incessant chatter and humor; her quiet and inward turn in the final episode of season 1 portends a shift in her character and values in the second season.

Ellie and Queer Theory

It's important to distinguish between two uses of the term "queer" within a philosophical context. We commonly use "queer" as an umbrella term for members of the LGBTQI community, whose gender or sexuality differ from the norms of our society. In contrast, contemporary philosopher Kim Q. Hall defines "queer" as an orientation within philosophy, a rejection of the "traditions, modes of being and knowing, that one is expected to reproduce."[2] In this context, Ellie's character doesn't simply offer us an example of queer representation due to her sexuality; she also embodies a queer approach to her world in a philosophical sense. Ellie rejects not only the traditions of patriarchal and individualistic pre-apocalypse society; she also defies the violently hierarchical, at times overtly fascist, rules of post-apocalyptic FEDRA, Kathleen's resistance organization, and David's cannibalistic religious cult.

In a telling moment for Ellie's values, Joel is nearly killed and falls ill from an infected stab wound. Despite his urging her to abandon him, and in defiance of egoistic expectations to care primarily for herself, Ellie takes over hunting and foraging, nurturing Joel, and even making a deal with David for antibiotics to save Joel's life. Along these lines, Kim Q. Hall defines a queer ethics as "the practice of radical care."[3] Care in this context means a conscious choice to connect with, support, and accept support from others; this conception of care lies in direct opposition to the individualistic, patriarchal norms of Western culture which value independence and dominance of others over mutual care or interdependence. Ellie demonstrates the queer conception of care pointedly in the television series when Sam, in a departure from the video game, confesses to her that he was infected. Rather than abandon or kill him, Ellie cuts herself and desperately presses her wound to his, insisting "my blood is medicine." She soothes this terrified, deaf child and promises to stay awake with him until morning despite the likelihood that he will become the very monster he fears. To care in this way is emblematic of Ellie's disruption of the individualistic, survivalist norms of the world in which she grew up. In caring for a disabled, infected child, Ellie models a queer ethic that pushes beyond an emphasis on merely caring, to "learning how to care about and for that which is deemed worthless" to those in power.[4]

Ellie and the Power of Imagination

Importantly, Ellie's queer orientation and subversion of social norms don't entail rejecting society altogether. Rather, they re-envision a transformed society. Ellie carries herself through the world in a way that gives us insight into her "otherwise" thinking: her reconception of a social order that privileges care and connection over individual dominance and violence. In *The Last of Us Part I,* when Ellie and Riley defeat the Infected in the mall, but realize they are both bitten, Ellie dismisses the idea of suicide and instead insists on the value of their remaining moments of life, accepting Riley's urging that "we can be all poetic and lose our minds together."

Violence and domination inevitably form part of Ellie's post-apocalyptic world, and we see her struggle with post-traumatic symptoms. After killing David in self-defense, Ellie is clearly traumatized. We see this when Joel tries to joke with her the following day, and she gives little facial expression and seems shut down and far away.[5] In the video game, *The Last of Us Part II,* we see Ellie struggle further with post-traumatic symptoms in the wake of killing members of the group who killed Joel. Ellie displays a multitude of symptoms of "moral injury," characteristic of traumatized people who have been exposed to, or committed, acts that violate their moral values.[6] In the first video game, Ellie draws on her comic book motto to "Endure and survive." But what is left of us after we endure so much? As Ellie progresses through her journey of vengeance following Joel's murder, she consistently responds to killing with worsening post-traumatic symptoms like flashbacks and nightmares that manifest after her killing of Nora and immediately after she realizes she has killed the pregnant Mel. The fact that Ellie experiences post-traumatic symptoms of moral injury after each instance of vengefully torturing or murdering another person points to a clash between those actions and her moral values.

Contemporary philosopher Alison Kafer expands our understanding of Ellie with her imagined "elsewhere," as a "political framework for a more just world that does not rely on a normalizing impulse."[7] Ellie's "elsewhere" would wait to see if people had immunity like her before preemptively killing them. She is drawn to Tommy and Maria's democratic and egalitarian community of Jackson as intensely as she is repelled by David's twisted, patriarchal cannibalistic survival cult. Ellie continues to forge her own path regardless of, or even despite, expectations.

Ellie's life is in danger both from those who scan her as infected and to be immediately killed, and those who see she's immune to the infection and to be immediately sacrificed to find a cure for the rest of society (or the elite and powerful within what remains of society). She also could face rejection or attack for her sexuality. In sum, Ellie must fear for her life because her physiology and desires fall outside the norm.

Survivors in the post-fungal world feel fear and pity for the disabled, and they are willing to sacrifice the life of a disabled person to save those whose "normal" lives matter. The utopian future they imagine is one without disabled or non-normative bodies and minds.[8] By making Sam deaf, the television show strengthens its critique of the injustice of the hierarchical norms that ruled society pre and post apocalypse. As contemporary philosopher Melinda Hall explains, the same stigmas against the disabled that block their access to social and political goods "implicates and flows into the medical realm, where persons with disabilities are especially vulnerable and regularly experience the barriers of marginalization and prejudice."[9] In situations of rationing, people seen as disabled go to the end of the line, in the regular, utopian, or dystopian worlds.

And the world of *The Last of Us* is clearly a dystopia, not only because of the Cordyceps pandemic, but also because of the monstrous response of human leaders to their situation. As Henry describes twenty years of FEDRA rule: "They raped and tortured and murdered people." In the same episode we see Kathleen, the resistance leader, casually order her second-in-command to skip a trial and just kill all the collaborators. "When you're done, burn the bodies. It's faster." In a world where the lives of those not in power matter little, disabled lives matter less than nothing. To access cancer treatment for his young disabled brother, Henry had to give something "big" to FEDRA—Michael, the leader of the resistance movement.

In a different society, where most individuals had symbiotic relations with the Cordyceps, perhaps individuals without the relation would be pitied and viewed as defective. In a future imagined differently, the lives of those labeled disabled (the Infected) would still be seen as worth living or at least worth preserving. Consider Riley's words to Ellie after they have both been bitten: "It ends this way eventually, right? Some of us just get there faster than others. But we don't quit, whether it's two minutes, or two days, we don't give that up." As Melinda Hall argues, only those with a perceived disability can decide their quality of life; discussions of who lives and dies based on society's view of the "norm" or ideal standard are notoriously biased and discriminatory.[10] Because Ellie takes Riley's words to heart, she gets more time with her beloved and survives to discover her own immunity. Ellie's willingness to embrace others in multidimensional radical care offers a new feminist "queer" model for living.

Integration of Queer Ethics with Ellie and Abby's Quests

In *The Last of Us Part II*, Ellie races to the sounds of Joel's tortured screams, only to be held down and forced to watch Abby viciously murder him with a golf club. After completing her mission, Abby leaves with her team. Ellie's life becomes consumed with hatred of Abby, and she promises Tommy that she will make Abby pay for what she's done. Her ability to think otherwise begins to wither away. When Ellie finally confronts Abby, she is left bloodied and sputtering, as an enraged Abby screams, "We let you both live and you wasted it!" By hunting down and murdering Abby's comrades, rather than accepting the mercy offered in being spared, Ellie forces Abby back onto the path of vengeance.

Halfway through the second video game, we switch perspectives from Ellie to Abby. We see Abby driven ruthlessly by her own quest to avenge her father, the surgeon Joel shot to free Ellie. When the Fireflies fold in the wake of the murders of Marlene and their leadership, Abby joins the WLF (Washington Liberation Front or "wolves"), a paramilitary group. She evolves from a slim young teenager to an adult with a hardened body-builder physique. Training relentlessly, she always keeps her desire to kill Joel in the forefront of her plans. In fact, she gives up her relationship with Owen rather than miss even one training session to spend time with him. Making herself into a weapon of war, Abby viciously tortures and murders Joel to avenge her father.

Yet when her teammates want her to kill the tied-up Ellie and Tommy, Abby limits her carnage to those she deems guilty. In sparing the innocent, she already distinguishes herself from Joel, who murders Marlene, lest she come after Ellie. And when two ex-Seraphites save her life, Abby begins saving them out of a sense of debt or obligation and ends up abandoning the wolves because, as she tells Lev, "*You're* my people!" Abby also ignores orders and rescues Owen, choosing relationships over hierarchy. After finding Owen and enlisting his aid in saving the life of Lev's sister, Yara, on the grounds that "they're just kids," Abby asks him "What happened to us?" Owen replies, "maybe we stopped looking for the light." Owen's fatigue with killing over territory, and his refusal to participate any longer, help Abby further shift toward privileging the feminine-coded values of relationship and connection, and rejecting patriarchal, masculine-coded violence and domination. In making this shift, Abby embodies the queer orientation described by Kim Hall.[11]

Having rejected the female sex assigned to him at birth, Lev values relationship over social convention. He returns to the mother who rejected him on religious grounds and gives her one more chance to accept him and escape the Seraphite community. Instead, she tries to kill him. Players might view Lev as following the path of many in the LGBTQI community, who make chosen families when their biological ones cast them out as deviant and sick (much like the treatment of the disabled) because of their sexuality or gender identity. And it's Lev who calls Abby out of a revenge-fueled assault on Ellie and Dina. As Abby prepares to slit the pregnant woman's throat, Lev calls her name and reconnects her to relationship rather than hierarchy and violence.

Ellie returns from her vengeance quest and chooses a different path in her ultimate fight with Abby, pointing to her gift for imagining "elsewhere." In a flashback in *The Last of Us Part II*, we see Joel take her to a museum for her birthday. Joel climbs with her into a space shuttle's cockpit and plays an audio tape of a launch, as Ellie's imagination takes over and we see her rocking side to side in a space suit amidst shifting light, as though she were herself launching into space. Ellie's penchant for imagination lends itself to her ability to conceive of a world with different norms than the world she grew up in. We can see both the queer, "otherwise" thinking of Hall and the imagined "elsewhere" of Kafer in Ellie's gift for imagining beyond the limits of her present reality. After the repeated disregard of her consent and autonomy, Ellie dares to take the reins of her own life and allows herself to let go of the patriarchal model of violence and vengeance in favor of forging new norms of relationship and connection.

Abby's refusal to fight Ellie until she threatens Lev's life, moves Abby into the role of protective parent (as Joel had been for Ellie). This parallel triggers the flashback to Joel that moves Ellie to also choose mercy over vengeance. The Fireflies themselves lost the light when they used FEDRA's brutal methods to allegedly work toward re-establishing democracy. To succeed this time, the Fireflies will have to draw on new ways to live and be human, building a society whose "aim is solidarity across difference in the creation of otherwise ways of living."[12] Consider Abby's words to Lev as they work to join the re-grouped Fireflies: "The goal was always to restore society. I mean there's all sorts of ways to go about it." Abby's love and acceptance of Lev's trans identity fits with a queer ethics that "makes room for other things to be thought, other ways of living that can be sources of new value."[13] Abby, like Ellie, has expanded the limits of her imagination to encompass new values and new ways of living. *The Last of Us Part II* closes with Ellie leaving her guitar from Joel behind in the mostly empty house she had shared with Dina and their son, JJ. The ambiguity and sadness of this scene lightens with the splash screen that appears of Abby and Lev's empty boat on Catalina Island. They've made it, and we can imagine an "elsewhere" where a former Wolf, former Seraphite, and a former vengeance-obsessed Ellie work in coalition to build a new world that embraces difference of all kinds, interdependence, and mercy.[14]

Notes

1. bell hooks, *Feminism Is for Everybody* (Cambridge, MA: South End Press, 2000), 1.
2. Kim Q. Hall, *Queering Philosophy* (Lanham: Rowman & Littlefield, 2022), 9.
3. Hall, *Queering Philosophy*, 115.
4. Hall, *Queering Philosophy*, 120.
5. For more on the importance of humor in the relationship between Joel and Ellie, check out Chapter 22 in this volume by Michael J. Cundall Jr.
6. Brandon J. Griffin, Natalie Purcell, Kristine Burkman, Brett T. Litz, Craig J. Bryan, Martha Schmitz, Claudia Villierme, Jessica Walsh, and Shira Maguen. "Moral Injury: An Integrative Review," *Journal of Traumatic Stress* 32 (2019), 350–362.

7. Alison Kafer, *Feminist, Queer, Crip* (Bloomington: Indiana University Press, 2013), 23.
8. See Kafer's insightful discussion of scholars' implicit acceptance of utopia as expunging disability in their celebration of Marge Peircy's novel *Woman on the Edge of Time*, Kafer, *Feminist, Queer, Crip*, 70–74.
9. Melinda Hall, *The Bioethics of Enhancement* (Lanham: Lexington Books: 2017), 131.
10. See discussion in Hall, *The Bioethics of Enhancement*, 92–99, 131–133.
11. Hall, *Queering Philosophy*, 9.
12. Hall, *Queering Philosophy*, 117.
13. Hall, *Queering Philosophy*, 119.
14. The authors would like to thank Joshua Horn for helpful edits and encouragement, and William Irwin for giving our abstract a chance. They would also like to thank Michele Skelton for getting Susan Peppers-Bates to watch *The Last of Us*, despite her horror of horror. Finally, they would like to thank the writers of *The Last of Us* for their otherwise thinking in bringing us the stories of Ellie and Abby.

PART IV
MONSTERS AND US

14

Kiss of a Cordy
Why Are Humans the Scariest Monsters?

Mariya Dvoskina

In *The Strange Case of Dr. Jekyll and Mr. Hyde*, a monster ravages the streets of London. As it turns out, Hyde and Jekyll are one and the same individual. They are the monster. This isn't a story of man defeating a monster, but rather a warning that all men have the potential to be the monster. In an exploration of reality rather than fiction, the philosopher Hannah Arendt (1906–1975) described how the capacity for evil lies terrifyingly in the most mundane of human actions. Arendt coined the phrase "the banality of evil" to refer to the Nazi regime, and more specifically to Alfred Eichmann, a man sometimes referred to as the "architect of the Holocaust." Eichmann's crimes were so atrocious and horrific that we wouldn't hesitate to call him a monster. Yet, Arendt suggests that Eichmann wasn't a sociopath, but an ordinary man following orders effectively. Arendt isn't excusing Eichmann's behavior. Rather, she is speaking to every human's capacity to commit and condone evil—all humans are capable of monstrous deeds.

In the world of *The Last of Us*, everyone has the potential to become a monster, both literally, by becoming infected, and figuratively, by committing monstrous acts. Over and over in the show and video game, we see examples of humans acting monstrously, and even taking advantage of others' humanity to steal, kill, or just get the upper hand.

Are We All Capable of Becoming Monsters?

In the very first episode of *The Last of Us*, the audience watches the transformation of an elderly wheelchair-bound neighbor into a violent attacker. In one scene, fungal tendrils can be seen protruding from her bloody mouth. The combination of human and monster is uncanny and disturbing. After Joel kills the infected neighbor, he flees with his family in their truck. Disturbed

The Last of Us and Philosophy: Look for the Light, First Edition.
Edited by Charles Joshua Horn.

by what she has observed, Sarah poignantly asks her father, "How do you know we are not sick?" The notion that anyone could be infected and could become a monster is terrifying. Yet, it's in the next scenes when Sarah is killed by the soldier that the true tragedy and horror of the episode unfolds. Sarah's death is indeed tragic, caused by a scared (presumably uninfected) soldier.

When we see FEDRA-occupied Boston for the first time in episode 1, we get a further sense that the humans, not the Cordyceps, may be the real monsters. We witness routine executions of both the Infected and those deemed enemies of the state. The heavily armed FEDRA soldiers, strict curfew, visible poverty, and the bent heads of the citizens are reminiscent of a fascist regime. When a soldier tells Joel about a FEDRA factory that only makes bullets and pills, Joel sardonically alludes to the consequences of losing one's humanity, stating, "Well, the more you shoot people, the harder it is to sleep, I guess."

In episodes 4 and 5, the audience is introduced to an alternative to FEDRA, the resistance group in Kansas City. Having overthrown their local FEDRA and taken the city, Kathleen, the leader of the resistance group, is brutal and merciless, killing hostages after promising them freedom if they give her the information she seeks. The irony is that the rebels and FEDRA have turned on each other, rather than coming together to fight against the Cordyceps fungus. Kathleen is later killed by a behemoth Bloater, the most monstrous-looking infected being we see in the entirety of the show. Yet, Kathleen is the true monster because her actions are cruel and intentional. It's humans who inflict the most suffering on other humans in *The Last of Us*.

In episode 8, we are presented with yet another example of the human capacity for horrible deeds. Possibly the most sadistic and clear embodiment of evil in *The Last of Us*, David is first presented as a caring and charismatic leader. In his interactions with Ellie, we are first convinced he may be trying to be her friend. Despite his revenge-hungry crew looking to murder Joel, David appears to want to save Ellie. The audience, though, soon learns his true motives for keeping her alive. David is a sociopathic pedophile, who, once his initial approach to Ellie fails, violently attempts to rape and kill her.

The Last of Us shows that individuals from all walks of life can become monsters and commit evil deeds. It seems that in the right context, whether in self-defense, or in the face of great loss, we may all be capable of turning into a monster. We often think of the world in an "us vs. them" way, where the monsters are always someone else. But why?

Why Do We Need Monsters?

Storytellers and philosophers may be onto something with the insight that we are all capable of becoming monsters. In fact, we struggle with becoming monsters daily. If you disagree, see what comes to mind the next time someone cuts you off in traffic. You'll likely find yourself attributing their behavior to a character flaw ("What an @$$#^%*!" you yell to your steering wheel) rather than a situational factor ("They are probably having a bad day"). When another human commits a terrible act, we begin to define them by their supposed difference from "the rest of us." We seek out a way to differentiate our own behaviors from theirs. "They" are the monster, and "we" are not because we are different from them.

The Last of Us regularly explores what defines a monster, but perhaps the most poignant example comes when the audience is led to reflect on monsters in the last moments of Tess's life. As a swarm of Cordyceps invade the abandoned building, one stands out from the crowd and kisses Tess. The kiss is a banal, plainly human action, yet shockingly, paralyzingly, terrifying. The audience is plunged into a morally grey area. Is there a last (part) of us somewhere still in the Infected? The kiss hints at a sinister "yes."

The Cordyceps is disturbing because the human part may still be "in there." Perhaps there is no dichotomy between alive and dead; perhaps the monster and the man are identical (as Stephenson and Arendt suggest). After he is infected, Sam gets to the heart of his fear in the conversation with Ellie, asking, "If you turn into a monster, is it still you inside?" The blurred line between monster and man carries profound moral implications for the characters in *The Last of Us*, as well as for the audience.

Compare the death of the elderly infected neighbor in the first episode with the death of Sarah. Even though both deaths involve the killing of a vulnerable victim, we don't consider the first killing as tragic. Like Joel, we have placed the elderly neighbor into the category of "them." This categorization makes Joel's actions morally acceptable and maybe even heroic. On the other hand, the actions of the soldier are complicated, as we can imagine that the soldier reacted rashly in fear, despite Joel's plea "we are not sick." We can put ourselves in the soldier's shoes. Since we have to weigh both our identification with Joel, and our identification with the soldier, we are sad. When we consider everyone as part of the "us," no choices are easy. Yet to see everyone as part of "us" requires great patience and much thought.

There is another important reason for the psychological tendency to create monsters of others. The more we dehumanize the "other," the more we can condone our own morally deplorable acts. In fact, the more monstrous others seem to us, the more monstrous we can be toward them.

When Kathleen is shown executing her hostages, she justifies her actions with an "us vs. them" mentality, saying,

I used to be so scared of these people. Now look at them. Did it feel good? Betraying your neighbors to FEDRA? Watching us get thrown in prison? Watching us hang, so that you could get medicine, alcohol, fucking apples? Did it make you feel better? Did it make you feel safe? How does it make you feel now?

The man Kathleen is hunting down, Henry, is on the run with his brother, Sam. We see Sam bonding with Ellie and feel sympathy toward the characters. Henry isn't fully honest with Joel at first, but eventually he discloses the reason Kathleen is after him:

> You know, I wasn't exactly telling you the truth before about me not killing someone. There was a man, a great man. He was never afraid, never selfish and he was always forgiving. You ever met someone like that? A man you'd follow anywhere. I wanted to. Yeah, but Sam ... he got sick. Leukemia. Yeah. Anyway, there was one drug that worked and, big shock, there wasn't much left of it and it belonged to FEDRA. If I wanted some, it was gonna take something big. So I gave them something big. That one great man. The leader of the resistance movement in Kansas City and Kathleen's brother. So, still think they should take it easy on me? Or am I the bad guy? I don't know what you're waiting on man, the answer is easy. I am the bad guy because I did a bad guy thing.

Both Kathleen and Henry justify their action with an "us vs. them" mentality and define who falls into each category. Once the line is drawn, it's easier to commit monstrous acts. Henry's actions seem understandable because we have gotten to know him. Henry is part of the "us," whereas Kathleen is a part of "them."

The order in which their stories are presented is important. We see Kathleen's despicable actions first, then we hear her story. But with Henry, we see his relationship with his brother first, then we hear the story about his despicable actions. Even though Henry himself tells us he "did a bad guy thing" we can relate to him, and therefore excuse his actions as morally justifiable. This scene also foreshadows Joel's situation at the end of the first season when he chooses to do something morally controversial.

David serves as another example of the difficulty of recognizing monsters. He seems to justify his murderous, cannibalistic, and pedophilic actions through a twisted sense of fatalism, telling Ellie, "And you think we have a choice? Is that it? You kill to survive ... and so do we. We have to take care of our own. By any means necessary." David also justifies his actions with an "us vs. them" mentality. At first, he attempts to convince Ellie that it's in her best interest to become part of his group, "That part of your life [with Joel], it's ending. And what I'm offering you is a beginning. But if you can't find a way to trust me ... then, yes, you are alone."

Ellie calls David an "animal" for his cannibalism, but David isn't fazed. He gives an eloquent explanation of how morality is contextual and depends on whose side you're on: "It was a last resort. You think it doesn't shame me? But what was I supposed to do? Let them starve? These people who put their lives in my hands, who expect me to keep them safe, who love me?... Didn't [Joel] take another man's life to save yours?... He was defending you." In this scene, David says that he was "shown the truth" by the Cordyceps: "What does Cordyceps do? Is it evil? No. It's fruitful.

It multiplies. It feeds and protects its children, and it secures its future with violence, if it must. It loves." In other words, as long as you're protecting your in-group, violence is justifiable, even necessary toward the out-group.

The more we dehumanize others, the more we can justify our own morally questionable actions. Murder, rape, and even cannibalism are acceptable to David. As the audience, we quickly place David in the "other" category and deem him the monster. So when Ellie kills him, we're glad.

Is Joel a Hero or a Monster?

Most of us root for Joel and Ellie. But this is precisely what is so worrying about being able to identify monsters. Like frogs who boil to death in gradually warming water, we don't notice becoming a monster when the change is slow.

In episode 2, we are taken back to the beginning of the Cordyceps pandemic. Ratna Pertiwi, a professor of mycology, is asked to examine an infested corpse. After her shock subsides, she tells the officer that there isn't a vaccine or cure, and the only solution is to "Bomb. Start bombing. Bomb this city and everyone in it." Dr. Pertiwi's suggestion is eerily utilitarian. The needs of the many (the world) are greater than those of the few (the infected city). Her words are made even more powerful by the fact that she doesn't choose to flee. She tells the officer, "if someone could please drive me home? I would like to be with my family."

Dr. Pertiwi isn't a hypocrite. After seeing what the future holds in episode 1 (not only of the Cordyceps-infected monsters, but also the human monsters who commit moral atrocities) we may be inclined to agree with Dr. Pertiwi's utilitarian worldview. If a couple thousand people must die to save millions, we may be willing to accept an atrocity. If only one person had to die to save millions, that would seem to be the obvious moral choice. But that perspective changes in the finale of season 1.

Joel is capable of great violence, and at the end of episode 1, he doesn't hesitate to kill the FEDRA soldier. This scene calls to mind the initial scene where his daughter is killed. In fact, we can almost see it through Joel's eyes. In episode 8, Joel tortures one of David's men. Once he retrieves the information he needs about the location of the compound where Ellie is held, he kills the hostage. The other hostage screams in horror and disbelief, "Why the fuck did you do that?! He told you what you wanted!... I ain't tellin' you shit." Joel kills him too.

Many of Joel's violent acts are committed in self-defense, or more accurately, in defense of Ellie. It appears that David was right after all when he told Ellie that we protect our own through violence, if necessary. In the finale of season 1, Joel acts proactively, killing innocent and defenseless individuals in order to protect Ellie, even killing Marlene in cold blood. Joel's actions also mean that the chance for the potential cure for the rest of the world is lost. Essentially, Joel's choice sentences thousands, if not hundreds of thousands of people, to death. Despite these facts, the audience sympathizes with Joel and condones his actions.

The utilitarian view we held in episode 2 with Dr. Pertiwi is gone. Because the story is told largely through the eyes of Joel and Ellie, the audience connects with them. We see Joel's pain at losing his daughter, and we feel the power of the bond that develops between him and Ellie. We may even wonder what we would do in Joel's shoes. Those of us who played the video game felt this bond on an even deeper level. As players we have come to see ourselves in Joel's and Ellie's shoes, and we condone Joel's final act in protecting Ellie.

The Monsters Lurking Within Us

The Last of Us leaves us to reflect on our own morality. Our tendency to try to separate the man from the monster likely has to do with who we put with the "us" and who we put with the "them." When the distinction is clear, we can engage in easy moral decision making. If they are one of us, we can justify nearly any moral choice, regardless of the consequences. If they are one of them, we can easily justify our own morally questionable behavior.

The Last of Us contains some thrilling jump scares, and it makes us uncomfortable to think of a fungus controlling our brains and behaviors. However, what is most horrific about the world overrun by Cordyceps is that it often brings out the worst in people. This lesson is even more important because the consequences of an "us vs. them" mentality are quite real. We should be mindful not just of the monsters "out there," but also of the monsters lurking in our own hearts and minds.

15

Self-Deception and Moral Failure in *The Last of Us*

Charles Joshua Horn

It's hard to do the right thing, and it's even harder when the human race is struggling to survive an apocalyptic pandemic. Sometimes the greatest obstacle is not Fireflies or Cordyceps. Sometimes it's us. We deceive ourselves into thinking our actions are right. *The Last of Us* explores this kind of self-deception with major characters like Joel, Ellie, and Abby, and also with minor characters like David, Manny, and Isaac. The series illustrates a vicious cycle of immorality where the characters cannot take the steps to become more virtuous because they do not properly reflect on their own wrongdoing in the first place. In short, they are deceived about their own moral behavior.

Joel's Self-Deception

For such a capable individual, Joel is often deceived about his own actions. He is most deceived about his feelings toward Ellie. After he loses his daughter, Sarah, Joel spends the next twenty years broken and isolated. When he is initially tasked with smuggling Ellie out of the Quarantine Zone in Boston, Joel wants nothing to do with the job in general or Ellie in particular. But over the course of their journey to Salt Lake City to find the Fireflies, Joel's feelings for Ellie grow in ways that he does not recognize. He eventually learns to trust her with a weapon, his safety, and even more important for Joel, his past. When they make it to Salt Lake City, Joel finally opens up to Ellie and starts to tell her about Sarah, something he had not done with anyone in two decades. Joel did not even want the picture of Sarah that Tommy offered him in Jackson. But for Ellie, Joel emotionally opened himself up again, telling her about Sarah, and eventually taking the picture he initially refused.

The Last of Us and Philosophy: Look for the Light, First Edition.
Edited by Charles Joshua Horn.
© 2025 John Wiley & Sons, Inc. Published 2025 by John Wiley & Sons, Inc.

Joel doesn't recognize how much he has grown to care for Ellie though. In one of the most memorable moments from the first video game and first season of the HBO show, Joel admonishes Ellie for running off when he tries to get Tommy to take her the rest of the way to the Fireflies. Ellie tells Joel, "Maria told me about Sarah. And I—" Joel cuts her off. In the video game he says, "Ellie. You are treading on some mighty thin ice here." Ellie pushes on though, "I'm sorry about your daughter, Joel, but I have lost people too." Joel retorts, "You have no idea what loss is." Ellie continues, "Everyone I have cared for has either died or left me. Everyone—fucking except you. So don't tell me that I would be safer with someone else— because the truth is I would just be more scared." For the moment, Joel explicitly rejects Ellie, insisting that she isn't his daughter and that he certainly doesn't care for her as one. He says, "You're right. ... You're not my daughter and I sure as hell ain't your dad. And we are going our separate ways."

Despite the growth of their relationship, Joel's feelings for Ellie are hidden even to himself until this moment. But once the hidden feelings become explicit, Joel's attitude to Ellie immediately changes. Of course Ellie isn't mere cargo to be smuggled—she has become his daughter in every way except blood. It's precisely Joel's recognition that Ellie is his surrogate daughter that compels him to sacrifice the possibility of a cure for mankind for one little girl. In Joel's mind, he didn't sacrifice the world for Ellie—she *was* his world. In the final moments of *The Last of Us Part II*, when Ellie reprimands Joel for not letting her die in Salt Lake City, he tells her, "If somehow the Lord gave me a second chance at that moment, I would do it all over again." Joel takes it as his responsibility to protect Ellie, even against her own wishes. Good fathers protect their children.

Not only is Joel deceived about his own feelings toward Ellie, but he's also deceived about his own motivations for saving her. Joel attacks the Fireflies to save Ellie partly because she is unconscious and cannot decide for herself whether she would want to sacrifice herself for the possible development of a vaccine. But Joel does not recognize that in lying to Ellie about the possibility of a cure, he isn't respecting her autonomy any more than Marlene and the Fireflies. Joel's actions reinforce the point that philosopher and theologian Joseph Butler (1692–1752) made in the eighteenth century—partiality to our own actions deceives us about our own morality and hinders our ability to become more virtuous.

Butler was a bishop in the Church of England who spread his moral teachings primarily through his sermons.[1] He discussed the pervasiveness and danger of self-deceit, arguing that overcoming this concern is critical for moral progress. According to Butler, self-deception arises because we often don't reflect on our own actions, and when we do reflect, we tend to be partial to our own behavior. He writes, "Vice in general consists in having an unreasonable and too great regard to ourselves, in comparison of others."[2]

Ellie's Quest for Justice

Like Joel, Ellie is emblematic of Butler's warnings. Self-deception looms large in her conversation with David in Silver Lake. When she's imprisoned, Ellie calls him a "fucking animal" for resorting to cannibalism. David responds, "Oh. You're awfully quick to judgment. Considering you and your friend killed how many men?" Ellie replies, "They didn't give us a choice." And David counters, "And you think we have a choice? Is that it? You kill to survive ... and so do we. We have to take care of our own. By any means necessary."

David's moral imperative to take care of his own by any means necessary is one that Ellie also accepts because she has learned it from Joel, and it will be reinforced by his choice to kill the Fireflies at St. Mary's Hospital later in the series. However, Ellie doesn't recognize that she's acting in a way not dissimilar from David. While it's true that she hasn't been reduced to cannibalism, she later resorts to torture and murder for the very same justification, to take care of her own, by any means necessary.

In *The Last of Us Part II*, Ellie is singularly focused on seeking what she perceives to be justice for the torture and murder of Joel by the Washington Liberation Front (WLF). On her search for Abby, Ellie kills (or is too late to kill) Nora, Manny, Mel, Owen, and others. And concerning those she isn't able to kill, Ellie is upset that she couldn't kill them herself. In a conversation with Dina at the TV station, the forward-operating base for the WLF, Ellie tells Dina that she would be upset if the people that killed Joel were killed in some other way than by her hand. Ellie says, "If those fuckers who killed Joel got taken out by some random Infected ..." Dina says, "Then they'd still be dead, Ellie." And Ellie responds, "I'm not sure that's justice."

Ellie is clearly deceived about her own actions here. Her driving motivation for searching for Abby and the WLF is to exact revenge (in her mind, justice) for their actions against Joel. And yet, she doesn't recognize that she is attempting to do the very same thing to the WLF that they did to Joel. The WLF is wrong for engaging in torture and murder, but Ellie is justified because they deserve it, whereas Joel did not. It isn't just that Ellie thinks that torture and murder are morally permissible and justified because the WLF deserve such treatment; rather, Ellie doesn't recognize that she is doing the very same thing as the WLF did.

Ellie's self-deception in these instances highlights another of Butler's claims—while some actions seem obviously wrong (like torture and murder), there are others which are more difficult to classify, and which can lead us to moral failure. He writes,

> It is to be observed then, that as there are express determinate acts of wickedness, such as murder, adultery, theft; so, on the other hand, there are numberless cases in which the vice and wickedness cannot be exactly defined, but

consists in a certain general temper and course of action, or in the neglect of some duty, suppose charity or any other, whose bounds and degrees are not fixed. This is the very province of self-deceit and self-partiality: Here it governs without check or control. "For what commandment is there broken? Is there a transgression where there is no law? A vice which cannot be defined?"[3]

If Ellie were more aware of Butler's point, then she would have realized that there are limits to seemingly moral imperatives like "take care of your own." The limits to this imperative are precisely the ones that are most ambiguous. Failing to see the limits is dangerous and hinders moral progress.

Abby's Quest for Revenge

Like Ellie, Abby is on a quest for revenge (in her mind, justice) for the murder of her father by Joel. The fact that Naughty Dog, the developer of the video games, juxtaposes these two characters and their violent journeys in the same video game, *The Last of Us Part II*, shows that they want to draw attention to the problem of self-deception. It isn't enough to see or even play as only one character who doesn't reflect on their own actions. In playing as both Ellie and Abby though, gamers can reflect on their own actions because they are explicitly seeing those actions from the perspective of both the aggressor and the victim. If we didn't play as both characters, it would be far too easy to view the other factions as the villains and the character we play as the hero. After all, as Butler reminds us in his sermons, it's far too easy to have special regard for ourselves. In the case of the video games though, we do not have to imagine what it would be like to be the victim to reflect on whether our actions are good or bad. We can embody the victim through the video game.

Butler believes we can guard against self-partiality and by extension, self-deception, by imagining our own actions being done by another. Toward the very beginning of their journey, Abby and her WLF compatriots, Mel and Manny, discuss the temporary truce between the WLF and the Seraphites (Scars), another political and religious faction.

ABBY: Getting nostalgic about the truce? Easier days, huh?
MANNY: Too easy. We let our guard down. And they strung up an entire squad.
MEL: That was in retaliation to us shooting those kids.
MANNY: Okay, but.... Those "kids" attacked our guys.... What would you do?
MEL: I don't know, not riddle them with bullets?
MANNY: I'd rather save our people.

MEL: Manny, they're kids ... it's not their fault.
ABBY: Not our fault either. Those deaths are on them.
MEL: Okay.

In their conversation, Manny engages in self-deception regarding the WLF actions against the Seraphites. As in the earlier conversation between Ellie and David, Manny doesn't recognize that the WLF isn't all that different from the competing faction. Mel, by contrast, is more mindful than Manny. She not only recognizes that the Seraphites are defending themselves just as the WLF is, but she also invites Manny to put himself in the position of those very Seraphites he is judging.

Like Manny, Abby also has moments of self-deception. Perhaps the clearest example is when Abby and Owen first get to the Aquarium and make their way upstairs to a room where a family has been staying. They find a corpse in a chair with a note describing how his children left him to join the Seraphites. Abby professes that she can't imagine how someone would be attracted to such a morally bankrupt group as the Seraphites. She says, "I just don't understand how anybody willingly joins the Scars." Owen says, "Why not?" Abby justifies her position stating, "Because they're an insane cult. That's why." But Owen retorts, "In the QZs, people would refer to the Fireflies as terrorists. Fanatics." Abby still doesn't admit the truth of Owen's claim here and responds, "We were naive. We weren't ... fanatical." But Owen doesn't give up the argument and replies, "We blew up checkpoints and assassinated soldiers." Even with this evidence brought to her attention, Abby remains in denial and deceived about her own actions. She responds, "It's not the same."

Abby implies that the Seraphites have no redeeming qualities and are basically terrorists, whereas the WLF and Fireflies are morally justified in their actions. But Owen responds that some people thought that their former group, the Fireflies, wasn't different from the way that she is characterizing the Seraphites. Abby is expressing here what Butler highlights as our ability to be strangers even unto ourselves. He writes,

> There is not any thing, relating to men and characters, more surprising and unaccountable than this partiality to themselves, which is observable in many; as there is nothing of more melancholy reflection, respecting morality, virtue, and religion. Hence it is that many men seem perfect strangers to their own characters. They think, and reason, and judge quite differently upon any matter relating to themselves, from what they do in cases of others where they are not interested.[4]

On the third day in Seattle after she discovers that Owen and the pregnant Mel have been killed, Abby finally makes it to the theater where Ellie, Tommy, and Dina have been hiding. Like Ellie, Abby is seeking revenge for the death of her friends and compatriots. In Abby's mind, Ellie has done something truly vicious in killing her friends, and especially a woman clearly and visibly pregnant. So, when Abby has Dina on the ground with a knife to her throat and Ellie pleads for her partner's life begging, "She's pregnant!", Abby doesn't relent. Abby doesn't acknowledge that she came for revenge precisely because she thought Ellie did something heinous and that she's about to do the very same thing—kill a pregnant woman. Abby responds to Ellie, "Good." Abby can't improve morally because she doesn't recognize that she's doing immoral actions in the first place.

In one final example of self-deception, there's a discussion late in the video game between Abby and Yara, a former Seraphite trying to escape the war. Yara asks Abby what Isaac, the leader of the WLF, hopes to gain with his assault on the island occupied by the Seraphites. Yara wonders what the goal of sending the entire WLF into hostile territory to kill another group of people could possibly be. Abby replies, "An end to the fighting." Yara questions, "But at what cost?" And Abby responds, "At this point.... Any cost." It's clear that Isaac isn't properly self-reflective and doesn't have the right perspective. He says, "This is bigger than any of us ... definitely bigger than Owen." Isaac doesn't realize the internal tension between desiring peace and using non-peaceful methods, including committing war crimes, to attain it.

Avoiding Self-Deception

The Last of Us highlights the problem of self-deception time and time again with both major and minor characters. If Butler is right that self-deception is such a significant hurdle to moral progress, then what can we do? Philosophers generally think there are two main strategies to avoid self-deception. Some insist that the best strategy is to follow Aristotle's advice and imbed ourselves in moral communities with friends who can help us act more virtuously.[5] (For more information about the need for a strong moral community, check out Chapter 12 of this book.) Other philosophers follow Butler's advice and suggest that we improve our intellectual virtues and thereby improve our actions.[6]

To become more virtuous, Butler maintains that we must be mindful of our own actions and try to evaluate them just as we would if they were done by others. Put simply, to avoid deceiving ourselves with respect to our own morality, we must become more reflective on our own thoughts, beliefs, desires, motivations, and actions. To avoid self-deception, we must be more philosophical. Many of the characters in *The Last of Us* neglect this key step. Even when their actions are questioned by others, they often express denial, insisting that their actions are fundamentally different than those they are judging. Butler makes the connection between self-deception and the strategy to be more philosophical. He writes, "And Solomon saw this thing in a very strong light when he said, 'He that trusteth his own heart is a fool.' This likewise was the reason why that precept, *Know thy-self*, was so frequently inculcated by the philosophers of old."[7]

While there are a few notable differences between HBO's *Last of Us* and the video games developed by Naughty Dog, the biggest difference is how we take in the tragic story of Joel, Ellie, Abby, and others. With the show, we watch their actions unfold on screen in a similar way to the other more explicit villains like the Infected, David, and Marlene. We have no more control over their actions than we do the Clickers. But in playing the video game, we are forced to not only watch Joel murder a hospital full of people helping to secure a vaccine for the Cordyceps, but instead to play *as* Joel while he commits these actions. Joel is not someone *else* whose actions we can evaluate—we *are* Joel. And because we identify as Joel, playing the video game makes it much easier to justify his (and our) actions. After all, as Butler so forcefully contends, we have a disposition to be self-partial to our own behavior. He writes, "There is one easy and almost sure way to avoid being misled by this self-partiality, and to get acquainted with our real character: to have regard to the suspicious part of it, and keep a steady eye over ourselves in that respect ..."[8]

The pervasiveness of self-deception suggests that it's one of the most serious moral problems in *The Last of Us* series. Self-deception is not a form of ethical relativism, the moral view that right and wrong vary from person to person, culture to culture, or time to time. It's not just that *beliefs* about right and wrong vary (a fact that any anthropologist or historian could verify); rather, it's that right and wrong themselves vary. These characters are not merely insisting that morality exists, and it varies from one faction or individual to another, or worse, that morality doesn't exist at all. Instead, they maintain that certain things are morally impermissible and reprehensible, like torture or murder, but then do not recognize that they are wrong for doing those very same actions.

Naughty Dog emphasizes self-partiality most when we play as both Ellie and Abby. For the first half of *The Last of Us Part II*, the gamer plays as Ellie as she plots revenge against Abby and the other members of the WLF for torturing and murdering Joel. We are meant to think that her actions are not only morally permissible, but that justice demands that Ellie seek vengeance on the individuals who committed such a heinous act against Joel, another "good" person who we play as in *Part I*.

In the second half of the video game though, we play as Abby and grow to sympathize with her, even though she is the same individual who tortures and murders Joel. And we do so, just like we did with Joel and Ellie before, because we *are* Abby. We control and give life to her actions through the act of playing the video game. By forcing the player to directly control two characters who are trying to kill each other, Naughty Dog invites the player to evaluate their own actions. They are asking the player to evaluate the morality of Ellie and Abby, and as a result, our own moral intuitions—in short, they are asking the player to be more philosophical.

In his sermon on self-deceit, Butler references a line in the book of Matthew which indicates that we must be mindful of the darkness we have within ourselves, and that our understanding is the light which can dispel that darkness. Understanding and self-reflection are the keys to over-coming self-deception. He writes, "Our understanding, and sense of good and evil, is the light and guide of life: 'If, therefore, this light that is in thee be darkness, how great is that darkness?'"[9] We find a similar message in *The Last of Us*, drawing on the same imagery. "When you're lost in the darkness, look for the light."

Notes

1. Joseph Butler, *Butler's Fifteen Sermons Preached at the Rolls Chapel; and, A Dissertation of the Nature of Virtue* (London: Society for Promoting Christian Knowledge, 1970).
2. Butler, *Butler's Fifteen Sermons*, 93.
3. Butler, *Butler's Fifteen Sermons*, 94.
4. Butler, *Butler's Fifteen Sermons*, 90–91.
5. Anna Elisabetta Galeotti, "The Attribution of Responsibility to Self-Deceivers," *Journal of Social Philosophy* 47 (2016), 420–438.
6. Amélie Oksenberg Rorty, "User-Friendly Self-Deception," *Philosophy* 69 (1994), 211–228.
7. Butler, *Butler's Fifteen Sermons*, 91.
8. Butler, *Butler's Fifteen Sermons*, 97.
9. Butler, *Butler's Fifteen Sermons*, 95; Matthew 6:23.

16

What Is It Like to Be a Clicker?
Consciousness and Cognition in
The Last of Us

Lucas Hinojosa-López and Remis Ramos Carreño

DR. NEUMANN: Viruses can make us ill, but fungi can alter our very minds. There's a fungus that infects insects. Gets inside an ant, for example, travels through its circulatory system to the ant's brain, and then floods it with hallucinogens, thus bending the ant's mind to its will. The fungus starts to direct the ant's behavior, telling it where to go and what to do, like a puppeteer with a marionette. And it gets worse.

"When You're Lost in the Darkness," the first episode of *The Last of Us*, provides important scientific information through a televised interview with Dr. Neumann, a mycologist who explains that a fungus like the Cordyceps could take control of its host and get it to act against its will. In the case of the ants, they latch onto a leaf at optimal altitude and humidity, which suggests a surprising degree of intelligence and agency for a fungus, an organism without a brain.[1] Worse, Dr. Neumann suggests that such a fungus could infect humans if it evolved and adapted to warmer temperatures. Indeed, the Cordyceps prove Dr. Neumann's prediction true, and the pandemic wipes out most of the population, leading to the quick downfall of society. The human hosts of the fungus, the Infected, don't aim to kill or eat other humans, but instead aim to spread the infection through biting. So, despite the gory violence, there's a method to the madness. Just as the fungus does with ants in its rainforest habitat, so likewise does the Cordyceps take control of its human host and issues specific orders for a specific goal. But how does that work?

For centuries, ever since René Descartes (1596–1650), philosophers have wrestled with the mind/body problem, the question of how an immaterial substance like the mind can interact and form a union with a material brain and body. Descartes' position, what philosophers today call "substance dualism," imagined that interaction between the mind and body occurred

The Last of Us and Philosophy: Look for the Light, First Edition.
Edited by Charles Joshua Horn.
© 2025 John Wiley & Sons, Inc. Published 2025 by John Wiley & Sons, Inc.

by animal spirits moving through the pineal gland in the center of the brain. Even in the seventeenth century though, Descartes' solution was flawed. After all, Descartes imagined animal spirits themselves to be material in nature. So, it's unclear how an animal spirit with a material nature could interact and form a union with a mind that has an immaterial nature.

The mind/body problem continues to perplex philosophers, but the consensus is that substance dualism isn't a good way to explain the interaction and union of minds and bodies. *The Last of Us* poses similar philosophical problems regarding our concepts of the mind and its properties. How can a brainless organism take control of a mind? To what degree are the Infected conscious? How can the Infected behave intelligently? Are the Infected a collective mind? Can there be intelligence or purposefulness without a mind?

Consciousness

To tackle these questions, we must try to understand the minds of different organisms, but this isn't without its problems. The contemporary philosopher Thomas Nagel used a thought experiment about bats to illuminate the difficulties of explaining consciousness in purely physical terms. We know much about how bats use echolocation (listening back to the echoes of their shrieks on surfaces) to hunt, navigate space, and make sense of their environments, but this biological explanation of their cognitive abilities doesn't help us to imagine *what it is like to be a bat*, how their conscious experience is different from ours. Nagel's insight implies that the scientific knowledge about how an organism's cognitive system works doesn't tell us *how* the organism's experiences feel or *why* they feel like they do.[2]

On an even more basic level, we don't know why or how living organisms are able to have qualitative experiences and feelings. The contemporary philosopher David Chalmers has dubbed this the "Hard Problem of Consciousness." The hard problem is the problem of explaining how purely physical states, like neurons firing in the brain, could give rise to a conscious mental state.[3] In a related thought experiment, Chalmers asks us to imagine a "philosophical zombie," a being that looks like, is built like, and behaves exactly like a normal human but has no consciousness, no inner life or experience. If such a creature is conceivable, then there's more to having a mind than what physical structure and biological facts can explain.

In *The Last of Us*, the Infected are symbiotes that can make sense of their surroundings, have shared goals, and collaborate to achieve them. In science and philosophy, the concept of cognition has widened considerably in the last few decades. The idea that animals don't have minds is a relic of the past, and we're starting to understand how cognition is an integral aspect of life itself. It might be that consciousness comes in many different flavors, and every living being might be conscious in its own particular way; so, we might not know what their experience is like, just as we don't know what being a bat (or a fungus or a plant) is like.

The contemporary philosophers Paco Calvo and Natalie Lawrence have argued that some plants and fungi exhibit fitness-increasing, adaptive behaviors.[4] Even without a central nervous system, they seem to be able to perceive their environment, form memories and learn from past experiences, make anticipatory decisions regarding their current state and the environment, and communicate and behave as a coordinated collective. Most of us fail to see plant behavior as intentional, intelligent actions because the actions happen on a different, much slower timescale.

All this leaves open the possibility of basic *fungal cognition*, sophisticated enough to explain the behaviors exhibited by the Infected in *The Last of Us*. Consciousness is difficult to understand in both humans and animals, and it may be even more difficult with respect to organisms like fungi.

What Doesn't Kill You ...

Is the Cordyceps fungus merely a parasite, or is there some degree of symbiosis between it and its human hosts? The emergence of behaviors that could be regarded as cognitive is currently being studied with respect to the plant–fungus relationship. Biologists Kaleda Denton and Dennis Krebs have studied mutualistic symbiosis, the close interactions that are mutually beneficial between members of the same or different species.[5] For example, certain birds associate with large mammals to feed on their parasites, as in the case of the heron and the buffalo. In the case of symbiosis between plant and fungus, this is enabled by a mycorrhiza: a union between the roots of a plant and the hyphae, the underground filament network of the fungus. Different plant species can be colonized by the same species of fungus, which can connect through a common underground network (known as mycorrhizal or mycelial networks) and share different nutrients necessary for their survival. In fact, Suzanne Simard and colleagues discovered that nutrients can be shared bidirectionally through this network between one tree species and another, according to their nutritional needs.[6] This fungal underground network serves as a hub for sharing nutrients, thus improving chances of survival.

In *The Last of Us*, some degree of mutualistic symbiosis between the fungus and its hosts must be in place. In the advanced stages of infection, Clickers and Bloaters presumably lose their ability to eat and drink, and the thick inner and outer layers of fungus integrated with their bodies must provide nutrients and energy to keep them going. The fungus's goal is to spread itself, but to do so, it must keep its hosts alive. So, while humans serve as a vehicle for fungus propagation, the fungus secures its survival by providing energy and probably also chemical substances to avoid other infections, like viruses, bacteria, and other fungi.

There are many other interesting properties of fungal colonies. For example, Kevin Beiler and colleagues discovered that mycorrhiza-forming fungi can link different trees and plants, acting as mediators between them, allowing the exchange of water, carbon, and other nutrients.[7] Previously, it had been unknown how interconnected these networks could be, but topological studies defined this type of interconnection as free-scale, identifying trees as nodes and fungal mycorrhizae as links. Simard suggests that the functioning of mycorrhizal networks is a lot like neural networks in the brain, with similar complex connectivity patterns.[8]

According to Darlene Southworth, in free-scale networks, some nodes are more densely connected than others, making much of the network easily accessible.[9] Removing a node doesn't compromise the rest of the network unless specific, densely connected nodes are removed. Nutritional resources transported through this network can be shared efficiently, and protecting densely connected nodes helps the system sustain itself. The HBO show incorporates mycorrhiza as a key element, providing an explanation of how the Infected sustain themselves.

Fungal Cognition

Yuan Yuan Song and colleagues conducted an experiment to prove that plants not only share nutrients through mycorrhizae but can also send stress signals that way.[10] She removed the leaves of a plant while analyzing the reaction of neighboring plants that were interconnected through mycorrhizae. To her surprise, the leafless plant "yielded" its carbon to the interconnected neighboring plants and, in addition, activated the response of defense enzymes. Her research seems to indicate that the plant "alerted" its neighbors, who hadn't been defoliated and yet showed signs of being stressed. The same experiment was replicated on plants that weren't interconnected by a mycorrhizal network, and the neighbors of the damaged plant did not show signs of stress. This suggests that mycelial networks also act as a means of communication between plants, allowing the spread and recognition of stress signals between them. It also suggests that sharing vital nutrients (such as photosynthetic carbon) occurs when the organism "evaluates" that after a certain percentage of leaf loss, it's more efficient to give up its nutrients rather than hoarding them. So, the current state of research suggests that plants, including trees, can perform certain actions that we could define as cognitive: perceiving, communicating with other plants, processing information, and even learning, remembering, associating stimuli, and adjusting their behavior. In *The Last of Us*, those infected by Cordyceps have these features, too, and act likewise.

Consciousness of the Infected

For contemporary philosopher Tim Bayne, cognition is the "capacity to understand, or process knowledge."[11] A plant, thanks to its symbiotic relationship with a fungus, could be characterized as a cognitive agent. Through mycorrhizal networks, a plant can collect information about the nutritional status of its neighbors and modify its behavior to share nutrients, recognize kinship, make decisions, remember, perceive, and share signals that alert and prepare neighbors for a threat. This suggests that plants make sense of themselves, their neighbors, and their environment.

The Infected in *The Last of Us* perceive stimuli and process information for the propagation of the fungus. They can tell the difference between themselves and their prey—the few non-infected humans that have survived. They can also recognize their location and navigate spaces, communicate, share information with other Infected, and use echolocation. In other words, the Infected seem to make sense of their position in the environment and coordinate their actions with others to achieve their shared goals, as occurs in a mutualistic symbiosis.

According to the neuroscientist Paul Cisek, the cognitive skills that can be assessed through behavior include attention, memory, thinking, intentionality, and decision making.[12] Strikingly, these skills can be observed in both the plant–fungus interaction and the Infected–fungus interaction, even in the absence of abstract or linguistic reasoning. Everything seems to indicate that the cognitive characteristics of the Infected in *The Last of Us* are enabled by the information provided by the fungi, which must travel through some kind of mycelial network, just like what occurs in plant–fungus interaction. The network seemingly supplements and even completely replaces the lost brain mass in the case of Clickers and Bloaters.

In *The Last of Us Part II*, the player can find a detailed account of the stages of those infected by Cordyceps. The FEDRA "Infected Stages Pamphlet" categorizes the Infected into four groups, each one rarer and more lethal than the former, and shows how the cognitive abilities of the hosts change the longer they are infected.

"Infected Stage 1: Cordyceps has taken over the victim's motor functions. Fast and agile. Stage 1 Infected usually travel in packs. DO NOT LET THEM SWARM YOU." Stage 1 describes "Runners," who are humans recently taken over by the fungus, with their perceptual and motor abilities still intact. They seem to pay attention to their surroundings and remember the location of a non-infected for at least a limited period of time. It's implied that their human minds might still be aware of their own violent behavior but are unable to do anything about it since the Cordyceps has taken over. Ed Yong describes this state as being "a prisoner in its own body. Its brain is still in the driver's seat, but the fungus has the wheel."[13] Tellingly, in the video game, some Runners are heard crying while eating a corpse.

"Infected Stage 2: Uses environment to hide and ambush victims. Will frequently flank and attack from behind. Approach with caution and check your surroundings." Stage 2 describes "Stalkers," who show a high degree of anticipatory reasoning and perspective-taking, abilities humans share with other animals. Yet, they don't show emotions or behaviors that imply the presence of their former selves. They seem to be humans devoid of humanity.

"Infected Stage 3: Completely blind, acute hearing, uses echolocation to seek out prey. Keep your distance. Stage 3 Infected are known for their ferocious attacks and are extremely lethal." Stage 3 describes "Clickers," those who are completely blind, with acute hearing. Clickers exhibit goal-directed, representational cognition in the mapping of their surroundings through their clicking (via echolocation) to track their prey. The loss of vision and the emergence of this new perceptual ability imply a radical change in their conscious experience. Assuming they are still conscious, the replacement of a large part of their nervous system by fungal structures means they are full symbiotes and possess a different kind of mind. As with Nagel's bat, we can't imagine what it feels like, at all.

"Infected Stage 4: Rare but dangerous evolution of stage 3 Infected. Incredibly strong and capable of throwing acidic projectiles. DO NOT ENGAGE UNLESS ABSOLUTELY NECESSARY." Stage 4 describes "Bloaters," who show a high degree of specialization. They are covered in thick fungal plates and can throw mycotoxin sacs attached to their bodies. They act as protectors to the other Infected.

The Last of Us Part II also has a type of Infected not described in the pamphlet. Ellie and Dina call them "Shamblers." Shamblers can't see (like the Clickers of stage 3), but are smaller than the Bloaters of stage 4, suggesting that they might be at a stage between 3 and 4.

Do the Infected at any stage possess free will? It's possible that the Cordyceps fungus doesn't modify the behavior of Runners and Stalkers by "commanding" them to act violently. Instead, the fungus might just inhibit prosocial/ethical behaviors, leaving its host reduced to a state of insatiable hunger for flesh, which makes the Infected even more terrifying because it's not the fungus ordering them to bite. The fungus's need to spread is just exploiting and unleashing our own, very human capacity for violence. So, there seems to be a radical change between Stalkers and Clickers. They have cognitive abilities, but they behave in ways that speak of a coordinated, specialized effort to spread the infection, with different roles and different strategies to accomplish their goals. The Infected may look mindless to us, but they might have different *kinds* of consciousness. They also might constitute a collective mind in which each interconnected individual exhibits agency only to preserve the integrity of the group. Indeed, the philosopher Bryce Huebner has argued that there might be several kinds of collective minds.[14]

It's noteworthy that while the Infected in stages 1 and 2 try to spread the infection through biting, stages 3 and 4 actively try to kill their prey.

This suggests that, despite being creatures devoid of human consciousness, they evolved to recognize the human survivors as threats to themselves and to other Infected and to react accordingly. All this implies that the Infected are not mindless creatures and that consciousness is not an all-or-nothing property of beings. Things can be *more or less* conscious, and they can be conscious in totally different ways from each other.

Consciousness and the Human Condition

Cognitive science, the interdisciplinary study of the mind, assumes that an explanation of higher human cognition must be based on, or at least be compatible with, the explanation of the basic sensorimotor cognition present in all biological organisms. The once popular *Computer Metaphor* as a model for explaining minds has given way to what is now called "4E Cognition," the idea that minds are not to be understood in terms of computational processes performed by brains but understood as *enacted, embodied, embedded,* and *extended* processes of sense-making that all living beings perform to adapt and thrive. As philosopher Daniel Dennett (1942—2024) claimed in his "Dangerous Memes" TED talk, viruses "don't need to have a mind to have a plan."[15] Certainly, Cordyceps fungi don't have brains, but they have goals—self-preservation and spreading by whatever means necessary. In establishing a symbiotic relationship with us, the Cordyceps piggybacks on our own penchant for violence. Indeed, in *The Last of Us*, other humans are as terrifying as the Infected—the demand for survival has turned most of the survivors into humans who are indifferent to all things human. The fungus is not evil, but humans are.

This double menace—the Infected and other humans—makes the rare moments of grace, growth, and genuine connection between Joel and Ellie even more precious. In our world, at a moment when the very concepts of consciousness and intelligence are being shaken to the core, it might well be that this capacity for empathy, kindness, and decency—against our worst instincts and primal impulses—is what makes us human after all.[16]

Notes

1. We highly recommend watching "Our Planet | Fungus | Clip," narrated by Sir David Attenborough, at https://youtu.be/ROQrbWkV4HI?si=eyPqo1Hufk NiyFqL.
2. Thomas Nagel, "What Is It Like to Be a Bat?" *The Philosophical Review* 83, no. 4 (1974), 435–450.
3. David J. Chalmers, *The Conscious Mind: In Search of a Fundamental Theory* (Oxford and New York: Oxford University Press, 1997).
4. Paco Calvo and Natalie Lawrence, *Planta Sapiens: Unmasking Plant Intelligence* (New York: W.W. Norton, 2023).

5. Kaleda Denton and Dennis L. Krebs, "Symbiosis and Mutualism," in Todd K. Shackelford and Viviana A. Weekes-Shackelford eds., *Encyclopedia of Evolutionary Psychological Science* (Cham: Springer, 2016), 1–4.

6. Suzanne W. Simard, David A. Perry, Melanie D. Jones, David D. Myrold, Daniel M. Durall, and Randy Molina, "Net Transfer of Carbon between Ectomycorrhizal Tree Species in the Field," *Nature* 388, no. 6642 (August 1997), 579–582.

7. Kevin J. Beiler, Daniel M. Durall, Suzanne W. Simard, Sheri A. Maxwell, and Annette M. Kretzer, "Architecture of the Wood-Wide Web: *Rhizopogon* Spp. Genets Link Multiple Douglas-Fir Cohorts," *New Phytologist* 185, no. 2 (2010), 543–553.

8. Suzanne W. Simard, "Mycorrhizal Networks Facilitate Tree Communication, Learning, and Memory," in Frantisek Baluska, Monica Gagliano, and Guenther Witzany eds., *Memory and Learning in Plants* (Cham: Springer, 2018), 191–213.

9. D. Southworth, X.-H. He, W. Swenson, C.S. Bledsoe, and W.R. Horwath, "Application of Network Theory to Potential Mycorrhizal Networks," *Mycorrhiza* 15, no. 8 (December 1, 2005): 589–595.

10. Yuan Yuan Song, Suzanne W. Simard, Allan Carroll, William W. Mohn, and Ren Sen Zeng, "Defoliation of Interior Douglas-Fir Elicits Carbon Transfer and Stress Signalling to Ponderosa Pine Neighbors through Ectomycorrhizal Networks," *Scientific Reports* 5, no. 1 (February 16, 2015), 8495.

11. Tim Bayne, David Brainard, Richard W. Byrne, Lars Chittka, Nicky Clayton et al., "What Is Cognition?" *Current Biology* 29, no. 13 (July 8, 2019), R608–15.

12. Paul Cisek, "Resynthesizing Behavior through Phylogenetic Refinement," *Attention, Perception, & Psychophysics* 81, no. 7 (October 1, 2019), 2265–2287.

13. Ed Yong, "How the Zombie Fungus Takes over Ants' Bodies to Control Their Minds," *The Atlantic*, November 14, 2017, at https://www.theatlantic.com/science/archive/2017/11/how-the-zombie-fungus-takes-over-ants-bodies-to-control-their-minds/545864/.

14. Bryce Huebner, *Macrocognition: A Theory of Distributed Minds and Collective Intentionality* (Oxford: Oxford University Press, 2013).

15. Daniel Dennett, "Dangerous Memes | TED Talk," February 2002, at https://www.ted.com/talks/dan_dennett_dangerous_memes.

16. This research was made possible by Proyecto Fondecyt regular no. 1221132.

17

Global Indigenous Philosophy
Remembering the "Us"

Matthew Crippen

HBO's *The Last of Us* begins with Dr. Neuman speculating that some zombie-ant fungus could evolve and spread to humans. The fungus makes ants climb trees where they sprout spores that rain onto new victims. If transmitted to people, Dr. Neuman frets the result would be "billions of puppets with poisoned minds permanently fixed on one unifying goal: to spread the infection..."

Now, we have fungal yeast and bacteria in us that affects our brains, and there's a pathogen that leads rodents (and humans) to behave riskily, making them easier prey for felines, inside of which the parasite reproduces.[1] But *The Last of Us* isn't solely about fungus-driven zombification. It also explores the contagion of ideas. Whether it's the fanaticism of FEDRA, the Fireflies, or David's cult, people become mindlessly obedient to the agendas of larger groups.

Does *The Last of Us* infect the viewer and gamer with a populist American ideology that elevates individuals over communities? With the complicated exception of the Jackson Community, the other collectives are mind-numbingly authoritarian. Despite occasional moralizing about Joel's or Henry's past misdeeds, we root for their survival, even if it means killing members of collectives. And let's not forget the main antagonist is the fungus, which dehumanizes the Infected by pulling them into a violent hive mind.

Collective existence isn't inherently dehumanizing though. Communities form the basis for importantly human traits like language, cooking, political reasoning, advanced tools, and religion.[2] In fact, Indigenous traditions from around the globe suggest that the individual "I" originates in the collective "us," and these perspectives shaped founding American philosophies.[3] Because *The Last of Us* celebrates popular American values, which are rooted not just in traditions stressing individual self-sufficiency, but

The Last of Us and Philosophy: Look for the Light, First Edition.
Edited by Charles Joshua Horn.
© 2025 John Wiley & Sons, Inc. Published 2025 by John Wiley & Sons, Inc.

those emphasizing collective existence, it invites explorations about whether humans can truly thrive in isolation or whether individual flourishing necessitates communities.

Now They Come

In real life, stinkhorn mushrooms crack through pavement, and *The Last of Us* depicts a fungus crunching through a basement floor. Like the depiction in the show, some fungus species hunt tiny worms with adhesive nets or by spearing them with spores that germinate into their bodies. In nature, fungal networks can span miles, sometimes using chemical impulses for rapid communication, and researchers are experimenting with mushroom computing.[4] The HBO series echoes this notion of communication when Ellie observes the Infected are "connected." Tess confirms the fungus "grows underground," with "long fibers like wires, some of them stretching over a mile," so that "Now, you step on a patch of Cordyceps in one place, and you can wake a dozen Infected from somewhere else. Now they know where you are. Now they come."

In episode 2, Cordyceps grow around an infected man that Joel has shot, signaling the diseased hoard outside, which surges in to hunt for new hosts. The setting is the Massachusetts State House, a real building in Boston. Boston was the location of one of the first major battles of the American Revolution. So, Boston is a symbol of American independence and contrasts the grotesque fungus that coordinates the Infected into mindless group violence.

Just in case we miss the contrast, there's a second scene in a Boston museum dedicated to the American Revolution. The museum is overrun by fungal growth and the Infected, reflecting long-standing anxieties about collectivist ideologies infiltrating the United States. To drive the point home, a bust of Benjamin Franklin topples when Joel fights the Infected. Before that, the camera sweeps across what may be a fallen sculpture of George Washington, with mushrooms protruding from its head. These images place American independence in opposition to collectivism, which is represented as a disease.

It's after the museum scene that Ellie, Joel, and Tess end up in the Massachusetts State House. The Infected attack, and Tess—who's recently been bitten—blows herself up to prevent the hoard from getting to Joel and Ellie. The Massachusetts State House, a historic symbol of the American way of life—erected shortly after the War of Independence—literally fractures. Still, the mind-rotting fungal collective doesn't win. The episode's last shot affirms the perseverance of America's victory over the collective ideals by showing Ellie standing alone in front of the ruined State House, which implausibly has an American flag waving on its roof, though the apocalypse is into its twentieth year.

Don't Tread on Me!

In the HBO version of *The Last of Us*, most characters are morally ambiguous, if not irredeemably bad. However, some characters, like Bill, are depicted as good without qualification. Bill, who embraces an individualistic libertarian philosophy, never kills innocent people, or tortures anyone for information, or eats those he captures.

In the United States, libertarianism traces to the Founding Fathers. But their views were possibly shaped by Indigenous Americans and definitely by Chinese ideas.[5] The libertarianism of the Founding Fathers diverges from today's popularly extolled versions. Though ironic because many Founding Fathers owned slaves, libertarianism prizes individual freedoms on the grounds that we want to do different things, so that the only shared wish is to pursue our individual interests without interference. Libertarians defend negative rights: the idea we're free to do anything that's not unjust, anything that does not interfere with others. Typically, libertarianism leads to a preference for small government because state authorities have historically interfered with freedom. The concern over strong governments is humorously highlighted when Frank complains that Bill lives in "a psycho bunker where 9/11 was an inside job, and the government are all Nazis." Bill screams, "The government *are all* Nazis!" to which Frank concedes, "Well, yeah now, but not then!"

The Gadsden flag, with the motto "Don't Tread on Me," is a libertarian emblem from the American Revolutionary period, and Bill has one in his workshop. Offensive speech doesn't count as treading on rights, but physical harm or theft do, and we're allowed to resist perpetrators. Libertarians also assert that mixing labor with unowned items makes them ours, like gathering apples from unclaimed land or purchasing items with our earnings.

Bill mostly upholds these principles. Instead of stealing, he merely salvages leftovers after the town is abandoned, akin to picking apples from an unowned tree. When he kills, it's because raiders are intent on murdering and robbing him. He's also within his libertarian rights to eliminate the Infected, who are aggressors and no longer people.

In the HBO series, Frank ends up in a hidden pit Bill has dug outside of his fenced perimeter. He's unharmed, and Bill releases him, though initially refusing to provide food. Charity is not mandatory for libertarians, but not releasing somebody who wasn't committing a wrong would be immoral. Bill eventually invites Frank for a meal, and their romantic relationship begins, aligning with libertarianism's support for free sexual expression between consenting adults. Their suicides also fit typical libertarian prescriptions, which see voluntary euthanasia as an individual right.

At the same time, Bill's psycho-bunker mentality contradicts the views of the Founding Fathers. Thomas Paine (1737–1809) extolled the moral teachings of Confucius (c. 551–479 BCE), equating them to those of Jesus,[6] which violate conventional libertarianism by mandating charity.

Thomas Jefferson (1743–1826) also appreciated Confucius's teachings, which Benjamin Franklin (1706–1790) published in the Pennsylvania Gazette.[7] Although Confucius's push for meritocracy fits libertarianism, his elevation of social goods over individual ones doesn't. And neither does Jefferson's mirroring proposal that university education be provided "at the common expense of all."[8] The reason is that today's libertarians overwhelmingly believe that using tax dollars for social goods like education is forced charity or theft.

John Adams (1735–1826) also stressed "public virtue"[9] and valued Confucian texts. These texts equate "public virtue" to "humaneness" by using a word (*ren*, 仁) that combines the Chinese characters for "person" (人) and "two" (二). Before the outbreak, Bill believed that the presence of more than one person necessitated rights to prevent harm from others. Paradoxically, he could only fulfill his libertarian duties to avoid harm when his community shrank to just one person, and the need for rights vanished.

After all, Frank was outside Bill's fenced area, not attempting burglary or property violation, so his confinement in the hole violates his libertarian rights. Frank additionally could have broken his neck in the pit or been killed by the same flamethrowers the raiders later set off. In short, Bill is only able to *mostly* uphold libertarian principles because he's in an extremely improbable situation that has removed almost all people and because Frank was lucky enough not to die or get injured.

Hunkering in a Psycho Bunker

It's not coincidental that Bill and Frank live in Lincoln, Massachusetts, named after a president celebrated for defending liberty. Lincoln is a five-minute drive from Walden Pond, famous for the cabin Henry David Thoreau (1817–1862) built there. Thoreau later published a book about Walden Pond, along with other writings like the libertarian tract, "Resistance to Civil Government."

Bill's isolation surpasses Thoreau's. *Walden* opens by saying that Thoreau lived but "a mile from any neighbor" in a dwelling he erected "on the shore of Walden Pond, in Concord," a town near Boston.[10] Thoreau and Bill believe we don't have to help others unless we're contributing to their oppression. A difference in their philosophical positions, however, is that Bill sides with libertarians like the contemporary philosopher Jan Narveson, who think it's "happily unusual" that we harm people far away,[11] whereas Thoreau saw it as common. He said the Northern economy supported Southern slavery. Today, he'd see our carbon emissions as harming uncontacted Amazonian tribes. He'd also regard Bill's bunker mentality as delusional because affecting others is unavoidable.

While Bill's bunker mindset conforms to survivalist stereotypes, his refined culinary and musical tastes defy them. Similarly, Thoreau challenges our expectations by bringing ancient Asian books into the woods at Walden. While there, he translated—from the available French—Confucian texts which talk about the interrelation between individuals and society. He cherished the Bhagavad Gita, which equates enlightenment to unity with the cosmos or the divine, a viewpoint echoed in Islamic Sufism. Before going to Walden, he helped publish part of the *Lotus Sutra*, a Chinese Buddhist scripture, highlighting that things are interconnected, akin to the networked fungus in *The Last of Us*, but without the terror. Maybe Thoreau was also exposed to Daoist thinking, where *yin* and *yang* symbolize the unity of contraries, as when presence and void comprise a valley or individual rights only gain meaning in communities.

Like the fungus which spread through contaminated food shipments, these philosophical views circulated along ancient trade routes connecting places such as Asia and Africa. A sub-Saharan perspective that's also found in North Africa is expressed in John Mbiti's (1931–2019) statement: "I am because we are, and since we are, therefore I am."[12] Mbiti suggests that language, morality, cooking, advanced tool use, religion, and other importantly human traits are enculturated. So, we can't realize our humanity in isolation. As Desmond Tutu (1931–2021) declared: "the solitary human being is a contradiction in terms."[13] One similarly finds Indigenous Americans claiming that all things are "animate and interconnected,"[14] a view that usually implies "the collective embodiment of the clanship experiences."[15]

In *The Last of Us*, the characters we root for learn of our deep interconnectedness in a limited way. Love for Sam shapes Henry's identity, and he kills himself when his brother dies. Joel's life revolves around his daughter, Sarah, and he attempted suicide after her death. Ellie becomes a surrogate daughter, and Joel makes increasing sacrifices for her. Bill's life changes when Frank arrives. Later, Frank wishes to die due to an irreversible illness, and Bill respects his choice. Unbeknownst to Frank, Bill adds a fatal dose of sedative to his own wine, saying, "I'm old. I'm satisfied. And you were my purpose."

It's Like a Spaceship

After falling in love with Frank, Bill's perspective shifts from a "world vs. me" mentality to a "world vs. the two of us" mindset. In a suicide note to Joel, Bill reflects, "I used to hate the world, and I was happy when everyone died. But I was wrong because there was one person worth saving. That's what I did. I saved him. Then I protected him." Bill concludes: "That's why men like you and me are here. We have a job to do. And God help any motherfuckers who stand in our way."

In *The Last of Us*, however, there's one attempt to explore the possibility of groups having moral precedence over individuals. It's revealed that Ellie has had Cordyceps in her brain since birth, which produces a chemical signal protecting her from harmful infections. The Fireflies plan to create a vaccine by cutting the fungus from Ellie's brain and killing her. They've kept her sedated and unaware of what's planned to prevent psychological suffering. The Firefly leader, Marlene, insists the procedure must happen for the *collective* good. Joel argues against it, aligning with a rights view that opposes killing Ellie without her consent and treating her as a mere object.

How, it may be asked, do the doctors know for certain they can make a vaccine from Ellie's tissue, despite only having a short time to examine her? Complex brain surgeries occur without death, so why not extract just a small sample, and try not to kill her? Since doctors can't be sure their vaccine will succeed, more so since they're working with extremely limited post-apocalyptic resources, wouldn't the more responsible and less hubristic course be to keep her alive for further study? And finally, why must she die within hours of arriving at the Firefly headquarters with almost no discussion?

The scenario in *The Last of Us* is so divorced from plausible reality that it's "like a spaceship," as Ellie says the first time that she's in an automobile. The situation mirrors objections that philosophy professors sometimes raise against utilitarianism, an ethical theory that considers actions good if they enhance collective well-being. Critics have presented fictional cases of slaves being happier, but the philosopher Richard Hare (1919–2002) responds that these imagined scenarios aren't relevant to the actual world. After all, if a society can ensure the contentment of slaves, it can surely make people even happier by abolishing the institution.[16]

Non-Western philosophies, like those found in China, favor compromise over binary choices. Responsible doctors would start extracting a sample of the fungus from Ellie's brain and work with that, rather than destroy their only source for study and murder a child. This course of action would show some respect to individual rights and simultaneously maximize chances of collective well-being.

Mind Infections

The Last of Us has one seemingly acceptable collective: the Jackson Community. However, Maria and Tommy disagree about whether their community is communist in structure. It's likely that Tommy's right because there's no state ownership or nationwide central government. The community, which has an American flag draped on its main street, is comprised of rugged individuals riding horses in frontier landscapes and toting guns. Jackson is also depicted as largely self-sufficient, so it's about as communist as *Little House on the Prairie* or *Davy Crockett*.

Though the Jackson Community isn't communist, it's a successful collective. Nonetheless it's outnumbered by at least four bad collectives: FEDRA, the Fireflies, the Kansas City Resistance, and David's cult. So, the primary depiction throughout *The Last of Us* is that collectives are usually bad.

The opening credits amplify the message. The sequence features eerie music and visuals of fungus taking over, growing into shapes that resemble city skylines, a decaying human head, and a map of the United States that stops at the Canadian border, hinting at the series' populist American-centric alignment. The credits end with silhouettes of Joel and Ellie surrounded by creeping fungi, all reminiscent of the 1950s communist paranoia since the disease pulls victims into a hive with no individuals.

Communist paranoia wasn't just about economic and political takeover of the American state and capitalist economy, but also a fear of ideas infecting American minds. Similarly, *The Last of Us* isn't a simple story of fungus-driven zombification; it's a tale that explores the mindlessness that arises from the contagion of ideas. The fungal-like spread of ideas parallels the contemporary evolutionary biologist Richard Dawkins's meme theory, which suggests that cultural elements, like beliefs, transmit between brains like viruses, regardless of their truth or usefulness.[17] Cult leaders like David equate blind loyalty to virtue, discouraging critical thinking. Dissenters face punishment in this world and probably the next, which promotes belief retention and spread as well as the surrendering of individual will to a higher authority.

To be fair, characters outside of collectives "lose" their minds sometimes. Joel has a flashback of a soldier shooting his daughter when a FEDRA guard points a gun at Ellie. This flashback leads him to uncontrollably beat and kill the man, even after he's helpless. But given the situation, most of us probably find his actions understandable, even if we believe he goes too far. Later, when Joel assaults the Fireflies to save Ellie, the haunting music, shots of the dead, and needless killing of wounded are clearly intended to express moral ambiguity. However, we're emotionally attached to Joel and Ellie, and barely acquainted with those getting slaughtered because of their idiotic scheme, so we're unlikely to root for the Firefly collective. Usually it's even more one-sided, as when Joel kills murderous members of the Kansas City Resistance. Most of the collective gets massacred because Kathleen, the leader of the resistance, fixates on killing Henry, while ignoring the zombie threat. In the resistance group, everyone falls into groupthink, obeying Kathleen's stupidly reckless orders.

The representation of collectives as a fungal disease indicates their undesirability and reiterates their foolishness. Their ignorance is explicitly stated when Joel denies Ellie's request for a fire on a cold night, and she wants to know whether it's because the Infected will see the smoke. Joel retorts, "Fungus isn't that smart," and intimates that he's worried about people.

Minding Interconnections

Although Confucianism includes elements Thoreau would disapprove of, such as the use of rituals to establish social harmony and prescribed roles in hierarchies, it doesn't imply the dissolution of individuals within collectives. Confucian philosophers even criticized governing through "coercive regulations"[18] and regard death as better than unworthy actions.[19] Thoreau agreed, stating *cost what it may,* a person shouldn't "resign his conscience to the legislator."[20] But harsh rules encourage just that. In the United States, however, Thoreau said that people "are commonly esteemed good citizens" for acting "as machines" with "no free exercise of the moral sense."[21]

In *The Last of Us*, however, it's primarily in collectives that people lose the free exercise of their moral sense. The Kansas City Resistance succumbs to a mob mentality, cheering as FEDRA prisoners are brutally executed. And neither Marlene, nor her soldiers, nor the medical team, question the wisdom of murdering the only immune person, who incidentally is a child. Bill at least weighs things and changes his mind to invite Frank in for a meal.

Despite the prevalent criticisms of collectives in *The Last of Us*, there are also criticisms of conventional libertarian arrangements. The fungal outbreak resulted from capitalist machinery supported by libertarians like Narveson, who argue that unrestricted food pricing will solve world hunger.[22] In the HBO series, Joel speculates that the fungus mutated and got into ingredients like flour and sugar, which are widely found in industrially processed foods. Most people got sick, but the fact that he ran out of pancake mix, the neighbors made raisin cookies instead of chocolate chip cookies, and that Joel forgot the birthday cake, spared him and his daughter.

The link between the outbreak and free capitalist exchange reminds us that, despite *The Last of Us*'s general emphasis on individuals over collectives, it's wise to acknowledge interconnectedness. The Chinese Buddhist luminary, Fazang (643–712), claimed that "one is all" and "all is one."[23] Using an architectural analogy, Fazang said that "the rafter is the building" and "the building is the rafter,"[24] suggesting the two define and make one another what they are, similar to how individual rights only make sense in the context of shared community existence. Though Thoreau didn't go as far as Fazang, he recognized and agreed that things are intertwined and that interconnectedness averts disasters, such as the one that occurs in the *Last of Us*. Thoreau's observation means appreciating that humans can't act without impacting the world. And that's the reason why they can't avoid affecting (and infecting) one another.

Notes

1. Matthew Crippen, "Enactive Pragmatism and Ecological Psychology," *Frontiers in Psychology* 11 (2020), 538644.
2. Matthew Crippen and Dag Lindemann, "Selective Permeability, Multiculturalism and Affordances in Education," *Philosophical Psychology* (2023, online first).

3. Matthew Crippen, "Africapitalism, Ubuntu and Sustainability," *Environmental Ethics* 43 (2021), 235–259; Matthew Crippen, "Chinese Thought and Transcendentalism: Ecology, Place and Conservative Radicalism," *Religions* 14 (2023), 570; Matthew Crippen, "Psychological Expanses of *Dune*: Indigenous Philosophy, Americana, and Existentialism," in Kevin Decker ed., *Dune and Philosophy* (Oxford: Wiley Blackwell), 108–118; Dave Wang, *China and the Founding of the United States: The Influence of Traditional Chinese Civilization* (London: Lexington, 2021).

4. Merlin Sheldrake, *Entangled Life* (New York: Random House), intr., chap. 1, chap. 2, chap. 4.

5. Charles Mann, *1491: New Revelations of the Americas before Columbus* (New York: Knopf, 2005), 278; Wang, *China and the Founding of the United States*.

6. Thomas Paine, *The Age of Reason* (London: Freethought, 1880), 10.

7. Wang, *China and the Founding of the United States*, chap. 1.

8. Thomas Jefferson, "A Bill for the More General Diffusion of Knowledge, 18 June 1779," at https://founders.archives.gov/documents/Jefferson/01-02-02-0132-0004-0079.

9. John Adams, "John Adams to Mercy Warren, 16 April 1776," in *Warren–Adams Letters* (Boston: Massachusetts Historical Society, 1925), 222.

10. Henry David Thoreau, *Walden* (1854) (Princeton, NJ: Princeton University Press, 2004), 4.

11. Jan Narveson, *Moral Matters*, 2nd ed. (Peterborough, ON: Broadview Press, 1999), 143.

12. John Mbiti, *African Religions and Philosophy* (Garden City, NY: Anchor Books, 1970), 152.

13. Desmond Tutu, *God Is Not a Christian and Other Provocations* (New York: HarperCollins, 2011), 21.

14. Anne Waters, "Introduction," in Anne Waters ed., *American Indian Thought* (Oxford: Blackwell, 2004), xxvi.

15. Ted Jojola, "Notes on Identity, Time, Space, and Place," in Waters ed., *American Indian Thought*, 92.

16. Richard Hare, "What Is Wrong with Slavery," *Philosophy and Public Affairs* 8 (1979), 103–121.

17. Richard Dawkins, *The Selfish Gene* (Oxford: Oxford University Press, 1976), 206–212.

18. *Confucius Analects*, trans. Edward Slingerland (Indianapolis: Hackett, 2003), 2.3.

19. *The Mencius*, trans. Irene Bloom (New York: Columbia University Press, 2009), 6A10.

20. Henry David Thoreau, "Resistance to Civil Government," in Elizabeth Peabody ed., *Aesthetic Papers* (New York: G.P. Putman, 1849), 190–193.

21. Thoreau, "Resistance," 191.

22. Narveson, *Moral Matters*, 154.

23. Fazang, "Essay on the Golden Lion," trans. Bryan Van Norden, in Justin Tiwald and Bryan Van Norden eds., *Readings in Later Chinese Philosophy: Han to the 20th Century* (Indianapolis: Hackett, 2014), 88.

24. Fazang, "The Rafter Dialogue," trans. David Elstein, in Tiwald and Van Norden eds., *Readings in Later Chinese Philosophy*, 82–83.

PART V
THE HUMANITY OF
THE LAST OF US

18

Better to Be Socrates Dissatisfied Than an Infected Satisfied?

Happiness, Flourishing, and the Good Life in *The Last of Us*

Steve Bein

Life in the Quarantine Zone (QZ) is pretty grim. The best you can say for it, really, is that life as a raider looks harder. It may not be solitary, but to crib from Thomas Hobbes, it's still poor, nasty, brutish, and short. Honestly, the best thing raider life has going for it is that, by comparison, being the zombified puppet of a mindless fungus seems even worse. But how sure of that can we really be?

Think about it. Fungi aren't complex enough to experience pleasure or pain. So there's a big difference between being a Runner (knowing you've contracted Cordyceps, but not yet feeling its effects) and being a full-blown Infected (completely under Cordyceps's control). The former is so bad that people who are otherwise sane prefer death. (Think of Anna, Ellie's mom, asking Marlene to kill her, or Marlene being willing to go through with it.) Being infected is dangerous to the uninfected, but how bad is it for the Infected themselves? Once Cordyceps takes over, your brain is offline, so ... congratulations? No more bad days for you.

Of course, you get no good days either. Which is better, to live a life with no experiences at all, or to live a life where the bad days outnumber the good ones? Does it matter if you can imagine being happy again? What if you can imagine being happy again, but you know you'll never get there?

On the other hand, maybe happiness isn't even the thing we should be striving for. Socrates could have said the unhappy life isn't worth living, but no, he said the *unexamined* life isn't worth living. What if a good life isn't measured in terms of how *happy* you are, but rather how *content* you are? Or how *powerful* you are? Or how *free* you are? Philosophers have been asking questions like these for a long time. *The Last of Us* twists those questions into new and interesting shapes. But it asks a novel question too: if it's possible to lead a life worth living even in the fungal apocalypse (which seems to be true; just look at Bill and Frank), then why do so many of us struggle with that in the real world?

Knock Knock, Anybody Home?

The *Zhuangzi*, one of the two foundational texts of classical Daoism,[1] has a story of two men standing on a bridge watching the fish in the Hao river. The first guy, Zhuangzi, looks down and says, "Don't they look happy?" His friend, a logician named Huizi, says, "You're not a fish. How do you know they're happy?" To which Zhuangzi replies, "You're not me. How do you know I don't know they're happy?" We can extend Zhuangzi's reasoning to the Infected: Do we *know* they're worse off than we are?

It's possible that they're neither happy nor unhappy, because they're what philosophers call a *zombie*. (Yes, that's really a technical term.) Philosophically speaking, zombies trace their roots back to a lovely little essay by the contemporary American philosopher Thomas Nagel, who asked the question, "What is it like to be a bat?"[2] Nagel said if you're trapped in a room with a bat who's trying to get out, you are in the presence of a truly alien mind. (Chapter 16 in this volume takes a deeper dive into Nagel and zombies, so I won't retread the same ground here.)

For present purposes, I'll just say being trapped in a room with a Clicker is not only more dangerous than being trapped with a bat, but also more philosophically complex. Is a clicker more like a *bat* or a bat's *ear*? Sometimes the Infected are described like sensory organs for Cordyceps— that is, not conscious beings at all, but more like motion sensors. The lights are on, but nobody's home. And that points to a crucial distinction between being a Clicker and being a bat: it's hard to imagine a Clicker being happy.

Of Unhappy Philosophers and Happy Pigs

The British philosopher, Jeremy Bentham (1748–1832) said, "it is the greatest happiness of the greatest number that is the measure of right and wrong."[3] Bentham is a founding father of *utilitarianism*, an enormously popular moral theory today. When Marlene shoots Anne, or when Tess waits until she's surrounded by the infected to blow herself up, they're acting on utilitarian reasoning. Usually their actions would be morally wrong, because usually it creates more harm than good to shoot sick people or to blow yourself up. But in their specific circumstances, these women try to maximize happiness for the greatest number by making the world a safer place for the uninfected.

That said, utilitarianism has its critics. One abiding counterargument is that you can use "the greater good" argument to justify all sorts of atrocious behavior. FEDRA violates human rights willy-nilly in the name of the greater good. In response, the Fireflies commit atrocity after atrocity in the name of toppling FEDRA. And why get rid of FEDRA? For the greater good.

Bentham's utilitarianism faced a counterargument in-house too, from another founding father of the movement. Bentham's successor, fellow Londoner John Stuart Mill (1806–1873), said we should promote not just the *most* good but also the best *kind* of good. In other words, Mill said it's not just the *quantity* of happiness that matters but also its *quality*. "Better to be a man dissatisfied than a pig satisfied," he said, "better to be Socrates dissatisfied than a fool satisfied."[4] So even if a Cordyceps infection felt like ecstasy, you should instead prefer higher-quality pleasures. (For example, you could take a leaf from Ellie's book and afflict the people around you with terrible puns.)

Despite objections like these, utilitarianism has shown remarkable staying power among philosophers and ethicists. After all, Bentham and Mill would ask, what else *should* FEDRA or the Fireflies be promoting, if not the greater good? Well, the German philosopher Friedrich Nietzsche (1844–1900) has an answer.

The Struggle Is Real

You've probably heard one of Nietzsche's most famous quotations: "That which does not kill me makes me stronger." He's got another zinger for the utilitarians: "Man does not seek happiness. Only the Englishman does that."[5] Nietzsche suffered from some pretty dramatic physical and psychological ailments, and they taught him there's more to life than just having a good time.

To Nietzsche, the greatest good isn't happiness. It's actually closer to "endure and survive." In *The Last of Us*, his philosophy is best exemplified by Bill, the paranoid doomsday prepper. In building his impenetrable compound, Bill exerts what Nietzsche calls the *will to power*. For Bill, happiness is just a byproduct of the real highest good: living and dying on his own terms. He wants to be in the driver's seat, not just a passenger in life.[6]

But is this kind of freedom enough to be the greatest good? Confucius (551–479 BCE) and Aristotle (384–322 BCE) would say Bill was pretty dysfunctional before Frank showed up. Confucius and Aristotle believed human beings are fundamentally social creatures ("political animals," to use Aristotle's term). Therefore, as long as Bill walled himself off from the rest of the world, he didn't lead a fully human life. Only by letting Frank into his community (and heart) did he regain his humanity.

Nevertheless, Nietzsche is surely onto something. To return to the earlier comparison between the Clicker and the bat, it's hard to imagine a Clicker being happy. But this isn't the case with a bat. We can imagine a happy bat, but there's still the deeper question: Is happiness the highest good for a bat? Picture a healthy bat, strong, fast, and cunning. Fleeing the bat is the world's juiciest, most delicious moth. The bat *almost* gets its teeth on the bugger, but at the last moment, the moth zigs and the bat zags. A simple utilitarian analysis says that's one frustrated bat—loads of energy wasted and no dinner as a reward. But a Nietzschean analysis would say—and Bill would likely agree—that this is a bat living its best life. The best prizefighters in the world want a worthy opponent, not an easy meal.

The ancient Greeks had a word for this pursuit of a valuable existence, one that Nietzsche and Bill would appreciate: *agon*, the agonizing joy of struggle. Aristotle's mentor, Plato (427–347 BCE), understood the value of *agon*.[7] He was the original UFC fighter, a champion in a martial art whose only rules were no biting and no eye-gouging.[8] Plato wrote his philosophy as a series of dialogues—verbal sparring matches—and sometimes set them in a gymnasium or other athletic setting, probably to emphasize the importance of struggle. Both Plato and Aristotle think there's a goal higher than the greatest good for the greatest number, and *agon* is a necessary part of it.

Being Happy and Living Well

I'll throw one more ancient Greek word at you: *eudaimonia*. This is mistakenly translated as "happiness," better translated as "flourishing" or "living well." That's because you can imagine a bat that's flourishing, but unhappy. (Say, the healthy but momentarily frustrated bat that *almost* caught the yummy moth.) You can imagine the reverse, too: a bat that's happy but not flourishing. (Say, a caged bat dosed with a teensy tiny amount of opium.)

Personally, I can't imagine what it would be like for a Clicker to flourish. They're not like bats, which can eat only so much before they get full. Clickers never get full because Clickers aren't even hungry. They're just looking to spread their infection. There is no *enough* for them, therefore no rest, no satisfaction, no condition they can meet where they—like you, me, or the bats—can put their feet up and call it a day.

A Clicker can perform its function well. Other mindless things can perform their functions too. Plant a bunch of apple trees in the right conditions and they'll produce truckloads of apples, just like a Clicker in the right conditions will spread Cordyceps like wildfire. But an orchard doesn't *flourish* in the way a bat can flourish, because trees don't do much other than sit there and grow. Bats flourish because they're *active*, and human flourishing is an even higher standard because our activities are so numerous.

Consider Jackson, Wyoming, where people do more than just endure and survive. They've created a lifestyle where residents have time to take on interesting challenges. They create art, try new things in the kitchen, and establish a government based on intangible principles like justice and fairness. These principles matter a lot to Aristotle. For him, flourishing is a *moral* ideal, achievable only by communities of morally good people. (For more on how communities are essential to goodness for Aristotle, see Chapter 12.)

Living in Jackson is still a hard life full of struggle. But Jackson is as close to a flourishing human society as anything we see in the apocalyptic world of *The Last of Us*. It meets Confucius's and Aristotle's requirement of social connectedness. It's not bad by utilitarian standards either; Tommy's not wrong when he tells Joel and Ellie they'll be happier there. Perhaps that's because Jackson's government does better than FEDRA when it comes to Nietzsche's standard: FEDRA is too controlling, while Jackson transfers more of that control to the citizens themselves.

But the people of Jackson *aren't* free. They can't come and go as they please. They can't opt out of contributing to the well-being of the commune. Honestly, the best we can say for them is they're as free as they can afford to be and still be safe from all their existential threats. Fear still governs their lives. Jackson isn't bad, but can humanity do better?

Keep Calm and Carry On

Siddhartha Gautama (563–483 BCE), better known as the Buddha, said the highest goal isn't happiness or even flourishing. He said we should seek equanimity.[9]

Happiness leaves a lot to be desired as an end goal. It's notoriously short-lived, for one thing. For another, we're pretty bad at judging what makes us happy. In fact, we may have *evolved to be bad at it*. Being happy doesn't help you pass on your genes—or if it does, it's not nearly as helpful as being anxious, suspicious, fearful, worried about the future, troubled by having limited resources, or dissatisfied with having just enough to get by.[10] So despite all the effort people devoted to make Jackson a safe, flourishing commune, it won't be long before they think it's not good enough.

If you doubt it, consider how unhappy so many of us are in the real world, with no mind-controlling fungi to worry about. As I write this, I am surrounded by angry people. They're upset because we aren't flying to Ireland today. Something broke on the plane and the airline can't get a new part here until later tonight. So, best-case scenario, we fly out early tomorrow morning. Second best, we take the next scheduled flight, which is tomorrow night. If you were supposed to be on this flight, how upset would you be?

It wouldn't bother Joel and Ellie. In their world, Ireland is a place you'd *sail* to. Getting there would take weeks. Imagine their reaction if I complained to them that, instead of crossing the entire Atlantic Ocean overnight, I'm "trapped" in an air-conditioned paradise with running water and plenty of food. Yet here I am, surrounded by angry, miserable people.

The Buddha tried to get to the bottom of the mystery of why suffering seems to be our natural state. You've already seen an evolutionary answer to that, but the Buddha was no scientist. He said it's all about setting expectations. When we expect things to turn out one way, we set ourselves up for disappointment. It's far better to suspend judgment, he thought, suspend expectation, and live in the present moment.[11] If we can do that, we'll see the right reaction isn't frustration when our flight gets canceled. We'd do better to react with acceptance (hey, no one *guaranteed* an on-time departure), or gratitude (hey, isn't it great they found the broken part *before* we took off?), or even compassion (hey, now that I'm not taking out my frustration on airline personnel, what can I do to relieve the suffering of all these angry passengers?).

Left to our own devices, we're bad at understanding what's dangerous to us and what makes us happy. Meditate deeply enough, the Buddha says, and we may discover the real threat to our continued well-being is our incessant attempts to be happy.

It's Not a Race—But Who Won?

So, who's living the best life in *The Last of Us*? One way to tell is to ask yourself, if you were forced to join a group in that universe, which population would you choose? Surely not the Infected, who may well be mindless. Even if they have minds, they can't exert their own will to power, they can't flourish, they can't seek equanimity in the present moment, and they sure don't seem happy.

Not the raiders either, I suspect. None of the Greeks who pondered *eudaimonia* concluded that a fundamental part of it is mugging other people and taking their stuff. Raiders fail the utilitarian test too: they inflict pain to get their pleasure. Whatever enjoyment they get from the loot they plunder, the original owners would probably have gotten similar enjoyment. And even Nietzsche would say raiders exert *force*, not *power*.[12] The Buddha would surmise it's probably the raiders' own suffering that drives them to cause greater suffering. These people haven't yet found equanimity.

The award for Best Life probably doesn't go to the QZ. FEDRA keeps making the same mistake the raiders make, exerting the will to force, not the will to power. No doubt they think they're trying to do good on utilitarian grounds, trying to maximize overall welfare, but clearly people don't flourish in the QZ like they do in Jackson. Tommy had good reason not to go back.

So the final contenders are Bill and Frank in their compound versus the people of Jackson in their commune. Which group is living the best life?

The answer to that might depend on your politics. Bill and Frank can do whatever they want, whenever they want. Libertarians will say that's the ideal. But Bill and Frank's libertarian commune only sustained two people, and it only sustained them because they were in love. (Lest we forget, Bill's first inclination was to let Frank die in a pit.) Plus, when a community ends in collective suicide, it's pretty hard to call that a good life.

On the opposite end of the political spectrum, socialists will say the government of Jackson chose the better ideal. The good life isn't about doing whatever you want, whenever you want. It's about belonging to a community that takes care of its own, with an eye for the well-being of future generations. But for everyone to benefit, everyone has to contribute. ("From each according to his ability, to each according to his needs," to quote Karl Marx's famous formula.) Jackson's socialist commune was sure to outlive Bill and Frank's libertarian commune, and if it collapses someday, it'll probably be due to someone rebelling against the security protocols.

That, or maybe humanity cures Cordyceps and there's no further need for walled city-states. Fingers crossed!

How to Live *Your* Best Life

The question of how best to live is a timeless one, and philosophers sharply disagree about the answer. But now you have some ideas at your disposal for how to live *your* best life. Maybe what you want is happiness, as the utilitarians recommend. Or maybe you think the Buddha is right and happiness is too fleeting, too unstable to be your life's goal. Maybe you side with Aristotle and Nietzsche, who agree that happiness is too low a standard for the good life. While Nietzsche says you ought to want to sit in the driver's seat, Aristotle and Confucius say this kind of freedom and control is pointless unless you've got other good people with you on the road trip. The choice is yours.

Notes

1. The other is the *Daodejing*.
2. Thomas Nagel, "What Is It Like to Be a Bat?" *The Philosophical Review* 83 (1974), 435–450.
3. Jeremy Bentham, *The Collected Works of Jeremy Bentham*, vol. 2, ed. J.H. Burns et al. (London: University College London Press, 1977), 393.
4. John Stuart Mill, *On Liberty and Utilitarianism* (London: Bantam, 1993), 148.
5. Friedrich Nietzsche, "Maxims and Arrows," in *Götzen-Dämmerung* (*Twilight of the Idols*) (Frankfurt am Main: Outlook Verlag, 2018), 12. The translation is mine.
6. There are deeper, more nuanced interpretations of the will to power. My favorite comes from the contemporary Scottish philosopher, Graham Parkes, who says it's not a matter of personal willpower at all, but rather "the matrix of forces that animate all sentient beings" (Graham Parkes, "Nietzsche and Zen Master Hakuin on the Roles of Emotion and Passion," in Joel Marks and Roger T.

Ames eds., *Emotions in Asian Thought* (Albany: SUNY Press, 1994), 227).
That means Bill, FEDRA, the Fireflies, and even the Cordyceps are all exemplars of the will to power. But that's a deeper cut than I can get into here.

7. Scholars disagree on the exact dates of his birth and death. He was probably born in 428 or 427 BCE, and probably died in 348 or 347 BCE.

8. Fun fact: Plato was a martial artist and Bruce Lee was a philosophy major. A coincidence? I think not.

9. Scholars agree his dates are a guess. They may be off by as much as a century.

10. For an extended (if somewhat depressing) argument in support of this thesis, see Rafa Euba, *You Are Not Meant to Be Happy, So Stop Trying!* (Queenstown: Crux Publishing, 2021).

11. This, of course, is a massive oversimplification of a philosophy that's quite complex. If you want a deeper dive, but still through the lens of pop culture, see my "Zen and the Art of Imagineering: Disney's Escapism vs. Buddhism's Liberation," in Richard Davis ed., *Disney and Philosophy* (Hoboken, NJ: Wiley Blackwell, 2019), 25–34, or my "Ode to Joi" in Robin Bunce and Trip McCrossin eds., *Blade Runner 2049 and Philosophy* (Chicago: Open Court, 2019, 59–65). Or, if you prefer a more scholarly but still readable overview, see Walpola Rahula's very accessible *What the Buddha Taught* (New York: Grove Press, 1974).

12. That's *Kraft*, not *Macht*, if you want the original German. Think of the difference between opening a safe with dynamite (force) instead of the correct combination (power).

19

Aesthetics at the End of the World
Uncanny Objects in *The Last of Us*

Enea Bianchi

All the promises at sundown,
I meant them like the rest …
—Ellie's Journal in *The Last of Us Part II*, Packing Up, Jackson

Ruins are everywhere in Seattle. The remains of a once-thriving metropolis have been eroded by the passage of time. Blue sky filters between the floors of skyscrapers that have been destroyed by bombs. Vegetation blown by the wind covers the roads. Reinforced concrete pillars, symbols of the capitalist urban expansion of the twentieth century, weakly support highways littered with the remains of cars, vans, and tanks. Ellie carries a broken watch that only serves to remind her of an unfortunate past—first Sarah's death, then Joel's. Everything bears the marks of trauma.

What is left of beauty in this world? Can beauty still be appreciated when what remains is fragmented and shapeless? As we'll see, the key to an aesthetic appreciation of *The Last of Us* centers not on beauty but on the uncanny.

Aesthetic Experience in a Decaying World

Aesthetics is the branch of philosophy that addresses beauty and related topics. The Greeks developed an enduring and influential theory regarding beauty, which is often referred to as "classical."[1] According to this theory, beauty is based on numerical and geometric relationships. Artists believed they could apply and reveal the laws governing nature in their creations, portraying the timeless essence of things, their unchanging properties and characteristics, rather than appearances and accidents.

In works such as *Discobolus* by the Greek artist, Myron, real-life imperfections are absent; instead, idealized human forms are sculpted. Beauty was considered independent of the observer. Indeed, beauty was a quality

The Last of Us and Philosophy: Look for the Light, First Edition.
Edited by Charles Joshua Horn.
© 2025 John Wiley & Sons, Inc. Published 2025 by John Wiley & Sons, Inc.

inherent to objects, and it was determined by the qualities exhibited by those objects. Order and proportion were considered beautiful and useful, while disorder and disproportion were thought to be ugly and useless.

Does any of this apply to *The Last of Us*? Well, if you google "Beauty and The Last of Us," videos, photos, and artworks appear, in which beauty is associated with post-apocalyptic ruins.[2] Instead of the classical ideal, *The Last of Us* portrays a different kind of aesthetics, connected to subjectivity.

With the Renaissance and the Baroque, the theory of beauty increasingly involved the artist's free expression, as well as the aesthetic reaction of the observer. In doing so, beauty slowly started to be perceived as a more relative and relational concept; it became more subjective, dependent on the aesthetic experience of the subject.

The search for beauty, in other words, shifted toward specific qualities within the observer's mind, such as their imagination, expression, and taste. For instance, something may be overwhelmingly sublime, evoking powerful emotions of terror and rapture, without necessarily being beautiful in the classical sense.

Neither the classical concept of beauty, nor the sublime—two corner-stones of traditional aesthetics—play pivotal roles in *The Last of Us*, which can be seen as an aesthetic representation of, and at, the end of the world. Throughout the video game narrative (but also in the series), nothing adheres to classical proportions; everything appears torn, shattered, and disfigured.

The visual disarray and the portrayal of the Infected—deformed and grotesque inside and out—starkly contrast with the canonical ideal of beauty. While the player's experience often features moments that could be described as aesthetic in a traditional sense—characterized by the melancholic contemplation of ruins and nostalgia for the past, often accompanied by Gustavo Santaolalla's evocative music—we shouldn't forget that the player's aesthetic experience occurs in the comfort of their home.

Sitting in front of our screens, we are moved by sublimity and boundless landscapes. Yet, this experience remains possible only if the sublime emerges when the magnitude of nature—compared to human insignificance—is observed at a distance, detached, with a disinterested attitude. For example, a storm at sea is sublime when seen from the safety of a lighthouse. If witnessed from a boat while we were in the direct path of peril, the experience would lose its aesthetic value, as fear and anxiety would override it.

Let's place ourselves in the shoes of Ellie, Joel, or Abby who are enduring extreme cold, inadequate sustenance, imminent danger, uncertainty of purpose, and emotional and relational desolation. In such a state of constant risk and ambiguity, the disposition and psychological distance needed to have an aesthetic experience of the sublime becomes difficult to attain. This departure from traditional aesthetic norms aligns with the video game's overarching theme of desolation and decay, and it paves the way for an aesthetic experience rooted in the notion of the uncanny.

Uncanny Forces

Sigmund Freud (1856–1939) introduced the concept of the "uncanny" (*Unheimliche*) to psychoanalytic theory, broadening the field of aesthetics by introducing the place occupied by ambivalent, negative, and more obscure phenomena.[3] The feeling of the uncanny emerges from impure, accidental, and displacing elements, as opposed to reconciling states where harmony and unity are central.

Traditional aesthetics pacify the gaze, while the aesthetics of the uncanny expose hidden and marginalized feelings. Literally translated, *Unheimliche* means "not familiar." *Heimlich* derives from *Heim*, meaning "home" and "family," but also "secrecy." The uncanny conveys both the familiar and the unfamiliar, evoking something known and secretive at the same time. It characterizes "all that should remain secret, hidden, but instead rises to the surface."[4]

The uncanny also represents confusion, where an object appears animate but is inanimate, and vice versa—the blurring of lines between life and death, or organic and inorganic. In *The Last of Us*, familiar environmental elements like trees, rivers, houses, streets, and people undergo an uncanny process: cars are wrecked, planes have been downed, buildings have collapsed, figures—human and infected—wander without purpose.

The tranquility one might expect in a deserted and decaying city is ruptured, punctured, and violated by the inescapable presence of this uncanny force. As a result, what initially appears as a placid atmosphere is transformed into a landscape bearing the scars of both physical and psychological upheaval, a vivid reminder of past order that has been irrevocably shattered.

The phenomenon of the uncanny informs *The Last of Us*, both in its gameplay and narrative. As players we have to continuously come to terms with a ruined world characterized by cities ravaged by floods, fires, and bombings, and we have to adapt our gameplay style to this kind of world. How can we cross a road that no longer exists? How do we descend from a building in which the stairs continually lead into dead ends filled with debris? *The Last of Us* allows the player to experience alternative forms of exploration on foot, within cities where we feel a sense of familiarity, but at the same time feel immensely distant from the everyday reality right before our eyes.[5]

Working with the Broken

Ellie, Joel, and Abby carry items like watches, revolvers, jackets, coins, and guitars—objects that often possess an eerie duality—they almost appear "sick." The Italian writer Alberto Moravia (1907–1990) wrote about the "malady affecting external objects and consisting of a withering process; an almost instantaneous loss of vitality—just as though one saw a flower change in a few seconds from a bud to decay and dust."[6]

Objects in *The Last of Us* often appear to be affected by a malady: the existential and physical catastrophe brought objects to the edge of misery, emptying them of their operational memory, namely their use and instrumentality, but also their communicative networks, and possibility of generating cultural practices. In doing so, "things become anonymous tombs, mass graves of the past."[7]

Consider the countless semi-destroyed buildings the player must traverse: desolate offices, non-operational computers and consoles, silent gyms, empty pools, vacant hotels, D&D games forever frozen on a table. These environments make us feel "at home" in the world—they represent our everyday life. But in *The Last of Us*, these environments undergo a process that renders them uncanny—they appear defamiliarized, as if they have lost a light from within.

Like objects, narratives and cultural practices are also affected by a malady. Consider the conversation between Ellie and Jesse in the bookstore in *The Last of Us Part II* in Seattle on the third day. In the children's section of the library, there are toadstools near the wall dating back to the pre-outbreak period. Jesse says to Ellie, "Pretty messed up, putting fungus in the kid's section," to which Ellie replies, "Mushrooms didn't exactly carry the same meaning back then."

Consider the drawings and thoughts that Ellie keeps in her journal, and the pages and the recordings scattered throughout the video game, frequently discovered in desolate homes alongside corpses. Standard books have become rare, but the world abounds with these fragments, each gradually offering a more in-depth understanding of the surroundings.

Also consider Joel's watch—an ordinary tool that tracks time, but is broken and useless in the context of *The Last of Us*. The watch introduces a temporal short circuit, as it is no longer aligned with rhythms of work and the predictability of the pre-apocalyptic world.[8] It's a watch that no longer tells the time, and yet it's always reminding Joel of the hour of Sarah's death. Significantly, Joel's watch serves to remind in order to forget, allowing life to come back after loss; it embodies absence through the memory of trauma. Although the object's original function vanishes, it leaves behind a mark of the past—a reminder of loss. This absence doesn't bring the characters to the brink of nihilism or desperation; instead, it fosters a meaningful life that connects characters and stories.

Whether it be the personal loss for Ellie and Joel, or the global devastation for other survivors, the past gives meaning that keeps the individual from becoming trapped in mourning and melancholy. Through its uncanny aesthetics, *The Last of Us* suggests that to "endure and survive," one must work with absences and voids, even starting from broken, non-functional, and purposeless objects.

Sarah's scream when she is killed by the soldier, and Joel's final glance at Ellie as Abby smashes his skull with a golf club, are traumatic events that produce terrible tears. Thus, *The Last of Us* concerns how to mend such tears, and how to open ourselves toward the future despite absences.

Uncanny Shadows

Another uncanny element can be found in the house at the end of *The Last of Us Part II*. In *The Farm* chapters, we experience a disquieting sense of (un)familiarity, switching from a fully furnished and happy home to the remnants of its past. Above the couch in the living room hangs a painting depicting a soothing mountain view. However, upon our return with Ellie, the house is empty, and the painting has vanished, leaving only rectangle-shaped residue on the wall. The object itself has dematerialized, yet it has left an indelible mark, a lingering testament to its prior existence. Thus, the imprint signifies the definitive loss of the object while simultaneously commemorating its prior existence.[9] As a result we experience the poignant interplay between absence and memory, where the vanishing object leaves behind a tangible echo of its existence.

In contemplating the loss of objects, one is reminded of the permanent shadows of objects and bodies left by thermal radiation following the bombing of Hiroshima, and the watch that was found, frozen at 8:15, the time of the detonation. Similar to Joel and Ellie's broken watch, the uncanny object becomes a symbolic artifact that encapsulates a kaleidoscope of feelings and experiences, allowing its material form to transcend and become a vessel for memories and a testament to their journey.

A place is truly deserted, *The Last of Us* seems to tell us, only when we believe that we are experiencing it by ourselves and only ourselves. On the contrary, the "other" still lives on through traces and memories, propagated in our habits and the objects we carry with us. Such objects remind us that we can move forward if we understand the world as the living history of the others. Those who came before might be long gone, but thanks to the dissemination of their traces we still can rebuild places—dwelling in, and inhabiting, a deserted world.

Both video games begin with a devastating loss, namely Sarah's death and then Joel's. Both narratives revolve around overcoming loss. While *The Last of Us Part I* is a journey toward hope, from a new "family" bond to the global vaccine, *Part II* is a story of vengeance. However, by allowing us to play as Abby as well as Ellie, the second video game invites us to explore the reasons of the "other." *The Last of Us Part II* makes us experience an uncanny phenomenon—it compels us to find the familiar in the unfamiliar and vice versa, playing with, and against, the same characters.

From this perspective, the shift in the characters we play as is significant. It's an emotionally uncanny experience to traverse the hallway of the

Firefly Lab, where Joel killed the doctors at the end of the first video game, reliving that same hallway in the traumatic memories of Ellie and Abby. A similar shift occurs in the aquarium: from coziness and intimacy, when Abby meets Owen, to the massacre carried out by Ellie. Or again, the theater that provides protection and shelter while playing as Ellie, and then becomes a displacing and disquieting environment when we experience it through Abby's vengeful eyes.

The Last of Us oscillates between individual and collective traumas, encouraging us to reconstruct meaning, bonds, communities, and cultural homelands by welcoming and working with the uncanny.

An Uncanny Aesthetics for an Uncanny World

In *The Last of Us*, familiarity with both urban and natural settings is persistently disrupted by elements beyond the ordinary. This ceaseless barrage of the uncanny shatters our perceptions of the surrounding world, making it apparent that this world is no longer within our command, as we have anthropocentrically believed for millennia. Through the relentless disruption of the real, an air of irreversible trauma is introduced into the narrative. *The Last of Us* introduces a world in which humans no longer sit at the center.

Cordyceps serve as both a turning point and a foundation for an alternative way of thinking and experiencing aesthetics. The Cordyceps aesthetic is uncanny, departing from human-centric definitions and distinctions (beautiful/ugly, harmonious/dissonant). This new aesthetic compels characters—and us, players or spectators—to reinterpret everyday life and to focus on unsettling, broken elements.

The pre-fungal world takes for granted the metaphysical distinction between subjects (those who act) and objects (those who are acted upon). Or, to put the distinction in the language of traditional aesthetics, the pre-fungal world takes for granted the distinction between subjects who decide what should be included or excluded within the notion of beauty and inert objects who merely possess given qualities (or not). The fungus introduces the idea of a world of movement, transmission, and infection. Entities are no longer isolated, but instead exist as temporary outcomes of encounters and networks.

The world in *The Last of Us* seems barren and desolate, especially when explored without human or infected presence.[10] However, this perception stems from an anthropocentric mindset that fails to recognize the countless lives of multiple species operating outside the human standpoint. Landscapes comprise patches, multiple temporalities, and a blend of human and non-human elements.[11] We aren't at the center of the universe, nor are we masters of Earth. As Freud would say, the ego does not reign supreme, not even within our own homes.

For millennia, we have acted as if the surrounding world was available for us to scrutinize, dissect, categorize, manipulate, exploit, and label. Cordyceps show us that we couldn't possibly have been more wrong, challenging us to imagine a world unshackled from human control, intellectual arrogance, and imperialistic justifications. The fungus reveals that our world doesn't need to be saved by humans—it persists regardless, as it persisted throughout the COVID-19 pandemic.

Fully experiencing the catastrophe in *The Last of Us* means feeling at home in the devastation, in the unfamiliar: working with the broken in a broken world.[12]

Notes

1. See Władysław Tatarkiewicz, *Ancient Aesthetics*, trans. Adam and Ann Czerniawski (Paris: Mouton; Warsaw: Polish Scientific Publishers, 1970).
2. On ruins in video games see Mathias Fuchs, "'Ruinensehnsucht'—Longing for Decay in Computer Games," in *Proceedings of the First International Joint Conference of DiGRA and FDG* (2016), at http://www.digra.org/digital-library/publications/ruinensehnsucht-longing-for-decay-in-computer-games; Emma Fraser, "Awakening in Ruins: The Virtual Spectacle of the End of the City in Video Games," *Journal of Gaming and Virtual Worlds* 8, no. 2 (2016), 177–196.
3. Sigmund Freud, *The Uncanny*, trans. David McLintock (London: Penguin Classics, 2003).
4. Mario Perniola, *20th Century Aesthetics*, trans. Massimo Verdicchio (London and New York: Bloomsbury, 2013), 115.
5. On *The Last of Us Part II* as a "postapocalyptic pastoral," see Melissa Kagen, *Wandering Games* (Cambridge, MA: MIT Press, 2022).
6. Alberto Moravia, *Boredom*, trans. Angus Davidson (New York: New York Review of Books, 1999), eBook ed.
7. Ernesto De Martino, *La fine del mondo: Contributo all'analisi delle apocalissi culturali* (Turin: Einaudi, 2002), 564.
8. On the relationship between time and objects in *The Last of Us* see Michael Fuchs, "Is This Really All They Had to Worry About? Past, Present and Future Hauntings in *The Last of Us*," *AAA: Arbeiten aus Anglistik und Amerikanistik* 44, no. 1 (2019), 67–82.
9. Massimo Recalcati, *Il mistero delle cose* (Milan: Feltrinelli, 2016).
10. For an analysis of *The Last of Us* in relationship with Donna Haraway's theory of "tentacular thinking," see Geneveive R. Newman, "Fungal Zombies and Tentacular Thinking: The Chthonic Mother in the Game *The Last of Us*," *Studies in the Fantastic* 7 (2019), 39–50.
11. Anna T. Tsing, *The Mushroom at the End of the World* (Princeton, NJ: Princeton University Press, 2021).
12. I would like to dedicate this chapter to Vittorio Filippo Dinca, Andrea Quintiliani, Emanuele Curcio, Paolo Bangrazi, Alessio Biancalana, Luca Salis, and Roberto Urbani, and to everything that video games have meant to our bond: no distance is unbearable.

20

Meaning and Emotion in the Music of *The Last of Us*

Lance Belluomini

In the first episode, "When You're Lost in the Darkness," Ellie discovers a musical code when she finds a note in *The Billboard Book*. Confirming it, she asks Joel, "The radio's a smuggling code, right? '60's song, they don't have anything new, '70's, they got new stuff. What's '80's?" Eventually, Ellie guesses correctly by telling Joel that Wham's 1984 single "Wake Me Up Before You Go-Go" played while he was sleeping, prompting Joel to lower his head with a worried reaction. Memorably she whispers, "Gotcha. '80's means trouble. Code broken."

The episode ends by cutting to Joel and Tess's apartment room with an ominous shot of the radio, which turns on and plays Depeche Mode's 1987 song "Never Let Me Down Again." The opening drum patterns and distinctive guitar riffs blare as the scene transitions beyond the wall to the crumbling ruins of Boston. Already, music is conveying meaning and imparting emotion to this story about the beautiful and awful things that can emerge from love. In light of the code, "Never Let Me Down Again" creates a dark undertone despite its upbeat sound, evoking feelings of fear and uncertainty for our protagonists, who face trouble ahead, in more ways than one.[1] The lyrics talk about taking a ride and getting high with a best friend, who actually may be the drug—after all, the song's original video shows a man driving alone. But the song's lyrics take on new meaning in the context of *The Last of Us*, foreshadowing Ellie's hope that Joel will never let her down, the ride they will take, and the fact that they will become best friends.

Of course, music doesn't just set a mood or provide a background. Philosophers think music can give meaning to our lives, arouse emotions, produce pleasure, and even cultivate virtue. Indeed, the music of *The Last of Us* does all this and more.

The Last of Us and Philosophy: Look for the Light, First Edition.
Edited by Charles Joshua Horn.
© 2025 John Wiley & Sons, Inc. Published 2025 by John Wiley & Sons, Inc.

"On the Nature of Daylight" by Max Richter

One way the music of *The Last of Us* arouses our emotions is through the pleasure we get from the beauty and clever artistry of the show's musical pieces, encouraging what philosopher Peter Kivy (1934–2017) calls emotions of appreciation (such as amazement).[2] Consider the gorgeous acoustic track, "Haven," by Gustavo Santaolalla, which surfaces in "When You're Lost in the Darkness" as Ellie enters and looks around Tess and Joel's Boston apartment—their "haven." The soothing and calming guitar notes plucked in the arrangement comprise the melody, exuding comfort, eliciting hopeful feelings, while anticipating the tender connection that Ellie and Joel will form along their journey. Notice, however, that it's the elegance of the music itself that arouses awe in us, an emotion of appreciation.

In "Long, Long Time," the powerful orchestral piece that plays for just over three minutes is called "On the Nature of Daylight" by Max Richter. It begins after Frank instructs Bill, "Then love me the way I want you to." As we hear the opening sustained sounds of the cello, we glimpse the charming farm and watch Bill pushing Frank in the wheelchair to the boutique. When the song transitions to the captivating violin melody, we're shown Frank's paint palette and the trap Frank had fallen into, the music and imagery working together to reflect the passage of time. The melody carries on as we witness their marriage and final dinner, replicating the first one they had shared together.

What impacts us most in this sequence isn't the wonderful imagery and fantastic acting performances. Rather, it's the beauty of the well-constructed musical composition itself, arousing a range of feelings in us: love, joy, comfort, sadness, grief, even triumph. We're moved by a combination of musical elements: the sustained musical phrases on the cello, the two-note melodic interval of the violin, and the warmth in the orchestral instrumentation. Unquestionably, it's the well-crafted music that arouses amazement for us, while aesthetically amplifying the emotional sequence and the episode's message: it's possible to give someone all the love you have, even in a dangerous world.

Well-designed music also has the power to establish relationships. Earlier in the episode, when Bill plays the piano and sings the Linda Ronstadt song "Long Long Time" to Frank, it sparks an emotional connection between them. Through the delicate piano melody, his voice, and the song's heart-wrenching lyrics, Bill openly shares his yearning to love someone. In effect, the song establishes Bill and Frank's relationship. *The Last of Us Part II* video game emphasizes this point too. After Joel plays and sings Pearl Jam's "Future Days" to Ellie (a solemn piece that speaks to the kind of father–daughter relationship they share), he gifts the guitar to her, reminding her that he had promised to teach her how to play. Later, Ellie frequently plays the song on guitar to remember Joel. The guitar and song represent the tender side of Ellie, symbolically connecting her to Joel through the medium she uses to wrestle with her feelings about him. Indeed, it's the instrument and well-made music that has helped in furthering their emotional bond. (Much more can be said about the song and the guitar, but we'll leave that for Chapter 21 of this book.)

"Fuel to Fire" by Agnes Obel

The music of *The Last of Us* not only arouses our emotions, it also comforts and pleases us. According to Aristotle (384–322 BCE), when we're emotionally moved by music, it has another benefit: influencing our moral character.[3] In fact, relaxing music leads us to enjoy what Aristotle calls well-ordered and balanced emotions (such as joy). And since relaxing music familiarizes us with balanced movements of emotions, it disposes us toward moral virtue.[4]

At the end of "Endure and Survive," after Joel buries Sam and Henry, he stares down and contemplates what Ellie wrote on the Magic Slate: "I'm sorry." Joel is likely reflecting on what he endured with the loss of his daughter twenty years ago and the dire situation he now faces: this beautiful father–daughter bond he's formed with Ellie and the intense fear he feels in potentially not being able to save her. The emotional connection Joel has with Ellie is evident. He buries Henry and Sam not for himself, but for Ellie, because he cares for her.

Ellie, ready to move on from this tragic event, then says to Joel, "Let's go." As they walk off together, the stunningly beautiful song "Fuel to Fire" by Agnes Obel begins to play. The song's mesmerizing rhythm, calming harmony, and slow-paced melody express a range of feelings. The opening hypnotic piano line has a melancholic quality, creating the feeling of moving on from tragedy (fitting with the sad demise of Henry and Sam). Yet, certain sections provoke perseverance and longing to care for others, characterizing Joel in a nutshell: he's persistent and isn't going to let his fears stop him from caring for Ellie. The alternating piano chords are beautifully complemented by plucked cello strings and Obel's soothing vocals (with layered hums and coos). The result is wonderful harmonies that also elicit joyful and loving feelings, corresponding with the emotions Joel and Ellie are experiencing in their bond. Because the piece imitates and familiarizes us with well-ordered emotions (love and joy), Aristotle would say it disposes us toward virtue; the song steers us toward being more caring, compassionate, and emotionally empathetic.[5]

The lyrics of "Fuel to Fire" perfectly describe Joel's predicament. The song is about taking risks in a relationship full of difficulties, and not letting fear stand in the way. Despite Joel's intense fear, the two words "I'm sorry" on the Magic Slate serve as a reminder of Tess's final words to him, "Save who you can save." They also remind him of Bill's letter stating that there was one person worth saving and protecting: "That's why men like you and me are here. We have a job to do." The Magic Slate words likely trigger these momentary reflections for Joel, supplying fuel to fire in embracing his identity and purpose—to keep persisting, caring, and saving who he can.

Undoubtedly, we are moved by this beautiful song. Most importantly, as mentioned, it familiarizes us with well-ordered emotional movements that direct us toward virtue and good ethical decision making, deepening our aesthetic admiration for the show.

"Never Let Me Down Again" Cover by Jessica Mazin

Aristotle says that music has a mimetic character, meaning that it imitates and arouses emotions in the real world, thereby affecting our behavior, helping us to properly govern our emotions and improve our rationality.[6] Clearly, the ancient Greeks were aware of music's effects. Similarly, the showrunners of *The Last of Us* are mindful of music's advantages. The instrumental tracks and pop-culture songs are well placed, transmitting layers of meaning while imitating the appropriate emotions our protagonists are experiencing, thus enabling us to better regulate these emotions in our own lives.

One of the show's best-placed songs is the "Never Let Me Down Again" cover performed by Jessica Mazin. The heartfelt rendition memorably surfaces at the end of "Kin." There's an emotional payoff to it, as earlier Ellie says, "I'm sorry about your daughter, Joel. But I have lost people, too." Joel snaps back, "You have no idea what loss is." To which Ellie exclaims, "Everybody I have cared for has either died or left me. Everybody … except for you!" Ellie reveals that she would be more scared without him, highlighting her greatest fear: ending up alone. In this emotional exchange, Joel lacks the courage to tell Ellie why she would be better off with Tommy: Joel's afraid of her, fearful of caring for someone, and terrified of the thought of trying to save someone and failing again.

At the end of the episode, when Joel falls off the horse, on the verge of death from being stabbed in the gut, Ellie crouches over him, and pleads for him to get up. She cries, saying she can't do this without him, that she doesn't know where she's going, or what she's going to do. Heartbreakingly she whispers, "Joel, please. Joel, please."

This is when Jessica Mazin's delicate acoustic rendition of "Never Let Me Down Again" begins to play. The reintroduction of this song with a female voice not only effectively serves as an echo of Ellie's plea for Joel to get up, but it also heightens the emotions, creates a mournful mood, and arouses tender feelings. Mazin's hauntingly beautiful slowed-down version of the song expresses the sadness, loss, and despair that Ellie is undergoing as she looks down at Joel—this father figure who has let her down again.[7]

Further, the lyrics take on a new meaning. Ellie has been taking a ride and flying high together with Joel (connecting with her best friend), who has taken her to where she wants to be (the Fireflies' base in the effort to find a cure to save humanity). Unfortunately, her hope of him never letting her down again gets shattered.

Aristotle would agree that the song's melody and complementing harmony of pleasant-sounding piano chords, coupled with Mazin's soothing and breathy vocals imitate a blend of emotions that evoke Ellie's feelings of hopelessness and fear. Aristotle would mention the educational value in listening to this piece. We feel comfort because the music imitates these emotional states, enabling us to improve our rationality in governing these feelings during real-life situations. Because the song achieves these things, in addition to injecting further emotion into this powerful scene, it elevates our respect for the show. (It's also poignant to reflect on the father–daughter relationship between the singer and the episode's writer.)

"The Last of Us (Vengeance)" by Gustavo Santaolalla

Beyond the comfort we feel from listening to music, and besides its educational value, Aristotle cites another pleasure we often experience from it: intellectual enjoyment.[8] Intellectual enjoyment from music occurs when we find joy in contemplating the appropriateness of the emotions or feelings imitated by the music. Aristotle states that our delight in sensing aesthetic order (between music's imitation of the feeling and the feeling itself) is fueled by our natural desire to know.[9]

In "Look for the Light," Joel saves Ellie from the Firefly-occupied hospital by killing the people attempting to save humanity. Shortly before Joel's killing spree, he shouts at Marlene, "You take me to her right now!" What follows is a heartbreaking scene, full of sadness and tragedy. Joel's horrifying behavior is driven by his love for Ellie and his parental instinct to protect his new "baby girl." It's Ellie he treasures more than anything else, motivating him to ugly violence.[10] He doesn't even think twice with any of his kills because he no longer cares about anyone else's humanity besides those he loves. His violent actions point to something Maria had warned Ellie about in "Kin" when she said, "Be careful who you put your faith in. The only ones that can betray us, are the ones we trust." Ellie has put her trust in Joel, and he has now betrayed the rest of humanity to save her life, something she wouldn't have agreed with if consulted.

Not to be lost amongst the chaos of the rampage is the sad and mournful music that plays over the scene in the hospital. The track, titled "The Last of Us (Vengeance)" by Santaolalla, is a powerful piece that expresses and arouses sorrowful feelings.[11] The musical cue doesn't glorify Joel's actions. Instead of sounding heroic or triumphant, it reflects the sadness behind Joel's gruesome behavior—massacring Fireflies who have dedicated their lives to saving the human race. As Joel begins to murder these innocent people to reach Ellie, the piece evolves into a slowed-down rendition of the show's main theme, "The Last of Us," carried by cellos and violins in low octaves. It's a grieving melody, containing solemn beats and soaring violin notes that ascend and descend in a higher key, eliciting regretful feelings. The track also expresses this disassociated feeling, corresponding with Joel's frame of mind throughout this sequence. He has disassociated himself from the rest of humanity, displaying a calm and fearless demeanor in his effort to save the person he loves.

The audience experiences intellectual enjoyment in realizing we are being appropriately moved by this musical piece in a way that mirrors the sadness of Joel's ruthless behavior. After all, we sense the aesthetic order between the composition's imitation of sadness and the feeling of sadness. Why, though, do we enjoy listening to music that expresses negative emotional states, such as sadness? Some philosophers have suggested that we can't comprehend the music we're engaging with unless we understand everything it expresses, which includes the negative emotions.[12] In other words, there's a payoff to engaging with a track that evokes negative emotions. The music that plays over Joel's brutal killing spree fills us with a feeling of sadness, but it's the price we pay to both understand the show's music and engage with the other pieces that arouse positive emotions. We don't just endure sad music to arrive at a good outcome, however. We also enjoy the experience of listening to it for some reason.

Aristotle offers an insightful suggestion for why we enjoy listening to music that evokes negative emotional states: his theory of catharsis. On this view, our negative emotional reactions to music (and other art forms) result in a positive psychological purification of the negative emotions.[13] Enduring the negative feelings caused by sad music in *The Last of Us* provides us with a positive psychological benefit—the cathartic experience gives relief from real-world sadness. According to Aristotle, when music imitates the negative emotion of sadness, we're able to safely release and engage with this repressed emotion and thus purify our soul, an experience we enjoy. Some philosophers have expanded on Aristotle's view, arguing that sad music allows us to experience negative emotions divorced from real-world consequences. Many of us get swept up in the sadness expressed in "The Last of Us (Vengeance)," allowing us to engage with sadness—a comforting and enjoyable experience—yet without the stress and anxiety that attend the sad events in our own lives.[14]

"The Last of Us" and "The Path" by Gustavo Santaolalla

The well-crafted instrumental tracks in *The Last of Us* score serve the narrative and move us, but they also arouse certain moods. Jenefer Robinson, a contemporary philosopher, rightly points out that, "Moods differ from emotions in that they are not directed at anything in particular but pervade experience as a whole."[15] Consider "The Last of Us" theme by Santaolalla, featured in the opening credits of each episode, the same iconic main theme featured in *The Last of Us Part I* and *The Last of Us Part II* video games. The piece is a driving force that gives the show and video games a musical identity, conveys the feeling of persisting along a journey, and arouses sad and hopeful moods, reflecting two important themes of the show and video games—grief and hope.

Yet another remarkable track by Santaolalla that arouses moods is "The Path." In the very last scene of season 1, Ellie asks Joel to swear that he is telling the truth about the events at the hospital. With little hesitation, Joel replies, "I swear." After a long pause, Ellie replies, "Okay." The screen then cuts to black and "The Path" begins to play, immediately projecting a mood of sadness, aligning with the sadness of Joel's lie and the sadness of Ellie's acceptance of Joel's lie and betrayal. But the majestic melody also creates a hopeful mood, appropriately imitating Joel and Ellie's hope that things will turn out alright between them. Santaolalla layers several stringed acoustic instruments to create these alternating moods. Much like "The Last of Us" theme, this track's melody and harmony starts in a minor scale, producing deep sounds that deliver sad feelings. It then switches to a major scale, producing tender, innocent, and hopeful sounds. A version of this piece plays in "Kin" during the lovely bonding sequence of Joel and Ellie traveling together on horseback to Colorado. Joel lets her know that, before the outbreak, he was a contractor. After Ellie says, "The contractor. That's pretty cool," we hear the delicate melody and harmony in major scale which captures their tender and sweet exchange. Of course, it's Santaolalla's poignant and intimate sounds that elevate the aesthetics of the scene, intensifying the emotions, while also creating a happy mood.

Clearly, the music of *The Last of Us* is vitally important to the show, arousing moods and emotions and performing a variety of other functions that benefit and delight us. Regrettably, there is no way to cover all the amazing music in the series, but at least we can see its philosophical significance and the ways it enhances our aesthetic appreciation of the show. Joel's comment to Ellie in "Please Hold to My Hand" regarding the Hank Williams cassette tape certainly sums up the music of *The Last of Us*, "It's a winner ..."

Notes

1. There are plenty of other 1980s songs in the show that signal trouble. In "A Long, Long Time," when Ellie and Joel enter Bill's bunker, Erasure's "Chains of Love" faintly plays, referencing the danger awaiting them in Kansas City. In "Endure and Survive" a cover version of the song "True Faith" by New Order performed by Lotte Kesner plays immediately after Joel and Ellie find themselves trapped by Henry and Sam, anticipating their tragic deaths. And in

"Left Behind," the A-ha song "Take On Me" casually plays as Ellie and Riley have fun at the abandoned mall, which includes riding a carousel to The Cure song "True Faith" covered by Rockabye Baby!—both songs signaling the imminent danger they face.

2. Peter Kivy, *Music Alone: Philosophical Reflections on the Purely Musical Experience* (Ithaca, NY: Cornell University Press, 1990).

3. Aristotle, *Politics*, trans. C.D.C. Reeve (Cambridge, MA: Hackett, 2017), chap. 5, 1339b40–1340a15.

4. Aristotle, *Politics*, 1340a16–a19.

5. Aristotle doesn't think that music can touch reason directly. Therefore, music doesn't make one virtuous; it can only provide familiarity with well-ordered emotions that guide us toward virtue.

6. Aristotle, *Politics*, 1340a23, b18–19.

7. Joel has already let Ellie down along their journey. For instance, in "Kin," Ellie feels let down by Joel when she realizes he intends to ditch her because he thinks it would be for her own good.

8. Aristotle, *Politics*, 1339a30–1339a34.

9. Aristotle, *Metaphysics*, trans. Richard Hope (Ann Arbor: University of Michigan Press, 1952), chap. 1, 980a21, chap. 2, 982a19.

10. Ellie has become Joel's purpose (just like Frank became Bill's purpose). Earlier, when Joel lets Ellie know the truth about how he got his scar, she remarks, "So time heals all wounds, I guess." Joel replies, "It wasn't time that did it."

11. A version of this emotional track, composed by Gustavo Santaolalla, also plays during *The Last of Us Part I* when Joel carries Ellie out of the hospital.

12. For more, see Jenefer Robinson, *Deeper Than Reason: Emotion and Its Role in Literature, Music, and Art* (Oxford: Oxford University Press, 2005), 348–378.

13. Aristotle, *Poetics*, trans. Stephen Halliwell (London: Duckworth, 1987), chap. 6, 1449b21–1450b20.

14. To explore this suggestion, see Jerrold Levinson, "Music and Negative Emotion," in Jenefer Robinson ed., *Music and Meaning* (Ithaca, NY: Cornell University Press, 1997), 215–224.

15. Jenefer Robinson, "Emotional Responses to Music: What Are They? How Do They Work? And Are They Relevant to Aesthetic Appreciation?" in Peter Goldie ed., *The Oxford Handbook of Philosophy of Emotion* (Oxford: Oxford University Press, 2010), 661.

21

"Some Folks Call This Thing Here a Gee-Tar"

Music Making, *Duende*, Schopenhauer, and Reconciliation in *The Last of Us Part II*

Per F. Broman

> The blessed end
> of all things eternal,
> do you know how I reached it?
> Deepest suffering of grieving love
> opened my eyes:
> I saw the world end.
>
> —Richard Wagner,
> "The Schopenhauerian
> ending to *Götterdämmerung*"[1]

On the campus of the University of Eastern Colorado in *The Last of Us Part I*, Joel confesses that, as a child, he dreamed of becoming a singer. "Shut up!" Ellie says. She laughs at this surprising tidbit, and then tries to get him to sing something. He declines. Despite having followed a different career path, Joel's music making, both as a singer and guitar player, is important to his identity and for the video game's narrative.

Music plays little role in the narrative of *Part I*. Gustavo Santaolalla's stunning non-diegetic score is featured, of course, and there are musical interactions between Ellie and Riley in *The Last of Us: Left Behind*. But music making and music listening are more prominently featured in *The Last of Us Part II*, and they are critical for the development of the narrative. Music helps characters like Ellie cope with the brutal post-apocalyptic world of *The Last of Us*. And it can also cultivate hate and fuel revenge.

The Last of Us and Philosophy: Look for the Light, First Edition.
Edited by Charles Joshua Horn.
© 2025 John Wiley & Sons, Inc. Published 2025 by John Wiley & Sons, Inc.

Moreover, musical creativity can have a powerful effect, doing more than just diverting our attention away from our own suffering.

The Guitar

Part II's prologue begins with Joel sitting in his chair, cleaning his instrument, revealing the most enduring storyline from *Part I* to Tommy: how he saved Ellie's life at the cost of depriving humanity of a possible vaccine. Shortly thereafter, he begins teaching Ellie to play the guitar, and she becomes quite accomplished. He starts by performing the first verse and chorus of Pearl Jam's song "Future Days," a somewhat sentimental and naive love song that will recur four more times in the video game. It begins: "If I ever were to lose you / I'd surely lose myself / Everything I've found here / I've not found by myself."

Despite Joel not choosing the best key for his voice, he sings a heartfelt rendition. Ellie looks somewhat moved, but with a hint of embarrassment, and states, smiling, when he finishes, "Well … that didn't suck." Ellie would eventually learn the song and internalize it, as she later scribbles down a fragment from the third verse in her notebook, "All the promises at sundown / I meant them like the rest …" below her sketch of an owl—an enigmatic statement, indeed. Clearly, Joel's music making had a significant impact on Ellie.

The guitar is featured in both the first and last frame of *The Last of Us Part II*, and the instrument is played by Joel, Ellie, and Tommy. The guitar manufacturer, Taylor, even made two commercially available models inspired by the game: one replica of Joel's iconic instrument in the Vintage Tobacco Sunburst finish with the characteristic luna-moth fretboard inlay, and one with artwork inspired by Ellie's tattoo that covers her bite mark.

Music making has several functions in the video game, but only plays a role for the people surrounding Ellie and Joel; music doesn't belong to Abby's world. Music enables Ellie to remember and reflect on her previous encounters with Joel. In Seattle's Pinnacle Theater, she finds a guitar and begins to play, leading to the flashback of her birthday excursion three years earlier. A similar flashback occurs at the end of the video game when she plays "Future Days" in the empty farmhouse and reflects back on a memory of being on the porch with Joel.

Music also allows Ellie to connect with Dina. In the music store in Seattle, she finds a guitar and plays a slow, mellow version of the A-ha dance song "Take on Me" for Dina, who sits mesmerized on the floor by her feet. In their farmhouse, right before the Santa Barbara chapter, Ellie plays Crooked Still's "Ain't No Grave" from their bluegrass album, *Shaken by a Low Sound* on a mechanical record player (and the entire B side of the album as long as Ellie stays in the room). The three of them, Dina, Ellie, and JJ, dance together, having a carefree and happy time.

Schopenhauer and the Will

In these scenes, music makes time cease to exist. The thoughts of the gruesome encounters with the paramilitary groups or the Infected stop, and the
characters are given space to contemplate, and to relax, to suspend what
the philosopher Arthur Schopenhauer (1788–1860) called the Will, the most
important concept in his philosophy. He considered the Will to be the
fundamental driving force of human existence and the underlying essence
of the world. According to Schopenhauer, the Will is an irrational, blind, and
insatiable force that compels individuals to act and pursue their desires. The
Will is the ultimate reality behind the appearances we perceive in the world.

Schopenhauer argued that everything we experience, including our own
thoughts and bodies, is a manifestation of the Will. While not inherently
bad, the Will is a ceaseless, constant striving for satisfaction and fulfillment,
which is ultimately unattainable. Furthermore, Schopenhauer believed that
the Will is the source of suffering. He argued that since our desires and
cravings can never be fully satisfied, the Will leads us into a perpetual cycle
of longing and disappointment. (For more on Schopenhauer's philosophical
pessimism, see Chapter 4.)

We see the cycle of longing and disappointment in Ellie's and Abby's
urge for revenge. If they could only eradicate their enemies, they believe,
life would somehow turn out fine. Both discover too late the error in their
thought—their unquenchable thirst for revenge led to Ellie's loss of Dina,
and Abby's loss of Owen. Schopenhauer put this fallacy of misguided striving in poetic terms with the help of Greek mythology, which resonates very
well with the game. Indeed, the intertwining storylines of *The Last of Us
Part II* read like Greek dramas, in which the characters act out their desires
in seemingly predetermined ways, only to suffer the consequences. They're
prisoners caught by their own Will. Not surprisingly, Schopenhauer ranked
tragedy among the highest of the art forms, second only to music.

Music and the Will

Schopenhauer argued that music is a unique art form because it directly
expresses the essence of the Will. Unlike other art forms, such as painting
or literature, which represent real objects and concepts, music represents
the innermost nature of reality itself. According to Schopenhauer, music
bypasses the intellect and appeals directly to the emotions, connecting
individuals with the universal essence of existence. Yet it also provides
intellectual satisfaction through the enjoyment of compositional features.[2]
Schopenhauer became influential for this insight, especially among musi-
cians, including the composer Richard Wagner.

Schopenhauer believed that music allows individuals to transcend their
individuality and merge with the underlying unity of the world. He saw

music as a source of solace and escape from the suffering and strife of everyday life. When we listen to music that we like, we temporarily transcend our individual desires and worries, and experience a state of deep aesthetic contemplation. The suspension of our worries is exactly what Joel has in mind when he tells Ellie in Salt Lake City in *Part I*, "on a day like this, I'd just sit on my porch, pick away at my six-string." It's a wonderful promise of a suspended Will.

Music making is also offered as a break for the gamer. In an otherwise highly structured video game, we're twice invited to pause to practice the guitar in Seattle's Pinnacle Theater. We're given the opportunity to develop our creativity, expanding on the previous opportunities to work on "Future Days," since we can modulate to different keys. The number of YouTube videos featuring covers created in the game suggests that this is a popular feature. (The only other opportunities to practice a skill relate to killing: at the Seattle football stadium's shooting range and during arrow shooting practice at a Hillcrest backyard.) Opportunities like these probably won't convince serious competitive gamers to take an extended music-making break, but for casual players it's a nice contrast to the intensity of the gameplay, to suspend the Will for just a moment.

Music and Emotions

Not only is music a kind of force, casting a calming spell on the psyche, but Schopenhauer also argued that music is uniquely capable of expressing human emotions, capturing the underlying psychological states that often remain inexpressible through words or other art forms. He believed that music, despite being non-verbal, has the power to communicate the full range of human experiences, including joy, sorrow, love, hatred, terror, hope, and the transcendent states of ecstasy and spiritual yearning.

How can music suspend the Will though, and at the same time represent all these emotions, including hatred and terror? The answer isn't that far-fetched. Although music itself can be full of rage—think of a Beethoven symphony or a Sex Pistols song—the emotions are not concrete or specific. They're not aiming for a particular target. Just as the Will can work in many ways, it's highly susceptible to musical influences. So, on the one hand, according to Schopenhauer, the beauty of music lies in its ability to suspend the individual's consciousness and allow them to directly experience the underlying reality of the world, but on the other, music also acts on the Will.

Schopenhauer was somewhat suspicious of combining words with music, but he admitted that poetry, through rhymes and rhythm, turns into a musical expression of sorts. Nevertheless, he thought that we need to tread carefully with genres in which music is combined with words. In an opera, for example, music should take precedence over language—words should always be subordinate to the music.

However, lyrics play an important role in the video game; the songs are well-chosen and have an impact, especially through the darker textual references. While music through the video game serves as a respite from the violent post-apocalyptic world, there are instances when it turns into an artistically dark space. In the video game, lyrics help us reflect on our emotions and the world.

Negative Emotions

The remarkable trailer for *The Last of Us Part II*, presents a scene that doesn't appear anywhere in the game, and features Shawn James's "Through the Valley"—with lyrics parodying Psalm 23 "The Lord is my shepherd." The lyrics foreshadow the main storyline from both Ellie's and Abby's perspectives. The narrator takes comfort in his gun and states: "I walk through the valley of the shadow of death. And I fear no evil because I'm blind to it all. And my mind and my gun, they comfort me. Because I know I'll kill my enemies when they come." Ellie is sitting on the bed with her guitar performing the song next to a dead body on the floor. After Joel walks in, asking what she's doing, Ellie puts down the guitar and responds, "I'm gonna find ... and I'm gonna kill ... every last one of them." This is certainly not a musically derived, Will-suspending statement—quite the contrary. The slow-moving folk-rock song features only vocals and a guitar in the first verse, and barely arouses terror. But the lyrics make it tick and appear to have been written for the video game.

The song also appears in the game's prologue, shortly after Ellie and Joel arrive in Jackson. Ellie listens to Shawn James's original version on her Walkman, faintly heard on the soundtrack, while she's sketching a bunny in her notebook. The bunny doesn't necessarily signify cuteness, but a source of protein, as in the beginning of the Winter chapter of *Part I*. Although this scene took place years before the main plotline began, music helps Ellie to internalize the revenge narrative that not only ruined her own life, but also Abby's, Dina's, and so many more.

Music's ability to focus our attention on something like revenge is not only far from Schopenhauer's view of music as a suspension of the Will, but also from his view on music and words. The music, along with the lyrics, enforce the need for revenge. So we're approaching the limit of what Schopenhauer can teach us.

Lorca and Duende

Spanish poet and playwright Federico García Lorca, or as his full name reads, Federico del Sagrado Corazón de Jesús García Lorca (1898–1936), is rarely thought of as a philosopher or an aesthetician of music or any other art form. But one of his texts, "Theory and Play of the *Duende*," originally a lecture he gave for the premiere of his play, *Blood Wedding*, reads like an aesthetic treatise on the conditions for creating deep, authentic, and emotionally rich works of art—performing arts, in particular. Lorca helps us understand the contradictory ways music works in the video game and complements Schopenhauer's aesthetic theory.

Originally a fairy or goblin-like creature in Spanish and Latin American mythology, *duende* became an aesthetic concept for Lorca. Citing an unnamed source, Lorca labeled the *duende* "A mysterious force that everyone feels and no philosopher has explained."[3] He makes several attempts to define *duende*, some of which are full of musical references.

> So, then, the *duende* is a force not a labor, a struggle not a thought. I heard an old maestro of the guitar say: "The *duende* is not in the throat: the *duende* surges up, inside, from the soles of the feet." Meaning, it's not a question of skill, but of a style that's truly alive: meaning, it's in the veins: meaning, it's of the most ancient culture of immediate creation.[4]

From this description, the *duende* sounds like a primitive Will of artistic creativity, working in the moment, something harnessed to create good, rather than something causing constant pain and disappointment. The *duende* is a creative force; it's not a spirit, religious or otherwise. It's not the devil, and, as Lorca makes very clear, certainly not an angel of creativity, nor is it a muse. While a muse and an angel are both sources of artistic inspiration and creative stimulation, acting as catalysts, providing ideas, visions, and insights that fuel the creation of various forms of art, unlocking the artist's creativity, they are insufficient, according to Lorca.

"The Muse," Lorca writes, "stirs the intellect, bringing a landscape of columns and an illusory taste of laurel, and intellect is often poetry's enemy . . . since it lifts the poet into the bondage of aristocratic fineness, where he forgets that he might be eaten, suddenly, by ants, or that a huge arsenical lobster might fall on his head."[5] In other words, a muse is simply too elegant, bourgeois, and yes, polished. "Angel and Muse come from outside us: the angel brings light, the Muse form." For Lorca, such art is academic and well meaning, but artistically superficial. He states, "the *duende* has to be roused from the furthest habitations of the blood."[6] Lorca emphasizes that an awareness of death is necessary for the *duende* to get to work, and, to him, Spain is a particularly fruitful place in this regard. "Every art and every country is capable of *duende*, angel and Muse: and just as Germany owns to the Muse, with a few exceptions, and Italy the perennial angel, Spain is, at all times, stirred by the *duende*, country of ancient music and dance, where the *duende* squeezes out those lemons of dawn,"[7] and the end of his testimonial of Spain could as well describe the post-apocalyptic one of *The Last of Us*—"a country of death, a country open to death."[8]

Duende is a necessity for an authentic performance for Lorca, not a cherry on top, an add-on spiffing up a work or performance. He quotes flamenco singer Manuel Torre telling a student, "You have a voice, you understand style, but you'll never ever succeed because you have no *duende*."[9] Think of an unplugged, live, imperfect version of a song performed at a small club compared to a version produced in studio with a drum-machine rhythm track, and a voice perfected with the lifeless, filtered autotune timbre. The first version of the song radiates authenticity, the second artificiality. This is an aspect of music making that Schopenhauer didn't consider.

A Reconciliation

If music in *The Last of Us* has been about getting a break from the hardship of the post-apocalyptic world and suspending the Will's urges for revenge, the very end of the game illustrates the *duende*, its emotional power, and ultimately a truly authentic musical rendition free of embarrassment, but full of pain.

In the epilogue, Ellie's again playing the beginning of "Future Days," but it's not cringeworthy any longer. She's performing it with great effort with the only remaining fingers on her left hand—index, middle finger, and thumb—as the others were bitten off by Abby during their last encounter. The chords are incomplete and accompanied by distorted dampened sounds from the instrument, stemming from her inability to firmly press down the strings. We can feel her pain. We know she's an accomplished player and that every note she plays takes immense effort. The most artistically deficient performance in the game turns into the most emotionally satisfying one—colored by her experiences from the ill-advised journey to Santa Barbara and return to the empty farm—a place in a "country open to death"[10]—and guided by memories from "the furthest habitations of the blood."[11] The scene is short and there is no singing, but in a way, all her experiences since Salt Lake City are encapsuled in this performance. And here, for the first time, the Will for revenge has finally ceased.

Again, the musical performance triggers a flashback during which Joel is "picking away" on his porch at night playing the intro to Crosby, Stills & Nash's "Helplessly Hoping." Ellie comes over to try and clear the air about what she perceives as his interferences in her life. Then she says, "I was supposed to die in that hospital. My life would've fucking mattered. But you took that from me." Joel responds, "If somehow the Lord gave me a second chance at that moment ... I would do it all over again." Ellie replies: "Yeah ... I just ... I don't think I can ever forgive you for that. But I would like to try." (For more on the nature of forgiveness, see Chapter 24 of the volume.)

Did the music of "Helplessly Hoping"—a song about a man's inability to deal with his feelings for, and inaction toward, a woman he loves—help the reconciliation between Joel and Ellie? Perhaps. It wouldn't take much effort to consider the lyrics as a representation of Joel's presently cold relationship with Ellie, where, in the second verse, he's waiting for her response, whether it be a goodbye or a hello.

It's certain though that, at the end of *The Last of Us Part II*, Ellie, triggered by music, has found a path to move on, a path to suspend the Will that has caused her to obsess over the events in Salt Lake City. For a moment, Schopenhauer's and Lorca's aesthetic theories come together as one. In the empty farmhouse, reflecting on her conversation with Joel, Ellie has abandoned the will for revenge, and at the same time, produced real art.

Notes

1. This was one of several endings of Wagner's libretto of the apocalyptic opera that he considered, but ultimately rejected.
2. Arthur Schopenhauer, *The World as Will and Idea*, 6th ed., vol. 3, trans. R.B. Haldane and J. Kemp (London: Kegan Paul, Trench, Trübner & Co., 1909), 227, at https://www.gutenberg.org/files/40868/40868-pdf.pdf.
3. Federico García Lorca, *Theory and Play of the Duende*, trans. A.S. Kline, at https://www.poetryintranslation.com/PITBR/Spanish/LorcaDuende.php.
4. Lorca, *Theory and Play of the Duende*.
5. Lorca, *Theory and Play of the Duende*.
6. Lorca, *Theory and Play of the Duende*.
7. Lorca, *Theory and Play of the Duende*.
8. Lorca, *Theory and Play of the Duende*.
9. Lorca, *Theory and Play of the Duende*.
10. Lorca, *Theory and Play of the Duende*.
11. Lorca, *Theory and Play of the Duende*.

22

Humor and Human Intimacy in *The Last of Us*

Michael K. Cundall Jr.

The human race has only one really effective weapon ... laughter. The moment it arises, all your irritations and resentments slip away and the sunny spirit takes their place.

—Mark Twain[1]

Joking around might seem out of place in a post-apocalyptic scenario, but it's not. In fact, season 1 of *The Last of Us* is a masterclass in the power of humor to bring individuals together and to make an audience care about characters. Joel and Ellie begin as strangers, but they end as surrogate father and daughter. This change is thanks largely to Ellie, whose sarcasm, teasing, and puns eventually get Joel to see her as more than cargo and get us to care deeply about them and their relationship.

Humor as Plot Device: Sarcasm, Teasing, and Real Laughs

Right from the beginning, humor is important in *The Last of Us*. It's part of Joel's relationship with his daughter, Sarah. Joel teases Sarah by volunteering her to visit the neighbors, and Sarah teases Joel about stealing his money to repair his watch. But by the time Joel meets Ellie, his fatherly teasing has all but vanished.

Over twenty years after Joel teased his daughter on the morning of the breakout of the Cordyceps infection, he gets caught up in the situation leading him to Ellie. His attitude toward Ellie is no different than the attitude he'd take toward the aluminum fencing he gets Bill, or the drugs he smuggles. Ellie, like the fencing, is cargo—a word used more than once to

The Last of Us and Philosophy: Look for the Light, First Edition.
Edited by Charles Joshua Horn.
© 2025 John Wiley & Sons, Inc. Published 2025 by John Wiley & Sons, Inc.

describe her. Joel wants nothing to do with her as a person—she's nothing more than cargo. Ellie, on the other hand, has a strong interest in not being seen as a person, as something more than mere cargo.

Sarcastic humor is Ellie's main weapon. We hear it in her interactions with Marlene when Ellie sarcastically counts back from ten, and we when she's dealing with Maria, Tommy's wife. In fact, the first few times Joel has anything like a conversation with Ellie, she responds with sarcasm. When Joel remarks that Ellie is "a weird kid," she throws it right back at him calling him a "weird kid." Taking what someone says and repeating it in an exaggerated tone is a classic teasing technique.

In contrast, Joel's use of sarcasm and humor is minimal early on. He's the gruff, tough guy that gets things done. His moral flexibility and strong desire to "finish the job" make him the ideal smuggler. Joel shuts down any attempt Ellie makes to interact with him. Even when she breaks the code of what the radio songs mean, he ignores her. Through most of the first three episodes, Joel is distant toward Ellie, rebuffing her at almost every turn and never playing along. The sarcastic, mean-spirited banter between Ellie and Joel persists early in episode 3, "Long, Long Time," but it radically changes toward the end.

When they finally reach Bill and Frank's home, finding it no longer occupied by the living, they prepare to leave. Ellie says that she'd like a shower and teases Joel that he "needs one. Seriously!" This is the first real time that Ellie's sarcasm isn't biting. Yes, it's a little dig at Joel, but it's a friendly dig. She's messing with him in a friendly way and we know this because the acidity of her voice is gone. Ellie's earlier use of sarcasm has her hitting Joel with verbal jabs. The shot about him needing a shower is prosocial. She's not making fun to hurt him, just to make him less smelly. She's trying to help.

It also marks a change in Joel's attitude toward Ellie. Rather than ignore her, he takes her advice, and some of Joel's crustiness begins to wash away. Joel isn't chummy with Ellie, but at least he isn't shutting her down. The relationship is opening up. This change marks the beginning of an evolution in the way humor functions between the two characters, heralding an important change in their relationship. Joel may have been softened emotionally by Bill's note telling him to protect Tess. Joel is a protector by nature, and Bill's note may have helped make a small opening for him to care about Ellie, the person now in need of protection. So Joel takes Ellie's good-natured shower prodding in the spirit it was intended. It's a positive sign that the relationship can become closer. After all, we play and joke with our friends, ribbing them and poking fun. As a result, our relationships are strengthened and deepened, made more intimate, as the philosopher Ted Cohen (1939–2014) argued.[2] Intimacy really begins to develop at this point in *The Last of Us*, as Ellie shifts from defensive to inviting with her sarcasm and teasing, and Joel becomes receptive and eventually engaged.

Puns and Penises: Humor in the Truck

Episode 4, "Please Hold to My Hand," is the pivotal moment of change in Ellie and Joel's relationship. In the first three episodes, they've interacted, but in a more guarded way. Sure, they've survived the Clickers and hiked past mass graves and downed airplanes, but it's pretty standard apocalypse-journey-stuff. The characters aren't flat, but they haven't bonded yet. Episode 3 shows how Ellie, despite all her defensive sarcasm, is still a kid who hasn't seen much of the world. She questions Joel, and he answers some questions, while letting others go answered. This slow build allows the audience to get a sense that Ellie is becoming something more than cargo. Joel wouldn't explain to cargo about the mass graves, nor would he take the time to show his disappointment in coach air travel. He sees Ellie as a kid. That change in perspective starts the process of having him see Ellie as a person, a person he'll eventually see as a surrogate daughter.

Episode 4 begins with a pit stop for gas. Any parent knows that taking kids on a road trip is annoying because they get bored and act out. When Joel admonishes Ellie not to wander off, Ellie momentarily sulks and then does something to break the boredom. She reveals to Joel and the audience *No Pun Intended: Volume Too*, a book she received from her close friend Riley. Ellie reads some puns aloud. Joel is annoyed, so of course Ellie just leans into it. But the playful character of the interchange is clear. Joel doesn't shut her humor down. He's a good sport about it. Ellie soon tires of the puns, and so does Joel. He did like the one about the Algae-bra—though he wouldn't show Ellie. Ellie playfully warns him of a more pun-filled future.

The scene switches to them back on the road. Ellie's in the backseat, like all kids on road trips, and boredom leads her to rifling around. She first finds a Hank Williams cassette and teases Joel that it will be nostalgic for him. He retorts that while Hank was before his time, it's still good music. Rooting around more, Ellie discovers Bill's porn rag *Bearskin* and announces her find to Joel. He's immediately uncomfortable. She finds Joel's discomfort delicious and pushes him even more. She asks, "How did he even walk around with that thing!?" Joel, acting as the adult/parent, tells her to get rid of it, but she persists—like any kid would when a parent or adult can't stop them. Joel is helpless. Ellie's going to mess with him just as sure as the sun will rise. Ellie asks about the pages being stuck together, furthering Joel's discomfort, and the ever-ready Joel, the smuggler who survives, is caught totally off-guard. He can only stammer. Ellie ends his discomfort by telling him "I'm just fucking with you," throwing the rag out the window.

The total screen time of the two interchanges is only a couple of minutes, but they're crucial to the change in their relationship. Ellie, by bringing out the book, invites Joel to play with her, sharing the enjoyment of silly puns. This sharing of humor is exactly the sort of cherished moment Ish's note from the video game reminds us of. Ish writes, "What's the point of surviving if you don't have someone to laugh at your corny jokes?" Joel doesn't laugh, but he lets Ellie pun. He doesn't fully play with Ellie yet, but he goes along. Once back in the truck, Ellie finds more ways to mess with Joel, and he reciprocates, showing us the radically different relationship they now have.

Joel's tacit acceptance of Ellie's humor allows Ellie to go further and reinforce the relationship's new direction. Ellie feels comfortable enough to tease Joel about his age and the male sexuality depicted in *Bearskin*. Age and sexuality are taboo subjects, but humor is one of the socially acceptable ways we can address taboo topics.[3] We don't directly ask our elders their age, and we certainly don't ask about the size of a man's junk. In this scene, we see humor being deployed in two ways in line with our everyday experience. First, it's a way to raise difficult topics and second, and certainly more importantly, it's a way to strengthen a relationship. By the time they reach Kansas City, Ellie is no longer cargo.

The shift in their relationship is heralded by Ellie bringing out the pun book. She needs to bond with Joel, and so she takes a chance that he will play along and not reject her. Like Ellie, we all need to connect deeply and intimately with other human beings to feel human ourselves. As Cohen says, "I need reassurance that this something inside me, the something that is tickled by a joke is indeed something that constitutes an element of my humanity. I discover something of what it is to be a human being by finding this thing in me, and then having it echoed in you, another human being."[4] Had Joel rebuffed her, Ellie would have felt hurt and the relationship would have been fractured.

The denouement of the changing relationship comes when they've stopped for the night before reaching Kansas City. Just before going to sleep, Ellie asks Joel "a serious question," which is just a cover for more punning. Joel waits and then answers her by finishing the pun. Ellie is amazed not just that Joel answered, but that he played along. He could have ignored her or refused her by getting angry and telling her to go to bed. He didn't. *He played with her.* Joel's active engagement in the joke signals his willingness to play with her from here on out. Puns are now a way to initiate and enjoy play through the remaining episodes. In addition to bonding, play provides "a release from the burdens of everyday activity," a necessity in the world of *The Last of Us* both for the characters and the viewers.[5] With the beginning of episode 4, roughly midway through their westward journey, sarcasm is no longer used only in an aggressive way. They are now able to "mess" with each other.

Think about that. You don't "mess" with strangers; you "mess" with your friends. One might go so far as to say that if you didn't mess with them, you're probably not particularly close. Ellie and Joel's relationship begins with sarcasm and that sarcasm transforms them from smuggler and cargo to intimate friends—friends who mess with one another, just like Joel did with his daughter. The humorous messing around is a kind of relaxation that's needed as a relief from stress, a kind that is not possible with just anyone. As the contemporary philosopher Noël Carroll says, "humour is indulged in moments of relaxation and leisure, indeed, riffing or joshing with one's friends, family and associates is itself a form of relaxation."[6]

Thus far, we've focused on the growth and development of Joel and Ellie's relationship, using humor as the lens through which we see the relationship evolve. It's one of the most important parts of the storyline between the two. Arguably, it's the most important part. But humor is also used in a more instrumental way throughout *The Last of Us*. Humor is a vehicle for lightening the mood prior to an intense or tragic situation—a pattern seen in many episodes.

Teasing, Growth, and Respite

This effect that humor has on Joel and Ellie's relationship can't be overstated. It's one of the main reasons that laughter is called the best medicine, and why this chapter begins with the Mark Twain quote. As Carroll says, "our laughter, through its endorphin-mediated opiate effect, in all likelihood boosts the tendency of cosmic amusement to facilitate social bonding."[7] This view is echoed by the journalist, Norman Cousins (1915–1990), who writes,

> It is a perversion of rationalism to argue that words like "hope" or "faith" or "love" or "grace" (and "laughter") are without physiological significance. The benevolent emotions are necessary not just because they are pleasant, but because they are regenerative.[8]

The sense that the good feelings we have are more than fleeting and have continued and sustained effects provides a partial explanation as to why humor is so instrumentally valuable: not just to writers and video game developers, but to all of us. When the writers use humor to raise the spirits of the audience, it's a clear indication that something intense looms. Humor can signal the calm before the storm, or rather the chuckle before the storm. I'd take the chuckle. Wouldn't you?

Humor propels the characters along, but also becomes a tool to guide or manage the audience's emotions. Back on the road after the campsite in episode 4, Joel and Ellie begin to talk. They engage in some light banter, but then the conversation turns to more serious matters. The subject of killing arises. Ellie shows a clear discomfort with the topic, and Joel expresses his sorrow for her having to kill someone.

We see the pattern of humor prefacing seriousness play out time and again. Ellie claims she's not tired on the drive to Kansas City, and then the next scene is her sacked out in the car—a little irony that relaxes the audience before the coming dangers. Ellie and Joel keep up their banter when they find a building in which to hide. Ellie is boosted in and when she opens the door she exclaims "Where would you be without me?" Joel sardonically responds "Wyoming." As they get settled for the night, Joel and Ellie have another round of pun sharing.

Humor provides respite for the characters and viewers early in the final episode. As Joel and Ellie move through Salt Lake City, they are cutting up with one another. The overall vibe is heavy, and Ellie is feeling a little lost. They've reached their destination and the mission will soon be over. The cargo will soon be delivered.

A new form of humor and play comes from Ellie, namely, the whimsical humor and enjoyment of the sort she shared with Riley through most of episode 7. When Ellie laughs at seeing and feeding the giraffes, her response is the laughter of delight. Joel shows her how to feed the animals and Ellie is giddy. Joel looks on as any proud parent would. As they move off from the giraffes, another heavy topic surfaces. Joel confesses to Ellie about his suicide attempt. In addition, Joel senses he will soon have to deliver Ellie. He will have to, in a very real sense, treat her as cargo again. He'll lose this new relationship. Joel asks if it might be time to dig out some puns. Absolutely thrilled that Joel has initiated play and asked to share something so dear to her, Ellie obliges. And then, literally, "boom!" they're captured.

You know the rest. Joel learns of the Fireflies' plans for Ellie, goes full-on Rambo and saves her. They make their way back to his brother's settlement. The final scene of the episode ends as they overlook the town. The audience knows about Joel's deceit and Ellie senses something's amiss. The hike to the overlook provides us with closure of the main arc of the first season, but it features humor in a different, more explicit way. During the hike, Joel is trying to get Ellie to perk up. He starts talking about his daughter and comparing her to Ellie. He notes differences, ham-handedly trying to draw in Ellie with limited success. He tells Ellie that the one thing he knows would make his daughter like her is her *sense of humor*. There's no humorous bit here, no pun, no sarcasm. Humor stands with them on that bluff overlooking the town almost a full partner in their journey.

Humor got them to Wyoming, and humor made us want to go with them. The story of a sullen teenager complaining at every turn to a callous smuggler concerned only about a reward would not have bonded us to these characters. Humor is the main mechanism that propels the characters in and through the story's development, bonds them together, and thus makes us care about them. There is much that is grim and intense in *The Last of Us*, but humor gives the characters and audience respite through laughter. Laughing together, as Cohen says, "is the satisfaction of a deep human longing, the realization of a desperate hope. It is the hope that we are enough like one another to sense one another, to be able to live together."[9]

Without laughter and humor, *The Last of Us*, and indeed our own lives, would be bland, dull, and unwatchable.

Notes

1. Mark Twain, John P. Holms, and Karin Baji eds., *Bite-Size Twain* (New York: St. Martin's Press, 1998), 36.
2. Ted Cohen, *Jokes: Philosophical Thoughts on Joking Matters* (Chicago: University of Chicago Press, 2001), 27.
3. Vladislav Maraev, Ellen Breitholz, Christine Howes, Staffan Larsson, and Robin Cooper, "Something Old, Something New, Something Borrowed, Something Taboo: Interaction and Creativity in Humour," *Frontiers in Psychology* 12 (2021), at https://doi.org/10.3389/fpsyg.2021.654615.
4. Cohen, *Jokes*, 31.
5. Noël Carroll, *Humour: A Very Short Introduction* (Oxford: Oxford University Press, 2014), 42.
6. Carroll, *Humour*, 42.
7. Carroll, *Humour*, 84.
8. Norman Cousins, *Anatomy of an Illness* (New York: Bantam Books, 2005), 38.
9. Cohen, *Jokes*, 29.

PART VI
RELIGIOUS
CONSIDERATIONS AT
THE END OF THE WORLD

23

God as a Survival Tool
Religion in a World of Desperation

Federico Dal Barco

A lot is missing from the dystopian world of *The Last of Us*, yet religion remains. It may not be as prevalent as it once was, but religious belief is central to some notable characters—David, Dina, and the Seraphites. Religion plays different roles in their lives, of course, but for all of these characters it is a survival tool for life under desperate conditions.

Survival Tools

Philosophers disagree sharply about the nature of religion. Some think that religions are defined by a set of beliefs, usually about God or the correct moral practices. Others argue that religions are instead defined by the practices of a given community. Most philosophers agree, though, that religions often include moral guidance about how to behave. The German philosopher, Immanuel Kant (1724–1804), wrote extensively about the relationship between religion and ethics. Kant thought that God was, by his nature, unknowable. And yet, he thought that belief in God was necessary for helping us make sense of an unjust world. In short, Kant's worry was one thematized in *The Last of Us*: What is the role of hope in our world?

Kant believed that we must hope for the existence of God and the immortality of the soul because these beliefs help us make sense of morality in this world. Without the possibility of an afterlife where the virtuous can be rewarded and the vicious can be punished, the universe would be unjust. Religion is thus a tool or instrument in Kant's terms. God is the instrument through which we are ensured that there is meaning in our actions and that it's not pointless to follow the moral precepts of a religion. Simply put, God grants us a reward for our good deeds and ensures punishment for those who act unethically.

Of course, for some people, religious belief may be more than just a way of making sense of the world. Some people have genuine religious beliefs

The Last of Us and Philosophy: Look for the Light, First Edition.
Edited by Charles Joshua Horn.

that serve a purpose beyond their instrumental good. Put differently, for some, religious belief may also be intrinsically good. Ultimately, religion plays a role in the lives of believers in both our world and the world of *The Last of Us*, giving them strength, providing meaning, and offering hope.

David's Religious Experience

Let's start with HBO's revised version of David, introduced in episode 8 of the TV show, "When We Are in Need." The first sequence of the episode powerfully introduces religion in the series. There, we see David reciting a section from Revelation 21:

> DAVID: And I saw a new heaven and a new earth. For the first heaven and the first earth were passed away. And I heard a great voice out of heaven say, "Behold, the tabernacle of God is with men. And God shall wipe away all tears from their eyes." That there will be no more death, neither sorrow, nor crying, neither will there be any more pain ... for the former things are passed away.[1]

David's small flock is supposed to be Christian. They live in a community where the pastor is the center; they pray before their meals; and they refer to the burial rite for the dead members of their community, even if it's safe to assume that they never really bury them. These people seem to have found a way to remain religious after Outbreak Day. Though most members of David's congregation seem unaware of the cruel practice reserved for corpses, it remains strange that a Christian pastor allows such a practice. Clearly the message of hope from the book of Revelation is undermined by the cannibalism and violence that fly in the face of the Christian message.

David's conversation with the imprisoned Ellie helps to elucidate his view of religion.

> DAVID: But then the world ended, and I was shown the truth.
> ELLIE: Right, by God.
> DAVID: No. By Cordyceps. What does Cordyceps do? Is it evil? No! It's fruitful, it multiplies. It feeds and protects its children, and it secures its future with violence if it must. It loves.
> ELLIE: Why are you telling me all of this?
> DAVID: Because you can handle it. The way the others can't. They need God, they need heaven, they need a father. You don't. You're beyond that.

David clearly uses religion as a tool to serve a purpose. For him, religion isn't about belief in a supernatural being or having the knowledge of certain moral commandments. Religion isn't even about the practices and traditions of a particular community. Rather, religion is merely a tool to help us survive. David understands one of the lessons from Hebrews 4:12: "For the word of God is living and active, sharper than any two-edged sword, piercing to the division of soul and of spirit, of joints and of marrow, and discerning the thoughts and intentions of the heart." The members of David's flock need paradise and a father (both heavenly and natural) to survive; they need a reason to continue to believe in the possibility of survival in such a harsh world. Put simply, they need hope, and religion is one way to provide it.

Whether they truly follow the moral precepts of the Bible or not becomes almost irrelevant. David wasn't a Christian pastor before the Cordyceps outbreak—he was a schoolteacher. With all the killing, stealing, and, to a certain extent, even cannibalism, David transforms Christianity into a wicked post-apocalyptic religion that seems to be only a useful lie.

The religious instrumentalism works on a different level as well. Not only does it help the flock survive by providing them hope and imparting meaning, but it also provides David a means of control over his flock. Perhaps this lie is no different than the other lies that David likely told his school children about Santa Claus to compel them to act in certain ways.

Dina's Faith

Dina's pragmatic religion is very different from David's cynical creed. In one memorable scene, Ellie and Dina explore a synagogue in Seattle. It's here that Ellie discovers Dina's Jewish faith and the way she draws on her religion for strength and meaning.

DINA: This place brings back a lot of memories. My sister used to drag me to a synagogue all the time.

ELLIE: You never struck me as much of a believer.

DINA: Nah. But I like coming from a long line of survivors.

ELLIE: You mean after Outbreak Day?

DINA: That ... and the Inquisition ... and the Holocaust. My family always made it out alive.

ELLIE: Barely.... Do you still pray?

DINA: Sometimes.

ELLIE: Really?

DINA: I said one when we left Jackson. I said one at Joel's grave. Sometimes I just ... say little ones to myself.

ELLIE: Does it help?

DINA: I think it calms me. Helps me put things in perspective.... It's a way to deal with grief. A way to show respect. It's what I know.

During a cutscene of the video game, we also see Dina giving a Hamsa hand, a symbol of protection in Jewish culture, to Ellie. After the outbreak, Dina didn't lose her faith practice entirely. But unlike David's flock or the Seraphites, Dina isn't part of a faith community. Her religious experience is deeply subjective and pragmatic. We can't tell whether she truly believes in the existence of God, but it's clear that Dina believes in the instrumental use of symbols and prayer. As she declares, she sometimes prays before dangerous missions. Prayer helps her to face the awful reality of her world. God is the instrument that helps Dina deal with the grief that results from her actions. Whether God truly exists is potentially irrelevant. Her faith helps her survive. Hence, this thoroughly subjective way of experiencing religion is another modified version of a pre-apocalypse belief that serves the purposes of the believers in the new world.

The Life of a Seraphite

In *The Last of Us Part II*, the Seraphites are a group governed by a leader who imposes rigid rules of conduct on subordinates. Their name has a religious inspiration: the seraphs are celestial or heavenly beings that appear in Judaism, Christianity, and Islam. They are usually represented as winged angels, so this could be the reason why they often refer to people's arms as wings. Male Seraphites shave their heads, and females all wear the same hairstyle. Most Seraphites wear similar clothing, and they all have scars near the mouth, suggesting that they undergo an initiation ritual. The universal scar hints at the horizontal equality between all the members, with the vertical exception of the leader. In addition to the initiation ritual, it seems that all Seraphites undergo rigid military training—just consider Lev's skill with the bow. Reverence for the natural world leads them to reject electronic devices and machines; they use hammers or arrows instead of guns. As for their God, it is difficult to know whether the female figure in their graffiti represents a prophet or an icon of their divinity.

The Seraphites seem to be a society based on religious ideas. To be part of the community, one must follow their strict religious tenets. This may have inherent value for some members. Clearly, though, there is also instrumental value in being a Seraphite. Although it isn't clear if the members of the religious group decide to join of their own volition or if they are forced from birth to participate, it's safe to assume that membership contributes to a greater chance of survival. After all, the training and community they receive as participants in the Seraphite culture would be preferable to living in solitude with the threat of violence at every turn. Hence, their religious beliefs are instrumental to their survival. In addition, the rules created and imposed by the leaders are instrumental, controlling the members and producing a functioning society.

The point isn't that the religion of the Seraphites is entirely a lie or that nobody really believes it. Rather, the point is that regardless of how the members of this religious group live their spiritual lives, they derive instrumental benefits. Being part of a strong group whose members help each other has real survival value.

Kant versus the Seraphites: What Must I Do?

What would Kant think of the Seraphites? Kant distinguishes between subjective religious experiences, those that originate from the individual decisions of a person, and heteronomous forms of belief, those that are determined by external dogmas.[2] For Kant, religious belief must be rooted in a subjective decision to conduct one's life in a specific way. Hence, a person's ethos, namely their rules of conduct, cannot be imposed by a religious dogma that isn't a creation of the subjects themselves.

This doesn't mean that Kant eliminates all forms of collective religious experiences. He and his parents were Pietists, a religious group that emphasized personal beliefs and practicing Christian teachings over theological doctrines and liturgical ceremonies. One belief about religion that Kant maintained over the course of his life was that religious conduct should freely come from the subjects. If we think about the examples of the Seraphites and Dina, we have two extremes. On the one hand, the Seraphites are a group of people who follow a dogma that a leader imposes on them. This means that they are not free to decide how they should behave. On the other hand, Dina represents the perfect example of a person who independently decides to pray because she needs to do it. It's a personal decision that Kant seeks, and it isn't a surprise that one of his famous mottos is "*Sapere Aude!* Have the courage to use your own understanding!"[3]

But what does Kant mean when he insists that you must think for yourself to be truly religious? After all, membership in many religious groups involves accepting some ethical limitations coming from above. Kant notes that humans are constantly struggling between two extremes.[4] On the one hand, humans are animals driven by instincts that result in selfish and generally evil action. On the other hand, we possess some faculties that animals don't have. One of these is rationality. Insofar as we are rational beings, we can create moral norms of behavior. In other words, humans realize they can limit their instinctive behavior by following rules.

The best part of Kant's theory is that we don't need a lot of rules to guide our conduct. One is enough (though there are several different formulations of it): "Act only according to that maxim whereby you can at the same time will that it should become a universal law."[5] Kant famously calls this rule the categorical imperative. Simply put, he believes that before deciding to act in a certain way, we should ask ourselves whether we would impose that same rule for action on every other rational being. If so, the action is morally permissible, obligatory, and can become a universal law.

By asking ourselves whether our actions would be universalizable, the obligation to follow the categorical imperative originates from ourselves.

The categorical imperative is, for Kant, a rational law that innately determines how every rational agent ought to act. The moral law is a self-obligation to act in a certain way if we want to be moral. The Seraphites don't follow a subjective process of this kind; they don't use their rationality to determine their choices. Seraphites follow the imperatives or rules of their leader. In this sense, their religion is dogmatic and, therefore, wouldn't be acceptable for Kant. Without freedom to think, there is no true religion according to Kant.

What Can I Know? Surely Not God

In the *Critique of Pure Reason,* Kant argues for the limits of human knowledge.[6] According to Kant, we can only have knowledge of objects in space and time, so things beyond the conditions of space and time, like God and the soul, are unknowable. Although God is beyond the scope of pure reason and beyond the scope of knowledge, this doesn't mean that belief in God is irrational or wrong. On the contrary, Kant insists that belief in God should be made on the basis of faith, not reason, and that such belief is required to help us make sense of justice in our world.

One might ask why we should believe in such religious concepts if we cannot know them. *The Last of Us* has an answer. God and religion have instrumental value. In the case of David, religion serves his egocentrism and megalomania, but, at the same time, it also raises the chances for his flock to survive. For Dina, prayers become a way to cope with the stark reality of her situation. And for the Seraphites, religion is an instrument for the construction and maintenance of their society.

Like the Cordyceps, religion survives because it mutates. In the world of *The Last of Us,* religion becomes a form of belief that prioritizes the use of God as an instrument for achieving specific goals. In this sense, religion can be just as powerful and meaningful in a post-apocalyptic landscape as it is today.

Notes

1. It's interesting to notice that David is not reading the entire passage, but he is selecting specific pieces from Revelation 21. Whether this has to do with his instrumental usage of the biblical message or is just a simplification imposed by television times is unknown.
2. This evaluation comes mainly from Immanuel Kant, *Religion within the Boundaries of Mere Reason,* trans. Allen Wood and George Di Giovanni (Cambridge: Cambridge University Press, 1998), 31–192.
3. Immanuel Kant, *An Answer to the Question: What Is Enlightenment?,* trans. Ted Humphrey (Indianapolis: Hackett, 1992), 1.

4. Especially Kant, *Religion within the Boundaries of Mere Reason*.
5. Immanuel Kant, *Groundwork of the Metaphysics of Morals*, trans. James Ellington (Indianapolis: Hackett, 1993), 30.
6. Immanuel Kant, *Critique of Pure Reason*, trans. Paul Guyer and Allen W. Wood (Cambridge: Cambridge University Press, 1998), 384–393, 551–623.

24

"I Don't Think I Can Ever Forgive You for That"

Forgiving the Unforgivable in *The Last of Us*

Peter Admirand

The Last of Us is drenched with seemingly unforgivable acts, and so questions spread like Cordyceps spores. Should Ellie have forgiven Joel for saving her from St. Mary's Hospital, even though he didn't regret his actions? Should Abby have forgiven Joel for murdering her father? Should Abby have forgiven Ellie for senselessly killing Owen, the love of her life? Should Ellie have forgiven Abby after watching her pummel Joel to death with a golf club? Should those crucified by the Rattlers forgive their persecutors? Should the victims of David's pedophilia and cannibalism forgive him? Do some of these actions reach the level of the unforgivable? What actions should be forgiven and why?

Forgiveness and the Unforgivable

Forgiveness is a journey for those wronged. The destination is a sense of peace, even if only foreswearing revenge against someone or something that has injured them. True forgiveness never condones the egregious harm as something ultimately beneficial or justifiable, nor is forgiveness free from pain, distress, and periodic angst toward the perpetrator. For these reasons, forgiveness is a process. We see this when Ellie tells Joel that she wants to try to forgive him for lying to her about the actions at St. Mary's Hospital.

There are many reasons why those wronged might forgive. Wrongdoers might genuinely express remorse, take responsibility for their action, vow (and prove) no longer to be the person who would ever do such an act

The Last of Us and Philosophy: Look for the Light, First Edition.
Edited by Charles Joshua Horn.
© 2025 John Wiley & Sons, Inc. Published 2025 by John Wiley & Sons, Inc.

again, and try to repair the wrong.[1] Sometimes the drive to forgive is rooted in self-survival and mental health, returning a sense of empowerment. A victim may have had no choice in the injury inflicted, but they can choose a response—and forgiveness may be essential to that response. Sometimes forgiveness is inseparable from pragmatic survival—perpetrators remain neighbors and collaboration may be required, even if wariness and distrust linger. In *The Last of Us*, there aren't any clear examples of this kind of pragmatic forgiveness—groups simply execute outsiders or rule-breakers. If the human race is to survive though, warring groups must, at some point, forgive.

Ideally, the victims don't forget the wrongs committed against them, but aim to remember the harm justly, neither embellishing nor diminishing it. Again, there's a delicate balance—some forgetting (or at least, letting go) may be necessary to live. Otherwise, the harm may haunt everything one sees, like it does with Ellie and Abby. How the wronged and the wrongdoer approach forgiveness may differ, which is why forgiveness should primarily highlight the needs and dignity of the wronged. We should not frame a situation such that the wronged must forgive or else be morally culpable if they can't forgive.[2]

Forgiveness is especially challenged by cases like what Marilyn McCord Adams (1943–2017) called the "horrendous" and what Claudia Card (1940–2015) called "an atrocity."[3] Examples of horrendous actions and atrocities are abundant in *The Last of Us*. Consider the innocent "tourists" slain by the hunters in Pittsburgh or the mass execution of unarmed civilians to control the outbreak. Terms like "atrocity" or "horrendous" point to something in the domain, or at least on the border of, the unforgivable, acts so pernicious and soul-destroying they seem beyond repair or recovery. These violations threaten the dignity and value not just of the wronged, but also the perpetrator. Unforgivable acts raise damning questions against an individual's moral essence (or humanity) and agonize religious believers, who wonder how God could create a world where such horrors are unleashed. *The Last of Us* invites us to think about the unforgivable in the context of what philosophers call the problem of evil: How can there be a loving, omnipotent God in a world where humanity is nearly annihilated and barely survives amidst infernal landscapes?

Unforgivable acts go beyond any reason or excuse. Nothing can justify the killing fields of Cambodia, the gulags of the Soviet Union, the Laogai in China, or the Nazi death camps. These atrocities involved systems of murder and unjust incarceration, but also the torture, rape, and killings committed by millions of people who supported and embodied the systems. The number of victims is staggering. In *The Last of Us*, beloved and hated characters commit inhumane acts too. Are unforgivable acts like these beyond hope?

The Torah, the Gospels, and the Unforgivable

To understand the unforgivable, let's explore forgiveness and the unforgivable in two religions referenced in *The Last of Us*—Christianity and Judaism. Christian iconography appears in *The Last of Us*; consider Joel's tombstone with its cross, for example. Likewise, elements of Jewish religion play a role, for example in the synagogue when Dina shares her feelings and memories of Jewish identity and belonging. Ultimately, the unforgivable among Christians and Jews will vary between and within the faith traditions, depending on context, sect, and time period. For example, what the Jewish sage Maimonides (1138–1204) deemed unforgivable in the thirteenth century wouldn't necessarily be held to be so by every Jew today.

In *The Last of Us*, many characters have biblical names: Joel, Sarah, Jesse, Dina, Ellie (perhaps from Elishiva, Aaron's wife), and David. In the Bible, King David loves God but is also a great sinner, committing adultery and murder. And yet, God forgives him. In another extraordinary story, Joseph forgives his brothers who sold him into slavery and sees God as merciful. In contrast, there are numerous passages in which God smites the various enemies of the Israelites. We even have God seemingly advocating genocide in the *herem* (Deuteronomy 20:17). Also morally messy is the punishment that should be accorded to those Israelites who commit certain sins, especially idolatry, or decrees demanding Israelites kill those who break various laws, like the infamous case of the rebellious son, who should be stoned to death if he doesn't heed the warnings from his parents and the community leaders (Deuteronomy 21:18–31). Such harsh laws resemble those of the Seraphites, who profess a zealous and unyielding acceptance of their doctrine. Recall how Lev's mother tried to capture her son and bring him to the elders—certain death—because he broke their rules.

Fortunately, the Rabbinic tradition emphasizes a merciful God. So, does the unforgivable exist in Judaism? Not surprisingly, views differ, based on both sect and individual. But on Yom Kippur, Jews are encouraged to express remorse in person to all those they harmed, and to repent for their sins against God. Thus, unlike Christianity, sins against fellow human beings and sins against God require different responses. While Jews are encouraged to be compassionate, wouldn't the Shoah, the mass execution of Jews during the Holocaust, be unforgivable?

Jesus, who was Jewish of course, famously forgives those who crucified him (Luke 23:34). When Peter sought to quantify suffering—"Lord, how many times shall I forgive my brother or sister who sins against me? Up to seven times?" (Matt 18:21–22)—Jesus stressed the limitlessness of forgiveness. When the elders want to punish the woman caught in adultery, Jesus forgives her, but also reminds her to sin no more (John 8:11). Consider also Zacchaeus, a chief tax collector for the colonial Roman power, who harmed countless people by his collaboration. Jesus calls him down from the tree where he was watching and invites him to discipleship—and Zacchaeus reforms his life (Luke 19:1–10).

Wounded characters like Abby, Joel, and Ellie were all harmed and haunted by violence, but they respond with more violence, taking them further away from self-acceptance and peace. If only they had someone to encourage them to come down from that tree and know they were loved, as with Zacchaeus; or to still see a path toward redemption, as in the story of Saul of Tarsus, a persecutor of the early followers of Jesus, who later became the Apostle to the Gentiles.

Yet, even in stories that sing of forgiveness, Jesus also identifies the unforgivable sin of blaspheming against the Holy Spirit (Mark 3:28–30). Jesus's parables about the afterlife also raise questions about the unforgivable (though the possibility of hell doesn't mean that God wouldn't forgive any sinner).

Atheist Forgiveness

Forgiveness isn't just reserved for those from Jewish, Christian, or other religious traditions. Forgiveness in a godless world can be courageous, cathartic, and genuine. How do those outside of a religious tradition, like Ellie, understand the nature of forgiveness? Believers can envision a God of love who seeks the redemption of even the most depraved (someone like David) or can suspend earthly vengeance by anticipating divine retribution and judgment. Atheist forgiveness operates without such mechanisms. According to atheists, there isn't an afterlife where the virtuous and vicious can be rewarded or punished for their actions, nor is there a cycle of rebirth.

In *The Last of Us*, remnants of religious beliefs smolder amidst questioning and doubt. While Joel is holding Sarah's dying body, he twice invokes God: First, "Oh, God," and then Joel's final words, "please, God," close the cold open before the title and credits. It can seem as if God also died in the video game at that moment.[4]

When Ellie and Joel later follow Frank into an abandoned church, no extended comment or dialogue ensues. Crosses and religious statues are just more post-apocalyptic debris. In *The Last of Us Part II*, we learn that Dina still prays, but mostly to continue Jewish ritual as a link with her people. Then there are new religious groups like the Seraphites, whose visionary founder inspired an egalitarian and ecological spirituality that degenerates into anarchic violence and isolationism. There are also religious hypocrites like David, a preacher turned cannibal. Does any character in *The Last of Us* suggest or display belief in a higher power who is kind, compassionate, and fair? Prayers are uttered, but the characters don't perceive signs of divine grace—though some viewers/players might highlight a certain scene (the giraffes!) or a loving act that embodies the presence of God. If *The Last of Us* is indeed godless, any act of forgiveness is extraordinary, particularly if it's also identified with something potentially unforgivable.

Marina Cantacuzino, founder of The Forgiveness Project, a charitable organization that collects and disseminates stories of forgiveness for the purposes of restorative justice, emphasizes that forgiveness can't just be the purview of religious believers.[5] Limiting the potent and essential lifeline of forgiveness to believers would be both immoral and destructive. Atheist forgiveness has much to teach religious believers, and *The Last of Us* can also be rewarding in this respect.

Forgiveness need not be restricted to humanity—forgiveness can also be applied to non-human animals.[6] In *The Last of Us*, human and non-human encounters provide some of the most spiritually rich interactions, from the giraffe scene in the first video game, to Abby, Owen, and Abby's father saving the zebra in the second video game. And then there are the dogs. Playing as Ellie, how many of us avoided, hesitated, or regretfully killed the dogs? Later we learn their names and even play with them. Clearly, unforgivable acts can also be committed against non-human species.

The Unforgivable (and Gameplay) in *The Last of Us*

Playing the video game is a different experience from watching the narrative of the HBO show. In playing the video game, the player must actively commit all sorts of potentially unforgivable acts, whereas the viewer gets to passively witness these actions. What could be unforgivable, then, when the player is "forced" to do things like have Ellie torture Nora?

You're probably a good person, but do you sneak past bad guys in video games? Or do you revel in creatively slaying them, even those who don't threaten your progress? This is an important distinction because when we come to Joel's saving Ellie in the Firefly lab, we have no choice but to kill Abby's father, Dr. Jerry Anderson. If we didn't kill the doctor, then Joel would be shot. But Joel (and the gamer) didn't have to maim or murder the other two cowering medics. Our gameplay decided whether the other medics needed to die as well. Smashing unarmed medics against walls or incinerating them with a flamethrower are crimes against humanity that many would deem unforgivable. Your Joel and my Joel may not be equally morally culpable, and may be committing distinct actions, only some of which are unforgivable.

While forgiveness doesn't always need to include reconciliation, it can sometimes help to restore a relationship. When Ellie confronts Joel about his actions in the Firefly lab, she demands to know why he "took that from me," believing this was her chance to give meaning to her life. A long silence follows as Joel seeks the right words. He doesn't regret his choice because, even though his actions have led to their estrangement, Ellie is alive. Her well-being matters more to Joel than the preservation of their relationship. Interestingly, he invokes God, saying: "If somehow the Lord gave me a second chance at that moment, I would do it all over again." Calling upon God here is a reminder of Joel's plea to God while Sarah was dying. He then looks Ellie in the eyes, stressing his conviction. Is it possible to forgive someone who doesn't regret what they did? Initially speechless and stumbling through her response, Ellie painfully admits: "I don't think I can ever forgive you for that." Here, Ellie labels Joel's action as potentially unforgivable.

If Ellie believes Joel committed an unforgivable act by saving her life, Ellie's views on Abby's murder of Joel barely need comment. Joel's murder propels Ellie into fanatical retaliation. Abby, meanwhile, got her revenge by killing Joel, but it provides little solace. She spends the rest of the video game seeking some meaning in her actions, if not redemption or self-forgiveness. She even risks everything to help Yara and Lev, enemies of her own group. Interestingly, it's Abby's attempt at repentance that foreshadows the emptiness of Ellie's quest for retribution. With their stories paralleled by murdered fathers and obsessive vengeance, Abby provides a vision and warning concerning what Ellie could become. If she kills Abby, Ellie will be even more alone and broken. But Abby is also Ellie's vehicle for moral growth and healing—made possible because of Abby's kindness and friendship with Lev. Any lasting process of forgiveness and redemption is always through, and with, others.

Both Ellie and Abby were traumatized and blinded by rage—and if those around them hadn't intervened, they would have committed other murders too. Owen prevented Ellie and Tommy from being killed in the lodge, and Lev stopped Abby from murdering a pregnant Dina and an incapacitated Ellie. In Santa Barbara, though, Ellie's blood on her arm and shirt triggers memories of Joel's torture and enflames the desire to kill Abby. Ellie takes a knife to Lev's throat (the person who ultimately saved her and Dina) and tells Abby she'll kill Lev if Abby doesn't fight. On the verge of drowning Abby, Ellie recalls a peaceful memory of Joel playing the guitar, and her love for Joel finally overpowers her desire for vengeance. She releases Abby, possibly forgiving her unforgivable act.

Seeking Forgiveness, Trying to Forgive

In *The Last of Us*, a world blotted with mass deaths from both the fungal pandemic and human depravity, mercy and forgiveness are fragile, rare, and rarely rewarded. Joel saved Abby before she killed him. Owen spared Ellie's (and Tommy's) life, but Ellie later kills him. And Abby spared Ellie who still sought revenge.

When assessing real, horrible suffering committed against innocent people, it can be enlightening (though also painful) to turn to the testimonies of survivors. Their responses range from Rwandan genocide survivor, Immaculée Ilibagiza, asserting that she even forgave those Hutus who murdered and raped her family members, to Auschwitz survivor, Elie Wiesel, who invoked a God of mercy to never forgive those who committed the mass crimes of the Shoah.[7] While there isn't a "right" path for when we should forgive, survivor's voices are vital.

Ultimately, little was resolved in *The Last of Us Part II* and there wasn't any clear indication of lasting healing. While Ellie's love and mourning for Joel signal a desire to forgive him, what does her releasing of Abby (and Lev) reveal? Is it only the suspension of vengeance or something more? Sadly, Ellie ends up as she most feared—alone. She's a survivor, but her astronaut and farm-dreams with Joel sought so much more. In addition to destroying Bloaters and hell-bent vigilantes, can a path of repentance and forgiveness (of herself and others) be a way back to those she loves? Since forgiveness is a process and journey, perhaps a continuation of the story, on TV or in a game, will follow the darkness of the second with a sense of the inbreaking of what true forgiveness can provide—peace and justice.[8] Until then, Ellie's words to Joel about forgiving him are promising: "But I would like to try." Sometimes, that's all we can do.

Notes

1. See Charles Griswold, *Forgiveness: A Philosophical Exploration* (Cambridge: Cambridge University Press, 2007).
2. Elie Wiesel and Primo Levi, the great witnesses to the Shoah, rebuked those who conflated the victims with the perpetrators by claiming if the context changed, so could the roles. While Alexander Solzhenitsyn's humble question—Could we not also become such an executioner?—is crucial, for Wiesel and Levi, many have proven the answer is no—and paid for that conviction with their lives.
3. See Marilyn McCord Adams, *Horrendous Evils and the Goodness of God* (Ithaca, NY: Cornell University Press, 1999); Claudia Card, *The Atrocity Paradigm: A Theory of Evil* (Oxford: Oxford University Press, 2002).
4. Phrases like "Oh, God" (Joel carrying Ellie while escaping the Firefly lab) or Ellie cursing "Jesus!" are spoken, but without any belief, especially in Ellie's case.
5. See Marina Cantacuzino, *The Forgiveness Project: Stories for a Vengeful Age* (London: Jessica Kingsley, 2016).
6. Beyond the question of intelligent life outside earth, non-human creatures have shown a capacity to something like forgiveness and other complex moral emotions. See Carl Safina, *Beyond Words: What Animals Think and Feel* (New York: Henry Holt, 2015).
7. Immaculée Ilibagiza, with Steve Erwin, *Left to Tell: Discovering God Amidst the Rwandan Holocaust* (Carlsbad: Hay House, 2006); Elie Wiesel, *And the Sea Is Never Full: Memoirs, 1969–*, trans. Marion Wiesel (New York: Knopf, 1999).
8. As Lev enabled Dina (and so baby JJ) to survive Abby's rage, perhaps Ellie's (and Abby's) restoration can come by teaming up to save Lev (and maybe working together for a higher good, like finding a cure or establishing a community like Jackson).

Index

The Last of Us and Philosophy: Look for the Light, First Edition.
Edited by Charles Joshua Horn.
© 2025 John Wiley & Sons, Inc. Published 2025 by John Wiley & Sons, Inc.